PRAISE FOR JANICE CANTORE

"Cantore's fast-paced and unpredictable suspense kept me burning the midnight oil for the next page and the next. Romantic suspense doesn't get better than this."

DiANN MILLS, BESTSELLING AUTHOR OF *AIRBORNE* AND *FATAL STRIKE*

"*Breach of Honor* is one of the best stories I've read in a long time! Pulling on her years of expertise in law enforcement, Janice takes the reader on an edge-of-the-seat journey that makes you willing to lose sleep to find out what happens next! This one is on my keeper list and I'm eagerly awaiting the next book from Janice."

LYNETTE EASON, BESTSELLING, AWARD-WINNING AUTHOR OF THE DANGER NEVER SLEEPS SERIES

"I can't remember the last time I've been so invested in the outcome of a story, or so satisfied with its conclusion. With *Breach of Honor*, Janice Cantore has crafted an adventure filled with brutal crimes, heartbreaking injustice, shocking twists, a gentle romance, and hard-won faith. Words like *page-turning*, *breath-stealing*, and *pulse-racing*, while accurate, don't begin to do it justice."

LYNN H. BLACKBURN, AWARD-WINNING AUTHOR OF THE DIVE TEAM INVESTIGATIONS SERIES

"In *Breach of Honor*, Janice Cantore tells a complex tale of deceit and back-room deals that leaves you wondering who the good guys actually are. . . . I could not wait to get to the end and see how it all tied together."

HALLEE BRIDGEMAN, BESTSELLING AUTHOR OF THE SONG OF SUSPENSE SERIES

"A fast-paced thriller with a strong Christian message . . . [*Cold Aim*] is an exciting and thought-provoking book."

CHRISTIAN NOVEL REVIEW

"A complex tale of murder, deceit, and faith challenges, complete with multifaceted characterizations, authentic details, and action scenes, even a subtle hint of romance . . . [all] well integrated into a suspenseful story line that keeps pages turning until the end."

MIDWEST BOOK REVIEW ON *LETHAL TARGET*

"Well-drawn characters and steady action make for a fun read."

WORLD MAGAZINE ON *LETHAL TARGET*

"Readers who crave suspense will devour Cantore's engaging crime drama while savoring the sweet romantic swirl. . . . *Crisis Shot* kicks off this latest series with a literal bang."

ROMANTIC TIMES

"A gripping crime story filled with complex and interesting characters and a plot filled with twists and turns."

THE SUSPENSE ZONE ON *CRISIS SHOT*

"A pulsing crime drama with quick beats and a plot that pulls the reader in . . . [and] probably one of the most relevant books I've read in a while. . . . This is a suspenseful read ripped from the front page and the latest crime drama. I highly recommend."

RADIANT LIT ON *CRISIS SHOT*

"Cantore, a retired police officer, shares her love for suspense, while her experience on the force lends credibility and depth to her writing. Her characters instantly become the reader's friends."

"An intriguing story that could be pulled from today's headlines."

"The final volume of Cantore's Cold Case Justice trilogy wraps the series with a gripping thriller that brings readers into the mind of a police officer involved in a fatal shooting case. . . . Cantore offers true-to-life stories that are relevant to today's news."

"Cantore manages to balance quick-paced action scenes with developed, introspective characters to keep the story moving along steadily. The issue of faith arises naturally, growing out of the characters' struggles and history. Their romantic relationship is handled with a very light touch . . . but the police action and mystery solving shine."

"Questions of faith shape the well-woven details, the taut action scenes, and the complex characters in Cantore's riveting mystery."

"[In] the second book in Cantore's Cold Case Justice series . . . the romantic tension between Abby and Luke seems to be growing stronger, which creates anticipation for the next installment."

"This is the start of a smart new series for retired police officer–turned–author Cantore. Interesting procedural details, multilayered characters, lots of action, and intertwined mysteries offer plenty of appeal."

"Cantore's well-drawn characters employ Christian values and spirituality to navigate them through tragedy, challenges, and loss. However, layered upon the underlying basis of faith is a riveting police-crime drama infused with ratcheting suspense and surprising plot twists."

"*Drawing Fire* rips into the heart of every reader. One dedicated homicide detective. One poignant cold case. One struggle for truth. . . . Or is the pursuit revenge?"

"This hard-edged and chilling narrative rings with authenticity. . . . Fans of police suspense fiction will be drawn in by her accurate and dramatic portrayal."

"Janice Cantore provides an accurate behind-the-scenes view of law enforcement and the challenges associated with solving cases. Through well-written dialogue and effective plot twists, the reader is quickly drawn into a story that sensitively yet realistically deals with a difficult topic."

"[Cantore's] characters resonate with an authenticity not routinely found in police dramas. Her knack with words captures Jack's despair and bitterness and skillfully documents his spiritual journey."

BREACH
OF
HONOR

Library of Congress Cataloging-in-Publication Data
Names: Cantore, Janice, author.
Title: Breach of honor / Janice Cantore.
Description: Carol Stream, Illinois : Tyndale House Publishers, [2021]
Identifiers: LCCN 2021006520 (print) | LCCN 2021006521 (ebook) | ISBN 9781496443090 (trade paperback) | ISBN 9781496443106 (kindle edition) | ISBN 9781496443113 (epub) | ISBN 9781496443120 (epub)
Classification: LCC PS3603.A588 B74 2021 (print) | LCC PS3603.A588 (ebook) | DDC 813/.6--dc23
LC record available at https://lccn.loc.gov/2021006520
LC ebook record available at https://lccn.loc.gov/2021006521

Printed in the United States of America

27   26   25   24   23   22   21
7   6   5   4   3   2   1

BREACH
OF
HONOR

JANICE CANTORE

Tyndale House Publishers
Carol Stream, Illinois

Dedicated to domestic violence awareness.

National Domestic Violence Hotline

1-800-799-SAFE (7233)

thehotline.org

"Lord, high and holy, meek and lowly,
Thou has brought me to the valley of vision,
where I live in the depths but see Thee in the heights;
hemmed in by mountains of sin I behold Thy glory.

Let me learn by paradox
that the way down is the way up,
that to be low is to be high,
that the broken heart is the healed heart . . .
that the valley is the place of vision. . . .
Let me find Thy light in my darkness."
ARTHUR BENNETT, *THE VALLEY OF VISION*

"You can never learn that Christ is all you
need, until Christ is all you have."
CORRIE TEN BOOM

PART
ONE

Adam-5, do you copy?"

"No, I didn't copy." Leah Radcliff grimaced before grabbing the mike and asking dispatch to repeat the emergency call.

"Can you 10-9?"

Preoccupied, her thoughts still simmering over the latest argument she'd had with her husband, Brad, Leah's mind was not on policing the city of Table Rock, Oregon.

"T-4, domestic violence call on Spring Street. Several reporting parties. Medics are also en route. Respond code 3."

Leah clenched a fist and almost screamed in frustration. She hated domestic violence calls. In fact, she'd rather handle a three-week-old dead body call than a domestic violence situation any day, but especially tonight.

The tornado of emotions that swirled around domestic violence made her head hurt. Anger, fear, accusations, and palpable pain often threatened to rip her off her own emotional foundation. She hesitated, pondering some way to avoid the call, but had no choice—it was in her beat, and she was in routine patrol mode a mere three blocks away. She let dispatch know she would handle the call.

Pressing the accelerator, she flipped on the emergency lights and siren and headed for the address given.

In a perfect world, *domestic* and *violence* were two words that wouldn't belong together. In reality, this was a typical summertime call. It had been a hot late-July day. Tempers were frayed, and there was a full moon. She'd had a training officer once who called them wife-beater moons. Maybe that was Brad's excuse.

Leah knew what domestic violence looked like in the field. The fight within herself was what it looked like in her own home. Brad had been furious. It wasn't the first time his hair-trigger temper scared her. Even now her stomach roiled over thoughts of just how frightening her husband could be.

In their two years of marriage this unpleasant side of her husband had surfaced more than Leah cared to think about . . . or admit.

"Adam-5, be advised: calling party says a subject named Carlos has beaten his wife severely."

Dispatch jarred her back to the here and now, and she pushed Brad and their fights as far away as she could.

"Is he still on scene?" Leah asked.

"Unknown. Suspect is described as a male white, late twenties, thin build."

Leah turned the corner onto Spring as she heard another unit answer up to assist. He'd be there in a few minutes. She slowed as she neared the address. This was a cluster of low-income housing units, and by the apartment number given, Leah knew the building she wanted was in the back, down a long driveway. She turned in to the drive and started down. A tall, lanky man was at the bottom of the drive, in front of the building Leah guessed housed the apartment number she was looking for. He raised both arms, crossing them back and forth frantically when he saw her.

She advised dispatch that she'd arrived on scene, jammed the car in park, grabbed her nightstick, and stepped out into a stifling hot night. The air was heavy and there was no breeze.

The man approached, clearly agitated. He was older, with gray hair at the temples, barefoot, phone in one hand, wearing shorts and a button-down shirt with none of the buttons fastened. Sweat beaded on his forehead. Leah could hear the South heavy in his voice when he spoke.

"He beat her. He beat her like a dog," he said, breathless.

"Where is he now?"

"Don't know. I hollered at him. He ran off. I was 'sleep. The screams woke me. Nobody should do a woman like that—nobody. You got to hurry. My wife is with her."

"You are . . . ?" Leah asked as she followed him into the courtyard, wiping sweat from her brow with the back of her hand.

She'd been here many times before. The complex was filled mostly with hardworking people, but mixed in were enough troublemakers now and again to make certain that the police were called often.

"Neighbor, Michael Haynes. I called. My wife is Lavinia."

It was well after 1 a.m., but lights were on in almost all the apartments and people milled about the fringe of the property. The complex was made up of several independent buildings, with four forming a square around a common courtyard. Concrete walkways surrounded the sparse courtyard, which contained a tired lawn, a couple of trees, and two plain wood benches on either side. Next to one bench she saw a woman she took to be Michael's wife bending over someone seated on the ground, who was half-leaning against the bench.

"Over here," Michael said. "Here."

Leah stepped toward the victim, coming up short when she saw the crumpled, battered figure on the ground. The beaten woman looked more like a girl, really, with her small frame. Her eyes were swollen shut and her face resembled raw hamburger. A low keening sound came from her, but Leah couldn't tell if it was a moan or the whistle of her breath through an obviously broken nose.

"Look what he did to her," Lavinia said. "He beat her within an inch of her life."

For a second Leah was paralyzed. Her knees threatened to buckle. She'd seen worse . . . but just barely. This hit home.

"I'm trying to stop the bleeding . . ." Lavinia turned her face toward Leah, tears in her eyes, bloody towel in one hand while she held the injured victim's left hand with the other. Her expression begged Leah to fix it.

Biting her tongue and tasting blood, Leah snapped out of it, pulled gloves out of her back pocket, and knelt down on one knee. But there wasn't much she could do. There was nothing spurting, no arterial bleeding. There was a lot of blood and horrific damage to the victim's face that she had no way to fix. It was pitted, cratered. What did this? she wondered. This was more than fists alone.

The victim's right hand caught her eye, her bloody fist clenching something. A pencil? A pen?

"Can you hear me?" Leah asked.

"Alex. Her name is Alex."

Leah nodded, but even addressing her by name got no response. A siren approaching told her that medics would soon be there to take over.

She turned her attention to the weeping Lavinia, placed a comforting hand on her shoulder. "Medics are close," she said gently. "You've done all you can."

"The poor girl . . . she's been a good neighbor."

"And you're being a good neighbor. What's her last name?"

"Porter. Alex Porter."

"Where is Carlos, the guy who did this?"

Lavinia's eyes darkened; she shook her head. "That worthless fellow, he ran off. I didn't see where he went. We just wanted to help her."

Leah heard the bounce and rattle of a gurney rolling across the concrete. She pulled Lavinia and Michael away from the victim to give the EMTs room to work. Relieved that the jarring image of the victim was no longer her concern, Leah readied her notebook to take down the witness information. Walking up with the medics was her backup, Clint Tanner, a low-key guy Leah barely knew. He had a couple of years more on the job than her, but he worked days, not the late-night shift, so they'd never worked together. Tonight he was filling in for someone.

"How can I help?" he asked, glancing at the medical activity going on around the victim.

"I just got a sketch of what happened," Leah told him. "I don't know where the suspect went. See if any of these people can help."

He nodded. Leah's attention went back to Lavinia. She and her husband had their heads together. They were praying.

Leah cleared her throat to get their attention. "Do you know Carlos's full name?"

Lavinia blew her nose. "He's Porter too, but they're separated."

Michael snorted and Leah turned toward him.

"That no-'count. Alex has tried to get rid of him. She stays in that apartment yonder." He pointed to an apartment across the courtyard. The door was open, and all the lights were on. "He just shows up once in a while, for money, you know?"

"Are there any children?"

Michael shook his head.

"Any guns or other weapons that you know of?"

Again, a headshake.

The medics had the victim loaded up ready to transport.

"How's she doing?" Leah asked.

One medic's expression told her more than words could. Leah felt sick to her stomach.

"Can we go to the hospital with her?" Lavinia asked. "I'll call her mother."

"If you wish. I'll be there as soon as I sort things out here."

The couple left and Leah located Tanner. He was talking to some animated people who must have witnessed the fight. They pointed this way and that, obviously affected by what they had seen. She waited a beat for him to finish.

"Tanner, let's check out the apartment."

He nodded and followed her. "Guy's full name is Carlos Porter, around twenty-six years old. He's the estranged husband. Has a possible address in West Table Rock, but no one here saw which direction he ran."

"So he doesn't live here," Leah said, half to herself. She couldn't concentrate, kept seeing the victim's face in her mind's eye.

When they reached the apartment's open door, she stopped. Obviously a fight had taken place. What sparse furniture was in the room was broken or torn. Just inside the door, on the floor, Leah saw something bloody. As she looked closer, she realized she was looking at a hard-plastic model horse, a realistic scale model with pointed ears and a long tail. All of the legs were broken off, and that stopped her cold. This was what he'd beaten Alex with. Carlos most likely reached for the most convenient weapon. And it was probably a piece of a broken leg that Alex had clenched in her fist. Anger welled up inside Leah and she clenched her own fists, shoulder aching where Brad had squeezed it a few hours ago hard enough to leave a bruise.

Tanner stepped around her and inside the apartment first. Frowning, he asked, "Do you hear water running?"

Leah tore her eyes away from the horse. They'd need to collect it as evidence, but she did hear water running.

"Bathroom's in the back." They started toward the rear of the apartment.

Tanner reached the door first and lurched inside. "It's the guy!" he said, alarm in his voice.

Leah followed him in and saw the reason for his quick reaction. A male subject was in the tub, head slumped on his chest, eyes closed. Water ran down the drain—blood-tinged water. He'd cut his wrists.

Tanner shoved the shower curtain out of the way and grabbed the guy's shoulders. He fit the description of Carlos Porter.

"Get some towels," Tanner said as he struggled with the deadweight. There was scant room in the tight space for Leah to move in and help.

She pulled a towel from the sink as Tanner draped the limp body across the bathroom floor.

"Here, take this," she said. "Is he breathing?"

"Barely." Tanner felt for a pulse at the neck, then took the towel. He wrapped it around one wrist, then checked the other. "Weak pulse. He cut the wrong way; bleeding is slowing."

Leah saw that. Keying her mike, she explained the situation and asked for a second ambulance. She opened the small cupboard under the sink and found another towel. This one she wrapped around the man's other wrist. The bleeding looked to have stopped, but she applied pressure anyway.

Squinting as sweat ran down her face, burning her eyes, Leah raised her arm and wiped the side of her face with her shoulder sleeve, a dull ache reminding her of her injury. Because of the warm night it was very humid in the tight space. She leaned over Carlos and Tanner to turn off the faucet, watching the last of the pink water disappear.

"What a coward," Tanner said.

"What?" Leah jerked around to face him. *Who was he calling a coward?*

"This guy. Any man who hits a woman is a coward. And he didn't have the guts to deal with the consequences of his actions."

Leah considered that as they waited for the paramedics. *Coward.* She agreed with him. But there was a disconnect. Her husband could never be called a coward. He was a cop—a good one. Yet he'd smacked her more than a few times in the last two years.

Was this her future? What she'd seen in the courtyard? Broken and beaten by Brad after he grabbed for the closest weapon?

No, she told herself. *My situation is entirely different. Brad was* sorry. *It was an accident. It's not the same thing.*

+ + +

At the station, as they filed their reports at the end of the shift, Leah was thankful that Tanner was low-key. He simply did his work, no useless chatter. He filed the evidence and the part of the report about finding Carlos in the tub. When they'd left the hospital, Alex was hanging on by a thread while Carlos was stable. Michael and Lavinia were still there, trying to comfort the girl, who was now comatose. Leah appreciated the couple and told them so. People not family were seldom so warm and caring.

Since there was a chance Alex might die, they'd handled the call like an attempted murder. Homicide investigators had been called out, and they did their own investigation at the scene. As a result, Clint and Leah had been on the call for the whole night.

Leah didn't believe Carlos meant to kill himself. Yes, he'd lost a lot of blood, but the cuts were shallow and across the veins, so the bleeding was easy to stop. She believed he did it for sympathy—after all, that's what a coward would do.

As she finished the last bit of the paperwork, she looked up at Tanner across the room. Her tired mind wandered, and she considered what she knew about him. He wasn't one of Brad's friends; therefore he wasn't in her social circle. She'd never heard any criticism of his work, just knew that he had the nickname Saint Tanner because he didn't drink, not even a beer after work. Brad always said you couldn't trust a guy who was a teetotaler. Leah didn't completely agree with that adage and at times thought Brad drank altogether too much. He blamed it on the job. She had the same job and couldn't keep up with him.

Saint Tanner wasn't a bad nickname; some guys had worse. Like Marvin Sapp. His was Pinky because of his complexion—any exertion caused his face to turn bright pink. Leah thought Saint was much better than Pinky.

Tanner was older than she was, but not by much. He had dark-brown hair with a hint of red, but she doubted he'd be called a redhead. His eyes were a pale color, almost green but more hazel, really.

He was handsome, she decided, in an understated way. Strong jaw, classic features, well-built. She did know that he played on the department basketball team. Though she herself had played ball in college, she'd never watched a department game. Brad hated basketball, liked to say the only real sport for men was football.

Tanner wore a neatly trimmed mustache, and right now there was dark stubble on his chin. She noticed that he had a long, light scar running from his right eyebrow down the side of his face toward his ear. She wondered about that.

She didn't know if he was married or not. He wasn't wearing a ring, but that didn't mean anything; Brad never wore one.

Tanner looked up and caught her staring at him. She looked away, knowing that she was blushing and unable to stop it.

"Something wrong?" he asked.

Leah sighed. "I'm tired. It's hard to focus."

He grunted and looked at his watch. "Well, we're EOW an hour ago. Why don't you go home. I'll finish up."

She met his steady gaze. He still looked as if he could work another shift without any effort. Her phone buzzed with a text. It was Brad.

Coming home? I miss you. He added several hearts and flowers. There. He *was* sorry. He'd never meant what happened earlier.

"Thanks, Clint, I appreciate that. You won't be long?"

"Nah, almost done."

Leah nodded and headed for the locker room. On the way she passed the wall where all the medal of valor recipients had their pictures hanging. Brad's was there. He'd dived in and pulled a drowning woman and her two children out of the Rogue River two winters ago, earning the medal.

He was no coward, Leah told herself. And she was no victim.

CHAPTER 2

Clint watched Radcliff until she was out of sight. Since he'd been working detectives and special assignments for the last three years and only recently transferred to patrol, this was the first time he'd worked a call with her, but he'd recognized Leah Radcliff from a different venue.

He smiled as a memory surfaced. Years ago, long before she became a cop, Leah Radcliff had been an all-American basketball player for Oregon State. Her play on the court had impressed him. He'd been a senior at OSU when, as a sophomore point guard, Leah was named MVP. The school newspaper had dubbed her "Mighty Mite." She was always the shortest, but back then her stats were consistently stellar. He'd often read her described as "quick-thinking and agile." Now she was a solid cop with a great reputation, but he could tell her mind was not on the job tonight.

He chewed on the top of his pen, powered down the laptop,

and tried to return his thoughts to the call. But all he could think about was Leah. To him she was strikingly pretty. Black hair and brown, almond-shaped eyes, sturdy build . . . She moved like an athlete; there was no frilly pretense about her. Her long hair was often pulled away from her face. Surprisingly feminine, even petite-looking in the uniform, vest, and gun belt, Radcliff avoided looking bulky like everyone else did with the accoutrements they had to wear nowadays.

He'd never had the courage to approach her while at college, though he'd seen her often on campus and thought about asking her out. He could feel his face redden as he recalled the crush he'd had on her back then. He knew that her major was business and not for the first time wondered why she eventually chose law enforcement as a career . . . and what she saw in a guy like Brad Draper. But then, she wasn't the only one who saw something in Draper that Clint couldn't see.

Clint leaned back and stretched before smoothing his mustache with a thumb and index finger. Draper was one of the few guys Clint had met in his life that he disliked immediately. He knew the man was a local legend. A star linebacker for the Oregon Ducks, quick and strong but too small to go pro. Awarded the medal of valor. From a family that had a history of public service—dad a retired cop, an uncle on his father's side also a cop, another uncle on his mother's side a firefighter. All in all, Draper's parents were wealthy, well-known, and pillars of the community.

But Clint couldn't get on the bandwagon. He'd worked around Draper and didn't like his manner or his tactics. There must be something there, though, for a smart beauty like Radcliff to have married him. *Is love truly blind?* Clint hoped that he was wrong and that Draper was a good and faithful husband.

✦ ✦ ✦

Leah's joy at seeing the contrite text from Brad was short-lived. As she drove home, the sun made her squint, and she realized she'd left her sunglasses at work. Two vehicles in the driveway turned the squint into a frown and made anger flood her veins like 100 proof caffeine. One belonged to Larry Ripley and the other to Duke Gill, two of Brad's best friends. And Leah didn't like either one of them.

Duke Gill worked for Brad's father, Harden Draper, who had business interests all over the valley. Duke was a kind of Johnny-on-the-spot, doing whatever needed to be done. Since he was the brother of her best friend, Becky, Leah tried to like him, but something about him rubbed her the wrong way. He encouraged Brad's baser traits, she thought, always egging him on for one more shot of whatever they were drinking.

The same was true for Larry Ripley, only more so. He was Brad's oldest friend; they'd grown up together. He'd been the best man at their wedding. And Leah could say that she hated him. A high-powered attorney—ambulance chaser to Leah's way of thinking—he was, in her opinion, oily and not to be trusted. He'd just been elected to the city council and she doubted that was a good thing for the city. Ripley was a bad influence on Brad, always only concerned about himself, nothing else.

Brad worked swing shift, so his EOW was 2:30 a.m. He usually got to bed around four and slept till about eleven. He should be in bed, text to her notwithstanding. That the guys were here now, at 9:30 a.m., meant they'd cut short Brad's sleep. She was certain Larry was the instigator here.

She'd learned to bite her tongue about the man, because it would only start a fight. And right now, the last thing she wanted was a fight.

Brad came out of the house to meet her before she reached the door, dressed and ready for the day, energy drink in hand. He smiled the smile that always melted her heart. She loved his dimples. He was Hollywood handsome, rugged and so very sexy. A cross between Brad Pitt and Jason Statham. A fleeting thought crossed her mind: He was the exact opposite of quiet Clint Tanner. Brad was outgoing, always the life of the party. If something was going to get started, it was Brad who started it. That quality had attracted Leah to him. Though now, nearly two years into their marriage, she often found it exhausting.

"Hey, babe, rough night?" He wrapped Leah in a tight one-armed hug while Larry seemed to slink out of the house. Duke shot her a grin, bordering on a leer, signature toothpick hanging out of his mouth, and climbed into his truck.

Brad didn't give her a chance to answer. "I got you some flowers. They're in the bedroom." Pulling back, he rubbed the side of her face with his thumb. "Hey. Duke has an emergency with his well. We got to go help him."

"Now? I was hoping we could talk," Leah said even as Brad was moving away from her and toward Larry.

"We will, I promise, when I get home." With that, he turned toward Larry's truck, he and Larry hopped in, and they were gone, Duke behind them.

Leah slowly walked into the house. She felt sticky from the heat and work, tired and beaten. Her heart hurt as she thought of Alex Porter and the broken plastic horse.

She and Brad had a plaque in the entryway: *This is a divided household* with a picture of a duck on one side and a beaver on the other. A joke because they were from rival schools, Leah from Oregon State and Brad, the University of Oregon.

But right now, it wasn't a joke or a laughing matter. Leah

felt as divided as if she'd been physically cut in half. She shed her clothes, hopped in the shower, and cried, glad the water washed away the evidence of tears instantly, much like water had washed away Carlos Porter's blood.

CHAPTER 3

L eah struggled to wake up as her phone buzzed. It seemed to buzz more insistently with each second.

Grappling with it as she sat up and squinted, she saw a police dispatch number, and fear immediately jolted her awake. *Something's happened to Brad.* Just as quickly she remembered he wasn't at work now. The phone told her it was 12:30 p.m. She'd been asleep for less than three hours.

She answered the call. The dispatcher spoke without greeting or preamble, normally calm voice clipped and tense.

"There's been a shooting, a state trooper on the I-5 just north of Grants Pass. Everyone is being called in early. Can you notify Brad?"

Wide-awake now, Leah answered, "Yeah, I'll call him."

"Tell him he's to report to the command post at exit 61. You need to come to the station."

The call ended and Leah stared at the phone. In her tenure at the PD she'd not dealt with an officer shot in the line of duty this close to home. And the dispatcher hadn't given his condition. She called Brad and got his voice mail, which was full.

"Huh." She blew out a breath as she switched to texting. Brad should already know about the shooting, she thought. He got alerts on his phone all the time. Leah had turned her alerts off, not needing to know what was going on when she wasn't working. She typed **911** and then hit Send, hoping he'd call her back.

Leah got dressed, waiting for her phone to chime. After throwing water on her face, she smoothed out the tangles in her hair, then paced her room for a minute before putting on her boots. She was halfway to the door when her phone finally indicated Brad had responded to her message.

Yes?

Furious, she bit back a curse. Where was he? Why was his voice mail full? What was going on? Pounding on the phone, she typed back, **Trooper shot. All ordered in early. Call me.**

Her phone rang almost instantaneously.

"I had my phone off," he said as soon as she answered. "What's going on?"

"Dispatch called. A state trooper was shot on the I-5 outside of Grants Pass. They want you at the command post at exit 61."

"How's the trooper?"

"Didn't say."

"And you didn't ask? Never mind. I'll head straight there, got stuff in my car. Don't cop such an attitude when you call me." He disconnected.

Leah almost threw her phone across the room. Instead, she hurried off to work, hoping against hope that the trooper was all right.

+ + +

The trooper's injuries were fatal. On the way into the station, Leah heard a radio news report that he'd died on scene. He was a young guy, two years on the force. She'd never met him. He'd pulled over a truck he suspected of carrying contraband and been gunned down as he exited his vehicle. The suspect was in the wind. Now she knew why they wanted Brad at the scene. He worked a special unit, SAT, smuggler apprehension team. His expertise was needed, she was sure.

With everyone on high alert, Leah made it through her shift and the extra hours operating on pure adrenaline. It was her Friday, and though the suspect had not yet been captured by the time she was EOW, she was told she would have her normal days off. Brad was still on duty, working with the state team. His uncle Dave was a trooper with the Oregon State Police, so Leah wasn't surprised. By the end of her shift she was too tired to be angry with him anymore, but there was a niggling question in her mind about what he'd been doing and why he'd had his phone off.

Leah woke up around four in the afternoon to an empty house and saw no indication that Brad had been home. Still tired, she napped on and off in front of the television before going back to bed in the early evening. The manhunt for the shooter moved north as it was believed his destination was somewhere in Washington State.

It was after two in the morning when Brad came home. The door being slammed open and the light flipped on woke Leah.

"What?" She squinted and turned toward Brad. Before her eyes fully focused, he was on her, his weight pinning her to the bed.

"Don't play dumb with me."

Wide-awake now, Leah saw the fury in his eyes as he squeezed her wrists so tight she feared they'd snap.

"What do you mean? What's wrong?"

"The attitude! How dare you talk to me like that on the phone." He squeezed her torso with his knees, pressing in. It got hard to breathe.

"I only—"

"No excuses! Never do that again. I'm the one in control here, not you. Don't forget it." He moved both of her wrists to one hand and slid off of her, rolling her to her side. As he got off the bed, he smacked her on the backside hard with his open hand, then let her go. "I mean it."

He stalked out of the room, and seconds later a stunned Leah heard the front door slam. Fighting angry, humiliated tears, she sat up, her pride and her rump smarting from the smack and her wrists aching. She stayed on the edge of the bed trying to process what just happened.

This is it, she thought. *I can't stay here. I can't put up with this.* Holding her wrists, bent over, resting her forehead on her knees, Leah crossed a line in her mind. *Brad is abusive.*

She had to say it; she had to tell someone. The image of Alex Porter's shattered face floated in her mind's eye.

The front door opened, and she looked up, afraid now he was coming back. Before she could stand, he was in the bed-room doorway.

"I'm sorry, baby. I'm so sorry." In two steps he reached her and swept her up into his arms, whispering over and over that he was sorry, kissing her neck, telling her he loved her and that it would be all right.

Leah wept on his shoulder as the resolve to tell someone faded. He loved her; he was sorry; things would be okay.

Brad was gentle and kind throughout the night, being the

man Leah remembered marrying. Nothing in his touch suggested abuse. As for the spanking incident, he was stressed about the dead trooper—that was how Leah justified it.

+ + +

"Justice served," Brad announced the next morning when he brought the paper in, his demeanor upbeat. "Dirtbag got what he deserved."

Leah saw the headline. The suspected cop killer had died at the Canadian border. He'd tried to drive through barricades and gone down in a hail of gunfire.

Brad called in to the station commander, and when he disconnected, he said, "There's still a lot of questions about this." He tapped the paper. "I have to go to work. Seems there was a boatload of synthetic fentanyl in his truck they think came from China."

"Do you know how long you'll be?"

He shook his head. "Nope. You know most of the junk we get here in the valley comes from Mexico. We have to find out how he got Chinese product up here."

He left to shower and change. Leah sipped her coffee, resigned to the fact that life would be busy at work until all the questions about the trooper's murder were answered satisfactorily.

The next two weeks were hectic. Brad was in and out, mostly out, as he was tied up with federal authorities investigating the smuggler. Work was tense as the law enforcement community struggled to cope with the loss of one of their own and to prepare for his funeral. Leah ignored the tension in her own heart about her marriage. *Brad is just a man who feels things deeply,* she told herself over and over. But no matter how many times she said it, it did nothing to quell the anxiety churning in her gut.

CHAPTER 4

Look, I told you I'm sorry. What else do you want?"

Leah stiffened, frozen with the fear of Brad getting angry again.

"You always say you're sorry and it happens again." She fought to control her shaking voice. The bedroom incident had stayed with her for days, and she'd teetered on the brink of coming forward and telling someone what had happened. In the end she decided to give her husband a chance to go for counseling. A formal charge of domestic violence would get him suspended at least and fired at most.

"We have a funeral to go to and you bring this up now?"

"It's been bugging me—"

"It's the job." He threw his hands up and she flinched. "When I'm under stress, just don't push it. A cop is dead! It could have been one of the guys I work with. What do you expect? *I'm sorry* will have to be enough."

"Maybe we should get some counseling—"

"For what?" He glared. "Our business is our business. Have you said anything to anyone?"

"No, but—"

"But nothing. We're fine. Chief Wilcox, Lieutenant Racer, Sergeant Forman—they won't believe anything different."

He finished polishing his boots with an angry flourish and Leah backed down. Maybe this was the wrong time to bring up counseling. That the trooper's death had exacerbated the tensions in her relationship with Brad was an understatement. He'd been tense and surly for days.

Every fiber of her being told her something had to change. What—and how to bring that change about—eluded her.

At the moment, she needed to finish readying her uniform for the funeral. Her boots were already shined, so she polished her badge, then grabbed her dress uniform and went out to the car to wait for Brad.

The trooper's funeral was in a few hours. Butterflies batted about in her stomach. Was it because of the funeral or because of Brad? When he came out to the car, his expression was hard, unyielding, and the ride to the station quiet, tense, leaving Leah wondering if she'd ever feel normal again.

Once in the locker room with other women and away from Brad's dark mood, she felt some balance return. Leah had seen funerals for police officers on TV, but this was the first one she would attend in person. Dress uniforms were the order of the day, and all the women helped one another be certain they looked their best before leaving the locker room.

When Leah stepped into the parking lot, the sight of all the uniformed officers, shoes shined and badges sparkling, took her breath away. She swallowed the lump rising in her throat and

quickly found Brad and his partner, Richard Chambers, standing by a black-and-white.

A large church in Eagle Point off of Highway 62 was the
venue for the service. The plan was for the officers to caravan to
the church in their police vehicles. Table Rock PD would team
up with Medford, Central Point, Talent, Ashland, Grants Pass,
and the Jackson County Sheriff.

Leah didn't trust herself to speak, so she simply nodded to
Richard.

"Okay, let's get this show on the road," Brad said, moving
around to the driver's side. "Babe, let Richard take shotgun.
He's too tall to sit in the back."

Leah didn't mind sitting in the back. Brad had just started
the engine when another officer stepped up and asked if there
was room. Brad said sure, but Leah could tell he was irritated.
She saw why when Clint Tanner climbed in and sat next to her.
Brad hated having to interact with people he didn't think were
fit for his circle.

"Leah," Tanner said as he fastened his seat belt, "how are
you holding up?"

"As well as can be expected," Leah managed to say. She'd
wanted to ride alone but decided she didn't mind having Tanner
join them. Maybe his being there would make Brad mind his
p's and q's. Still, she felt no need to talk, and except for Brad
and Richard speaking in low tones, the drive to the church was
quiet, even peaceful.

Once at the church, officers from each department formed
up together. All around were somber faces. Grief was as heavy in
the air as a wet winter fog. The service itself was heart-wrenching
as the trooper's parents and his young, pregnant wife paid him
heartfelt tribute. Leah couldn't stop the tears and she didn't try.
Brad wasn't pleased; Leah could tell by his expression. Tears

were weak—she knew that was his opinion. His go-to emotion was anger.

After the service, officers milled about in the parking lot. The trooper had been cremated and no graveside service planned. Leah spoke to one or two officers, then searched for Brad and Richard, wanting to be home and away from all the grief of this horrible, no-good, bad day. As she looked, she walked slowly toward the black-and-white, feeling tired and wrung out after all the tears. She caught sight of Richard first. He was off to the side of the church, Brad with him. She almost walked over to them but saw that Brad was having a heated discussion with his uncle Dave. She stopped, too exhausted to deal with her husband's mercurial moods at the moment. Let him vent at Uncle Dave.

"Have you heard anything about Alex Porter?"

Leah jumped. She'd been watching Brad and hadn't heard Tanner walk up.

"Sorry, didn't mean to startle you."

"Oh, it's just been a hard morning."

"Yes, it has." He followed her gaze and she looked away.

"I haven't heard anything, no." The name brought the battered face into Leah's mind. The last thing she'd heard was that Alex was in a drug-induced coma.

"I've kept her in my prayers," Tanner said. "I think it would be nice to see a miracle."

Leah nodded and was about to ask him more, but Brad was coming. His expression said he was not in the mood for small talk. The ride back to the station was tense, and as soon as they got home, Brad left again without saying where he was going. Leah went to bed, closing her eyes, but sleep wouldn't come. She hadn't prayed in years, and she found herself wondering if God would listen to anything she did pray.

CHAPTER 5

A few days after the trooper's funeral, Alex Porter died. Leah received a note from homicide in her mailbox at work telling her. It had been touch and go with the girl—she'd had extensive damage to her face, but there was a bleed on her brain and that was what killed her. She never regained consciousness. Carlos Porter's arraignment for murder was scheduled in a couple of days.

Though the note brought Leah close to tears, she fought them. It was just another call, she told herself. Alex had never even spoken to her. Leah thought of Michael and Lavinia. They'd be crushed.

She needed to compose herself before squad meeting, guessing that her emotions were so close to the surface because of Brad. He'd been in and out, and they hadn't had much time together while he worked with the feds on the smuggling case.

When they discovered that the smuggled fentanyl had likely arrived through the port of San Francisco, the feds released all local law enforcement, and the investigation headed south to California. With the shooting suspect dead, the trooper buried, and the investigation out of Brad's hands, Leah hoped the stress on Brad would ease and she'd be able to connect with him.

She was wrong. In the few days since she'd asked about counseling, the day of the funeral, Leah had barely seen her husband. His demeanor whiplashed between pleasant and contrite to surly and threatening, and he always had an excuse to be somewhere else—usually helping Larry and Duke with something or other.

She'd kept quiet and let the resentment build. Now she was fairly simmering with anger of her own. The note about Alex dying merely popped the cork. This wasn't an entirely new thing; Brad did spend a lot of time with friends where Leah was not included.

Leah had friends, but Becky Blanchard, Duke's sister, was the only one Brad approved of, so she was the only friend Leah saw regularly, usually for lunch. She was a stay-at-home mom with a two-year-old. Leah liked Becky. Married to Grady, a deputy sheriff, she understood law enforcement. Becky had wanted to be a cop instead of married to one, she confided in Leah once, but a congenital defect in her back made it impossible to pass the physical requirements. "I just live it through Grady," she'd said once.

Becky was the only person Leah could or would confide in.

"Lately, this thing with Larry is taking up all of Brad's free time, and that is odd. It kindles all of my suspicious cop instincts," she'd explained to Becky over lunch one day. "He and Larry are up to something, and it doesn't have anything to do with a faulty well."

"What do you think he could be up to?" Becky asked.

"I don't know. It just bugs me." She stopped short of saying that Duke was also included. Becky worshiped her brother, and Leah knew she'd get defensive. They'd survived a horribly abusive childhood, and Becky considered herself his protector, kind of like a mama bear. No one could ever talk bad about Duke to Becky.

"Maybe it's something political. Rumor has it Larry has higher aspirations."

"Brad's never been concerned with politics. I just don't trust Larry." Leah had picked at her salad. She and Becky were close, yet there was one big secret in her life she was loath to share with anyone—even Becky. Even thinking about the last time Brad hit her made the heat of shame rise in her face, and Leah gulped her iced tea, hoping Becky didn't notice.

"If I were you, Leah, I wouldn't worry about Larry."

"Huh?" Leah looked Becky in the eye. "What do you mean?"

"Brad's the leader; he's always the leader. Yeah, Larry's a weasel, but Brad is the head honcho no matter what. I think you know that at heart."

Leah continued to replay the conversation as she dressed for work. Some part of her did know that Becky's assessment was true, but she ignored that part. It was easy to hate Larry and easier to blame him.

Monday night her and Brad's shifts overlapped. Sometimes, on quiet nights, they'd meet for coffee. Since the manhunt for the cop killer was over and the trooper had been laid to rest, Leah hoped she and Brad could do that tonight. By the time she logged on to her car computer, it was close to 11 p.m. Brad had been at work since 3:30 p.m. She immediately checked unit status, looking for where Brad and his partner, Richard Chambers, were. They showed out for investigation outside the city limits, not far, but over the line. It was an area close to the interstate, and it made sense considering what had happened to the trooper.

Leah pulled out of the station lot and drove to an empty strip mall parking lot in the center of her beat to park and think. Brad and Richard had been out for investigation for over thirty minutes. If they were a regular patrol unit, dispatch would be checking on their well-being. But with the task force, they could be out there all night if they wished. SAT had a lot of leeway; they worked citywide and were not confined to a beat.

Sergeant Erik Forman was the supervisor for SAT. Some supervisor, Leah thought. Forman logged on and disappeared every night. He was a disgrace to the uniform to her way of thinking. Brad liked him, of course, because Forman let him do whatever he wanted.

The department talked about putting GPS monitoring in all patrol cars so dispatch would always know exactly where the units were, but that hadn't happened yet, so Brad could say he was anywhere, really. She thought about texting him, but if he was involved in something, she didn't want to interrupt. Besides he could type anything in a text.

She double-checked everyone who was logged on the system, but no one else was out with Brad and Richard. In fact, even though the sky was bright with a three-quarter moon, it was a quiet night, not much was going on anywhere that she could see, and radio traffic was sporadic. It would be risky for her to leave the city boundary, especially if she got a call. And she could drive right into a major operation.

Leah decided it was worth the risk and took the chance, heading out of the city to where Brad said he was. He might be angry, but she was angry as well, and tired of being ignored.

The word *abused* echoed in her mind, but she pushed it away, shaking her head in an effort to erase it like you would a drawing on an Etch A Sketch.

She reached the spot Brad had given as his location, and he wasn't there. True, the intersection he'd indicated could just be a general area, but he still should be close. She cruised the area slowly. Nothing was going on within blocks. The only person she saw out was Netta, a local homeless woman.

Frustrated, Leah stopped and grabbed one of the extra water bottles she always carried with her in the summertime. She got out of the car. "Hey, Netta, how are you doing tonight?"

Netta gave her a vacant stare and then managed a smile. "Fair to middlin'. Righty all right." She nodded.

Leah handed her the water. "Hot day today. Here's some water."

Netta squirreled the bottle away in her volumes of clothes. Body odor, sweat, dirt, and urine formed an aroma around Netta as solid as a shield. Leah felt sorry for the woman; she survived on the streets and resisted all help. Leah thought she was probably smarter and more aware than she let on, so she tried to help in small ways.

Leah climbed back into her car and pondered her next move. Brad was nowhere to be found. A knot formed in her stomach. Where was he? An affair? Leah had heard stories about cops years ago taking advantage of quiet nights to visit girlfriends. In the good old boys club of the day, cops covered for each other for good behavior and bad. Rumor was that mistresses were a matter of course back in the day when women were not allowed on patrol.

And Leah knew well enough that the good old boys club survived. Brad, Richard, Terry Racer in IA, and three or four guys from SWAT were the modern-day incarnation of the club—they called themselves the Hangmen. She couldn't prove they covered for one another, or even if they had as much power as they thought they did, but she knew that you didn't get special assignments unless they liked you. It wasn't something she was supposed to know, but she'd heard Brad and Racer joke about it at a party once. At the time it made her glad she was married to Brad. But lately she thought about how unfair and chauvinistic it was.

Was that what was up with Brad? A mistress? Her body fairly vibrated with the fear of betrayal. But would Richard put up with that? Chambers always struck her as a straight-arrow kind of guy. Yet he followed Brad around like a puppy. His nickname was Shadow.

Leah parked, window open, patrol car motor humming. This had to do with Larry, she was sure, whatever it was. Larry was the problem, not Brad. She waited a few minutes, half-expecting Brad to drive by. She checked his status again and it had not changed. He had to be close in case dispatch asked for him—at least she thought he should be. Now she feared that if she did text, he wouldn't answer and would claim later that his phone was off because he was working something.

Frowning, she tapped on the steering wheel. Then it hit her. Larry had rental units all over Table Rock and neighboring Medford. There was one not far from here, just inside the city limits. Leah had taken lunch to Brad there one day about a year ago when he was helping Larry refurbish the place.

She made a U-turn and headed for the rental house. It was in a rough section of town, an area she knew Larry wanted designated for redevelopment. He'd make a killing off of his real estate holdings if that happened.

She didn't drive directly past the property. One block over as she crossed an intersection, she thought she saw Brad's plain car parked at the curb. Her throat tightened, and even on this warm night her hands felt numb on the steering wheel.

Leah parked a couple of blocks away. On the computer, she put herself out for investigation—but at a location still in her beat—before she got out of the car. She'd spent nine months with narcotics before she and Brad married, so she knew a little about how to make a stealthy approach and do some surveillance.

Leah went over in her mind what she'd say to Brad if he caught her. Fear pulsed through her, her mouth went dry, but she had to know what was going on. There was no way this was police business.

She turned her radio down, crossing her fingers that she didn't get a call. There was a long travel trailer parked across the street and about two doors down from Larry's rental. Leah crossed the street and used the large vehicle as cover.

From behind the trailer she peered across the street. She had a clear view of the rental. Parked in front sat the nondescript Ford that had caught her eye in the first place. She couldn't see the plates, but it was most likely the SAT plain car. The lights were on in the rental, and she recognized Larry's truck in the driveway. She began to wonder about the wisdom of coming here. Brad and Richard had been "out for investigation" now for nearly an hour. Whatever he was doing, he'd probably already done it or was doing it in the house.

Frustration ratcheted up in her chest. She wanted to go beat the door down and confront her husband, but a thin shred of self-restraint said that wouldn't happen. She waited around ten minutes watching the house. Nothing happened as time ticked away. Leah was amazed she hadn't gotten a call.

Just as she was about to give up and admit defeat, headlights swept down the street and reflexively she ducked. A panel van drove past, slowing and stopping right behind the plain car. After a very long minute a thickly built, blond, bearded man climbed out of the driver's seat.

He stopped at the end of the driveway and made a call on his cell phone. A few seconds later, three men came out of the house and walked to where the bearded man stood. Leah recognized Larry immediately but almost didn't recognize Brad. He wasn't in uniform, his clothes were dark, and he had a ball cap on, but the way he moved, turned, and surveyed the street . . . it was Brad, she was certain.

With Richard, like Larry, there was no guessing. Chambers was a big man. He'd played football with Brad in college and had actually gone on to play a year in the pros, for the Chicago Bears, before being cut and joining the PD. He kind of trailed after Brad and Larry, earning his nickname.

Leah's heart beat faster. This couldn't be a sting. Larry wasn't a cop, not anywhere close. The men talked, but she was too far away to hear what was being said. Leah wondered briefly at them being outside in full view of neighbors, but she realized that the houses were dark. The house directly across from Larry's had a For Sale sign and appeared vacant. The men were next to a hedge, and the only illumination was from the moon, so they probably were cocky enough to think that even if someone did see them, they wouldn't care.

Suddenly Brad stepped forward forcefully and drew a weapon from behind his back. Leah gasped as he grabbed the bearded man's shirt and jammed the gun into his face. She put a hand over her mouth, hoping she hadn't been heard, and then held her breath. What on earth was Brad thinking? What had been said?

After what seemed an eternity but was certainly only a few seconds, Brad stepped back and lowered the gun.

The bearded man then pulled an envelope out of his back pocket and handed it to Brad. Letting out a rush of air, Leah bet the envelope contained money. But she couldn't tell for sure from this distance.

Brad simply looked inside and nodded once. The bearded man turned, climbed into his van, and drove away.

Her knees felt like water. Looking down, she leaned against the trailer. She'd just seen a payoff, but for what? When she turned back, Brad, Richard, and Larry were gone, and she knew she'd better get back where she belonged.

Anger, fear, bewilderment, betrayal, a sense of being blindsided—so many emotions swirled through Leah as she hurried back to her car and then to her beat. There'd be a confrontation—there had to be. Leah had to know what her husband was up to . . . no matter what.

CHAPTER 6

After Leah returned to her beat, she kept watch on Brad's status. When she saw it go from out for investigation to back in service, she pulled over to call him—only to be interrupted by a burglary call. Groaning in frustration, she hurried to the burglary, hoping to finish it quickly and have some time to contact her husband.

It was not to be. The burg situation was involved, and she couldn't reach out to Brad. He texted her when he was EOW, telling her to be safe and that he looked forward to seeing her at home. It was so easy for him to be nice in a text.

Leah struggled to finish her shift, a million different possible scenarios explaining what she'd seen going through her mind. None of them were good. When she pulled into her driveway, tense, worried, angry, and unsure, she sat for a few minutes, chewing on the inside of her cheek, before getting out and walking up the path to the front door.

The light was still low outside, brightening slowly. The house was quiet. Brad should be asleep. She set her kit inside the door, put her gun on the credenza in the entryway, and walked back to the bedroom. He was asleep but he stirred when she stepped into the room. Leah's resolve became weak-kneed. Did she really want to confront Brad now?

Yes, everything in her screamed. This was too important. Besides, it was too late to turn back now.

Yawning and wiping sleep from his eyes, he sat up on one elbow, blinking when she turned on the light.

"Hey, babe, turn that off and come to bed. I missed you."

"We need to talk." Leah swallowed, hoping her courage held.

"Sleep now. Talk later." He smiled and patted the bed.

"Where were you tonight?"

"Huh?" His face scrunched in bewilderment. "At work, like you. What's up?" A tinge of anger entered his voice as he came fully awake.

"You weren't where you said you were. You were at Larry's rental. What's going on?" Leah's heart pounded. Her palms itched with sweat.

His features hardened, eyes narrowed, mouth a thin, taut line. He threw the blanket off and swung his legs over the edge of the bed. "Are you checking up on me?"

There was danger in his tone, and she could see the muscles in his arms tense, but she forged on.

"I wanted to talk to you. You weren't where you said you were. I saw you at Larry's rental on the west side. I want to know what's going on. You owe me an explanation."

He stood, wearing only boxers. Though weighing about seventy-five pounds less than his playing weight, he still pumped iron like he had when he played football. His entire body was tense. A vein pulsed at his forehead and another across his deltoid. There was fury in his eyes as he pointed an index finger at her. His anger could be volcanic.

"You followed me?" He stepped forward and she retreated. "How dare you."

"I—" Leah was fast, but Brad was faster, and the slap caught her full on, causing her to see stars and taste blood, sending her into the wall.

Brad was on her before she could blink away the pain. His thick hands went around her throat. "What did you see?" He didn't squeeze, but she couldn't move. Both of Leah's hands grasped his forearms, which were as hard as iron.

"You're hurting me." She could barely speak, and shock slowed her thinking

"This ain't nothing. I want to know what you think you saw." His eyes seemed to throw off sparks.

Leah coughed. "It looked like you took a payoff. What—?"

He cursed. "I can't believe this!" He was fairly foaming at the mouth. Spittle struck her face. "You had no right to stick your nose into my business."

Now he did squeeze, and as the pressure on her throat increased, Leah scrabbled at his wrists, unable to loosen his grip of iron. She looked into a face she didn't recognize, and the edges of her sight blurred.

"You saw something you never should have seen," he hissed through clenched teeth. "What happens now is your own stupid fault."

The pressure he applied on her neck cut off the airflow completely. Leah couldn't breathe and felt consciousness ebb. She fought as hard as she could but was weakening. She tried to go for his eyes, but he batted her hands away with one hand, the grip on her neck unbreakable. Then he shifted his weight and she had the briefest of openings. With her last bit of strength, she brought her knee up hard into his groin and connected.

He howled and fell back, releasing his death grip. Leah gasped for air, coughing and choking as if she'd just come up from being held underwater. Her knees crumpled and she fell, knocking the nightstand over. The lamp shattered and Brad's phone and gun fell to the floor. She scrambled for the phone, but her hand closed around the gun.

He recovered and grabbed her ankle, yanking her toward him, cursing. "You'll pay for this, all of it!"

Leah turned toward him, gun in her hand. Seeing his face twisted in violence and anger, she realized that if she didn't pull the trigger now, she would be dead.

So she did.

CHAPTER 7

I n short order, Leah found herself on the other side of 911.

The first officers to arrive were Marvin Sapp and his rookie, Vicki Henderson.

"Slow down, Leah. Slow down." Sapp gripped her shoulders. "Just tell me what happened."

Haltingly and painfully, voice hoarse, throat burning from being constricted, she did. Marvin held a cop face in place as long as he could, but Leah saw the shock and disbelief move down his features like a shade.

More officers arrived, and paramedics, though there was nothing they could do. The chatter of police radios and whispers filled the house, a disjointed melody she'd heard often at the scene of tragedies. Leah caught snatches of conversation, reminding her of voices from a distant television.

"Sit with her, Henderson. Don't let her talk to anyone," Sapp ordered as he guided Leah to the living room couch. Leah let him direct her to sit down.

"What about an official statement?" Henderson whispered.

"Per policy, she only has to give one to the shooting team; she shouldn't talk to anyone else right now. Not anyone. I've got to secure the scene in the bedroom." Marvin left Leah with Henderson.

The minutes ticked away in a blur of agony, regret, fear, grief, all whipped together as if in a Ninja blender. They hit Leah in changing and shifting degrees, like the colors of a kaleidoscope.

As the police work swirled around her, Leah kept wiping her hands together, rubbing her palms to get the blood off. It was long gone now because of her constant rubbing, but the image of Brad in her mind was indelible. She'd tried CPR on her husband, though recognizing immediately that it was useless.

"Radcliff."

Leah turned.

"The lab guy is here for photos."

As her neck, face, and hands were photographed, Leah said nothing. There were no words. The glares of officers who'd loved Brad did not escape her notice. But she felt disconnected from her body and the situation, hoping against hope that this was a bad dream and she would soon wake up.

"We'll need your clothes," Sapp said gently.

Leah looked down at the blood drying on her shirt and shorts.

"I'll get you some clothes to change into," Henderson said. When she returned, she accompanied Leah to the guest bedroom. Henderson put the soiled clothes in an evidence bag. Once changed, Leah went back to the couch.

Detective Patterson from homicide arrived about the same time the chief and DA Arron Birch did.

"What happened?" Patterson planted himself in front of Leah. He'd been one of Brad's groomsmen at their wedding.

"I-I told Sapp."

"Tell me."

"Sir, I don't think that's appropriate right now," Henderson said.

"What?" Even in her shocky state, Leah heard the fury in his voice and saw his angry, twisted features as he turned on the rookie. "You've been on the force since breakfast and you're telling me how to do my job?"

Henderson didn't back down. "Policy says that officers involved in shootings will give one statement to the investigative team—"

"That's for on-duty shootings. Does this look like an on-duty shooting to you?"

"Still, Officer Radcliff needs representation, some protection for her rights."

"You listen to me, little girl—"

"Patterson, that's enough," DA Birch spoke up. "We have a scene in here to look at. Why is she still here?" He looked to Wilcox, who nodded.

"Someone should transport Radcliff to the station," he said. "Sapp, see to it."

Leah watched and listened to all of this, eyes going back and forth between each speaker. She was certain it couldn't possibly apply to her. She took people to the station, not the other way around. A part of her still hoped the nightmare would end. Someone would snap their fingers and her world would return to normal.

Sapp and Henderson led her to their patrol car. She sat in the back, on the hard-plastic bench, looking into the cage. It was broad daylight, but Leah had the sensation of being stuffed into a cave.

Waiting at the station was an attorney who said he was affiliated with the police officers association and, surprisingly, Clint Tanner, in civvies.

"Would you like me to be your peer support officer?" Tanner asked.

Leah could only nod.

Sapp and Henderson left for a cubicle to file their report. Tanner took Leah up to the homicide offices, where they settled into a conference room.

"How about some coffee." Tanner pulled out a chair at the conference table. "The DA's team will be a while getting here."

Leah found her voice, but it was hoarse and her throat sore from where Brad had nearly crushed it. "Thanks. Black please."

"You sound awful. Maybe medics should take a look at you."

Leah shook her head.

"Leah, it might be a—"

"No." She did not want to be touched, poked, or prodded. Thankfully Tanner left to get coffee without further comment.

+ + +

Clint watched Leah for a moment, then went on his way to get the coffee, a thousand unanswered questions roaring through his mind like a blast from a fire hose.

When he'd gotten the call from Marvin, Clint couldn't process what he heard right away. It was only when he reached the station, saw the anger, sorrow, shock in people's faces and heard the gossip already flowing, that the full impact of what had happened hit him square in the forehead. *Leah Radcliff shot and killed Brad Draper.*

And seeing Leah, he knew from the bottom of his heart what the gossip wasn't saying: this was justified. He poured coffee and tried to quell his own rising anger. Domestic violence was rarely a one-off event. Leah had been a victim long before this night. Why hadn't she said anything? Why hadn't anyone noticed?

Why didn't I notice?

Before he started back to where Leah waited for him, he stopped and prayed. She didn't need a lot of questions from him; she needed peer support. And anger at Brad was futile at this point. So Clint prayed to be the best support he could be. To help Leah stand up to the questioning she would face and hopefully bring stability to a woman who'd obviously just had the worst night of her life.

✦ ✦ ✦

When Tanner returned, Leah accepted her cup with a nod. The first sip burned her raw throat.

They waited for about an hour. Neither of them spoke. Leah found the silence, and Tanner's presence, comforting. She had transitioned from fresh, raw pain to a kind of numbness. The world around her felt nebulous, disconnected, but she knew now it wasn't a dream she'd wake up from.

Brad was dead.

The comfort shattered when DA Birch and his shooting team arrived, including Patterson and Chief Wilcox, but by then Leah found she could shift to her cop persona and feel some semblance of control return. She was read her rights, and the interview was taped, Leah doing the best she could with her scratchy voice. Wavering between disjointedness and shock, she gave her statement and answered every question the POA attorney allowed.

When she was finished, Patterson asked her and Tanner to wait outside the conference room while the team had a discussion.

"You think I'll be booked?" she asked Tanner.

Tanner shook his head. "I don't see how. It's self-defense. They might convene a grand jury to determine if filing charges is needed, but that would just be a formality."

Leah looked at Tanner—a man she barely knew, yet he'd steadied her. There was none of the shock and disbelief she'd seen on Sapp's face. Tanner had simply been matter-of-fact and helpful. A thought flashed: Brad would ask what his angle was.

Sighing, she leaned against the wall. "How'd you get here so quick?" she rasped. Her voice felt stronger to her but it was rough. "Weren't you off?"

He nodded. "Sapp called me. I called the POA attorney. Sapp knows I'm a peer counselor and that you'd need one."

"He knew no one else would want the job. Brad was, well . . ." Her voice faded.

"A fellow officer?" Tanner finished for her. "So are you. And whatever Brad was, it's obvious he hurt you, badly. It's not your fault."

"What?"

"That's what I tell victims of domestic violence. The only person at fault is the one who does the abusing. Don't make this your fault, Leah."

Victims of domestic violence. Leah gripped her arms tight about her, so tight it hurt. But she couldn't move because if she did, she'd lose it. She'd break into a million pieces all over the police department floor. She held her breath as the door to the conference room opened.

"You're suspended indefinitely," the attorney said, "but you'll remain free while a grand jury convenes." He handed her a card.

"Here's my information, cell phone number. Call me if you need anything."

Leah managed to take the card and stuff it in her pocket before giving as much of a nod as she dared.

"You'll need to turn in your badge," he continued. "I'm told they already have your gun."

"I'll see that it gets turned in," Tanner said.

"You're free to go home; just don't leave Jackson County."

The attorney left and Tanner turned to Leah. "I can take you home, unless there's someone you'd like me to call."

Swallowing, barely trusting her voice, Leah said, "Call my dad."

"Sure." Tanner went to do that. Leah knew he could get her father's phone number from personnel. At the moment, she wished she didn't have to wait, that she could fly home. She wanted her father, but she dreaded seeing him. They'd been mostly estranged for more than two years. He'd never approved of Brad, always thought he was disingenuous, unfaithful, and wild, so after the wedding she'd mostly cut him out of her life, visiting only occasionally. His words came back to her from the night she'd told him they were engaged.

"A loose cannon, that one. Leah, please reconsider. I see only problems. He doesn't even believe in God. Surely there must be a strong believer out there for you if you'll just wait."

"I love him, Dad, and you're wrong about him. You'll see."

Brad never visited her father when Leah did, and for the entire two years of the marriage, she and her dad had drifted further and further apart. What would he say now?

When Randy Radcliff arrived to take her home, his face was a study in shock and bewilderment. He looked years older than she remembered.

As Leah climbed into the front seat of his truck, her father got out, and Tanner gave him a brief explanation of what had happened. Was this an "I told you so" moment? she wondered.

"Are you okay?" her father asked when he sat back in the driver's seat. His tone was laced with worry.

"I'm so sorry, Dad." Leah couldn't hold back the tears.

"What are you sorry about?" He grabbed her in a sideways hug. "I love you, baby, no matter what. From what Tanner said, it was justified. What in the world was going on?" He held her for a long moment, and Leah took comfort in his grip, his presence, and the strong, sure beat of his heart.

Oh, if only she'd listened to him.

When he relaxed and let go, she sat back. He gave her some Kleenex and she blew her nose. Dad started the truck, and on the drive home Leah told him what she'd put up with from Brad for the bulk of their two-year marriage. The slaps, the intimidation, the times he'd hold her down just to prove he could, and the threats that no one would believe her if she told anyone. Her dad's expression went from horrified to angry. But he didn't say, "I told you so."

"Why didn't you tell me? I wish you had. Brad and I would have had words. I would have put a stop to it."

Leah had no answer. And as she wept in the front seat, her father kissed the top of her head and patted her shoulder and told her he'd be with her and that it would be all right. Time would heal all wounds. The knot of pain in her heart screamed that he was a liar. Nothing would ever be right in her world again.

CHAPTER 8

Clint watched Leah and her father drive away. He recognized Randy Radcliff from church, where Randy had a reputation as a man who helped people when they needed it. He decided he would be there to help Randy any way he could.

With Leah gone and his duty finished for now, he fought his own rising anger about the violence done to her by her husband. He remembered the day of the funeral, how tense Leah had been. At the time he'd chalked it up to grief, but now he wondered. The redness on one side of her face today and the nasty bruising on her neck were proof enough to him. Besides, she could barely talk, Brad had squeezed her throat so hard. He was angry with himself for not seeing a problem, for not being able to rescue her.

Even as the word crossed his mind, the anger eased some-what, and a rueful smile creased his lips.

"You can't rescue everyone, Clint." His father's voice rang in his head. *"It's not your job. God can rescue everyone—that's his job. You must learn to pick your battles."*

He'd gotten the lecture after being beaten within an inch of his life trying to rescue a girl from human traffickers in Kyrgyzstan, where his family were missionaries. Unconsciously, he ran a thumb down the knife scar on his face from the wound he'd received that day. At fifteen years old, he'd waded into a group of six men to save the terrified girl. They'd taken the girl and left him bleeding and unconscious in the gutter.

"But God didn't do his job," he'd told his father through swollen lips. "They took that girl. Don't we have to do more than just pray?"

His father nodded. "When we're sure that is what we're called to do." He held up an article. Clint could read the Russian headline: *Border Confrontation Ends with Two Dead.* And below, "Girls freed from trafficking ring. Four in custody, two shot by border police."

"She's safe at home. You can't run off half-cocked. Prayer is your first, best weapon and defense."

Clint had prayed, but he admitted now that at the time he didn't believe prayer worked. The beating and the aftermath led to major changes in his life. First, he had to leave the mission field. The trafficking network put a bounty on his head, and his parents' church sponsor wanted him stateside. That brought him to Oregon, where he moved in with his aunt GiGi. That eventually led to the second major change. He went from an angry teenager with no direction to a young man with a goal to become a police officer. A profession where he could be a rescuer when the situation called for it. Most of all, his attitude toward prayer changed, as he came to trust his father's wisdom: that prayer was a powerful weapon and should be the first one drawn in any fight.

As his anger ebbed, he hoped that understanding and peace would come as all the facts emerged. Going forward, the road was going to be rocky for Leah and for the police department. From what he'd heard and seen, the shooting was clearly self-defense. Yet some of the whispering he'd heard going on as he waited for Sapp to arrive with Leah worried him. Brad was thought to be a cop's cop, a macho guy without fault. A lot of people couldn't believe Leah had been abused. And with this coming on the heels of the trooper's death, hearts and emotions were still raw.

"Whose side are you on, Tanner?"

Clint turned and saw Erik Forman glaring at him. Forman was off duty and looked as if he'd rolled out of bed and driven to the station in a hurry.

"What do you mean?"

Forman spit tobacco juice on the ground. "One of our own was just murdered and you're playing peer counselor?"

"From what I saw, it was self-defense. But neither one of us is going to adjudicate it today."

Forman jabbed his index finger into Clint's chest. "Brad was in his underwear. She shot him in his sleep. There's no way she'd get the best of him in any other situation, and I hope she fries." He pushed past Clint, brushing his shoulder as he did so.

The gossip information superhighway traveled code 3, lights and sirens. Forman already knew the details of a crime scene he'd not even been at.

On the way to his car, Clint called his prayer partner, Deputy Sheriff Jack Kelly, part of a group he belonged to called Iron

Sharpens Iron. Leah's world had just been shattered, and Clint knew all he could do at the moment was pray.

✦ ✦ ✦

It took three weeks to impanel a grand jury. In Oregon, the grand jury was made up of individuals from the juror pool and consisted of seven people. At least five were required to make the decision to return an indictment. Since the grand jury only recommended charges be filed—they did not come to a guilty finding—the burden of proof was lower than in a jury trial. All the evidence would be presented by the DA. In this case, DA Arron Birch was a close friend of Brad and his family. Clint heard from Randy that Leah's lawyer tried to argue the DA should recuse himself from prosecuting the case, but it got nowhere.

The grand jury would consider the evidence Birch presented. Leah would not testify, nor would her attorney present any evidence. The old adage about how a grand jury could indict a ham sandwich had a ring of truth to it because it really was a one-sided hearing.

Clint stayed close to Randy, knowing that supporting him was supporting Leah.

"Randy, even if they vote to indict, remember, they are only hearing one side of the story. At trial, Leah's attorney will be able to tell her side."

"I know you're right. I just wish I had the money for an attorney with more experience."

The POA attorney from the day of the shooting was out of their price range, so Randy had found another. The new criminal defense attorney Leah and her father had hired was young, but he was earnest and, like her father, a Christian.

Clint stopped by after work one night. It pained him to see Leah looking pale and still a little shocky. Randy had voiced worry about the new attorney's experience.

"Are you saying you don't have confidence in the attorney?" Leah asked.

"Not at all." Randy appeared to be mustering up as much confidence as he could.

Leah caught Clint's eye, and he wished he saw more light there.

"What about you? What do you think of the new guy?" she asked.

"Since I know the shooting was justified, I'm sure he'll do fine," he said, smiling and wishing he could reach across and hug her and make all of the sadness, pain, and fear in her eyes disappear.

✦ ✦ ✦

"I know the shooting was justified . . ."

Clint's words reverberated in Leah's ears. She could only nod, recognizing at some level that Tanner was being supportive. While the fog had lifted from her mind, it didn't provide clarity about the situation; it only opened the floodgates of pain, remorse, and guilt. She knew in her head that Brad would have killed her, but her heart was harder to convince. She couldn't sleep because as soon as she lay down, the incident replayed over and over in her mind. Was there something, *anything* else she should have done?

How could she convince a jury she wasn't guilty when she couldn't convince herself?

She believed her life hung on what the grand jury decided. Leah was fatalistic about her chances with a trial jury if the people on it believed that she should have known better, she should have reported the abuse if it had really happened. Somehow, because she'd never said a word to anyone, that made her look guilty. She knew it made her feel guilty.

Prison looked inevitable.

"Have faith in the system," Tanner told her. And she wanted to believe like he did. Something about the way he looked at her, as if he could see right down into her soul, she found comforting.

Tanner had been a rock for Leah while everyone else kept their distance. She didn't blame them. She didn't know how to feel about what had happened, so how could she expect people who had worked around her and Brad for years to know?

Tanner was different. He went to the same church her dad did, so he was more than willing to help and to pray. Leah had been raised in the church. Her mother sang on the worship team. Leah began to back away from church after her mother died in a car crash. The move accelerated when she went off to college. Then God lost his importance in her life. Church attendance was sporadic, mostly when she was home on weekends to make her father happy. Eventually, when she met Brad, Leah stopped going to church altogether. He'd mocked faith when he saw her Bible. *"Where does all that get you? Reading about all the dos and don'ts and all those thees and thous?"*

Chastened, Leah remembered that all she could say was "Peace."

His response was typical Brad. "Aw, you can get that from a couple of cold beers."

Her father had asked her to go to church with him two weeks after the shooting.

"No, I don't want to go anywhere."

"You need to get out, a change of scenery."

"No."

"Well, we'll be praying for you, sweet pea."

When she heard her father's truck start up and head down the drive, Leah let out an anguished cry and threw her coffee cup across the room. It shattered against a picture frame and knocked the picture off the wall.

"Why? Why? Why?" Leah clenched and unclenched her fists as waves of anger rolled over her. All the grief and shock from the night of the shooting had morphed into a deep, dark fury. She looked up while the tears fell. "Why am I asking? You won't answer—you never do!"

She wasn't even angry at Brad anymore; she was angry with God. She'd never been a bad person. Why had he let this horrific thing happen to her?

Ignoring her tears and sniffling, she bent to clean up the mess. Ironically, the picture she'd smashed was her own work. It was a pencil drawing she'd done of her father and mother. She'd presented it to them on the last anniversary her mother was alive. In her preteens and teens, she'd done quite a bit of sketching with pencils. Her mom had always loved her work and once mentioned art school might be in her future. After her mother was killed, Leah put her pencils away.

What a metaphor for my life, she thought bitterly, *always me doing the destroying.*

Her anger festered and only a thread of control kept her from venting all the rage she felt toward God at her father. His presence and his house had become a cocoon of safety. He was the thin lifeline that kept her from opening the door in her mind that said, *End it all.*

As much as she fumed and hurt, she couldn't do that to him. This added to the frustration. She couldn't get an answer to the why, she couldn't change what had happened, and she couldn't see any way forward in her now completely shattered life.

CHAPTER 9

Curled up in bed one Monday morning, curtains drawn, room dark though it was almost midday, Leah had her eyes closed, but she was awake when her father knocked on the door.

"Leah, you up?"

Resisting the urge to pretend she was sleeping, that she didn't hear him, she unknotted her hands from the bedsheets and turned her head. "Yeah, Dad, what is it?"

"Can I come in?"

Leah bit back a snarky response. "Sure, give me a minute." She forced herself to sit up. It seemed as if she were encased in cement. She got out of bed and put on a robe, then opened the door. "What is it?"

The expression on his face really made Leah wish that she'd consulted a mirror.

"You were still in bed?"

She sighed.

"We have to go get your things today."

"That's today?" Leah didn't know how she'd forgotten. This was a river she did not want to cross. She wanted to beg off. But she had to face reality.

Furious from day one because she'd not been arrested, Brad's parents were clamoring for her head in the newspaper and on TV every day. They'd taken her to court immediately after the shooting, trying to get an emergency restraining order. Their stated purpose was to protect Brad's estate. They were told that they jumped the gun; Leah had not yet been charged with a crime. For her part, Leah didn't want Brad's estate. She had her own bank accounts; she and Brad never comingled money unless they made a purchase together. They'd bought a Jet Ski and a couple of kayaks, but that was about it.

But the Drapers' actions forced her to make some decisions, one of them being what to do about the house. It was in Brad's name; she'd simply moved in when they married and had never given it another thought. He'd not left a will and his parents wanted the house and his life insurance. She didn't want either. Turned out, Brad hadn't listed her as beneficiary to anything, not even the small life insurance policy the PD provided. Harden Draper was Brad's only beneficiary. For the house, the probate judge recommended a third-party mediator.

In the end, the mediator gave her permission to remove her things while the rest of the estate was in probate. And today was the day she'd return to the house—their house—where Brad had died. Where she'd killed him.

She hadn't returned since the night of the shooting. Staying in the home was untenable for a lot of reasons, one big one being that it was right down the road from Brad's parents.

Leah had told her father she didn't care about the house, but he thought she should fight to keep it, that it should be hers by marriage. "You earned it by putting up with that man. I sure wish you'd've told me what was going on."

"It was his house, Dad. I know his parents will go after me in civil court no matter what. They'll get the house one way or another, and I just don't want to fight this battle now."

Reluctantly he agreed. It would be enough to just retrieve her things. Brad's house had been a bare bachelor pad when she moved in. Since she liked oak furniture and had nice stuff, he'd let her redecorate.

"The truck's here," her dad was saying now, "and I've got help lined up." Leah's nice stuff included some heavy furniture, which was why they needed muscle. "I know you don't want to go to that house, but you have to tell us what's yours. That nasty lawyer for the other side will be there."

She closed her eyes. *Rachel Clyburn. Nasty* was the word but *spurned* also fit. Brad had broken up with Rachel when he began dating Leah. She'd then moved to Portland to practice law. But every time she came to Table Rock, she'd make a point to see Brad in some capacity.

There was enough orneriness in Leah to muster up the strength to get dressed. Rachel couldn't win this.

"All right, Dad. Give me five to shower and change my clothes." It took all of her strength to do just that. The only saving grace was that her father waited with a mug of steaming coffee for her when she left her room.

There in the driveway stood Clint Tanner and a couple of men from church.

On edge and instantly defensive, in spite of all the help Tanner had been to her, Leah said, "Wouldn't think you'd want to be seen with me. This might just ruin all your career aspirations."

Tanner shrugged. "All I've ever wanted to be is a good beat cop. If that's all I ever am, I'm fine with that."

"You're a good man," her father said. "A good man. I'm amazed that we went to the same church for years; too bad it took a crisis for us to meet."

"I'm the crisis," Leah mumbled under her breath before climbing into the truck with her dad. Tanner drove the U-Haul. The other men followed in their own car.

They rode in silence and Leah knew her father kept glancing her way. *Pull it together,* she told herself.

"I'll be okay, Dad. I promise. Rachel will be as mean as a snake; it's her nature."

"Don't worry about her. Just tell us what needs to go, and we'll get it done." He patted her shoulder.

Leah said nothing.

She felt as though life after the shooting was one insult after another. It still stunned her that she'd had to shoot Brad. How on earth did it come to that?

As they neared her home, her mind switched to the here and now. Leah braced herself for a confrontation with Rachel. They'd never liked one another. Thankfully, when she and her dad arrived, the only people present were Ivy, Brad's twin sister, and a Jackson County deputy sheriff, "to keep the peace," he said. He, Clint, and her father worked out the ground rules. Leah watched from the truck. She realized Ivy had a list of items that were not to be removed. That was fine. Leah didn't want anything that belonged to Brad.

Ivy's eyes shot daggers at Leah, but she said nothing. The sound of another vehicle pulling up caught Leah's attention. Maybe Rachel would appear after all. But it wasn't Clyburn; it was Larry Ripley. Anger sparked inside and Leah got out of the truck.

Larry cast her a glance but stepped up to Ivy. "Hey, Ivy, now that the police seal on the door is cut, before she gets inside, Brad had something that belonged to me. Can I go in there and get it first?"

The deputy answered. "Why don't you tell me what it is, and I'll get it for you."

"I don't know exactly where he put it. I'll have to look for it." He appealed to Ivy. Leah knew that Ivy didn't like Ripley any more than she did.

"What is it?" Ivy asked.

"Just a gym bag."

Ivy snorted. "Yeah, right. You're not going to rifle through my brother's things to find a stupid gym bag."

"Ivy, Brad was my best friend. I only want what's mine."

"No."

"What?"

"You heard me, no. The estate is in probate. Besides, you're a snake. I never understood Brad being your friend. You're not getting anywhere near his house."

Leah almost smiled. Larry started to argue, but the deputy cut him off.

"Sir, you have your answer. I'll have to ask you to leave."

"This is crazy! I want my property back."

Clint stepped forward to where the deputy stood, as if to provide support, Leah thought, somewhat perplexed. Ripley was close to hysterical.

"I want my brother back," Ivy retorted. "Guess we both lose."

Ripley jerked back as if slapped. Leah watched as he regained control, wondering all the while what was so important about a gym bag.

He held up both hands as a sign of surrender. "Fine. Sorry." He turned and trudged back to his car, not giving Leah another glance.

"You all can go in now," the deputy said.

Ivy stepped back and made no move to go inside the house. The deputy did. As for Leah, once she was inside, her hard-fought composure crumbled. A musty, unused smell permeated and something else—was that blood? She nearly fainted. Tanner caught her.

"Whoa, you okay?" he asked as he helped her to the couch.

"I can't go in there. I can't go back into that room. My dresser is on the left. Same with the closet. My stuff is on the left." She looked up into his worried face. "Can you just pack the boxes for me?"

"Sure. Just rest here."

Clint said something to the deputy, and then he and everyone else went into the bedroom.

"Can I get you some water?"

"What?" Leah looked up at the deputy. His expression was neutral, his eyes kind. "No thanks. I'll be fine. I just . . ." Her voice trailed off. She stayed on the couch while moving activity went on around her. Every so often someone would ask her about a piece of furniture. Ivy never came inside, Rachel never showed up, and for that, Leah was grateful. She and Ivy had never been friends, but they'd been cordial. She didn't think Brad and Ivy were very close, even though they were twins. Obviously her brother's death had hit her hard.

Once the truck was loaded and Leah and all her movers were out of the house, the next stop was a storage place her father had rented. Here, things went faster, and Leah was even able to help a bit. The fog on her brain lifted somewhat with the physical activity. After they finished, Leah felt hungry for the first time in days. Clint said he'd drop off the U-Haul and return to their house with pizza. She didn't argue.

Leah looked forward to returning to her father's quiet

manufactured home. On five acres, no neighbors in sight, it was the best place for her at the moment. She felt safe there. She was in limbo physically and emotionally. The bruises on her neck had faded, Brad had been laid to rest, and now the house was empty of all her belongings. Still, there was a question always at the forefront of her thoughts: *What if the grand jury votes to indict?*

"You defended yourself. The grand jury will see that," her father said. "Besides, we're praying, and God hears."

She remembered Michael and Lavinia praying for Alex Porter. A lot of good that did her.

"I don't believe that. If God really listened to anything, this never would have happened."

Under the anger bubbled guilt. She'd killed her husband; maybe she needed to be found guilty.

Brad had been a cop for six years to her three and had a large cadre of friends and admirers. Their opinion that she was guilty of murder seemed to keep everyone else away. She'd long since stopped reading the local paper. The publisher was a close friend of Brad's folks and had practically made the paper a daily memorial for Brad, rehashing all of his victories in football and in life. If the grand jury did indict, the best Leah could hope for was a change of venue.

When Clint arrived with the pizza, Leah felt something, finally, almost glad. He was the only silver lining in the entire situation. She hadn't known him well at all before the shooting, but he was the only officer openly supporting her. Tanner had shown himself to be a man of integrity, believing in and supporting Leah, promising to stand by her through everything.

She met Tanner at the door, ready to eat a full meal, even one classified as a junk food meal. Maybe getting her things out of the house had been the right thing after all.

But the expression on his face stopped her cold. "You've heard something, haven't you?"

He nodded, shifting the pizza to one hand. "I'm sorry, Leah. I just got the message. It was five out of seven, but the grand jury voted to indict you for murder."

All of Leah's composure fled. She grabbed the pizza from Clint's hand and flung it across the driveway.

"*Aggh!* Your God did this! The God you say you pray to! I don't want any more of your useless prayers. I don't want to hear about your vindictive God! I never want to see you again. Stay away from me and stop praying."

She turned on her heel and stormed into the house, pushing past her stunned father.

CHAPTER 10

Table Rock Officer Indicted: Radcliff Accused of Shooting Her Husband, Also a Table Rock Officer, in His Sleep.

After the indictment was handed down, Leah and her father reported to the city jail. She was booked and fingerprinted, but Judge Revel, citing jail overcrowding and Leah's spotless record while an officer, allowed her to be released on house arrest, with an ankle bracelet, over the vociferous objections of Harden Draper. It seemed as if Brad's father gave an interview every day saying he believed she'd murdered Brad. Rachel Clyburn stood right next to him, nodding with a serious expression on her face. When given the chance, she called Leah a "rogue cop" who thought she answered to no one. Cable news outlets picked up the story, calling the incident a cop-on-cop killing.

DA Birch also seemed to enjoy the spotlight. He made it

clear that he believed Leah had murdered Brad. Her attorney promised a vigorous defense.

The months leading up to the actual trial were surreal with Leah bound to stay inside her father's house, ankle monitor secure. Her dad had to battle the press from time to time, and he lost work over the situation, but never did his confidence flag that Leah would be acquitted.

The trial itself was nightmarish, unlike anything she ever imagined. Leah had to walk the gauntlet of reporters every day as she entered the courtroom. She ignored every shouted question.

"Your husband was in his underwear; did you shoot him while he slept?"

"Was there another woman?"

"Brad Draper was a hero. Why would anyone believe you were abused?"

"Did you abuse your husband?"

In the courtroom her attorney tried everything to refute the cold-blooded murder allegation. The photos of the crime scene did not support it, but Birch continued to hammer it home. Along with the fact that Brad was a medal of valor recipient and a true hero. Nearly all of the witnesses he called praised Brad and his character. In one glitch devastating to Leah's defense, the tape of her hoarse-voiced interview could not be presented. It had been lost—all the jury had was the transcript.

Tanner and Vicki Henderson both testified for Leah, as did Becky, but no one could say Leah had told them she was being abused. Leah herself chose not to take the stand; she didn't trust herself to be coherent, and neither did her attorney.

The trial lasted a week, and after four excruciating days of deliberation, twelve jurors convicted Leah of murder. Oregon didn't assign degrees to murder; it was either murder or aggravated murder, which could have led to the death penalty. It was aggravated murder to kill a police officer, but they still found Leah guilty of only the lesser charge.

"That's a good sign," her attorney told her. "I'll file an appeal; I promise this is not the end of this case."

As it was, Leah received the maximum sentence of twenty-five years to life. She was denied freedom while the appeal went forward and would serve her time at the Coffee Creek Correctional Facility in Wilsonville, Oregon.

PART
TWO

When the guilty verdict came down, shock shrouded Clint as if he were buried in tons of new snowfall. He'd told Leah to trust the system and now the system had found her guilty of murder. As a witness, he'd not been able to sit through the entire trial. When he was on the stand, he'd told the jury how serious Leah's injuries were. The pictures should have proved what he said, but for some reason they didn't depict the seriousness of what he remembered. A picture might be worth a thousand words but not in Leah's case. The severity of the bruises didn't show through. When he learned that the recording of her raspy-voiced interview had been lost, he tried to emphasize how bad she'd sounded.

He had to admit Birch was a pit bull for the prosecution, something Clint had admired in the past. But when it came to

Leah, Clint knew Birch had it all wrong. He hounded Clint on the stand about not being at the scene, and all Clint could say was no, he hadn't been on scene; he'd only seen Leah right after.

"Then how could you possibly know exactly what happened?"

No matter what Clint said after that, Birch dismissed it. Obviously the jury had as well.

The judge had ordered that no officers attend in uniform for fear they'd influence the jury, and that kept some away. Others attended every day they could. Most of the officers who attended the trial were on Brad's side. Marvin Sapp was the only one Clint knew who was on Leah's side.

"Her attorney was just outclassed," Marvin told Clint. "He made no impact on the jury. Birch is good—great, maybe. Leah's attorney was mediocre."

"But the injuries . . ." Clint held up his hands. "There wasn't even a clear motive."

"The pictures certainly didn't tell the whole story." Marvin shrugged. "And Birch painted Brad to be some kind of god. He kept pointing out all the awards and accolades Brad achieved over his lifetime. Leah was the wannabe.

"She didn't get any help from Judge Revel either. He always sided with the prosecution. She was hit by an avalanche." Marvin rubbed his face with both hands as Clint digested what he'd said.

He knew from Randy that the criminal defense attorney he'd hired was the best they could afford. He'd been recommended by the POA attorney who'd helped Leah the day of the shooting.

Was it really the attorney's fault? A defendant is entitled to a speedy trial. Was this trial a little too speedy? He was at a loss. He'd trusted the system, but something went wrong and it rocked his faith to the core.

He needed to find out what had happened. How on earth

could twelve people see those injuries on her face and neck and not say self-defense?

Clint went into investigator mode. He requested a copy of the court transcripts, but while he waited, he reviewed the grand jury testimony, which was already available to the public.

The most important part of the transcript to him was the part about Leah following Brad and seeing what she thought was a payoff—it was the incident that precipitated the argument with Brad.

Grand Jury Testimony—Larry A. Ripley

Q: Ms. Radcliff said in her statement to investigators that she witnessed Brad Draper receive what she believed was a payoff, in the early morning hours of August 6, while you and Richard Chambers stood by. Is that what she saw?

LAR: No, no, that's not what she saw. I realize it was a bit unorthodox, and out of policy, but I was accepting a large amount of cash, first and last months' rent for one of my commercial properties. Officer Draper and his partner merely stood by to make certain it all went well. Officer Draper took the money and then gave it to me. The help of these officers was approved by their sergeant.

Q: Why did your renter pay in such a way and so early in the morning?

LAR: Grant Holloway is a busy man. I simply tried to accommodate him.

Q: Did Officer Draper threaten Mr. Holloway with a gun?

LAR: No, never.

Q: Would Officer Draper's wife finding out about this "out of policy" meeting, as you called it, cause Officer Draper to become so enraged that he'd want to harm her?

LAR: No, not Brad.

When Clint read Larry Ripley's explanation of the incident, it sounded lame. Yet Grant Holloway gave testimony to corroborate Ripley's, as did Richard Chambers. Were they all lying?

Clint pondered how to proceed. He had no authority as an investigator, but he wanted to ask questions, gauge answers, find out if someone was not telling the truth. Leah deserved that.

In his head, he heard his father's voice: *"Pick your battles."* That gave him pause. What was the battle here? The jury heard all the evidence. Could he be wrong?

No, I'm not wrong. Leah is not a cold-blooded killer.

CHAPTER 12

E ach step of custody stripped away everything that Leah was. She was handcuffed in the courtroom, not allowed to hug her father, and led away to the very cells she herself had locked people in. People she'd worked with for three years gave her stone-cold hate stares. When she left the custody of the Table Rock city jail, remanded to the state prison, everything familiar was gone.

"You'll do what you're told when you're told and how you're told" was the admonition from the intake officer at Coffee Creek Correctional Facility. There was a strip search and a haircut because short hair was easier in prison. Her personal clothes were taken away and exchanged for the prisoner uniform. She was given jeans and a T-shirt emblazoned with *Oregon Department of Corrections* to put on.

When she entered the custody area, there were all kinds

of catcalls from the women behind bars, echoing around the enclosure. Leah ignored them as she followed the corrections officer down a long hallway, carrying her state-issued bedding and a package of toiletries.

Inmates entering the Oregon Department of Corrections system underwent a monthlong assessment period. Medical, dental, mental health, and educational needs were among the areas assessed for each inmate. For male inmates the time was also used to determine where to send them, as they would not remain at Coffee Creek. For the female inmates the assessment period would determine which facility at Coffee Creek the woman would be housed in, minimum or medium security, and any programs that would be helpful: drug treatment, parenting, education, etc. During the assessment period the women were housed in a dormitory situation—except for Leah. She followed the intake officer as they left the populated section of the prison for the segregation unit.

"We've never had a female cop killer in custody," the intake lieutenant explained. "We have determined that none of your arrestees are currently incarcerated here, and we don't anticipate problems, but it's best to play it safe."

Leah was placed in a segregation cell. At first, she believed that was what she wanted, that it would be best for her to not have to worry about physical assaults. Plus, she wouldn't have to talk, explain herself, or socialize, and that sounded like the best situation. But after only a couple of days, the walls of her seven-by-fourteen cell began closing in. Her thoughts tortured her, like the dripping of an interior water faucet, never stopping and echoing louder with each drop.

You murdered your husband. . . . You murdered your husband. . . . Brad is dead. . . . Brad is dead.

Even the sounds around her—doors clanging, inmates yelling, conversations going on, guards making their rounds—did nothing to mute her thoughts.

She was allowed out to shower and to exercise in a small area where all she could do was walk back and forth. And to attend her assessment meetings.

"You're in a position to help women here," her intake counselor told her. "You're educated. You could teach, maybe even mentor women with less education, fewer life skills. Would that interest you?"

Leah thought for a moment. "Would that get me out of segregation?"

"For periods of time. But I have no control over your housing situation."

"I'd have to think about it."

Later, she wondered why she didn't jump at the chance to do something outside her small cell.

What could I possibly teach anyone other than how to mess up their life?

By the end of the second week, Leah was certain she would lose her mind. Her appetite disappeared and she felt like sleeping all the time. Feeling desperate, she dropped a kyte—prison terminology for a request—for the institution psychologist.

"Are you suicidal?" the psychologist asked.

Leah studied the woman, who barely looked up from her notebook. She didn't answer because she wasn't sure how to answer.

"Are you suicidal?" the woman repeated.

The drab gray office mirrored how Leah saw herself, how she felt, and how she saw the future: drab, gray, hard, and unyielding.

She could hear the woman's clock ticking and felt as if she were on *Jeopardy!* with seconds to come up with the right answer.

She knew what suicide watch meant in prison. She would lose everything: her clothes, bedsheets, and the only bit of privacy she had, which was lights-out. Suicide watch meant the lights on 24-7 and guards monitoring everything she did. That would push her around the bend.

"I don't want to live—is that the same thing?"

The woman finally looked up from her notebook. "Have you tried to hurt yourself?"

Leah shook her head. "No, because if I did, it would hurt my father. I don't want to hurt him any more than I already have. But I still can't see around the corner. I can't see how I will last in this place."

"Don't try to see around the corner. Take one day at a time, one step at a time."

Leah studied her shoes as the clock ticked. "Do I have to stay in segregation?"

"You're there for your own protection."

"It's punishment, hell. I'd rather take my chances in the general population."

The woman wrote in her notebook. After a moment she said, "I'll see what I can do, but I'm not making any promises. You have to do something for me."

"What?"

"Start eating and acting like you do want to live, whether you feel like it or not."

Leah gave a weak nod, wondering how to accomplish that. Life as she knew it was over. Would she be better off in general population? She didn't know. All she knew was that segregation was not where she wanted to be.

Another week passed before her transfer was approved. By then Leah was hanging on by her fingernails. When the guard came to escort her to the medium security side of the prison, she was ready with all her belongings stuffed in a prison-issued duffel bag. As she left segregation, there were catcalls and obscenities tossed her way from the women incarcerated there for disciplinary issues. They told her she wouldn't last a day where she was going. *Maybe yes, maybe no,* Leah thought. *But I absolutely would not last another day here.*

As she followed the guard down a long hallway, carrying her bag, more insults and predictions were tossed her way when they reached the medium security custody area. None of it scared Leah because at this point fear couldn't penetrate the numbness. It only made her want to hurry; the noise gave her a headache.

Once they reached the cell that was to be her new home, Leah stood and waited for the door to open. On the other side was a tall, heavyset woman with short hair shaved close to her head, an unreadable expression on her face.

As Leah stepped inside and the door clanged shut behind her, she wondered if she'd just jumped from the frying pan into the fire.

CHAPTER 13

L eah stood, staring at the woman, considering what her
next move should be.

Her new cellmate made the first move and stepped
forward. "Name's Nora. I know who you are. Leah
Radcliff." She pointed to the left bunk. "That's your
bunk. And everything on that side of the cell. Everything
on the other side is mine. I like things clean, so make sure you
keep things clean, stay outta my stuff, and we'll get along."

"Thanks." Leah tossed the duffel bag on the floor near the
bunk and pulled out her bedding, a little befuddled because
there was something familiar about Nora. As she went about
making the bed haltingly, she kept glancing at her from the
corner of her eye, struggling to remember how she could possibly know this woman. Leah had been informed that none of
her arrestees were here at Coffee Creek, so it couldn't be that.

"You got something to ask, ask it."

"You look familiar."

"All criminals look alike?"

"No, that's not what I meant," Leah protested, only to realize Nora was teasing her. Then it hit like a sledgehammer. She knew the woman from basketball. But not as Nora. She was Leonora Lyons, nicknamed Leo the Lion for her aggressive play on the court. At one time Leah had idolized her and tried to emulate her. Two or three years older than Leah, Leonora had skipped college and gone straight to the pros, playing for several years with the Seattle Storm.

Leah remembered why Nora was here. Four years ago, she'd gotten behind the wheel drunk and driven onto the freeway going the wrong way. She hit another car head-on and killed a family of three. Her license had already been suspended for DUI, and Nora got the maximum sentence of fifteen years.

"You remember?"

"I do." Leah would never forget. She hated drunk drivers. Her mother was killed by a drunk driver. She didn't know what else to say. What were her options? She couldn't go back to segregation. Finally she fell back to basketball.

"You were a great ballplayer."

"So were you. And here we are. Are we going to have a problem?"

The question hit Leah sideways. After all the stress and the drama, the pain and the guilt, Nora's question made her laugh, and once she started, she couldn't stop. She had to sit down on her half-finished bed while Nora gave her the side-eye.

"What's so funny?"

Leah held her stomach and worked to regain her composure. "We're both in prison for a very long time—what other problems could there be?"

"Oh, believe me, a lot. You've never been on this side of the bars before, honey. You don't even know the true meaning of the word *problem* yet."

Her tone sobered Leah. She realized her new cellmate was 100 percent correct and it was nothing to laugh at.

✦ ✦ ✦

After Leah finished making her bed and putting her meager belongings away in her space, she sat down on the bunk. Nora was reading a familiar book, the Bible. It made Leah want to scream. Reality hit her like a blow between the eyes. She'd wanted out of segregation and here she was, with a Bible-reading drunk driver killer for a roommate. Her father's God was not only vindictive, he had a sick sense of humor.

"Can I ask you a question?"

Nora put the Bible down and looked over at Leah. "Shoot."

"Why did they put me with you? Because we're basketball players?"

Nora shrugged. "Don't know. My last cellie was released two days ago, so there was an open bed. That might be all there was to it. But God works in mysterious ways."

"You're a Christian?"

"I am."

"You're not going to preach to me, are you?"

"I don't preach to nobody but myself."

"God hasn't done much for you, has he?"

"Honey, God has done everything for me. You got a problem with God?"

Leah shrugged. "It's just not my favorite subject."

"Fair enough."

"Does everybody here know about me? Know that . . . ?" Leah couldn't bring herself to finish the sentence.

"That you shot your hubby? I don't know everyone. But I suspect most folks do. Not a lot to do here but talk. And most ladies like to talk, tell tales, true or not."

"And I was a cop. Am I going to have trouble?"

Nora sat up and faced Leah. "You might. Depends on how you carry yourself. You're not a cop now, so don't act like one. But don't take any guff either."

A buzzer rang, made Leah jump.

"That's the dinner bell."

The cell door opened, and the sounds of women exiting their cells, laughter, talking, footsteps on the pavement filtered in. Women walked by, peering into the cell but continuing down the hallway. Suddenly Leah felt fear.

"Don't show it." Nora closed her Bible. "They smell fear like sharks smell blood. You toughen up and put on your game face." She stood.

Leah swallowed and followed her, pasting on a stiff, blank expression, knowing she had to do as Nora said and wondering what would happen if she was tested.

As they walked down the hallway, along the line they were directed to stay on, she was cognizant of the stares. Once they reached the dining hall, some women fell into step with Nora, greeting her as if they were friends. They ignored Leah. The dining hall filled with chatter, reminding Leah of a flock of parrots. Organized, chaotic fellowship. That's what she was hearing here.

They'd just gotten their food and were walking toward a table when a woman approached. "Hey, Nora, who's your little friend?"

Leah turned and saw a thickly built woman with a crew cut and tattoos all over her neck walking toward her.

"Not your concern, Pat. Not your concern." Nora kept walking.

"Really? She ain't got a voice?"

"I have a voice." Leah stopped. A hush spread across the hall, as if Leah had tossed a silent pill into the pond and the ripples rolled across the sea of chatty women, quieting them.

"Oh." Pat folded her arms. "What do you have to say for yourself, stinking cop?"

Leah knew she had to think fast and talk smart.

"That you're not my counselor or my lawyer, so I have nothing to say to you. I'm going to eat my dinner." She moved to walk around Pat, careful to keep her eyes up and on the woman. Pat glared and jerked as if she was going to knock Leah's tray from her hands. It took all of Leah's self-control not to flinch. She passed within a hair's breadth of the woman and followed Nora to a table. It wasn't until she sat that she realized she'd been holding her breath.

"Not bad, Radcliff," Nora said before she lowered her head to say grace over the meal.

Leah bowed her head as well, not to pray, but to try to calm a heart that pounded in her chest as if it wanted to escape. How would she survive twenty-five years of this?

CHAPTER 14

Brad Draper had been dead for nearly a year, and Leah had been in prison for over a month. Clint shook his head as that truth sank in. He'd received the trial transcripts and read them over a few times, frustrated not so much by what they said, but by what they didn't say. Leah didn't take the stand, so she did not personally spell out the abuse she'd been subjected to. The attorney did the best he could, but Clint knew that if he'd been on the jury, he'd have wanted to hear from Leah.

A lot of time was spent on the photos from the morning of the incident. The attorney obviously thought that would be enough to prove self-defense. But so many people testified about what a great guy Brad was, the idea that Leah would have to defend herself from him seemed unlikely. It broke Clint's heart, but one fact hurt Leah more than anything: In the months, weeks, and days before the shooting, she never told anyone Brad was abusive.

He wanted to conduct his own investigation, talk to the people who'd testified, at least those who would talk to him, and he'd had a month to mull over his options. Clint decided the direct approach was called for. Richard Chambers was his best bet. Their shifts overlapped. On his Friday he looked over everyone's status and found Chambers on his lunch break, eating at a favorite place of cops, a diner near the river owned by a retired officer. Clint didn't change his status, leaving himself available for any calls that came in, as he made his way to the diner.

The big man regarded Clint warily as he approached.

"How are you doing?" Clint asked as he stepped up to the table.

"I'm fine. What are you doing here? I didn't hear you ask for code."

"That's 'cause I'm not on my lunch break. I came here to talk to you."

"What do we have to talk about?"

Clint turned a chair around backward and sat facing Chambers. "I'm sorry about your partner."

Chambers said nothing, just kept chewing.

"I'll be blunt. I don't believe you told the truth on the stand. Not you or Ripley for that matter."

Chambers swallowed, took a sip of his soda, his face betraying nothing. "Yeah? So what do you think the truth is?"

"Leah was a victim of abuse. I saw that for myself."

"Whatever. A jury saw it differently." He hiked a shoulder. "You need to suck it up and accept it. You were wrong."

"What is it you guys are hiding?"

For the first time Clint saw a reaction in Chambers's face—surprise, maybe. He hoped he'd hit a nerve. He heard the door open and Chambers looked toward the entrance. Clint turned and saw Sergeant Forman striding their way. Forman used to run SAT, but that detail was disbanded after Brad's death. He now supervised day patrol.

"You're out of your beat, Tanner."

"That's what I was trying to tell him," Chambers said.

Clint heard something in Chambers's tone—irritation? No, he decided, it was fear, Chambers was afraid of Forman.

Realizing he would get nothing from the man at this point, Clint stood to leave. "Just on my way out."

Forman gripped his arm as he went to pass. "Stay in your own lane. I mean it."

"No problem," Clint said, jerking his arm free and leaving the restaurant. He got into his patrol car and left the area, anger vibrating through him. Something was way off here, and it grated on him. But then, did he really expect Chambers to admit that he'd lied under oath? Cops were guarded under most circumstances, and he admitted to himself that he was on very shaky ground. But at the moment all he could think to do to help Leah was to ask questions.

He had one shot left, and that was in the civilian world. Maybe if he caught the man off guard, he'd get more out of the insurance salesman and planned for that while he worked to calm down.

+ + +

On his next day off Clint paid a visit to the insurance office of Grant Holloway.

Holloway was a tall blond man with a thick beard. He smiled like a salesman and gripped Clint's hand in a tight handshake when he entered the office.

"Good morning, how can I help you today, Mr. . . . ?"

"Tanner, Clint Tanner."

"Mr. Tanner. Looking for insurance?"

"Not really. I guess you could say I'm looking for answers. I'm a friend of Leah Radcliff and—"

"I have nothing to say about that." Holloway's posture changed as if someone had flipped a switch. The smile disappeared and he took a step back.

"I only wondered if—"

Holloway cut around him to the office door and opened it. "I think you better go."

"Do you always pay your rent at two in the morning?" Clint asked as he stepped toward the door.

"I have nothing to say to you."

Clint slowly exited the office and held the man's gaze as he did so. Holloway looked away first.

Boy, asking questions about the trial sure seemed to bring out anxiety in people, Clint thought.

Two days later, when Clint reported for duty, there was a summons in his mailbox from internal affairs. Frowning as he read the complaint, Clint reported there as soon as squad meeting ended.

He was directed to Lieutenant Racer's office. Clint didn't know Racer well, but the man had been tight with Brad Draper. Clint had heard rumors about the man, that he was a petty micromanager, eager to fire good cops for no reason, because he was never a good cop. Clint hated to rely on rumors for anything.

"Have a seat, Tanner."

Clint did as instructed. He couldn't read Racer at all and decided not to try. His conscience was clean. He'd not crossed the line anywhere that he could remember, so there was no reason to get worked up about this summons.

"Today is your first day back to work after the weekend." It was a statement, not a question.

Clint nodded, wondering if he was going to be read his police officer bill of rights.

"I guess you managed to irritate someone on your days off."

"Sir?"

"Grant Holloway filed a complaint, claiming you harassed him the day before yesterday."

Clint almost laughed but caught himself. Racer was deadly serious.

"I only wanted to ask him a question. Never even got to. He kicked me out of his office. That was the extent."

"He's pressing me to charge you with conduct unbecoming. That's a fireable offense."

"Pressing? Am I being charged with something? I was off duty and I did nothing wrong."

Racer stood, walked around the desk, leaned his hip on the corner, and glared down at Clint. "Leah Radcliff is gone. A jury convicted her. Case closed. Drop it unless you want to find yourself looking for another job."

Clint refused to be intimidated. "Is that a threat?"

"A warning. Stay away from Holloway and anything to do with the Leah Radcliff case. That's an order. If you disobey my lawful order, you'll be facing insubordination. Understood?"

Clint nodded.

"I can't hear you."

"Yes, sir."

"Good. You're dismissed."

Clint got up and turned to leave, knowing that arguing with Racer was not in his best interest.

"You don't want to be on my bad side," Racer said to his back.

CHAPTER 15

Leah learned two things pretty quickly.

First, prison was all routine. They had meals, recreation time, and three head counts at the same times
every day, lights out at ten, lights on at five.

And second, the prison was really just a collection
of cliques. Some were along racial lines, others on sentence lines, and others were people who knew each other out
of prison and reconnected in prison. Nora was in a religious
clique. Leah figured that for the rest of her life she would have
bad luck. Being stuck with Nora, a prayer-believing Christian
like Tanner, was just that, bad luck. She even called herself Nora
because of the Bible.

*"People in the Bible had their names changed after important
life-changing events. Jacob became Israel; Sarai became Sarah;
Abram became Abraham. When I found God in here, I decided to
become Nora, a new person. Leonora is my past."*

Leah thought that was a bit extreme, but Nora wasn't a threat, so she decided to try to make the best of them being cellmates.

Being around Nora reminded her of Tanner. She'd told him in no uncertain terms to stay out of her life, and she doubted she'd ever see him again. More bad luck that she'd alienate the only guy who seemed to be on her side.

After a week in general population, she felt a little better than she had in segregation. True, her thoughts were more distracted now because she always had to be on guard against an attack. Pat, the woman with the tattooed neck, seemed to always be watching her. Leah was a long way from getting her balance back. Inside she ached. She stayed close to Nora, ignoring the prayers and the God talk, knowing that there was safety in numbers in this place.

She'd been in jail for a little over a month before her father's first visit. It had taken that long for him to be approved. When the day came that she could see him, Leah thought her heart would burst.

"Oh, sweet pea, you look so thin." He hugged her, and Leah fought the tears. She had lost fifteen pounds. "You're skin and bones."

They sat at their assigned places at a table in the visiting area, the noise of families reuniting all around them.

"Sorry, Dad. The food isn't great here," she said, though she really had no opinion about the food. Her world right now was flat and gray, the food and everything in it. Though at the moment, her dad was three-dimensional and in color.

"They put you in general population. Is that going okay?" His forehead crinkled with worry, and it pierced Leah to see how he'd aged five years in a month.

"Yeah. My cellmate is Leonora Lyons. Remember her?"

His eyebrows went up. "The basketball player?"

Leah nodded.

He smiled and the tension fell away from his face. "That is answered prayer. She's someone you can relate to."

He kept a grip on her hand and began to tell her what was happening at home. Prayer was a big part of what he had to say, and Leah barely listened, still amazed that anyone, especially her father, believed in prayer.

"Praying for a new attorney . . ."

"We'll file an appeal as soon . . ."

"Got a big group at church . . . every Sunday . . ."

Leah simply savored the sound of his voice, like a bandage on an open wound, and the feel of his calloused hands on hers. Eventually he fell silent.

"Talk to me, Leah, please."

She looked up and saw the tears in his eyes, and something broke inside. The wound ruptured and the bandage fell away. Grabbing her gut, she leaned forward, head hitting the table.

"Oh, Dad, I feel so empty inside," she moaned. "It's as if someone carved the middle out of me with a jagged spoon. I can't believe Brad is dead."

Though she thought she'd cried all the tears possible, more fell. She felt her dad's hand on her back. He began to pray, but she hadn't the strength to tell him to stop. By the time she composed herself, the tone sounded that indicated their time was almost up. She wiped her face with her sleeves.

"I'll be okay, Dad. Sorry—"

Voice sharp, he said, "You have nothing to be sorry for." He reached into a bag he'd brought with him. Leah had noticed it but said nothing.

He laid a notebook and a Bible on the table. "I got permission to give these to you."

She started to protest but stopped. He was all she had.

"Take it," he said. "Maybe you don't want to read it right now, but you never know how you'll feel in a few days or a week. There's also a notepad if you feel like writing or drawing."

Too tired to fight, she nodded and picked up the items.

He wiped his eyes with his palms. "I'll be back next week. I love you, sweet pea. Never forget that."

+ + +

"It's always harder after family visits," Nora said when Leah was slow to get up for mealtime.

Leah sat up with her feet on the floor, head in her hands. "How do you do it?"

"My family is all in Seattle. I don't see them much."

"That's not what I meant." She looked up. "How do you act so normal, so content here in this place?"

"What do you want me to do, mope? The only thing I have control over is my attitude. I got to be here. I ain't gonna cry about it."

"You killed three people! How do you live with that?" Leah asked the question partly to get a rise out of Nora. She didn't believe the woman had successfully put her crime behind her.

But Nora was unfazed. "Since you asked . . . when I first got here, I was a lot like you. Drowning in self-pity and wanting an easy way out. But my first cellmate recommended I drop a kyte for the chaplain. I did and it changed my life. I'm sorry for my crime, wish it had never happened. But I can't take it back. All I can do is move forward and live a better life. My faith helps me do that."

"You weren't a Christian before you got arrested?"

"I thought I was. But I was drunk or high so much of the

time, I thought I was a lot of things. Chaplain Darrel helped me get my head on straight. He can do the same for you."

Leah shook her head. The door opened; it was mealtime. "He'll just tell me to trust God and pray. I don't believe in either of those things."

"Suit yourself. You can do hard time if you want. I think you'll find it exhausting in the long run."

CHAPTER 16

C lint went into service seething after his talk with Racer. Something was wrong with everything: Grant Holloway, Terry Racer, Leah's conviction. He had to calm down or he'd make a mistake.

His computer beeped with a message. It was from Sapp and Henderson. They asked to meet at a Dutch Bros. Coffee shop. Clint agreed and soon arrived at the location. Dutch Bros. was a drive-through and Clint didn't see them in line. In a second, he spotted the other patrol car at the far end of the lot with Sapp and Henderson standing by the trunk, drinking coffee.

Clint was not in the mood for coffee, so he pulled up next to them and got out of the car.

Instantly he forgot his problem when he saw Vicki's face. She was upset about something.

"Hey, what's up?"

"Big mess," Sapp said as he opened the trunk. He pulled out an evidence bag with a dead rat inside. "Vicki found this in her mailbox this afternoon."

"What?" Clint felt a new flash of white-hot anger.

"It's not just this. I've been getting nasty, hateful phone calls, and my tires were slashed. It's because I testified for Radcliff, I'm sure, but . . ." Her voice trailed off and she looked at Sapp.

"I testified as well, and nothing has happened to me," Sapp said. "What about you?"

"Nothing unprovoked." He told them about his chat with Chambers.

"Maybe you should leave it alone," Sapp said. "The jury spoke."

"Something's not right. You were there that day."

Sapp just shrugged.

Clint turned to Vicki. "You have the least time on; maybe that's why you're being targeted. Someone wants you to quit."

"Well, I'm not going to. I like this job."

"Good for you. Go to the POA. This is something the union should know about. Harassment in any form is wrong."

Henderson shook her head. "I'm already being called a rat. I don't want to add whiner to the mix. I just wondered if it was happening to you. I got my answer."

Clint saw determination in the young officer's face. "Okay. But let me know if anything else happens."

"We will," Sapp said. "You do the same."

Clint left the meeting, mind whirring about the injustice that was piling up. Leah wronged and now another woman, Henderson, feeling unjustified wrath. What on earth was happening?

Later in his shift, since the radio was quiet, he decided to make another stop. His first training officer had retired three years ago, and he lived in Clint's beat. Clint took a chance he'd be home and available. When he turned the corner, he was rewarded by the sight of Parker out mowing his lawn.

The older man looked up and smiled when Clint pulled to the curb. Then he turned the mower off.

"Out here mowing your own lawn?" Clint chided. "Don't you have grandkids for that?"

Parker smiled and mopped his brow. "They don't do it the way I like it."

Clint laughed. Parker was OCD—that was for sure. It was good to be trained by him. He was a stickler for crossing t's and dotting i's.

"To what do I owe the honor?" Parker walked to where Clint stood next to his patrol car. They shook hands.

"Oh, this and that. I had a question for you."

"Shoot."

Parker listened while Clint gave him the highlights about Leah, about Holloway, and about Racer and the complaint. Parker let Clint finish before he said anything.

"Hum" was all he said at first, but Clint waited.

"I remember Radcliff. I thought she had a lot going for her. I was sorry to see her hook up with Draper." He folded his arms across his chest and sighed. "You know you're dealing with the Hangmen, don't you?"

"The Hangmen?" Clint was genuinely perplexed. "That sounds like something a group of cops in the 1890s would call themselves. Back when law enforcement was less civilized."

"That's probably where they got the name."

"They? Cops in Table Rock?"

"Yep."

"Why would a group of cops call themselves the Hangmen? Are they trying to dispense justice in a frontier sort of way?"

Parker chuckled. "You still don't gossip, huh? That's generally a cop's second pastime."

"I never saw the point in it."

"Maybe it's just as well. Racer, Draper, Patterson in homicide, and a few others, they consider themselves the official gatekeepers, or Hangmen, of the PD."

"Gatekeepers?"

"They decide who gets what special assignments, plum transfers, who stays, who goes, who gets in trouble, who doesn't, who hangs, and who doesn't." He shrugged. "It's a good old boys club."

A light went on. "I have heard about it; I just didn't believe it. We have a command structure—"

Parker snorted. "The brass are politicians at heart. Politicians often don't want to make the hard decisions. Nature abhors a vacuum, so the Hangmen step in."

Clint looked hard at his old partner and mentor. "Wait, you condone this nonsense?"

Parker held up a hand. "It's not that black-and-white. Yeah, they're egotistical jerks. But every once in a while, they step in for the greater good. You remember that gal they hired a few years back, the one who looked as if a stiff breeze would knock her over? Had no business in a uniform with a gun, but she knew someone."

Clint thought for a minute. Vaguely he did remember a woman who'd failed just about every field training parameter.

"She bombed out of field training, right?"

Parker shook his head. "She did, but they weren't going to fire her."

"If she graduated the academy—"

"She was a protected class, a woman, and they eased every test they could to get her out of the academy, to help her graduate. She was a hazard in the field. It was only a matter of time before she got herself or someone else hurt. The Hangmen solved the problem."

"How?"

"I don't know the specifics, but she quit."

"You're okay with that?"

"Look, should it work that way? No. I'm not against gals, worked with lots who were qualified. Police work is dangerous enough for cops who pass everything with flying colors. That poor trooper from last year is a case in point. The brass wasn't doing that girl any favors bending rules to keep her in order to satisfy a quota. It was all politics. Would you rather she stayed on the job and got herself or someone else killed because she wasn't up to the task?"

"No, but—"

"I remember: you're a Boy Scout. You're right—it shouldn't work that way, but it does. Until the brass gets tough enough to buck politics and do the right thing for officer safety, groups like the Hangmen are going to operate below the radar."

Clint struggled to keep his tone level. This was wrong in so many ways. "Suppose they don't just cull officer safety problems? Suppose they start acting in their own self-interest?"

Parker nodded. "That is a problem. Brad Draper was heavy-handed in the field and at times a liar. The fact that he was never investigated is the answer to that question. He was dangerous, but he was a Hangman."

+ + +

The conversation with Parker bothered Clint. He kept praying for an answer and heard nothing.

After work he got together with his friend Jack, a Jackson County deputy sheriff.

"Am I that naive?" Clint asked after telling Jack about the conversation.

"Nah, you just concentrate on the job at hand. A lot of people don't." He hiked a shoulder. "I'll admit sometimes I like to stand around on slow nights and tell stories with other cops, listen to gossip, talk about arrests. I've heard rumors about the Hangmen for years."

"You never said anything."

"It was innuendo. I know you don't take much stock in that."

"Innuendo, but you believe they exist."

"I guess I do." Jack paused and played with his coffee. "I don't believe they affect the sheriff's department yet."

"Yet?"

"Well, this is 975." Jack lowered his voice, using a code that meant confidential information. "You know Duke Gill?"

Clint nodded.

"He was tight with Draper. I think he's one."

"Noncops are Hangmen?"

"If they serve a purpose. The rumor is the Hangmen aren't only about street-level police work. Gill works for Harden Draper, so the Hangmen have reach in business. He concerns me because he's related by marriage to Grady Blanchard. Some of us think they might try to spread the club to the sheriff's department. But we have a contingency plan—that's all I'll say."

Clint sat back and sighed. "Wow. How many officers in my department do you think are involved in, uh . . . ? How many guys are Hangmen?"

"Hard to say. I'd bet it's a small number. I heard they all have tattoos of an old-fashioned gallows somewhere on them. Don't worry, bud; you're not surrounded by people who make their own rules and get people fired or not."

"But to have the power to get anyone to quit or get fired . . . you'd think a lot of people would have to be involved."

Jack tilted his head. "Just the right people with clout. It will be interesting to see if the Hangmen last without Draper. He had a lot of juice because his family is so politically connected, the head of the snake, so to speak."

Clint considered this. "What about Leah? Did the Hangmen have the juice to influence her trial?"

"That's a tough one. She certainly didn't make them her fans by killing Draper. A lot of us in the sheriff's department didn't think that self-defense was so far-fetched. Gossip on the grapevine is sixty-forty Leah acted in self-defense. But DA Birch is tight with the Drapers. I was surprised he didn't recuse himself."

"You believe the Hangmen could have influenced the prosecution."

"No doubt. How do you prove it?"

Clint didn't have an answer.

CHAPTER 17

One gray day after another ran together for Leah. The hardest month was August and the one-year anniversary of Brad's death. Her father's weekly visits helped steady her and, surprisingly, so did the rigid routine of prison. September and October passed in a blur. There was no opportunity to retreat and bury her head in the sand. The need for a sweatshirt in the recreation area reminded her that time was moving on and they were swiftly moving toward winter. She kept to herself but still stayed close to Nora. One day during recreation a woman approached her. She had the look of a speed freak: bad teeth, sallow skin.

"I'm Donna." She held out a hand. "You the one who killed her husband 'cause he was beating you?"

Leah tensed. "Yes."

"Good. 'Bout time we won a round. It's always the man that kills the woman. I had a man beat me once or twice, wish I could have done the same as you."

In her peripheral vision, Leah could see other women watching the exchange. She hesitated a second. She wasn't proud of shooting Brad, far from it. And she certainly didn't want it to be a win for feminists. Yet she understood this woman's sentiment. Leah had seen her share of women victimized by men.

She took the extended hand. "Leah."

"Glad to meet you." Donna looked over at Nora. "I know your cellie. This is my third stay here. We met before. She's a Jesus freak. Harmless and nice, though." She sat down on the bench next to Leah and continued to talk.

"I was wondering . . . There's a running program here in the prison, organized by a nonprofit, called Reason to Run. I enrolled. Tried everything else to keep me off drugs. Maybe this will do the trick," she said. "You interested in joining up too?"

Leah had heard about the group. It was all about women encouraging one another to form healthy habits that they could continue once they were released. The women in the program trained together for a 5K run. It didn't interest her in the least.

"No, jogging is really not my thing."

"It might help. You're depressed—I can tell. I was so depressed my first time in."

Leah looked at Donna out of the corner of her eye, wondering who had put her up to this. "Sorry, not interested."

"If you change your mind, let me know." She got up and trotted off for the track. Leah watched her leave and then noticed for the first time that there was a basketball hoop in the yard. Maybe she needed exercise, just not jogging.

After recreation ended, on the way back to her cell, she asked Nora, "Will they give me a basketball?"

"Sure, you can sign one out."

A few days later she did just that. As she rolled the ball around in her hands, the feel of the taut orange leather evoked long-forgotten memories. While basketball had dominated her early life, Leah had played very little since she graduated from college. Playing at the collegiate level spoiled the game for her. She loved having fun on the court, she liked to win, but the push to win at all costs left a sour taste in her mouth. And Brad hated the game. When she bounced the basketball for the first time in the recreation area, she couldn't remember when she'd last played.

It felt awkward at first, but better with each bounce. To limber up, she just walked up and down the length of the blacktop, bouncing the ball. Memories flooded back: winning the state championship in high school. Her mother was alive then. She was killed two months after the championship game.

Leah started shifting the ball from hand to hand, stepping up her pace. Then she did some dribbling between the legs, snappy and quick down the length of the yard. Finally, breathing hard, she pivoted, turned, and shot her signature twenty-foot jumper. Air ball—she missed the basket by a mile.

Standing there, heart racing, Leah watched the ball bounce away. She could hear her mother's encouragement from years ago when Leah was just starting to play. All the other girls were so much taller.

"Try again, Leah. Size doesn't matter. Practice will level the playing field. It's the only thing that will help you get better."

Mom was right. Leah practiced hard and eventually made varsity squad, then all-American. Then college. She'd always been able to work hard and do better.

Now, what was the point?

Defeat set in and tears threatened. Taking a deep, shuddering breath, Leah felt like she was the air ball, off target and useless.

"You want to play?"

Leah turned. Nora had been watching.

"Don't think so."

Nora picked up the basketball and walked toward Leah. "Some one-on-one? Might do us both a lot of good."

Leah hiked a shoulder. "I'm too rusty."

"Change your mind, let me know." Nora tossed the ball back and walked away.

Later, back in their cell, listening to Nora snore, Leah curled up in her bunk, wishing she could close her eyes and make the nightmare go away.

Wouldn't happen. Brad was dead and he would stay dead.

Another of her mother's sayings floated through her thoughts. *"With the wrong attitude, everything can look dark. Change your attitude and you change your circumstances."* Nora had said almost exactly the same thing.

Tears flowed. "I can't, Mom. I can't," she whispered. "Things seem dark because they *are* dark. I'm in a pit I'll never be able to climb out of."

She saw the Bible on the floor in her corner where she'd tossed it. She'd scribbled a bit in the sketch pad her father had brought, and it was on the tiny portion of the desk area reserved for her use. But she had no interest in the Bible and had thrown it on the floor.

Just before lights-out, Leah got up and retrieved the Bible, careful not to wake Nora. She sat on the bed and opened it. Written on the inside cover was a note from her father.

Whether you like it or not, I'm praying for you. I always have, and I always will.

Leah stared at her father's writing until the lights went out and she couldn't see it any longer.

CHAPTER 18

N ew Year's Day, Clint sat in church and barely heard the message. He'd told Leah to trust a system that was likely rigged against her. He'd wanted to give her hope, not mislead her. But the first anniversary of Brad's death had come and gone, and Clint knew he'd soon wake up one day to the realization that Leah had been in prison for a year. Yet they were no closer to seeing her freed. The appeals process was on a snail's pace. Where was God?

The question stabbed at him. Almost immediately an answer stabbed back—God was right with her, every step of the way. He remembered when Randy had shared that Leah asked to be moved to general population and Clint almost lost it. Reliving that moment helped him to focus and calmed the turbulence in his soul. God had provided for Leah then when no one else could; there was no reason to think he wouldn't keep providing.

"Why take her out of segregation?" he'd asked at the time.

"She wanted out, said she didn't like being by herself," Randy told him. "They did give her a cellmate I've heard of, Leonora Lyons. She played basketball too. I'm praying that it's a good, safe change for Leah."

Clint had researched Lyons and discovered that he couldn't have picked a better cellmate for Leah. Lyons was genuinely repentant and apologetic. She also claimed to have found God in prison. Clint grudgingly gave thanks for that. He went from "maybe God is working" to acknowledging that "yes, of course God is working." In spite of that knowledge, the New Year had him back in struggle mode. Why hadn't she been cleared yet?

And when he met Randy for lunch after church, things were worse than he thought.

"I had to let the attorney go," Randy told him over coffee. "While he charged less than the POA attorney, it was stretching my resources. As far as the pending appeal goes, he said it could take up to eighteen months to be heard. I have time to search for a new lawyer."

Clint bit his tongue when a bitter, impatient comment threatened. Taking a deep breath, he searched for something positive to say. Randy had become a good friend; Clint needed to help any way he could.

"We'll start a GoFundMe page or find an attorney to work pro bono. My parents are familiar with a lot of Christian firms that might take the case," Clint offered.

"Leah's conviction was not about religion; it was pure injustice. Maybe we need to look toward those organizations that look into criminal justice wrongs."

Clint nodded. "That's an idea, but let me exhaust all my avenues first. Maybe my folks can give me some recommendations."

"Thank you for all you're doing, Clint. At least my fears

about Leah leaving isolation never came to pass. She is doing good despite the move."

"How is Leah getting along with her cellmate?"

Randy shrugged. "I'll say good, because she doesn't complain about her. Still, she looks so lost."

Clint wondered if Lyons was the problem or if it was simply being in jail. When he looked in Randy's eyes, he saw the uncertainty there and knew he had to offer some encouragement, even if he didn't feel it.

"I researched Leonora Lyons on the Internet. I remembered her name from basketball."

"What did you find out?"

"That she was truly repentant after the accident. She asked the family and God to forgive her for what happened."

"Repentant?"

"Yeah, Randy. Think about it: we're all worried, but God is there watching over her while we can't." After he made the statement, Clint prayed that the confidence would infuse his own heart.

For the first time Clint could remember, Randy smiled. "Why, thanks for that. I know it, but I needed to be reminded. Bless you for reminding me."

"No problem, Randy. I wish I could do more."

As they ate breakfast, Randy told Clint all about the latest visit. Clint didn't tell Randy about the Hangmen; he was still working out how to deal with the clandestine organization. Cops enforced laws; they didn't make up their own set and ignore what they didn't like. Depending on how widespread the Hangmen really were, it would be a scandal that could tear his department apart.

He also decided it was time to promote. The sergeant's test was going to be given soon, and Clint felt confident that he was ready to take the next step in his career. The administration was considering starting up a new smuggling task force, and Clint wanted to be part of it, hopefully as supervisor.

When he returned to work on Monday, there was another note in his box from IA. This time it was a formal complaint. In disbelief Clint saw that a woman he'd arrested a month ago filed a complaint that he'd sexually molested her. He reread the name and remembered the arrest. It was of a meth addict. Her family had paid for her to spend the weekend in a Motel 6, to clean up and eat well for a change. The addict repaid their kindness by trashing the room and then threatening the manger with a knife when he tried to throw her out. Clint arrested her as she started to come down off her high. She fell asleep two minutes after he left the hotel parking lot. That she would make such a claim was outrageous.

He could feel his face redden with anger, and his first inclination was to storm the IA offices and choke the life out of Racer. This was bogus on steroids. And a serious IA complaint would definitely derail his chances at promotion.

"You okay?"

Clint looked up from the paper. Marvin Sapp stood in front of him.

Clint swallowed, working to tamp down his temper. "Fine." He waved the paper. "IA."

"Anything to do with Leah?" Sapp asked.

Clint shook his head. Sapp continued on his way.

The complaint said Clint was to report to Racer at 3 p.m. It was only 9 a.m., so he had the whole day to stew over the false charge. Taking a deep, calming breath, he walked out to the lot, climbed into his patrol car, and went to work.

Sapp's question rang in his head. *Anything to do with Leah?* The more he thought about the complaint, the more he realized that maybe it did have to do with Leah indirectly. He'd probably gotten on the wrong side of the Hangmen. He prayed for the truth to prevail as he drove. He'd learned after the beating he'd received as a teen never to wade into fights when he was overmatched. Racer had him by rank and position. Clint needed the Lord to fight this battle.

About halfway into his shift on this subdued January day, he cruised past the 7-Eleven on Manor Avenue and noticed something off. Making a left turn, he drove around to the back and parked his car. He radioed his location and then turned down his radio, wanting to scope out the store, not really sure what the problem was. As he reached the front, he peered into the window.

He almost didn't believe his eyes. It was like a scene out of a movie. People were on the ground, and there was a masked gunman.

Clint's heart rate spiked. "Boy-87, I have a robbery in progress." He asked for a code red to keep radio traffic at a minimum while he waited for backup.

Drawing his weapon, Clint saw movement from the corner of his eye. He inched forward to gain a better view inside the store, holding his breath that the crooks did not look his way. There were two armed men he could see. One was waving a pistol around like a crackhead while the second had a young woman by the hair, dragging her toward the back of the store.

This was bad. His backup hadn't arrived, but they must be close. Clint had to act; he'd never forgive himself if someone died while he waited.

He did a quick survey of the parking lot, looking for a layoff man, but saw no one.

Stepping forward, he kept his eyes on the gunmen, who were looking at each other, not toward him. Gun in a two-handed grip, he took three long steps and shouldered the front door open.

"Police! Freeze!" He raised his gun, targeting the man who had the woman, keeping the second man in his peripheral vision. Time slowed.

Both thugs did freeze for a split second, staring at him. Number one flinched first, releasing the woman to bring his gun up.

Clint fired two shots in rapid succession, ducked to his right, and turned the gun on the second man. Thug two moved backward and fired, but so did Clint. The window behind Clint shattered with a loud booming crash even as the second thug fell, knocking over a display rack and sending candy and chips everywhere.

✦ ✦ ✦

The aftermath of an officer-involved shooting is controlled chaos. Backup arrived seconds after Clint had fired and helped him get a handle on things. The thug who'd had the girl was dead on scene; the second thug was alive when the medics picked him up, but he died at the hospital.

The only other seriously injured party was the store clerk. Before Clint's arrival one of the criminals had pistol-whipped the man into unconsciousness. He was found behind the counter bleeding and unconscious.

"He wanted to rape me," the girl sobbed as soon as Clint reached her. Eyes red from crying, hair completely disheveled, she clung to Clint.

"What's your name?"

"Christie."

He barely understood what she said. Christie was on the verge of hyperventilating. He did his best to console her as officers dealt with the bloody crime scene around them. Vicki Henderson came to his aid, pulling Christie away to calm her down and take her statement. Marvin Sapp grabbed Clint.

"Wow." He pulled Clint aside. "Good job, but you need to take a break. The shooting team will want to talk to you. How are you holding up?"

Ears still ringing from the gunfire, pulse jumping, Clint took a deep breath and blew it out. "I'm okay, really. They gave me no choice."

And he spoke truth. The people who'd been in danger were safe now—he'd done his job. That was the most satisfying thing to know.

t was early morning before Clint got home. He was tired but his mind wouldn't shut down. He took a shower, closing his eyes as hot water ran down his head and over his whole body. He wanted to drown out the images of the shooting that kept replaying over and over in his mind. Clint had hoped he'd never have to shoot anyone. He knew he might have to, and he was ready, but deep down he was one of those cops who prayed that in his entire career he'd never have to fire his duty weapon. Now he knew he'd have to get a handle on this, or it would be an issue that haunted him.

After the shower, he made some coffee and sat down at his desk, checking the time. It was 5 a.m. here in Oregon, so that meant the time in Indonesia was 8 p.m. He turned on his computer, hoping he'd be able to catch his aunt GiGi for some Skype time. She was more technologically savvy than his parents, and he really felt the need to talk to her.

He'd lived with her from age fifteen to nineteen. Once he was accepted to college, she quit her job and threw in lock, stock, and barrel with Doctors Without Borders. Indonesia was a good base for her. From there she was flown to poorer countries that needed a doctor.

"You can take of yourself," she'd told him, "or at least I know that God will take care of you. It's time for me to go where I'm really needed."

Clint understood. GiGi was a general practitioner whose heart bled for people in third world nations. He knew that as soon as she'd paid off her college loans, Doctors Without Borders was what she wanted. His coming to the States had delayed her dream by a couple of years. At the time, she insisted Clint's parents stay where they were, and she gladly took Clint in. He loved GiGi as much as he loved his mom and dad and was glad for the time they'd had together.

Since she'd left, Clint could count on one hand the number of times she'd been back to the States. His parents had returned more, though they now considered Kyrgyzstan their home. GiGi flew all over the world at first, wherever doctors were needed. Recently she'd been more stable, spending long periods of time in Indonesia, Thailand, Vietnam, and many of the islands in that area of the world. Clint hoped he'd catch her at one of the rare times she was seated and taking a rest. He scored when she answered immediately.

"Hey, what a nice surprise! How's my favorite nephew?" She looked tired and grayer than he remembered, but the sparkle and light in her eyes were still there.

"I'm your only nephew. And I'm well, so glad I caught you."

"Great, but it's 5 a.m. there, so something must be on your mind. I have plenty of time to chat today. Tell me everything."

The connection was great, and Clint told her about the

shooting, about Leah, and about the Hangmen. He'd only wanted to talk about the shooting, but once he got going, it all came spilling out. GiGi interrupted once or twice, but mostly she listened, which was what Clint loved about his aunt.

"You talk so nonchalantly about your shooting—" she patted her chest—"but you made my heart race. I know that's your calling and God has you in the palm of his hand, but for once I'm glad news is slow here. I would have hated to read about something like that without having talked to you first. Also, glad you saved the day. You'd better call your mom too."

Clint smiled, feeling so much better. "I will, I promise."

"Now, about this other officer—Leah? You say she was being abused and that her husband was in some secret club called the Hangmen?"

"Yeah, I saw her the morning of the shooting. She'd practically been choked to death."

"And you think this Hangmen club may have perverted justice somehow?"

"That's what I'm afraid of. I think I got on their bad side by asking questions." He told her about the IA complaint.

"What will happen with that?"

"Not sure. I got involved in the shooting, missed my appointment, haven't heard from them."

"I'm thinking you need to stay out of it. If such a club really exists, it sounds dangerous. Get these Hangmen off your back by staying away."

"I don't know if I can do that, GiGi." He took a deep breath. "This is all so wrong. I keep asking how God could let such a great injustice happen and I don't get an answer."

"Clint, you're asking the wrong question."

"What do you mean?"

"God works in ways none of us understands. If we completely

understood everything that goes on in the world, then we would be God, or at least we'd make ourselves gods. Have faith that God knows the big picture and it will all work out the way he intends it to. The right thing to ask is 'Show me how you're working and what my job is in all of this.'"

"Wow." Clint pinched the bridge of his nose and felt a great weight lift from his shoulders. "Thanks. I knew that, but I was lost in the moment and not thinking of the whole picture."

"That's easy to do, especially if you're too close to the situation. As for your friend Leah, you need a lawyer, someone outside who can review her trial transcripts and tell if anything was off. A good lawyer can also get ahold of what wasn't presented at trial and will work through this situation faster and easier than you can."

"I'm guessing you have a suggestion for a lawyer."

"I do. Gretchen Gaffney. She happens to be from Oregon, a lot further north, though—she's in Bend, if I remember right. Specializes in domestic violence, is affiliated with a nonprofit called No Violence at Home. I met her at an international domestic violence conference in Singapore a couple of years back. She made an impression. She'll help—I'm sure of it."

Clint felt another weight lift, his prayer for Leah answered. "I knew you were the person to call."

"Of course you did. Now I'll text you Gretchen's information. You call your mom; then you go straight to bed, young man. You look exhausted."

Clint laughed. "Love you, GiGi."

"Love you too."

He signed off, then called his mom. By the time that call was over, he was dead tired. The text came in from GiGi, and Clint obeyed his aunt and went to bed.

+ + +

The phone ringing woke Clint up around noon. It was Jack, checking up on him.

"I'm fine," Clint told him. "I was sleeping."

"Well, wake up. Check out the news online. A lot has happened in the last few hours."

"You're not going to tell me? You're going to make me get up and look for myself?"

"What are friends for?"

Even as Jack hung up, his phone beeped with another call. Clint didn't recognize the number, so he let it go to voice mail. Yawning, he went back to the computer.

The headline for the *Table Rock Tribune* website floored Clint: *Hero Cop Saves Daughter of Prominent Judge.*

Clint read the story. The sobbing girl from the robbery was Christie Revel, the daughter of Judge Revel, the very same man who had presided over Leah's trial. He was big in the county, had been a judge for a very long time. The story contained eyewitness statements from the shooting, people raving with praise for Clint's bravery.

He moaned, even as his phone went off again. *I just did my job,* Clint thought. *I don't need to be called a hero.* He picked up the phone. This time it was a number he did recognize, his supervisor, Lieutenant Haun.

"How are you holding up, Tanner?"

"I'm tired but okay."

"Things have kind of exploded around here. The cable news services have even picked up the story. You're gonna be famous."

"Not something I relish."

Haun laughed. "Well, I saw the video. You were an action hero, my friend."

"The store had cameras?" He'd had tunnel vision for the bad guys. Hadn't noticed the cameras.

"Yep. Good ones too. Caught the whole thing, from the time the robbery started to the time you ended it. Witnesses say the guy who grabbed the judge's daughter was planning on taking her into the office, having his way with her, and then destroying the camera."

"He really thought he'd have that much time?"

"Drug-induced thinking. Both crooks were bad actors from California. A two-man crime spree over the last three days. We think we can connect them to robberies from Redding to Medford to Table Rock. They were working their way north. I think everything will be fine for you."

"What about the IA complaint?"

"What IA complaint?"

That gave Clint pause. Haun should have known about the complaint. "I got it yesterday morning, was supposed to report to IA yesterday afternoon."

"I heard nothing about that. I'll contact IA and get back to you."

A few minutes later, Haun rang back. "If there was something, it's been withdrawn. I spoke to Racer himself. Hey, the chief wants to milk your heroics. He thinks the department got a black eye over the Radcliff/Draper thing. And really, we need more videos of cops like this out there. It's unambiguous—you did your job, saved the day. They want you to be the face of the PD now. You on board with that?"

Nonplussed by the missing complaint, Clint needed some clarification. "What do you mean by that?"

"The press is clamoring for the tape of the shooting to be released. I know it's early in the process, but it really shows a lot of courage on your part to bust into a situation like that and take out two gunmen. You'll be Hollywood Tanner now. Judge Revel would like to personally thank you, and community relations would like you to give at least one interview."

Clint ran a hand over his head and blew out a breath. This was the last thing he wanted. "Is that an order?"

"No, I can't order you. All I can say is that you did a great job and if the judge wants to thank you, let him. It's not right away anyhow. Everyone wants you to take your mandatory time off and decompress."

"All right, great. I've got a trip to make. I'll be in Bend visiting a friend—is that okay?"

"Sure. If you need anything at all, call."

+ + +

Clint picked Randy up on his second mandatory day off after the shooting, and they made the three-hour drive to Bend to speak to Gretchen Gaffney. Because Gaffney knew Clint's aunt, he'd made the call for Randy. While she didn't sound overly excited about speaking to them, she did sound interested.

Once they got there, Clint liked her immediately. A short, round woman with a head of curly red hair, Gretchen welcomed them into her cluttered office. Everything looked well-worn and well-used, not messy or beat-up. It was just obvious that someone worked a lot of hard hours here. She opened the meeting with prayer, asking for guidance and clarity.

"I'm glad to meet the both of you," Gaffney said, prayer finished. "I followed the story of Leah Radcliff—" she nodded toward Randy—"your daughter, with some interest. It's difficult sometimes to convince a jury that a spouse was killed in self-defense. In Leah's case maybe more so because she never told anyone she was experiencing abuse."

Randy shook his head. "She never said a word. I didn't like the guy, and Leah pretty much cut me off after the wedding. I knew it was because of him. . . . All I could do to bring her back was to pray." His voice broke and he cleared his throat. "I sure wish I had an inkling about what was happening."

"In my experience, there are myriad reasons why women say nothing and simply accept the abuse. And make excuses for the abuser. In your daughter's case, perhaps she knew a charge of abuse could cost her husband his job. It hadn't gotten to the unbearable stage. She was most likely in denial."

"There's something I'd like to throw in the mix," Clint said. "Maybe something else was at work in the trial. Maybe it wasn't just the evidence the jury saw that convicted Leah."

"What do you mean?" Gretchen raised an eyebrow. "You know of evidence that was withheld?"

"Not directly, but I think you should know something that might have played a role in her conviction." He glanced at Randy, swallowed, and then shared with Gretchen what he'd heard about the Hangmen. When he finished, he said, "I know it's rumor and innuendo, but there is a chance the entire trial was rigged against Leah, that nothing about it was fair."

Randy came up out of his chair, face red with anger. "Good old boys club? Protecting Draper and railroading my daughter?"

A glance from Gretchen calmed Randy and he sat back down.

"That's interesting." She steepled her fingers, a thoughtful expression on her face. "Getting a judge to grant a new trial, as the two of you are hoping, is a rare thing. There are three reasons a new trial would be granted. First, to fix a legal error. Second is the discovery of new evidence. And the third is to correct an injustice. Proving the existence of 'the Hangmen' is one thing. We'd also have to prove that they had a direct effect on the trial. I'll be honest—it's a long shot."

"My daughter did not murder Brad in his sleep. That is not Leah. She shot him because she saw no other way," Randy said.

"I'll try to help any way I can," Clint offered.

"I have my own investigator and I wouldn't want to put your job at risk. First, I have to decide if I can take the case on. That would mean reviewing the trial transcripts and meeting with Leah. Can you talk to your daughter and see if she is amenable to a meeting?"

"You bet I will," Randy said.

"I'll clear some time on my calendar and travel to Wilsonville then."

CHAPTER 20

As the months progressed, Leah felt a certain comfort in the prison routine. It kept her from having to think too hard about anything. Even holidays faded into the backdrop of routine, Christmas and New Year's having passed with a whimper. Every minute of her life was regulated: meals, showers, free time, sleep. Since she still didn't feel very balanced, the strict timetable helped her feel propped up.

Normal morning lights on was five. Leah woke earlier than that because Nora worked in the kitchen preparing breakfast and the cell door opened for her to leave for her assignment. Leah would lie in her bunk, awake, until the cell lights came on and it was time to get dressed for breakfast. The cell doors opened at 5:45, and Leah would fall into line for the dayroom and the meal.

Once the last full meal tray was picked up, the women had twenty minutes to finish their food. Nora's friends stayed close to Leah, which didn't bother her. Pat, the woman who'd confronted her the first day, continued to send hate stares her way. As long as Leah surrounded herself with friendlies, as Nora called them, Pat kept her distance. Leah sat with Nora's group at meals or during free time. Donna, the woman who'd introduced herself to Leah and tried to convince her to join the running program, fell in with the group and made it a point to chat with Leah.

"How are you holding up?" she asked one morning.

"I'm surviving."

Donna nodded. "Good. Place can't beat you unless you let it." She then chatted on about the rehab class she was in, about the running program, and about other women in the prison. Leah only half listened and nodded from time to time. Donna seemed to like to hear herself talk.

After breakfast triage lines formed for women with medical issues or on medication. Once the lines finished, the women cleaned the dayroom and then it was time to return to their cells for the first count of the day.

The same routine continued for the midday meal, starting at 11:45. After this meal they were given free time to either watch TV or, weather permitting, go out to the recreation yard for forty-five minutes.

Leah played basketball every time she was in the exercise yard. The exertion simply took the edge off of her frustration. At first, a little bit of dribbling and shooting the ball had her out of breath. She'd not realized how out of shape she was. Once she and Brad got serious, she'd stopped playing ball completely but had continued a fitness routine in the gym. After a few days in the rec yard she felt better, especially once her timing improved and she began to sink her twenty-foot jumpers.

"Looks like you worked out the rusty." Nora picked up the ball. "One-on-one now?"

Hands on her hips, Leah caught her breath. While physically she felt better, her emotions were still all over the map. Was she ready for competition? What would it hurt?

"Sure, I'll play some one-on-one."

Nora passed the ball to Leah, who passed it back, and the game started. Nora surprised Leah. While she was overweight and older, she still had moves, showing shades of Leo the Lion, and Leah remembered the player she'd loved to watch. Five minutes in, six points down, Leah knew they had a game. But in the end, Nora was more out of shape than Leah. After about twenty minutes, Leah had her and the game.

Breathing hard, she faced Nora, who was bent over, catching her breath. "We both need to do some working out."

Nora nodded without looking up. "We should do this more often. It was hard, but it felt good."

Unable to resist, Leah had to ask, "What happened, Nora? You had game—how'd you get caught up in alcohol?"

Nora straightened up. "My game slowed down. I got old, then cut from the team. I was a second too slow and it rocked my world. I never thought basketball would stop. Drinking, smoking pot were ways to dull the pain."

"You coached for a while if I remember right."

"Yeah, but it was never the same for me as being on the court myself. Then the bottle got me." She wiped sweat from her face. "You didn't go pro—heard you had the chance."

Leah shrugged. "I hated the thought of traveling all over the place."

Nora's breathing slowed. "You took the wiser route there, yet here we both are, guilty of crimes."

Fiddling with the basketball, Leah looked away. *"Here we both are, guilty of crimes."*

She didn't know what to say to that. Free time was over. She put the ball away, but Nora grabbed her arm as they walked back inside.

"Look, it's not easy being here, but I've come to terms with what I did. Made peace with it, if you will. If you need help with that, let me know."

Leah pondered the woman's words for the rest of the day. *My crime was killing the man I loved who was trying to kill me. How do I come to terms with that?*

+ + +

One thing hadn't changed even with the passage of time. Like Nora said, things were always toughest for Leah after her father's visits. He came every Saturday even though she knew it had to be a hardship for him. It took all day to drive up and then home again. Gas, loss of work, plus the stress . . .

Leah struggled the most with everything about her life after her father left. Playing basketball when she could helped somewhat.

She noticed that playing was good for Nora as well. After a couple of weeks, she'd dropped a few pounds. And they drew a crowd when they played. Several other women eventually joined them, and they started playing full games regularly. At times it was more like jungle ball than basketball, but it helped Leah to not dwell on the pain, loss, and humiliation that dogged her daily. Her sleep was always shredded by nightmares of the shooting; the activity helped exhaust her so she could fall asleep. But some days, not even basketball helped.

"Off your game today," Nora commented after Leah's second missed jumper.

Something snapped. Leah shoved the ball back to her. "Yeah, I am. I'm done for today." She stalked off the court, angry that tears threatened and frustrated that the game hadn't distracted her today.

"You just gonna quit?" Nora called out.

Leah waved her hand without turning around and kept walking.

Nora caught up with her. "Hey."

Leah whirled. "Hey what? I don't want to play anymore."

Nora held both hands up. "I got that. I've got an assist for you, something I think will help."

Leah glared and said nothing, fearing the tears would start, and that was the last thing she wanted. As always, Pat was watching, and she was determined not to show weakness.

"You asked me once how I came to terms with what I did?" Nora did not give Leah a chance to answer. "I had to let go of everything. I had to find someone bigger than me, someone who could forgive me and show me how to keep on living. Coming to prison was the best thing that ever happened to me."

Leah's expression must have shown the shock wave such a statement caused.

Nora gave a mirthless chuckle. "Yep, that's what I said. I found God here, Leah. I found God and he gave me peace. Drop a kyte for the chaplain. God can help you too—I know it."

"I told you I've got no use for God," Leah said.

"You might not always feel that way," Nora said. "And for sure you'll never be free of what's dogging you until you let it go." She turned and trotted back to the game, leaving Leah standing, fuming, and hating the fact that wherever she turned, someone seemed to throw God in her face.

Clint Tanner popped into her head. Saint Tanner, the good guy who'd helped her during the darkest time of her life. He'd made her so angry with his prayers. She tried to drum up that same anger, tried to force the tears away with anger, but she couldn't. A part of her realized she was exhausted from holding on to all of her bitterness.

Would talking to a chaplain really help?

The thought kept her up that night. Before she fell into a fitful sleep, Leah decided maybe it would. The chaplain would be someone she could vent to. Since she knew from personal experience that God did not answer prayers, that he heard nothing, maybe it would be helpful to talk to someone who *could* hear. She didn't expect any answers; she just hoped that venting would help her feel better.

The next day she followed Nora's suggestion. A few days after that, a guard escorted her to the chaplain's office. They'd barely left her cell when she began to get cold feet.

Can I really vent to a total stranger?

"What's the problem?" Hastings, the corrections officer who interacted most with Leah, asked when her gait slowed.

Leah looked at her. The woman always had a frown on her face. Not having the words to explain the feelings raging within her, Leah simply shook her head and kept walking.

When they reached his office, Chaplain Darrel was not at all what she was expecting. He stood to greet her, and Leah, at five foot seven, could look him right in the eye. With a craggy, well-worn visage and sandy-colored hair, he looked more like a weather-beaten cowboy than a chaplain. But then, what was a chaplain supposed to look like?

He offered her a chair next to his desk, and she sat while Hastings stepped out into the hall and closed the door.

"I hear you're depressed," he said without preamble, catching Leah off guard.

She wiped sweaty palms on her thighs. "Who told you that?"

"Your dad."

Leah wasn't sure how she felt about that. "You talked to my dad?"

"I have. I spoke at his church a couple of weeks ago. He introduced himself."

"Oh, well, I guess you could say I'm depressed." Leah fidgeted, looking around the small room. Wondering how to get out of the meeting.

"How's that working out for you?"

"Huh?" Her gaze rested on the chaplain. Pale-blue eyes gazed back at her. There was no judgment in the gaze, but Leah had the eerie feeling he could see right through her, so she turned away from him, glancing toward the door.

"Where's it getting you? You're a young woman with a long life ahead of you. How's being depressed and broody going to get you anywhere?"

Leah frowned, gave an exaggerated wave of her hand, then fixed her eyes on the clearly delusional man. "I'm not going anywhere. In case you forgot, I'm in prison for twenty-five years."

His lips curved into a slight smile. "You're breathing. Got two arms, two legs that work. Using prison as an excuse to check out is pretty weak." Amusement played in his features and Leah got mad.

"Is this a joke to you? You think my situation is funny?"

He shook his head. "No, I don't. Your situation is serious. I think it's strange that you choose to live in the past. Can't get anywhere always looking in the rearview mirror. You need to turn your head around and move forward."

Furious, Leah tensed and almost shot to her feet. "There is no forward for me. What is wrong with you?"

He didn't flinch, just stayed where he was, gaze fixed on her. "There's a lot ahead for you if you'll open your eyes."

"What, if I turn to God and prayer?" She spit the words out bitterly. "I'm done with this meeting." Calling toward the door, "Ms. Hastings?"

"Turning away from God hasn't done you much good."

"He turned away from me! That's why I'm here." She held her hands out, palms up. "Look what your God did to me. I didn't ask for any of this or do anything so horrible to deserve it."

"I didn't say you did. But if he's my God, why do you blame him for your troubles? And can you honestly say you have no responsibility for anything that has happened to you?"

"Is that what you and your God do? Blame the victim?"

"It's not about blame. It's about breaking free of self-pity and taking an honest look at your circumstances so you can move forward."

For a minute Leah was speechless. But the pain and unfairness of her situation provided the words to fire back at the chaplain. "He's a vindictive God! He lets evil people prosper and punishes innocent people like me for fun."

"I don't believe that, and I'll bet you don't either, really. God is good all the time; all the time God is good. His message to you is one of hope, even here—especially here—if you'll listen."

Anger boiled and she stood at the same time Hastings opened the door. "Everything okay?" the woman asked.

"We're good," the chaplain said, his calm posture never changing.

"I'm ready to go back to my cell."

Later, on her bunk, arms wrapped around her knees, which were pulled up against her chest, Leah fumed anew about God and his betrayal. It brought back all the pain and loss from the day of the shooting. But under the anger and the pain, barely audible, was a voice that told her the chaplain was right. Focusing her anger at God had gotten her nowhere.

Drowning in a sea of bitterness and self-pity, she buried her head in the pillow, not wanting to let go of what had become a crutch. What hope could there ever be for her again? She'd lost everything. The world would never hold hope for Leah, not now and not in twenty-five years.

Would it?

CHAPTER 21

After her visit with the chaplain, which Leah felt was a waste of time, she worked hard to stay positive if for no other reason than to keep her dad happy. On his Saturday visit her father told her about the possibility of a new lawyer, someone Tanner had found.

"I waited a little bit to tell you. We had to be sure she could clear her calendar. Her specialty is domestic violence, and she'll be here to see you as soon as she finishes up some cases she already has going."

Leah smiled and tried to feel it. "That's great, Dad. I look forward to meeting her."

By Monday her doubts were already overtaking any hope she might have gotten from her father. The day started out like any other. Leah simply followed her routine, the one she had no choice but to follow. After lunch she grabbed a basketball and headed to the court. There were a lot of women milling around, a lot of normal conversations, when a strange sound assaulted her ears. It was like an animal's strangled cry.

Leah turned and saw a woman, someone she'd noticed around but had not interacted with, come screaming around the corner straight for her. Trained to always look at a subject's hands, Leah spotted the shank. Reflexively Leah pushed the ball toward the human missile.

The weapon came down into the ball, which popped with a whoosh of air. Leah squeezed it, trapping the knife, and twisted right, using the woman's momentum to send her stumbling that way. In the process, she lost her balance and her grip on the ball. The woman fell back, grabbed the ball, and worked to free the knife.

Leah backed up to put distance between her and the crazy woman. Heart pumping, a cold, icy feeling injected straight to her bones: This person wanted to kill her.

Hastings jumped into the fray. Turning to Leah, she said something Leah didn't hear because Leah was still focused on the threat.

In the split second Hastings directed her attention toward Leah, the guard didn't catch how quickly the crazed woman repositioned herself. She'd yanked the shank from the ball. Leah saw her raise the weapon and run straight for Hastings, who stood between them. Leah knew the guard would get the shank right in the back.

She pushed her shoulder into Hastings, shoving her out of the way, and caught the frenzied woman's wrist in both her hands as the weapon thrust toward her. Leah caught a look in the woman's eyes. Her pupils were huge—she was high on something. She was also very strong.

Leah kept the shank from impacting her face by twisting

sideways, but the woman overpowered her and jammed the weapon into her midsection. The sharp punch to her stomach took her breath away.

Hastings reentered the altercation and grabbed the attacker by the shoulders, pulling her away, causing the woman to yank the knife out of Leah. An alarm sounded and several more guards surrounded the knife-wielding woman, wrestling with her for control of the knife.

Leah looked down at the spreading blood on her shirt. Astonishingly, she felt no pain. She put both hands on the wound and fell back into a seated position. Blood oozed through her fingers and she felt queasy. Her vision faded, and the last images her eyes registered were Hastings and other guards turning to check on her after they subdued the crazed inmate. Then the world around her faded to black.

+ + +

Leah woke up in the ambulance.

"She's coming around."

Leah turned toward her left and a paramedic smiled at her. "You're in good hands. Relax and enjoy the ride."

"I'm not dead?"

His smile widened. "No, and we have no plans to lose you."

She relaxed slowly, remembering the crazed woman, a hundred questions running through her mind. *Why* being the biggest and brightest question. *Why did that woman want to kill me?*

Leah woke up in recovery after a short surgery where the doctor determined that the shank had not done any serious damage.

"You were lucky," the surgeon told her. "You'll need to take it easy, but the stitches are dissolvable and will take care of themselves. You'll also be on a course of antibiotics for seven days."

After an overnight stay, medics transported Leah back to the prison infirmary. There, she was allowed to phone her father and tell him what happened. It was the hardest phone call she'd ever had to make.

"You were *stabbed*?" The fear and anger in his voice made her breath catch in her throat and she fought tears.

"Yeah, but I'm okay. They took me to a hospital, and the doctor who treated me said I'm going to be fine."

"But they told me there was no threat to you, that's why you weren't isolated. What is going on?"

"They don't know why the woman did what she did." She explained what she knew about the situation to him.

"I still can't believe it. Leah—"

"I'm okay, Dad. Please don't worry."

"That's like asking the sun not to shine." He paused and Leah wasn't sure what to say. Finally she heard him sigh. Then with resignation in his voice he said, "You are in God's hands. I won't forget that. I love you, sweet pea. Your new lawyer will get to you soon."

"Dad, can you afford—?"

"She's offered pro bono work, and she's good. Cheer up— I'm truly hopeful now."

"Okay, then I am as well. I love you too, Dad."

"See you Saturday."

While Leah was in the infirmary, the police officer investigating the assault visited her.

"You don't know this woman?" He showed Leah a picture of the woman, Tracy Dunham. She looked decidedly sane in her booking photo, not at all like the drug-crazed attacker who stabbed her.

"Sure, I saw her around, but we never spoke." It was three days later. She was ready to be transferred back to her cell. Her midsection felt as if she'd done about a thousand too many crunches. But she was healing.

"She was arrested in Table Rock eighteen months ago for possession of meth. She failed to complete drug court and was sent here two months ago."

"She's still not familiar to me. Who arrested her?"

He gave her the names of two narcotics officers she knew, but the names did nothing to illuminate why the woman attacked her.

All Leah could do was shrug.

The investigator got up to leave. "Quick thinking to push Hastings out of the way," he said. "I believe she might have been stabbed simply because she was in the way if you hadn't shoved her." He pointed. "You got stabbed instead."

Leah shrugged. "I didn't want to see anyone get hurt."

He started to say something, then stopped and left the infirmary.

When she was sent back to her cell, she soon discovered that the incident was the talk of the prison.

"I knew Tracy," Nora said. "She had problems, but I've never seen her violent."

"She sure had a head of steam that day," Leah said. She'd relived the attack over and over every time she closed her eyes. While it seemed to her that it had gone on forever, she knew it had only been a matter of seconds. For her part, the attacker kept fighting after Leah fainted. Four guards struggled with her while everyone else was ordered back to their cells.

The aftermath of the attack was a whole prison lockdown. The yard where the attack happened was covered by cameras, so it was clear that Leah was not an aggressor. In fact, she was credited with saving Hastings from getting a shank in the back.

The question was, what made the crazed woman, in for a drug crime but assessed as very low risk, go after Leah? Blood tests showed she was pumped full of illegal stimulants. Where did she get the drugs? The stabbing instrument was a shard of metal honed to a sharp point. Where did she get the shank?

Tracy couldn't tell anyone. She fought with the guards who took her into custody until she went into cardiac arrest. CPR was performed to no avail, and she died on the way to the hospital. Cause of death was ruled a drug overdose.

Back in her cell for the first time in days, Leah picked up the Bible again. The next morning, she dropped another kyte for the chaplain.

+ + +

"Hear you had a serious scrape." The calm chaplain eyed Leah as she sat gingerly in the chair. Her midsection was still sore, like a very badly pulled muscle, and she didn't need to be reminded to take it easy. In his office, Leah felt unsettled and more relaxed at the same time.

Attempting to lighten the mood, she said, "She had very poor aim."

"Unusual here. Medium security. Tracy wasn't known for violence."

"First time for everything."

"Hmm. And what made you call me back? Last time you were here, you didn't like what I had to say."

Leah swallowed, mouth suddenly dry. What did she want? "When that woman—Tracy . . . when she came screaming at me with the knife, all I could think was, *I don't want to die*."

"I can understand that."

"But before that, I didn't want to live. I . . ." Something caught in her throat. "My whole life is ruined—it's over. Everything I ever dreamed of is gone. So why at that moment did I not want to die?"

"You tell me."

"I'm trying to figure it out. . . ." Leah studied her hands for a moment. "I remembered a call I went on once. A woman killed herself the day before Christmas. She shot herself in her husband's workshop."

She wiped her eyes. Strength returning, she found Darrel's presence calming, fortifying. "The note she left was scathing. She blamed everyone, even God, for how horrible and what a failure she felt her life had become. Her final fervent wish was to hurt everyone she left behind."

Leah swallowed a lump and forced her voice to steady. "I don't want to hurt my dad. I don't want to hurt anyone. But I don't want to go on feeling like this, empty like a hollowed-out shell." She paused. "I'm so tired of crying and wishing things could be different, because they never can be. And I'm tired of asking why because I don't believe that question will ever be answered."

Darrel watched her. After a couple of beats, he said, "You're right about the why questions. A lot will never be answered in this life. I can't help you there. I can help you with the future. But to move forward, you have to let go of the past, make peace with it. Can you do that? Can you let go of Brad?"

Leah looked at him, exhausted. Her shoulders sagged. A thought flashed through her mind. *I've been holding on so tightly to all the anger, regrets, and self-pity that it's sapped all of my strength. What would it feel like to really put it all behind me?*

"I'd like to try," she whispered.

He scribbled something on a piece of paper. "Here's an assignment for you. I want you to read these passages in the Bible. Write down any questions you have, and we'll talk about them at our next meeting. We'll set it for next week. Does that work?"

Leah took the paper and nodded.

Leah couldn't play basketball until the doctor said it was okay. She had nothing but time, so for the next week she read and reread the passages Darrel had given her. She also read other passages she remembered liking when she used to go to church.

"We have a weekly Bible study you're welcome to attend," Nora told her when she saw her looking up the verses the chaplain had given her.

"I don't know yet," Leah said truthfully. "I used to go to church a lot when I was a kid. My mom sang on the worship team." So many good memories came flooding back. She paused as they hit her in the center of the chest, drowning her with warm feelings.

"There's a good church service here as well."

Leah looked at Nora, not sure what was holding her back. "Maybe I'll go with you this Sunday."

When the cell doors opened for rec time, Nora left to hit the snack bar and replenish her supply, so Leah had some time to herself. She sat back and thought about her mother. *I used to love the sound of her voice when she sang.* In a couple of seconds, she was humming the only two songs she remembered because they were her mother's favorites: "In the Garden" and "Trust and Obey."

Sadness enveloped her when she tried to pinpoint why she walked away from church. She'd never been baptized. Her mother asked her one day if she wanted to, and she'd said no.

"One day you'll have to proclaim your own faith," Mom said. *"God doesn't have grandchildren, only his much-loved children."*

Truth was, Leah was always drawn more to life outside the church. For some reason she thought all the excitement was somewhere else.

Then the what-ifs invaded: What if her mother hadn't died in that car crash? What if Leah had never met Brad? What if she'd never followed him that night?

Tears flowed and Leah got angry. *I'm so tired of always falling apart. The chaplain is right. I can't stay in the past. It will just keep dragging me down. But can I really let go of Brad?*

That question drew her back to the Bible and the promises she'd read of forgiveness and peace. She stepped up to the little sink, looking at herself in the faux metal mirror. She barely recognized her face, and not just because the mirror distorted her features. She was looking at a prison inmate.

"No, no." Her mind wouldn't let her stop there. "I'm not only an inmate. I'm a survivor. Brad didn't kill me; being sentenced to prison didn't either. Tracy tried and failed."

Breathing in deeply, Leah stood up straighter. "I may be in jail for twenty-five years, but I will survive." *Twenty-five years* still stung deep in her soul like acid. "I can't keep looking down the road. Only what is in front of me matters." That thought lessened the sting.

With new resolve, Leah rinsed her face off and vowed to stop the crying.

A thought crept into her mind, tiptoeing on stockinged feet. *Maybe, just maybe, God isn't responsible for what happened to me. Maybe I just made a series of poor choices.*

She wrote her thoughts down in the notebook her father had given her.

1. *I can't change anything that's already happened.*
2. *Blame is irrelevant. It will change nothing.*
3. *I have to move forward and make better choices.*
4. *I need to remember what it felt like to walk with God, not away from him.*

Then she sat down on her bed, Bible in her lap. For the first time in longer than she could remember, she prayed.

She prayed for forgiveness, she prayed for peace, and she prayed to be able to move forward, even if every step for the next twenty-five years was going to be in prison. She also prayed to be able to let Brad go, to stop tormenting herself because she'd had to shoot him. Even as she whispered the words, she knew she couldn't, not completely. There was still a spark inside, a flashing neon *WHY?* Yes, Darrel had said that a lot of whys would never be answered, but there were two questions Leah had to ask and one she'd have to find some way to get the answer to.

What was Brad doing the night I followed him, and why did my knowing make him so angry he wanted to kill me?

CHAPTER 23

You're getting good at that."

Leah looked up from her drawing, surprised to see Donna during free time. She should be at her drug rehab class or running on the track. Nora was off to the rec yard, but Leah still felt a little weak, so she'd opted to stay in the dayroom and draw.

"Don't you have a training run today?"

Donna laughed. "Door's been open for nearly forty minutes. You been drawing all that time?"

Leah nodded and had to stretch, realizing she was stiff from bending over her drawing.

Donna peered down at the sketchbook Leah's father had given her. "That's great."

"Thanks." Leah rubbed her neck. "This is the most relaxing hobby I've ever had. I learned to draw in junior high. I stopped for a while. I just picked it back up again."

"Who is that?" Donna pointed to the top sketch.

"My dad." She flipped through the pages. "This is my mom and—"

"Chaplain Darrel." Donna laughed. "That's a great likeness. You did that with just a pencil?"

"Yeah. I'd like to work with color, and my dad is going to get me some colored pencils."

"Who's the last one?"

Leah flipped to the last page and held the drawing in the light. "This is the guy I saw my husband threaten with a gun. It was dark, and I was far away, so right now this is the best I can do." Leah knew that an insurance salesman named Holloway claimed he was the man there that night. But her instincts screamed he was lying. Sketching helped her remember every detail about the man she'd seen.

"He looks evil."

"I don't know if he's evil or not. All I know is I'd like to talk to him."

"That will be tough."

Leah chuckled mirthlessly. "Don't I know it."

"Think you can draw me?"

Leah arched an eyebrow and regarded her only other friend besides Nora. "Probably. You want me to?"

Donna shrugged. "You do good work. Maybe I can send it to my kids. They might get a kick out of it."

"I'll give it a try."

"Great."

Free time over, it was time to go back to their respective cells. Leah studied the tall, bearded figure she'd been trying to draw. After the second meeting with the chaplain, Leah felt better emotionally than she had in a long while. And when she looked back over the drawings of the last couple of months, she could see improvement. But the details of the bearded man's face eluded her.

"Radcliff."

Leah looked up. She'd been so engrossed she'd not heard the footsteps. There at the door to her cell stood Hastings, the officer she'd shoved.

"Yes?" Leah closed her sketch pad, got up, and stepped to the door.

"My first day back to work after the altercation." She'd sprained her wrist in the struggle with Tracy.

Leah nodded, not sure where this was going. They'd never had a conversation before; it had always been officer and inmate orders and acknowledgments.

Hastings held up the package in her hand. "Your father left these, and they've just been approved for you to have."

Leah reached out and took the package. Colored pencils. "Thank you." Leah knew these would help her sketch more clearly. She expected Hastings would move on, but the woman made no move to leave.

"I want to ask you a question," the officer said, face blank.

"Sure."

"Why'd you shove me the other day? If you hadn't, you might not have been stabbed."

Leah frowned. "Why wouldn't I? She was after me, not you. I saw her coming—you would have gotten it in the back."

"Because I'm a corrections officer."

"So? You're not my enemy."

Hastings seemed to consider this. The woman held her gaze, and Leah was puzzled.

Finally she took a step away but turned back. "Your husband was really trying to kill you?"

That question jolted Leah. In nearly a year in prison, no

corrections officer had asked that question; they all assumed she'd shot Brad in his sleep, which had been the cry of the prosecutor at trial.

"Yes, he really was."

Hastings's expression softened a bit. "Thank you. I might have gotten that shank instead of you."

Leah was at a loss for words. But she didn't have to speak; Hasting went on. "You have a visitor."

Surprised because it wasn't Saturday, the day her father always came, Leah hesitated before she moved.

"Name's Becky Blanchard," Hastings said. "She's a friend?"

"Yeah, she is." Surprised and suddenly anxious, Leah followed Hastings to the visiting area, wondering what Becky had to say. She hadn't heard a word from her since Brad's death.

She also realized that Hastings's whole demeanor had changed. It was less stiff, more friendly. *Maybe she doesn't think of me as a cold-blooded killer anymore,* Leah thought. She realized there would be many people who would always only see her as a killer. The evidence presented at trial had convinced twelve people that she was. Despair started to creep into her soul like the fog over the San Francisco Bay.

Leah stopped it. *I will not return to the pit. I changed Hastings's mind; I will change other people's as well.*

She entered the visiting area and saw Becky Blanchard waiting.

Becky smiled tentatively. "Leah, I . . ."

Leah stepped forward, also unsure, a flash of shame rippling through her. Then Becky lurched forward and gave her a hug. Leah flinched when she squeezed a bit too hard.

"Oh! I'm sorry. You're hurt?"

"That's okay. It's better today and I should be fully recovered in no time."

"So sorry this happened to you," she whispered in Leah's ear.

Leah fought tears and hugged her friend. When Becky let go, they both stepped back and wiped tears from their eyes.

"I don't know what to say," Leah started. "I never expected anyone but my dad to visit."

"Sorry it took so long, but with Grady and the baby, it's hard to get away. It also took me a month to be approved to visit. We're friends, Leah. I knew Brad, remember? I never thought it was anything but self-defense."

Leah felt the tight ball within her loosen. First Hastings, now Becky. It felt good to know that others besides her dad believed the truth.

"Thanks, Becky. That means more to me than I can say."

They sat at one of the tables, and Leah let Becky prattle on about life with an almost three-year-old and what was going on at home. Larry Ripley was considering running for state senator.

"He was always interested in politics and higher office," Leah said.

"That's true. That's why I'm pushing Grady to run for sheriff when the current sheriff retires."

"No kidding? He'd be good," Leah said and meant it. Becky was always pushing Grady for something.

"I agree. Duke's even thinking of running for county commissioner."

"Really?" Leah listened while Becky went on about her brother and her husband. Her world revolved around the two men. Leah remembered Becky telling her how it was love at first sight when she met Grady.

"I didn't think I'd ever get married—I was happy single—but Grady walked into my life and made me laugh, and I knew my life wouldn't be complete without him."

Leah made no comment about Larry Ripley or Duke. Becky didn't seem to notice.

"Any news on your appeal?" Becky asked.

The statement caught Leah off guard. She and her father had only briefly talked about the appeal, which she knew could take over a year to be heard. Filed about a month after she began her sentence, it hadn't even been eight months yet. Could the new lawyer he'd found speed up the process?

"I'm told it will take time."

"Well, I hope it changes things. One brain-dead jury shouldn't be the end of it. Grady is pulling for you. So is Duke."

Leah nodded, but the thought of the appeal scared her. What if it wasn't just a brain-dead jury? What if no one would believe she shot Brad in self-defense?

In that same instant, one of the verses Chaplain Darrel had recommended invaded her thoughts. *When you walk through the waters, they will not overflow. When you walk through the fire, I will be with you . . .* Losing every appeal would be like drowning, being overflowed.

But I'm not alone anymore, am I? She remembered Nora saying that going to jail was the best thing that ever happened to her.

Could I ever say that?

CHAPTER 24

Two days after Becky's visit, after making certain she was on the road to recovery, Leah's dad told Leah a little more about the new attorney.

"She'll be coming to see you; I think you'll like her."

Leah listened as he talked about Gretchen Gaffney. Since Tanner had found the lawyer, she hoped that meant he wasn't mad she'd told him to stay out of her life.

"Dad, I'll talk to her, but don't get your hopes up."

"What do you mean?" He frowned. "You're innocent."

"I know, but—"

"No buts about it. For some reason the first jury was blinded. A new trial will fix that."

Leah wanted to ask if he was certain about that but couldn't. Her father was hardly objective. A lawyer would be objective. When she got a chance, she'd ask the lawyer.

A chance to do just that came sooner than she thought. The lawyer her father had so much faith in came to see her the next visiting day. Gretchen Gaffney had a sharp, penetrating gaze. Leah felt like there was nothing she could hide from this woman.

"You're going to be my new lawyer?" Leah asked.

"Maybe," Gaffney said. "First, convince me." She pointed at her chest. "Convince me you didn't murder your husband in cold blood, that you truly were defending yourself."

Leah studied the redheaded lawyer and wondered where to begin. She decided to start at the beginning. "We had a couple of good months. Then I made a mistake. Brad had a man cave. I was not to enter it without being invited. He'd warned me, but I didn't take him seriously. One day I did go in because he had a phone call. He was furious. He used a police takedown and pinned me, warning me to never do that again. It was terrifying. And it progressed from there."

"Why didn't you tell anyone?"

Leah sighed and rubbed her forehead. "I've had a lot of sleepless nights to think about that question. I don't know if I can convey the shame I felt."

"Try. If we are granted a new trial, you'll have to convince a second jury."

"You want me to testify?"

"I think you have to. If you truly were in fear for your life, then you have to convince the jury. No one else can do that."

Leah thought hard about the question before answering. "I couldn't admit to myself that it was truly abuse. He was careful not to leave marks anyone would see. He'd apologize, and we'd be fine for a time . . ."

Leah sighed, thinking back. "My dad never liked him. . . . I guess the bottom line is, I thought I could get a handle on it.

Women who were true victims of domestic violence were just too weak to get a handle on things, so I had to tell them to leave their abusers."

She paused while Gretchen scribbled notes on a yellow pad. "Every time I responded to a domestic violence call, it was like walking on razor blades. I always told women what the literature and my training said: He won't stop, and it will get worse. I could never apply that to myself."

"How about now?"

The question gave Leah a start. A lump formed in her throat. "I was a victim of domestic violence. I hate that. It still hurts." Fists clenched. "How could I have been so stupid?"

Gretchen shook her head. "I don't come here to condemn you or to make you condemn yourself. I just want you to be able to articulate the issue clearly and believably with the jury."

"You're sure I should testify?"

"You don't want to?"

"It's not that. In the first trial the lawyer recommended against it, said Birch would destroy me."

"Like I said, and I firmly believe, you are the one who has to do the convincing. Your life was in danger; the jury needs to believe that."

"Do you really think I have a chance at a new trial?"

"I do. And you have to be all in."

Leah nodded.

"Now go on. What else can you tell me about your life with Brad?"

"In retrospect, it was all about him. I stopped seeing my father because Brad didn't like him. We spent a lot of time with his folks, which was always rough."

"How so?"

"I never cared for my father-in-law, but I tried because Brad and Harden were close. Harden treated Blanche, his wife, like a servant. I remember feeling sorry for her but never having the courage to speak up. Usually when we had dinner together, Blanche would drink herself into a stupor and Ivy, Brad's sister, would put her to bed."

Leah paused, remembering something Blanche often said. "After dinner Brad and his father would retire to Harden's den. Women weren't allowed. One time early on I objected. She took my arm and led me to the bar. 'Let the men do their men things,' she said. It was a phrase she repeated often."

"Do you think she was abused?"

Leah took a deep breath. "She had to be. That's what the literature says: Abuse is a learned behavior. Brad probably learned it from Harden." Tears started and Leah swallowed them back. "Maybe if I'd said something, I could have helped her as well."

"Hindsight is twenty-twenty. Let's go back to you and Brad. How was he about money?"

Leah tensed, fighting the wave of recrimination and regret that threatened to engulf her. "He kept his finances private. His money was his money, my money was mine, and he didn't want the two to mix. And my friends, he was prickly about that, only wanted me having certain friends. At one point, I did think about telling a woman I played basketball with what was going on. Even though we'd stopped playing, we'd get together from time to time. I think Brad thought we were too close because he told me to cut her out of my life. After that I almost went to talk to the department shrink, but I knew Brad would find out."

"Why? Isn't that confidential?"

"It's impossible to keep a secret like that at the PD. And I didn't know who to talk to outside the PD."

"You referred women to outside agencies all the time."

"You're right—I did—but that was for victims. Like I said,

I refused to see myself as a victim. Somehow, calling myself a victim made me weak."

"Have you ever heard of the Hangmen?"

The question took Leah by surprise, and it must have shown in her face.

"You have. Tell me about it."

"It was what started the first fight, the first time Brad pinned me down until I couldn't breathe." She thought back to that day. "I'd invaded his domain, he said. I went into the man cave without being asked. He kept it locked. He was talking about the Hangmen with someone on his cell phone." Leah shuddered as she remembered what it had been like to be pinned by Brad. He was all muscle, hard as iron.

"Where was the man cave?"

"In the basement. Our house had a walk-out basement, so people could come and go without me seeing them."

"Was that where the Hangmen met?"

"I think so. But not the only place."

"What exactly were the Hangmen?"

Leah sighed. "A good old boys club? Brad said they were just a private group, a guy thing. I don't know for sure. I heard rumors, and once in a while I'd overhear something about 'his crew stepping in.' I really thought it was mostly chicken-chested boasting. Brad called himself the executioner. All of the Hangmen had a tattoo of a gallows on them somewhere. Brad's was on his right shoulder blade. He believed he controlled who made it in the PD and who didn't."

"Made it how?"

"He claimed he and his buds had the final say on who was hired, fired, or who promoted. One conversation I heard had to do with someone who wanted a slot in narcotics. Brad didn't like the guy, so he didn't get the promotion. Brad believed he was the reason, but I'm not sure he really had the power he thought he did."

"Were you in the Hangmen?"

"No, it was all guys. I didn't want to be in it. Too much testosterone."

"Do you know all the members?"

"I'm not sure I know all of them. Brad, Terry Racer in IA, Chief Wilcox—"

"The chief is a member of the Hangmen?"

"Yeah, he's a good friend of Brad's family, Brad's dad."

"Who else?"

"Patterson in homicide, Larry Ripley, and Duke Gill."

"So it included nonpolice officers?"

"Yes. In the basement, Brad had a bar top made out of an old log, and they all carved their names in it. I wasn't supposed to know that, but I saw the carvings one day. Why are you asking about the Hangmen?"

"It's been suggested to me that the Hangmen may, in part, have been responsible for your conviction."

"What?" Leah felt her jaw drop. Heart racing, she stared at Gaffney. "But the jury convicted me on the evidence—"

"Did you murder your husband in bed?"

"No!"

"What makes you believe the jury was correct?"

"They weren't. But trials are a game; people can be made to believe anything. The jury didn't believe me."

"I know. But what if I can prove that they didn't believe you because someone had their hand on the scale?"

CHAPTER 25

Clint returned to work two weeks after the shooting. He took extra days off because even after his return from Bend, the incident was still generating a lot of media attention. It was a distraction. And he was tired. The shooting had affected him more than he wanted to admit. And then there was Leah's stabbing. That news jolted him to the core in spite of Randy's assurance that she was okay. It increased his resolve to pray for her every day until she was home. He used the extra time off to study for the sergeant's test.

On his first day back, before briefing, he took the summons he'd gotten the morning of the shooting to Lieutenant Racer. After waiting twenty minutes to see the lieutenant, the reaction he got perplexed Clint.

"It's been dropped," Racer said with a disinterested shrug. "Be happy; go back to work."

"This was a serious charge that I deserve the right to refute."

"Look, there is no charge. I guess the crackhead decided to forget everything."

Clint studied Racer for a moment and got a withering stare.

"What?" Racer asked.

"I would never, ever do what was suggested in that complaint." He held up his digital recorder. "From now on I carry this, and I use it. No one is going to be able to file false charges on me, ever."

Racer regarded him with thinly veiled disdain. "Don't you have work to do?"

Clint left, resisting the urge to wipe the smirk off Racer's face. He went back into service, glad the complaint was gone, but not unprepared. He wasn't going anywhere without the recorder. The department had talked about body cameras for all officers, but that hadn't happened yet, so Clint decided to be proactive. It wasn't long before he realized he wasn't the only person who needed to be careful.

At EOW he found himself in the patrol parking lot facing off against one of Brad's biggest defenders, Erik Forman. Whoever was after Vicki had upped their game since the dead rat. She'd received death threats and her car had been vandalized with spray paint.

Forman was just coming on for the new shift when he made a comment to Richard Chambers that Clint overheard. *"Weak sisters don't belong in police work."*

Clint stopped. "Hey, Henderson doesn't deserve what's happening to her."

Forman turned, faced Clint. "You talking to me?"

"If you're harassing Henderson, I am. Hazing has no place in police work, period."

Forman smirked and approached Clint. Chambers hung

back, and Clint noticed that everyone who'd been in the parking lot, including Henderson and Sapp, was now listening and watching.

"The rookie who disrespected a senior officer at a crime scene?" Forman said. "That Henderson? Things getting too hot for her, she needs to get out of the kitchen. I hear TruckMaster is hiring." That garnered snickers from at least one officer.

"She doesn't need to have her property damaged, be bullied, or fear for her life."

"You're saying I painted her car? Threatened her? You're crazy, Tanner."

"I don't think you did it, but I think you know who did. This has to stop. Brad's dead. Leah's in jail. We need to move forward like adults."

"You're wrong about what *we* need. If she can't take it, maybe *she* needs to quit."

"I'm not quitting. Not because of your childish behavior." Henderson was fired up, but her boyfriend, a fellow officer going off duty, stopped her from getting in Forman's face.

"We all depend on one another," Clint said, holding up a hand. "At least we should all be able to depend on one another."

"You and she both should have thought about that before you took sides with a cop killer. You're both rats."

Another Brad supporter stepped up, and then things got out of hand. Vicki's boyfriend got in his face and the fight started. They traded punches and then grappled with one another. Clint grabbed the boyfriend and Chambers stepped forward to grab the other guy.

"We need to get past this—we really do," Clint said once the two had been separated.

Forman just told the instigator to get to work, and with that the night shift officers dispersed.

Clint looked at Vicki's boyfriend, who was wiping a bloody lip. "You okay?"

"Yeah. I'll be fine."

"Thanks, Clint. I appreciate your defense," Henderson said. "But they're not going to make me quit."

"Glad to hear it."

He turned to leave but stopped when he saw Chambers watching him from the edge of the lot. "You have something to add to the conversation?" Clint asked.

Chambers shook his head. A few seconds later he disappeared into the night.

Clint went home, still troubled. The idea of faked internal affairs complaints troubled him for a long time after.

A few days later a phone call from Randy improved his mood immensely.

"Gretchen took the case." Randy was a happy man; his joy reverberated over the phone.

"Ah, great news. I believe she'll find the problem and get Leah a new trial," Clint said, thinking of GiGi and her advice to try to see how God was working in tough situations rather than moaning about what had already happened.

"She and Leah hit it off. I have hope. Most of all, during my visit yesterday I saw hope in Leah's eyes."

"I'm glad to hear it."

Clint thought a lot about Leah, every day. He also thought about how the verdict had rocked his faith, couldn't imagine how she was coping. Certainly, the day she'd lashed out at him when the grand jury voted to indict, she was having her own crisis of faith. Where was she at now?

He hated thinking of her behind bars. He'd considered writing to her, maybe even applying to visit, but the last time he'd seen her, she'd told him to stay away from her and out of her life. While he knew most of it was stress talking, he figured she had enough on her plate, and he'd have to be satisfied with simply hearing about what was going on through Randy and praying for her.

At the office, first thing in the morning, Clint asked the president of the union to organize an emergency meeting. It was bad enough that Leah was unjustly behind bars, but the situation was destroying the department and the coworkers he respected and loved working with. At least neither of the officers had sought to file a complaint against one another. That would have opened up a whole other can of worms. The POA president agreed with Clint about the meeting and promised to set one up.

Other than the blowup in the parking lot, work had, for the most part, returned to normal after Clint's shooting. The shooting itself was eventually ruled in policy. He'd spoken to the department psych once. Most of the talking he'd done was to his prayer group, Iron Sharpens Iron. They understood his perspective better than any shrink. Yeah, he'd hated to take two lives, but the bottom line was, he had absolutely no choice. He did one cable news interview like community relations requested, surprised and irritated that they micromanaged the interview. He was given statement guidelines, orders of Chief Wilcox. *The image of the PD was everything,* the chief said. Clint stuck with them because he didn't want to give anyone any reason to target him.

Meeting Judge Revel was interesting. Clint wanted to ask if he was a member of the Hangmen, but he didn't. Revel wasn't much different in person than he was on the bench. There was an imperial air about him. But his heartfelt thanks to Clint for saving his daughter was real.

"One hears about such horrible ordeals in other places,

happening to other families. This incident has driven home for me how important law enforcement is," he said.

Through it all, Clint couldn't emphasize enough that he'd only been doing his job.

+ + +

Months passed before Gaffney contacted Clint and set up a meeting with her investigator. Ironically it was on the first anniversary of Leah's prison sentence. He discovered that she was someone he already knew. Jenna Blakely had been a sheriff's deputy for Multnomah County. Clint had met her once or twice at training. She was sharp as a tack and a solid Christian. She was also personally invested in putting a stop to domestic violence. Jenna had been injured on a domestic violence call, ironically by the woman she'd been called to protect. When Jenna arrested the husband, the woman had gone after her with a golf club. The incident cost her her left eye and eventually she'd retired because of it.

"Good to see you again, Jenna." Clint gave her a hug. Jenna was tall, six-one and slender. She was a paddler, into all kinds of extreme kayaking, in spite of her injury.

"Likewise, Clint. Impressed now that I know a true hero."

Clint felt himself redden. "Don't start that. You know what I'm going to say."

"I do. You were simply doing your job." She arched an eyebrow. "Most guys wouldn't have been that gutsy."

"I'm praying you'll be the hero for Leah."

"I've read through her file once, plan on doing it again. If she got a raw deal, Gretchen will figure it out."

"Where're you starting?"

"Background first. I'll be interviewing Leah as soon as

possible. I'm also trying to snag an appointment with Birch, but he is elusive. Gretchen is now the attorney of record, so I hope that frees him up. You know, it's best you let us handle things. Gretchen doesn't want you to become a target of the Hangmen."

"I know—she told me. Can't help it, though; I hate sitting on the bench."

"I gotcha. But this could take a long time, years. The wheels of justice move, but they move slowly."

Clint knew what she meant.

+ + +

Thinking about justice a few weeks later, Clint was happy to hear from Henderson that the hazing had stopped. The union meeting seemed to do the trick. But he couldn't help but think that something completely unrelated also had a hand in it. Sergeant Forman had been suspended for two weeks.

"You can even hear him snoring." Sapp was laughing so hard he had difficulty speaking. "It's karma."

Clint tried not to laugh, but it was hard. And he didn't believe in karma.

They were both looking at Sapp's phone. A citizen had taken cell phone video of Forman sleeping on duty. The sergeant had parked his car behind a business, maybe thinking he'd wake up and leave before they opened. The video went viral on social media, and an investigation into the sergeant's behavior began. This was on top of an ongoing investigation about some of the time cards Forman had filed for the SAT officers. Though the unit had been disbanded over a year ago, the probe had been working its way through channels. The sergeant was in real trouble, and Clint couldn't laugh about that. As much as they clashed, Clint didn't want to pile on. He trusted IA to sort it out.

A couple of days after Forman's suspension, Clint came to work, only to learn that Chambers was in the hospital. He'd gotten hurt chasing a suspect.

"How bad is it?" he asked Lieutenant Haun, who had given him the news.

"Might end his career. It's his knee. He'd hurt the same knee playing football."

"Are visitors okay?"

"He didn't say no."

After he logged on, Clint drove to the hospital to see how Chambers was doing. Were Chambers and Forman getting what they deserved?

No, he decided. That would be too pat, too simplistic.

He poked his head into the hospital room. The big man looked to be asleep. His right leg was elevated and swathed in a cast. There was purplish bruising on Chambers's face. Haun had said he'd fallen while chasing a suspect. He must have fallen on his face.

Clint stepped into the room and Chambers jerked awake, irritation crossing his face for an instant before he focused on Clint.

"What are you doing here?"

"Just wanted to see how you're doing, if you need anything."

"Not from you I don't."

The animus surprised Clint. "Okay." An awkward moment passed.

Chambers raised a hand. "Hey, sorry, didn't mean that." He shifted in the bed, wincing. "I'm just not at my best right now."

Clint relaxed. "I get it." He stepped closer.

"You still tight with Radcliff?" Chambers asked.

Clint shrugged.

"Think she'll get a new trial?"

"I hope so."

Chambers looked as if he was going to smile, but it came out as a grimace. "What goes around comes around."

Clint frowned. "What do you mean?"

"Nothing. Pain pills are kicking in. Maybe I hope Leah gets another day in court." His eyes closed and he was out.

Clint stood by the bed for a minute. "I hope so too," he whispered.

CHAPTER 26

W e're filing a second appeal."

In spite of the hope in his voice, Leah's father looked older, and it broke her heart. She'd heard from Gretchen that the appeals court had denied their first appeal. Surprisingly, after twenty months in prison, Leah would say she was fine. She would never say she wanted to stay in prison for the rest of her sentence, but she had a sense of peace with her circumstances. She wanted her father to have that same peace.

"Dad, I want you to know that I'm okay. Right now, I feel like me being here is harder for you than me. Please, I feel your prayers holding me up; let my prayers do the same for you."

"I'm being preached to by my daughter, and you know what?"

"What?"

"It feels good. I hate that you're here, but I'm so glad you found your faith again."

"Me too."

+ + +

Leah told Nora and the Bible study group about the failed appeal.

"You're taking it well."

"I guess I am. You think maybe being in this Bible study has helped me get my balance back?"

The ladies laughed.

"That happened as soon as you decided to stop fighting God," Nora said.

"You're right. By the way, I'm thinking of asking Chaplain Darrel if there's any way I can be baptized in here."

A huge grin split Nora's face. "I was baptized in a laundry basket."

"No kidding?"

"That's right. We could do the same for you."

Everyone agreed.

A little while later, Leah was in the infirmary for an analgesic—she'd overdone basketball the day before—when the intake counselor she'd talked to during the assessment period stopped in.

"How are you feeling, Radcliff?"

"I'm fine. No ill effects. I think this is my last scheduled recheck."

"Things are working out in general population?"

"Yeah, I have a great cellmate. Thanks for arranging that."

"I had nothing to do with it—simple luck of the draw."

"Oh." Then Leah remembered her father saying that Nora was answered prayer. She smiled.

"I have a question for you, Radcliff."

"Shoot."

"I know you and Lyons have been playing impromptu basketball games. You've got a regular group of ladies working out with you."

Leah nodded.

"What would you think about starting a formal basketball program?"

"A basketball program?"

"Yeah, something like the running program we have, for women who need exercise but are not interested in jogging. Giving people something they can succeed at, something healthy that they can continue after their release, is worthwhile. I'm thinking of something along the lines of a clinic. I asked Nora to do something like that a while ago, but she wanted more help than we could give her. I ran it by her again, and she's game if you are."

"You are 100 percent cleared if you need my opinion," the nurse offered.

Leah thought for a second. "I guess if Nora is on board, then I am too."

"Great, I'll draw up some guidelines."

CHAPTER 27

They fired Vicki!" A distraught Marvin Sapp pounded the locker next to Clint.

"What?" Clint stopped what he was doing, not believing what he heard. The hazing had stopped over a year ago. What was happening now?

"For what?"

"She's been in and out of IA for the last month regarding a report she filed a while ago. They say she made false statements."

"You're kidding."

"I wish I was. We're meeting later—want to join us?"

"You bet."

Clint met Sapp and Henderson at a restaurant in Medford, outside Table Rock.

"It was a simple theft report," Vicki said. She was shattered; Clint could see it in her eyes. The fight he'd seen before was gone. "They say I added to the loss to benefit the homeowner."

"The homeowner complained?" Clint hoped Forman was not the problem. After his suspension and embarrassment over being caught sleeping, he'd been a different man. And Clint wanted to believe that the man could change.

"No, it was their insurance agent. He contacted IA."

Clint felt his gut tighten. "Who is the agent?"

Vicki frowned. "Grant Holloway. I know that name. . . . Why do I know that name?"

"He testified for the prosecution regarding Leah."

"What? Why on earth is he after me?"

"I don't know, but I think we need to find out."

+ + +

"You think the Hangmen are behind this?" Gretchen asked after Clint told her about the firing. Since Leah's first appeal to the Oregon Court of Appeals had been denied, Gretchen had immediately filed a second appeal to the Oregon State Supreme Court.

"I do. Marvin told me that Vicki got into it with Patterson the day of the shooting. And Leah told you he was a Hangman. I think they've had it in for her since then and finally got their chance."

"This bit about Grant Holloway being involved—that's very odd and too big a coincidence. There is a possibility that the denial of Leah's appeal emboldened the Hangmen."

"I hadn't made that connection," Clint said, wondering why he hadn't. "It makes sense."

"This has been a difficult few months. We've hit a big blue wall in trying to discover more about the Hangmen. Leah said secrets were hard to keep at the PD—well, this one sure isn't. If Vicki will talk to me, maybe this will be a way to get our foot in the door. Proving that she was targeted because of this group might help."

"Great," Clint said, mood improving somewhat.

"I believe there were errors in Leah's case, even without the Hangmen," Gretchen told him. "Not the least of which was Prosecutor Birch. He has a long, close history with the Draper family, so he should have recused himself."

"But the court of appeals didn't think that was reason enough for a second trial."

"There's more just coming in from my investigator. Brad was used as a hammer in the first trial. Birch painted him as a hero of heroes. That should have opened up the other side. Leah's attorney should have been allowed to show that Brad was not the saint he was thought to be. Jenna has found several people who claim they suffered abuse by Brad and that their complaints were never followed up. One man even has a paper trail. I've just asked the PD for records I believe they withheld from the first trial."

"Blame the victim?"

"In a way, yes. But it is only fair for the jurors to see all the evidence, even that which was not favorable to the victim. It goes to why Leah felt in fear for her life, and it adds dimension to the self-defense argument. I believe Birch withheld such evidence, which is unfair, maybe illegal, depending on his reasons." Gretchen put a hand on Clint's shoulder. "I know the denial hit you hard. Don't give up hope—I haven't. Leah will be free one day. My advice to you is that you be ready to tell her how you feel."

"What?" Clint felt his face flush.

Gretchen chuckled. "Clint, it's nothing to be ashamed of. And as circumspect as you try to be, it's obvious that you feel for her. She'll need your support when she's free again."

"Thanks, Counselor. I'll take your advice."

Clint left the meeting hopeful for the first time in months. The knowledge of how hard Gretchen was working on Leah's appeal was encouraging. The surprise at having his feelings outed faded, though he really thought he had a better cop face than that.

It's time to write her a letter, he decided. *I'd like to get information from her firsthand anyway.* Always pumping Randy for news was not a good thing.

Once home, Clint prayed and then sat to write out, longhand, a letter to Leah.

+ + +

The next night, Clint was about to go EOW when he heard the call go out—a fatal accident on Highway 62. His buddy Jack was on the way, so Clint decided to see if he could lend a hand. It was described as a vehicle versus logging truck, and Clint braced himself—it would not be pretty.

And it wasn't. It looked as if a small sports car had hit a fully loaded logging truck head-on.

"How can I help?" Clint asked when he reached the scene.

Jack was already laying out flares. "Talk to the truck driver. He's in my car, distraught."

Clint hurried to Jack's car. A tough-looking bearded man fidgeted in the back.

"He drove right into me. I couldn't avoid it!" The man was animated, talking to Clint before Clint even asked a question.

"Was he swerving to avoid something else?"

"Not that I saw."

Clint noted that he did not smell alcohol or pot. This driver was most likely not impaired. Was the other one?

"Was he passing someone else?"

"No, no. It was as if he wanted to be hit."

Curious now, Clint left the truck driver and was walking to the mangled wreckage when he saw the license plate. It had come off the sports car and lay in the middle of the highway. He stopped dead in his tracks. It was a personalized plate, one everyone on the PD would recognize.

I PRO U—I prosecute you. This was Arron Birch's car. As he got closer to the car, he could vaguely make out the body of the silver Porsche Birch was so proud of.

Two state police vehicles rolled up to the scene code 3.

A sergeant approached Clint. "This is ours, occurred on a state highway. We'll be handling."

"I'm just here to help—"

"Thanks, we're good. You can return to service."

Clint saw no grounds to argue but left scratching his head, as did Jack and the other deputies on scene.

The next morning he read an article about the crash and learned Birch had been behind the wheel. The investigating officer, Sergeant Dave Draper, had already ruled the crash a suicide.

"We found a note," his quote said. *"He emailed several people outlining his intentions. Clinical depression drove Arron Birch to kill himself."*

"Wow" was all Clint could say as he remembered what Gretchen said about Birch concealing evidence in Leah's trial. It was connected—it had to be. The thing was, Arron Birch had never seemed to be the depressed type. He was a fighter, a pit bull. Was it really suicide?

+ + +

At work that day, most everyone was talking about the Birch situation. In spite of how wrong Clint thought he was with

Leah, Birch had been a popular prosecutor for the city. People were having a hard time with the suicide angle, but that was what the investigation put forward.

A few days later he learned that Gretchen had officially signed on as Vicki's lawyer. It created a subdued buzz around the PD.

"She's not going to get her job back. She could hire a hundred lawyers." Clint overheard Erik Forman talking to another officer. The other officer concurred as the two men left the squad room. Forman's opinion was not the majority. Vicki was respected and well-liked. There were a lot of officers who thought she got a raw deal.

Clint caught up with Vicki over coffee. She'd called him, saying she needed his advice.

"Gretchen says my case for firing looks weaker and weaker with every page she turns," Vicki told him. "I'm really glad I found her."

"Me too. What is it you need my advice on?"

"Gretchen thinks now is the time to try and shake something loose."

"What did she mean?"

"She wants to go public by holding a press conference to talk about the Hangmen. Throw it out there that we know what's going on and we plan to stop it."

Clint sat back and thought about what that might mean.

"It's likely to stir stuff up," Vicki said. "Good and bad."

"Can you handle that?"

"I've got nothing to lose and everything to gain. Would you be ready for something like that?"

"Oh, I'm ready. I've been ready ever since the jury said *guilty*."

CHAPTER 28

L eah checked off another day on the calendar, trying not to be depressed by how much time had passed while she lived behind bars. It helped to be surprised, and that happened when she received a letter from Clint Tanner. It came out of the blue. Her father hadn't even told her to expect one. And it was handwritten, not printed out from a computer. That made it more personal somehow, and to say it brightened her day was an understatement.

> *Leah, I've thought long and hard about writing you this letter. The last time we spoke, you said you wanted me to stay out of your life and to stop praying for you. I hope you'll forgive me since I have to confess I've not stopped praying for you. I'm happy to say that I helped find the attorney now representing you, and I have high hopes your*

new appeal will be allowed and you'll receive a new trial. Maybe I've taken too long to say this clearly, but I was there that morning, remember. I know your injuries were real, and I know you only shot Brad because you were in fear of your life.

I hope your anger with me is past. I decided to write you because, frankly, I was expecting, after almost two years, to see you in person. That your appeal failed was frustrating for me, though I'm sure more so for you. I told you to trust the system and I fear the system has failed you—again. It encourages me to see Gretchen optimistic, so I pray that encourages you as well. Please know that there are many of us who have not given up hope, so don't you. I believe in you, Leah, and I pray that one day I'll be able to say that to you in person.

If there is anything I can send you or do for you here, please let me know. I remain your friend, Clint Tanner.

"No way." Leah held the letter in both hands, amazement flowing through her.

"What?" Nora asked.

Leah swallowed, realizing she'd spoken out loud. "I just got the best letter."

"Boyfriend?"

"No, a coworker. . . . He, uh, has been a big help to me and to my dad. I told him to stay out of my life once."

"Why?"

Leah grinned. "He's one of those praying Christians—you know, the annoying ones?"

Nora laughed. "Yeah, I remember how that used to bother you. Just be careful, my friend."

"Careful how?"

"Build a good relationship with God before trying to build one with another man, no matter how good he makes you feel."

Leah nodded, thinking she was doing just that.

She read the letter over and over, straining to hear his voice in every word. She had long ago forgiven him and sat down to write back and tell him so. From that point on, he was no longer Tanner; he was Clint.

+ + +

"You're pretty chipper today," Chaplain Darrel commented a couple of days later when she sat down for their meeting.

Leah grinned. She told him about the letter and Clint.

"I'm happy for you. I would, however, urge caution."

"Caution?"

"I'm a chaplain, not a shrink. My interest is in your spiritual growth. My wish is for you to focus on your foundation, your worth as a child of God."

Leah laughed.

"That's funny?"

"Only because Nora said almost the exact same thing."

"Smart woman, Nora. God first. Then you'll know not to put up with behavior from a man that you shouldn't put up with."

Leah thought long and hard about his advice after their meeting. She remembered the classes she'd taken on domestic violence. A lot of women stayed in abusive relationships because they didn't believe they could make it without the man. Brad had been her everything, and because of that she'd put up with aggressive and demeaning words and actions from him that she should have rejected outright. At the time, there was a part of her that said she wasn't worthy of someone like Brad. If she lost him, she'd have lost everything.

Well, I have lost him, she thought, *and I'm still standing on my own two feet. I don't want to follow the same pattern with someone else, especially since I'm in here and he's out there.* She knew she had needed to have balance in her life. Even here in prison with nothing, she was still a much-loved child of God. That knowledge must keep her upright; it had to be enough for the next twenty-five years.

"Hey." Nora came rushing into the cell, face flushed with excitement. It was free time and she'd been watching TV. "Come on out. They're talking about you on the TV."

"What?"

She grabbed Leah's arm. "Just come."

Leah let herself be dragged into the TV room. On the screen was Gretchen Gaffney. She was talking about the Hangmen.

". . . there's a problem in Table Rock, Oregon. Not just for Officer Henderson or Officer Radcliff. A clandestine club is operating within the police department, subverting justice."

"Do you have proof?"

"I'm gathering proof as we speak. If I can't get the city of Table Rock to cooperate, then I'll go higher."

"What does that mean?"

"The FBI is always interested in police corruption and the systematic violation of people's constitutional rights."

"She said your name before," Nora said. "She believes you were railroaded. Were you?"

Leah nodded. "She's my attorney." Her heart beat hard in her chest as she realized this would turn her department upside down. Would it put anyone in danger? She thought of her dad, and she thought of Clint. She prayed for their safety, then realized how natural prayer had become for her . . . and how comforting.

+ + +

Clint watched the press conference when he got home. He already knew that since the conference had been held, the city attorney had contacted Gretchen and offered a settlement where Vicki was concerned. Gretchen had declined the offer, telling the attorney that Vicki would take her chances with a judicial hearing. Clint planned to be there when that happened.

He'd just been promoted to sergeant. He'd scored number one on the test, sailed through all the interviews. If he was on the Hangmen's list, they hadn't messed with him. He wondered if the Hangmen were lying low or if they really were toothless in most things. And he also wondered if all this talk of the Hangmen and their power was making him paranoid.

His phone rang.

"Tanner."

"You're a dead man."

"Excuse me?"

"And you won't see it coming."

The line clicked.

Proof the Hangmen were alive and well?

Clint set his phone down, pulse racing. *You're not paranoid if they're really after you.* He'd known Gretchen's announcement would overturn the apple cart; he just hadn't known it would dump on him.

Two weeks after Gretchen's press conference, Clint was at the courthouse bright and early for Vicki's hearing.

"What's going on?" he asked Gretchen, who was seated in the hallway outside the hearing room.

She stifled a chuckle. "Seems the city's case is falling apart. Grant Holloway got cold feet about testifying at this hearing."

"Cold feet?"

Vicki smiled. "Now he's mistaken about the loss he claimed I added."

"So the city doesn't have a case?"

"The hearing judge is speaking to the city attorney now."

Just then the door opened. "You all can come in now," the bailiff said.

Clint followed Vicki and Gretchen into the room. The city

attorney, a recent hire, was already seated, and he didn't look happy.

"Ms. Gaffney—" the judge addressed Gretchen—"I've been informed that the city no longer has a case against your client. Therefore, I'm dismissing all of the charges, and at this moment I'm ordering the city to bring your client back on board without delay and without further penalty. It's to be as if she was never terminated. And I assume, at some later date, you'll want to address back pay."

"Yes, Your Honor."

"Very well. This hearing is adjourned."

Vicki beamed and Clint gave her a hug.

"I knew it was all bogus."

Later, when Vicki left, Clint asked Gretchen, "What do you think happened? Why the change?"

"I'm not sure, but there's been a cable news reporter in town, asking questions about the Hangmen and whether or not Vicki was the victim of a good old boys club. Holloway obviously didn't want to be recorded under oath, and the city had the good sense not to press the issue."

"What does this mean for Leah?"

"It means there are breaks in the wall, movement forward. We're making progress. I think it's good news for Leah."

"I truly hope you're right."

+ + +

Election Day was the day after Vicki's vindication. It was a special election because of the death of a state senator and two early retirements. There were three names on the ballot that Clint was concerned about: Grady Blanchard, Larry Ripley, and Duke Gill. When the results were tallied, they'd all won their races. Grady Blanchard was elected sheriff of Jackson County, Larry would serve as state senator, and Duke was voted in as a county commissioner.

"Are you happy with the outcome?" Clint asked Jack the next morning.

"I don't have a problem with Blanchard. His wife is a little annoying, but he came up through the ranks."

"Annoying how?"

"Just pushy. She reminds me of a Hollywood stage mom—you know, the kind always pushing their kids? Sometimes the way she talks to Grady, I want to say, 'Hey, why don't *you* put on the uniform?' Grady is a different person when she's not around, a better person. Funny and lighthearted."

"No chance he's one of the Hangmen?"

"I don't see it, so I hope not. Told you before he's tight with his brother-in-law, Duke Gill. Gill is a piece of work."

"Yeah, and surprise, Gill's a county commissioner now."

"How can so many people not see how slimy he is?"

"I don't know. He said a lot of the right things."

"Did you believe him?"

Clint hiked a shoulder. "No. How about Ripley, our new state senator?"

"He's worked his way up the ladder as well. He didn't do anything offensive as a councilman. I voted for him."

Clint sipped his coffee and said nothing. He knew from Gretchen that Leah didn't like Larry. She believed he was a Hangman. Jack was right: Larry had been a good councilman, often on the same side as Clint on things. Was that how the Hangmen did it? They stayed in the shadows by not being obvious, by only striking where people least expected it?

After coffee with Jack, Clint had a meeting scheduled with Jenna. She'd called him to say she'd hit a gold mine of information. Gretchen had set up a tip line, and they'd received a lot of calls, some worthless, but some had panned out. The gist of it was a common thread: a lot of abuse claims had been ignored, not just for Brad, but for his partner and a couple other guys he was close to.

After Jenna's call, Clint had drawn up a chart of men he suspected of being Hangmen. They were clustered in IA and detectives. Maybe that was why he was able to promote to sergeant. No suspected Hangmen had anything to do with interdepartmental promotional testing. Frowning, Clint looked at everyone on the chart. Five names. He still found it hard to believe they had the power Parker, his old partner, thought they did.

That was the topic of conversation when Jenna showed up.

"I can see them covering up for Brad or stopping people from getting on the SAT team or into homicide, but I can't see them having the power to get people fired."

"The primary objective of the club just might have been to save Brad," Jenna said. "I've spoken with four officers who retired and moved out of state. They tell me that the Hangmen were actually started years ago by Harden Draper—and he is still actively involved."

"Brad's dad?"

"Yeah, he was a cop for a time. These old retired guys said he was always free with his nightstick and his department-issued flashlight. His favorite target was the suspect's head."

"Really?" This violated all training about the use of force and contact weapons. Never aim for the head, spine, or groin. It was too easy to kill or seriously injure someone.

"They say he was always in trouble and on the verge of being fired, so he came up with the Hangmen to save his own skin. The rumor was that he got some dirt on the chief at the time and used it."

"Blackmail?"

"Apparently his specialty, a close tie with bullying. He retired after only ten years, the same time the chief did, maybe because he had nothing on the new guy. The guys I talked to said he'd never have made it to thirty years and a service retirement because policing was changing. His heavy-handed ways were under scrutiny."

"And after he retired, he founded Table Rock Home Security. They're all over the valley now."

Jenna nodded. "He started the company, sold it after ten years, then invested in the import-export business that has been so lucrative for him."

It was Clint's turn to nod. Harden imported all kinds of goods from China and supplied almost all the outdoor, furniture, appliance, and general hardware stores in Oregon and neighboring states. He'd heard a rumor years ago that big box stores like Costco were going to put Draper out of business. But there was a big Costco in Medford, and Draper was still going strong. Maybe his real estate holdings kept him afloat; he owned half of Table Rock.

"So he starts the Hangmen but leaves the department, and Brad resurrects it?"

"When Brad was hired, a few of Harden's pals were still in the department—Chief Wilcox, who had been Draper's trainee—plus there were several in the community, in influential places . . . Judge Revel for example."

"Judge Revel?"

Jenna nodded again. "He was a police officer in Table Rock for only three years, until he graduated from law school."

Clint folded his arms to consider this. "If Revel was biased because of his relationship with Harden Draper, that should strengthen Leah's second appeal."

"Agreed," Jenna said and went on. "From all I've heard, Brad was every bit the bully Harden was. A few guys believed, but couldn't prove, that Harden used his influence to keep Brad on the job. Eventually Brad took over running the Hangmen."

"This is all fascinating and disturbing, but how will it help Leah?"

"At first Gretchen was simply interested in showing the other side of Brad. Jurors didn't see the plausibility of Brad the hero also being Brad the abuser. Now there's more. Gretchen believes the jury was tampered with."

Clint's voice fled and he stared at Jenna.

"One of the tips we received. Even though it was anonymous, the caller knew some specifics—about a juror being bribed to vote guilty and influence the other jurors. I'm not naming names, but this will be big. Not only that, a lot of people believe there's a good chance Harden Draper was behind it and will find himself behind bars."

Clint was stunned. What Jenna and Gretchen had discovered could only help overturn Leah's conviction, he thought.

As he and Jenna finished their coffees and left the shop, Jenna reached out and touched Clint's arm. "It's been really good reconnecting with you, Tanner."

"Likewise."

"I was wondering . . . are you seeing anyone these days? I'd love to get together and talk with you about anything other than work."

The question caught Clint off guard. One word flashed through his mind: *Leah*. The woman he'd carried a torch for since college, the woman who'd told him to stay out of her life forever. He'd just received a letter from her and was amazed at how happy it made him. It opened a door he'd been praying would open.

*I'm embarrassed I told you to stay away. I even threw away
your pizza. I'm very glad you ignored me and took the
time to write a letter. All things considered, I'm doing okay.
While it's not pleasant being behind bars, it's bearable. I
have a good cellmate and the knowledge that even in here
I'm in God's hands. We play basketball a few times a week.
Please keep the letters coming. I'd love to stay up-to-date
with what is going on in Table Rock PD.*

He liked Jenna; they connected on many levels. But he
needed to see what this opening with Leah would bring.

He cleared his throat, working for time to formulate the
right answer. "I enjoy spending time with you as well, Jenna.
But there is someone else on my mind right now. Hope we can
still work together well."

She dropped her hand. "I'd be lying if I said I wasn't dis-
appointed. . . . But I'm sure we'll still crush crime together. Just
remember me if the other doesn't work out."

CHAPTER 30

The cloud of corruption over Table Rock PD had Leah angry and on edge.

Why didn't I pay more attention to what Brad was doing? Or at least make a note of all the Hangmen?

If I'd snooped more, I might be able to help Gretchen more.

How are the department and all the good people I worked with for three years doing in this mess?

The questions ran through her thoughts, and she really couldn't answer any of them.

Out in the recreation yard, she and Nora were shaping up a group of women on the court. Leah and Nora had started the basketball mentoring program. They'd trained up two good teams of women and played a regular once-a-week game. Teaching rules and sportsmanship was a good thing. They'd worked away from jungle ball and even had a surprising referee of sorts. Pat, the tattooed woman who'd tried to intimidate Leah, had played high school ball. She couldn't play now because of a bum knee, so she'd walk up and down the court and call fouls.

Leah gave pointers and helped the less athletic women with game skills. Sometimes it amazed Leah how well she fit in. These were all women she would have arrested if things were different. Most of them had substance abuse issues, one was in for manslaughter, two were arrested for solicitation, and a couple had been convicted of armed robbery.

Yet on the court they had fun together, helped one another, and for forty-five minutes could forget that they were behind bars.

Besides basketball, Leah had church. For Sunday chapel, she and three other women made up the worship team. They told Leah she had a beautiful voice. She really couldn't hear herself; all she knew was that she loved to worship and would sing all day if she could.

But in spite of these good things, the routine of jail chafed, and there were dark nights when she would have given anything to be out on her own, under the stars or simply at a fast-food restaurant for a midnight snack. On the whole, though, Leah felt at peace, and surprise coursed through her when she realized that she could say, along with Nora, that prison was the best thing to ever happen to her. A part of her felt as if she was the real Leah now, without the facade of the person Brad thought she should be.

If only she had found herself before having to shoot him.

Wednesday afternoon Leah and Nora were warming up while waiting for the rest of the women who formed the two basketball teams to arrive. On any given day they had quite a few spectators. Leah noticed some new faces, fresh from the intake period. Nora missed a jumper and it caromed off the rim, over Leah's head toward the onlookers.

Leah came down from leaping up and missing the ball and turned. One of the onlookers—a thin, blonde woman Leah didn't know—had picked up the ball. A feeling jolted inside Leah, like an alarm going off. Brad would have called it her spidey sense. Something was not right with the woman.

Leah hesitated, then held her arms out to receive the ball. For a second Leah didn't think the woman was going to throw it back. Then in the blink of an eye the woman reared back with the ball in both hands and threw it at Leah with as much force as she could muster.

Leah sidestepped easily, but like a bad dream, the blonde charged her, something glinting in her hand. A razor blade.

Not again.

This time Leah was prepared and in better shape. The woman slashed at her face with the blade, missing Leah by inches. Leah grabbed her assailant's wrist in both hands, then brought her knee up as hard as she could into the woman's midsection.

The small blade dropped from the woman's hand as the breath rushed from her body in a whoosh and a groan. Keeping a grip on the woman's wrist, Leah forced her to the ground even as in her peripheral vision she could see guards rushing toward them.

After releasing the woman to the first guard who reached them, Leah stepped back and let them gain control.

The woman screamed something in a different language—not Spanish, maybe Russian. Leah couldn't tell. As her heart rate settled down and the woman was taken into custody, all she could do was wonder what was up this time.

+ + +

There was another lockdown after this second attempt on Leah's life. So many questions.

Like the first woman to try to kill Leah, Trina Kotov had been arrested in Table Rock, but this time Leah knew the officers, Marvin Sapp and Vicki Henderson. Kotov, who'd emigrated from Russia when she was a child, had been sentenced to six months for dealing drugs. As to why she tried to kill Leah, she wouldn't say. All she would say was that she wanted a lawyer.

She was charged with assault and transferred to a women's prison outside of Oregon. Leah was troubled by the attack, but while on lockdown, something happened that changed her mood in a good way. She received a second letter from Clint.

> *Leah, thank you for writing back and sharing with me*
> *what it's like behind bars. I'm glad you're playing ball*
> *again; you definitely have a gift there.*

He answered a lot of her questions about what was going on in the department and closed with the line: *Still believing in you and still praying, Clint Tanner.*

The letter brought tears to her eyes at the same time it brought joy to her heart. She didn't know how Clint knew that those words were what she needed to hear—that he believed in her and he was still praying. She got busy and sat down to write him back.

CHAPTER 31

Clint got Leah's second letter just before a big meeting the mayor and chief had called. All 103 sworn members and 33 civilian members of the department were to be in attendance, with Jackson County Sheriff agreeing to cover Table Rock so even those on duty could attend. Clint arrived early to the fairgrounds; the meeting place was in one of the exhibit halls.

He knew the gathering was necessary. Table Rock PD was in turmoil. Since Vicki's reinstatement, national reporters were asking questions that local reporters never would. Rachel Clyburn, the Draper family attorney, was all over the news trying to mitigate the Hangmen story and make certain Harden was kept out of it. The Hangmen were the number one topic of conversation. Whenever asked, Chief Wilcox continually denied that the organization existed.

When Clint arrived and looked around, it appeared to him that everyone was in attendance. Including Vicki Henderson. She looked uncomfortable and he caught her eye. Smiling with what looked like relief, she hurried his way.

"Have you seen Marvin?" she asked.

"Not yet." He held out his hand. After his promotion he'd been sent to a couple of different schools and hadn't been in patrol to welcome her back. "Good to see you, though."

She grinned and shook his hand.

"Has it been difficult?"

"Not really." She hiked a shoulder, still searching for Marvin Sapp. "Most everyone has been supportive. It helps that the judge ordered them to bring me back as if I'd never been fired. Got my same shift with my same days off. I'm back working with Marvin. Curing him of all the bad habits he developed in my absence."

Clint nodded. He spied Marvin out of the corner of his eye. "Here he comes."

"See you found my boot." Marvin clapped Clint on the shoulder, teasingly referring to Vicki as a very green rookie.

"Ha-ha." She rolled her eyes.

"Quite a crowd," Marvin said, surveying the room.

"No kidding," Clint agreed.

Chief Wilcox, Lieutenant Racer from IA, Sergeant Forman, and Detective Patterson in homicide were at the front of the room with patrol supervisor Lieutenant Haun a little off to the left. Clint fought his surprise as he saw Harden Draper saunter in the door.

"Hey—" Vicki elbowed him in the ribs—"is that who I think it is?"

"It is," Clint said, watching the man like you'd watch a snake. Draper shook hands here and there. The older guys were more familiar with him, but Clint could see a bit of awe in the eyes of some of the younger guys. Draper was a local celebrity, no two ways about it.

"He walks around the place like he owns it," Sapp said. "Guy's been retired for way more years than he ever worked."

Draper made his way to the front of the room. At one point, he leaned close to Wilcox as if asking a question. They both turned and looked in Clint's direction. There was no mistaking the animosity in Draper's visage. Clint refused to be intimidated. It was Draper who looked away first.

"Wow." Vicki turned to Clint. "Did he just give you the hate stare of all hate stares?"

Clint simply shrugged.

Wilcox called the meeting to order. "I'm glad to see everyone here. I don't have to tell you why we called this meeting," he began, though there were still ripples of whispers rolling through the room. "All of the nonsense you're reading in the press. There is no such group as the Hangmen."

The room erupted as the whispers became louder and a bunch of cops started to speak at once. Some spoke in agreement, but Clint also heard some disbelieving comments.

"Quiet, quiet!" Wilcox ordered.

The murmurs died down.

"This noise about the Hangmen is just a smoke screen." He paused, glancing to Draper, then went on. "This is about one thing and one thing only. Radcliff lost her appeal. Her new pot-stirring lawyer is grasping at straws, trying to shift blame. Radcliff killed one of our own in cold blood, and she had her day in court. These false allegations will fade away if we don't put any more wood on the fire."

"Mind if I say a few words, Chief?"

Wilcox, Racer, and Patterson all turned as Harden Draper

stepped forward. He'd phrased it as a question, but it was clear he wasn't going to wait for an answer.

Draper faced the room. He was a big man, at least six-four, with a full head of steel-gray hair. His frame held weight that came with age, but his posture was straight. He reminded Clint of old-time actor Lee Marvin.

"You all know who I am, what I lost." He paused, Clint figured for effect. "And you know that I once walked in your shoes. Table Rock PD is a great department, staffed by fine men who want to do right by their community. This *fe*-male lawyer just wants to smear fine men to help someone we know committed a crime. Let it roll off your backs, boys. Just do the jobs you're paid to do, the jobs you're good at." He waited, but if it was applause he wanted, he didn't get it. Finally Draper nodded and left the room.

Clint looked around at his coworkers. Had Draper rallied them? Sergeant Forman started to clap. A couple more joined in, but for the most part there were folded arms and blank stares. Clint knew then that if there was such a thing as the Hangmen, they were a minority, and that gave him hope.

Wilcox looked to be at a loss, and Racer stepped up and took over, admonishing everyone to say nothing to the press.

"Any offhand comment could be taken the wrong way. Nobody wants the FBI in here poking around."

Murmurs of agreement floated through the room. Clint felt as if Racer were speaking directly to him, but he didn't flinch. The hotter the fire was under the PD, the greater the chances that something would break loose and help Leah's case.

+ + +

Later, at home, Clint reread Leah's letter.

> *I'm worried about what all this Hangmen stuff will stir up at the department. I gave Gretchen a list of everyone I thought was in the group, but there may be a lot more. Watch your back. I'd like to think that they don't have as much power as Brad thought they did, but be careful anyway.*
>
> *I had a bit of excitement here myself...*

She went on to write, rather nonchalantly in his opinion, about an attempt on her life. Someone came at her with a razor blade!

Clint felt his heart stop again. He took a deep breath and reread the account.

> *... it was a clumsy attempt. I've gotten in pretty good shape, and the muscle memory of weaponless defense really helped. Please don't worry. I've told my dad the same thing.*

In spite of her mitigation, the thought of another attempt on her life made the hair rise on the back of his neck. The danger was real. In his next letter he asked her permission to visit her.

✦ ✦ ✦

Another internal investigation was underway regarding the second attempt on Leah's life. Where the woman, fresh out of intake, got the weapon was a huge question. Two weeks into it, Hastings told Leah something huge.

"Trina Kotov brought the razor blade to jail with her," she said. "One of the intake officers admitted taking a bribe to go easy on her search."

Leah frowned. "Bribe? From who?"

"She can't say. Or won't. But she got four grand in cash to do it. This investigation is not over."

Leah eventually found out from Hastings that an officer named Helen Jones confessed to being approached by a man with an accent and given the money in cash in an envelope. She believed she was only making it easy on a girl who'd never been arrested, claimed she had no idea the woman was hiding something like a razor blade. And she'd never seen the man before or since.

Sobered by the news, Leah now knew someone outside the prison wanted her dead. Harden Draper's name rose to the top of her list. Sadly, Leah realized that she couldn't put it past her ex-father-in-law. In retrospect, she'd never liked Harden. Brad idolized him, and the feeling was mutual, so she did her best to get along. But Harden had always made her nervous. He didn't really think much of women. Reflecting on how angry he was with her during the trial—and how, if looks could kill, she'd already be dead—she didn't doubt that he would really pay someone to try to kill her.

The lockdown ended after three weeks, and Leah had a surprise visit from Gretchen's investigator, Jenna. Leah knew Jenna had been a state cop and how she'd lost her eye, but she'd never met her. Tall and blonde, she moved like an athlete with confidence and purpose.

"Glad to finally meet you, Leah."

"Likewise. I guess I can thank you for uncovering good evidence for me. But I confess that I'm worried about the ramifications."

Jenna frowned. "Ramifications? If you mean that the Hangmen might retaliate for being uncovered, let them try. I look at them as bullies, ones that need to be confronted. I know you talked to Gretchen about the Hangmen. Is there anything else you can tell me?"

Leah blew out a breath and tried to think. "Brad took a lot of cues from his dad. Harden would talk about the 'good old days' as a cop when he could intimidate people to his heart's content. I'm embarrassed that I never spoke up. I even laughed at his stories. But Harden had some sexist and racist views. I can't say he was a Hangman, but it wouldn't surprise me if he was."

Jenna nodded. "I believe all of this started with Harden. What do you know about Melody Draper?"

The question surprised Leah. "Not much. She's Brad's older sister. They never talked about her. I only knew about her because Brad's sister Ivy got drunk one night and mentioned her. Brad wouldn't. All he'd say was that she left years ago and then he called her names. Why do you ask about Melody?"

"I'm thorough. She's a loose end. I'm trying to find her and talk to her."

"If I remember right, Harden and Blanche tried hard to have kids and couldn't. They hired a surrogate and . . ." Leah paused.

"Go on."

"This is conjecture on my part—I'm reading between the lines. They were certain the baby would be a boy up until it was delivered. Along came Melody. Harden didn't want a girl, but it was the only time Blanche put her foot down. They brought Melody home. Five months later, Blanche found out she was pregnant with twins."

"Brad and Ivy."

Leah nodded. "I'm not surprised Melody left, more surprised that Ivy stays. As far as Harden was concerned, there was only Brad. Where Melody went to and when . . ." Leah shrugged. "I wish I could help you."

They went on to talk about the case. Leah gave Jenna the names of a few retired police officers to talk to.

Later, back in her cell, she sat down to answer Clint's latest letter, to respond to the request to come visit her.

+ + +

Clint met Jenna after work. She'd called him and said she'd uncovered something huge.

"You heard about the latest attempt on Leah's life?"

Grimly Clint nodded. "Leah mentioned it in her latest letter. Randy said an officer was in custody."

"Yes. Helen Jones is related to Marcus Jones."

"So?" Clint asked.

"Marcus Jones was on Leah's jury."

"What?"

"He was the foreman. I tried to talk to him and got the door slammed in my face. Gretchen made a formal complaint to the state police alleging jury tampering."

"Wow, great thinking connecting Table Rock to Wilsonville, with a name as common as Jones."

"It felt like too much of a coincidence. And now the full force of the investigation will be handled by the state police."

"That's a good thing. They have the power to compel cooperation and get answers."

"Let's hope."

Clint did hope, and he prayed. He also kept corresponding with Leah. He'd asked permission to visit her, but she didn't want him to.

"It's a vanity thing," she wrote. *"I don't want you to see me wearing clothes emblazoned with 'Oregon Department of Corrections.'"*

CHAPTER 32

Though Leah felt as if she was getting to know him better with every letter over the last several months, the correspondence with Clint was wonderful and painful at the same time. Bitter and sweet. Leah could see his face as she read his writing. She smiled at the bits of self-deprecating humor. He told her about his time on the mission field and how he got that scar on his face. He also wrote about his aunt GiGi, a woman Leah hoped to meet someday.

She read each letter over and over again. While they were breathtakingly refreshing, they also stung like lemon juice on a paper cut. She wanted to be free, sitting across from Clint, listening and sharing face-to-face. The ache of that want sometimes took her breath away.

Leah remembered how her mom had always handwritten her letters. *"It's the personal touch,"* she'd say. Her cursive writing was beautiful, a work of art. Leah couldn't say the same of hers, but she was working at it. Clint always handwrote his letters. Not cursive, but in clear, readable block printing. And in the letters Leah heard Clint's heart.

> *I went to State, just like you. I was there when you played, two years ahead of you. I caught every home game and most away games even after I graduated. You were a great point guard. The games were always exciting and worth the price of admission. I have to confess, once I thought about approaching you—okay, the truth: I had a crush on you . . .*

A crush! Leah's knees went weak. She thought about her time in college. It was all basketball, all the time. Because of her size she'd always felt she needed to work twice as hard as everyone else. She hadn't walked away from God completely yet. How would her life have been different if she'd met Clint then?

+ + +

> *Playing basketball for four years in college totally burned me out. The game was not fun anymore, so after I graduated, I rarely played. Brad hated the game . . . Needless to say, after we started dating, I stopped completely. It took prison for me to pick up the game again. There's a joke in there somewhere. I've also started to go to church here regularly. Another regret—why did I ever walk away from church and God? The service here is really beautiful, considering . . .*

Clint was glad to hear the part about church. He enjoyed reading every word from Leah. She was three-dimensional and real in her letters, but sometimes he sensed a subtext that made him angry and sad. Brad was never, ever the right man for her.

He remembered well the day Leah graduated the academy and joined Table Rock PD. That was the first time he realized he really had been carrying a torch for her. He'd rehearsed asking her out, trying hard not to sound like a lovesick puppy or worse, some kind of strange stalker. He wanted to wait until she passed probation, figuring there was just too much going on in training, and he didn't want to distract her.

But in waltzed Draper the month before she would have been off probation, and Clint saw his chances evaporate like snow off a hot pavement.

His phone rang and he saw it was Randy.

"Hey, Randy, what's up?"

Randy was breathless. "We did it."

Clint sat up straight. "What?"

"You heard me. Leah's been granted a new trial. A juror confessed to taking a bribe to ensure a guilty vote. The new trial date is pending."

"Amen!" Clint exclaimed, standing to his feet. Answered prayer. He knew that soon he'd be seeing Leah face-to-face and not just in the inked lines of her letters.

PART
THREE

CHAPTER 33

Sergeant Clint Tanner suppressed a yawn as he prepared his notes for the first briefing of his newly minted task force. He'd barely slept in the last thirty hours and had about six more to get his team briefed, staged, and on task—raiding a suspected smuggling operation.

Four years ago, after the death of Brad Draper and an unrelated scandal that rocked the smuggling task force with the acronym SAT, the unit had been disbanded. Since that time, the department had made only sporadic attempts to interdict smuggling operations on the I-5 corridor. There was infrequent talk about forming a new task force because of the uptick in human trafficking.

When Clint arrested two Russian nationals driving a truck loaded with an absurd amount of marijuana bound for states where it was still illegal, talk became reality, and he was tasked with getting the new task force up and running. With individuals brazen enough to try to move a mountain of marijuana, there were undoubtedly worse things going on along the interstate.

Interim Chief Haun poked his head into the briefing room. "You nervous?"

"A little," Clint admitted. He'd been a sergeant for eighteen months, but this was his first gig as a task force leader. And while he was excited about the opportunity and anxious to get going, it pained him that he would miss the last part of Leah's trial. He'd already missed the first part because of training. There was no way around it. Her second trial was being held in Salem, four hours away, and he'd never make it. He prayed Leah would understand.

"You'll do fine," Haun told him. "With all of that intelligence you gathered, I have high hopes this will be a huge success." He held up a thumb. "Be safe."

Clint nodded. In spite of the butterflies and the regret over missing the trial completely, he was confident about the operation. When he arrested the two men in the truck a day and a half ago, he'd overheard a conversation. The men were speaking Russian, apparently believing they were safe from anyone understanding. But Clint spoke Russian—not well enough to pass for a national, but well enough to understand what concerned the men. That led him to scrutinize paperwork he found in the truck and on their persons, a lot of it in Russian. Through the two information sources, he pieced together an address in Sams Valley, a place called Larkspur Farms, and he picked up on a strong desire in both men to reach a phone quickly, as there were people they needed to warn that their mission had been compromised.

The arrested men were allowed by law to make one phone call each, but the judge recognized the need for secrecy, so he agreed to let the police hold the men incommunicado pending booking—but for no longer than thirty-six hours.

A little bit of intelligence gathering while the men were in a holding cell awaiting booking uncovered a farmhouse and barn on a large piece of property. Neighbors reported trucks coming and going at all hours. Most believed the farm was owned by a large commercial enterprise. But the kicker was, the farm and land were in foreclosure; no one should be there at all. That gave the PD enough time to get a warrant and mobilize a strike team before the judge's deadline expired.

There was also the coincidence regarding the woman who attacked Leah in prison; she too was Russian, though a naturalized citizen now. Clint hated coincidences. The men he arrested might have absolutely nothing to do with the woman who attacked Leah, but he planned to make sure one way or another. So Clint beat back his fatigue with a strong cup of coffee and told himself to suck it up. He could sleep for hours when this was over.

As the team—including four members of his own department, two state cops, and two county deputies—began to file in, Clint checked the clock. In thirty minutes, they'd be breaking down doors. TRuST, the Table Rock Smuggling Team, would serve its inaugural warrants and hopefully be in a position to interdict a lot of illegal smuggling in southern Oregon.

+ + +

Daylight was two hours away when TRuST reached their destination and Clint deployed his personnel. He'd decided against bringing in SWAT, both because of the time it would require and because he was reasonably certain these people couldn't know their cover was blown.

The place was dark and quiet, and Clint wondered at that. He pushed any niggling concern to the back of his mind. He knew the men in custody had not been able to call and sound the alarm. They hadn't been booked, so they weren't even in the system. The people in this farmhouse should have no idea what was about to hit them.

He led a team to the front, and his friend Jack Kelly, a deputy sheriff, led the team that would go around the back. His radio crackled that Kelly's team was in position, and Clint gave the go signal.

His team roared up the drive in two vehicles. They came to a stop and he and his men bailed out. Clint and Vicki Henderson and Marvin Sapp took the front door while the other two officers took positions of cover. Clint was on the porch steps in one leap.

He pounded on the door with a knock and notice. "Table Rock PD! We have a warrant—open up!"

He waited a beat and then nodded to Sapp, who had the battering ram. In two quick strikes, the door splintered and fell open. Clint and his team rushed in.

The rooms were dark except for the team's flashlight beams. Clint and Henderson went left, while Sapp and another officer went right. Clint heard something that sounded like crying, and for a minute he wondered if they'd stumbled into human trafficking.

He held up a hand to quiet Henderson. With the sound of the rest of his team in the distance, Clint heard crying for sure, but it wasn't human. It was coming from the last room to be cleared. Signaling Henderson to cover him, Clint pushed the door open and stepped in, gun up and on target.

The whining increased exponentially, and in the corner he saw the source. A small brown-and-white puppy of questionable heritage sat on a dirty pillow, obviously terrified. Aside from the pup, the room was empty.

"Ah, poor thing," Clint said as the all clear was given and he holstered his weapon. Somehow, seeing the miserable creature took his mind off the incredible failure this raid was.

Henderson crinkled her nose. "He's filthy, and it looks like he's been using this room as a toilet."

"Not a dog person, Henderson?" Clint asked as he knelt down near the frightened animal.

"Afraid I'm a crazy cat lady."

Clint held his hand out and clicked his teeth. The frightened dog's body vibrated with fear, tail tucked between its legs. It looked as if its meals hadn't been too regular either.

"Here, sweetie," Clint cooed. The dog came to him and he scooped it up.

"Want me to call animal control?"

"Nah, I'll handle it. Let's just go see how badly we've been hosed today."

The dog settled into the crook of his arm, and for a brief second, Clint forgot his disappointment.

After all their hasty planning, in a few minutes, they'd cleared an empty house.

Clint wiped sweat from his forehead and contacted Jack's team.

"All clear out here. Not a sign of anyone," he said. "We'll check the barn."

"10-4," Clint said, then bit his bottom lip, frustration washing over him like acid, harsh and stinging.

"Hey, Sarge, come in here," Sapp called from the kitchen.

Clint stomped into the kitchen.

A half-eaten pizza was on the table, plus several cans of beer.

One of the cans had been knocked over and there was a puddle of beer on the floor.

"They were tipped," Sapp said. "Probably left not long ago." He pointed at the dog. "But you caught one desperado, heh?"

The dog had stopped shaking. Clint nodded absentmindedly and knew Sapp was right about the bad guys being tipped. He also knew that neither of the Russians had gotten near a phone.

That could only mean one thing. They had a traitorous leak.

ou're going to wear out a path," Gretchen chided Leah as she paced the conference room.

"Can't help it. I feel antsy and it's nice to have the room to pace."

They were waiting in an attorney-client room outside of the courtroom. Her second trial had started just after the forty-first month of her incarceration. It lasted a little over a week, and today it ended early in the morning session. After lunch, the jury had broken to deliberate. If they didn't reach a verdict by 5 p.m., Leah would be sent back to a holding cell. Pacing served two purposes: it calmed her nerves and it stretched muscles that ached from sitting in court. She fully expected to be back in a holding cell at the end of the day. The jury in her first trial had taken four days to come to a verdict—it was anyone's guess how long this jury would take.

"I think we did fine," Gretchen said. "I'm not worried."

Leah looked at her. Gretchen was the picture of peace. *Why can't I be that still?* she wondered. Patting her hands together and continuing her pacing, Leah couldn't shake the butterflies. It felt good to be moving.

Gretchen's cell phone buzzed with a text. She read it, then stood. "I'll be right back. I promised a cable news outlet a brief interview. You'll be okay?"

"Fine."

Gretchen nodded and went to the door and knocked. The deputy on the other side opened it and let her out, and Leah was alone with her thoughts.

With her attorney gone, she reflected on the quiet, real quiet. Prison was never, ever quiet. Here, compared to her cell, it was monastery quiet. Taking a deep breath, she was finally able to calm her nerves. She had done the best she could on the stand, and this time Gretchen had been a pit bull on her side, but the outcome was in God's hands.

She didn't remember much of her first trial. Decimated by shock and grief, she'd assumed a mental fetal position and let things happen. Now she paid attention to every detail, often sketching her own rendering of the proceedings and the people. It helped to steady her nerves.

Remembering her sketch pad, she pulled it out and opened to her current in work in progress. The subject taking shape under the pencil in her hand was the judge presiding over her new trial. A petite woman, she wore a formidable expression that during the entire trial never changed no matter which side she was dealing with. Leah prayed that meant the woman would treat both sides equally when it counted, and the trial proceedings had answered that prayer. She carefully filled in the outline of the woman's face from memory, placing her on the bench, gavel in hand.

Leah's pencil sketching had come a long way in the nearly four years of her incarceration. The figures and scenes she drew now were clear, the faces human and recognizable, even lifelike. Donna had been over the moon with the drawing Leah had done for her. That couldn't be said of the drawings in the first part of her sketchbook, when she'd begun to relearn the skill she'd honed in high school. She liked to think of the progression of her sketching as a visual representation of the progression of her soul, first blurry, ugly, and misshapen, then later clearer and more defined. The change didn't happen overnight, either.

At the moment, the activity helped center Leah. It was difficult not to be nervous and anxious even though the new trial was clearly necessary given what had happened during the first trial.

Leah had to trust, a skill she was learning could be difficult to master. She knew in her heart that what she'd had to do was justified. Now she prayed this second jury saw the same thing.

+ + +

Leah hadn't quite finished her sketch when the quiet was shattered by a commotion in the hallway outside the room she was in. She put the pad and pencil away and wondered what was happening. The clock said the jury had only been out two hours—was it possible they'd reached a verdict?

She doubted that was what had happened. But what? She stood, tense.

A few minutes later the door flew open and in burst Gretchen. "This is it, Leah. They reached a verdict. We're being called back to the courtroom."

Leah felt her breath leave her. How was that possible? Not even a whole day of deliberation. Was this good or bad? Not having the strength to form the question, Leah grabbed her notebook and followed Gretchen out the door.

Once seated, Leah looked around the packed courtroom and took in as much of the crowd as she could. One face was missing. Her dad had relayed Clint's regrets, but Leah realized she'd been hoping something would change, and it surprised her how strong the disappointment was.

The press area overflowed. Thankfully, the judge had denied the request that the proceeding be televised. It was bad enough that for a week the courtroom artist had been sketching Leah and everyone else involved. She thought the sketch of her resembled a short-haired gremlin and wished she could have given the news organizations her own work.

Whether or not she prevailed in this second trial, everyone in the state now knew her face, and she wished that wasn't the case. It was difficult having your image flashed across every cable news channel 24-7 because you'd shot and killed your husband, been convicted of murder, and now won a new trial. Listening to so-called experts debate her guilt or innocence was crazy making. A couple of times she wished she could call Nancy Grace and set the record straight but knew it would do no good. Everyone had an opinion.

One unfortunate result of all the work her legal team put into finding a reason for the new trial was the discovery of Brad's history of brutality. Leah had been shocked; she'd had no idea. Gretchen and her investigator, Jenna, had been meticulous in digging up hard evidence. They were able to prove Lieutenant Racer had been covering for Brad his entire career. The floodgates opened after Vicki Henderson's firing was dismissed. When people saw that the Hangmen could be thwarted, lips started to loosen. Henderson's case became a wedge that unlocked the evidence eventually leading to Leah being granted a new trial.

There was one notable absence on the witness list. Arron Birch, the prosecutor who died in a car crash a year and a half ago, couldn't answer allegations of withholding evidence, jury tampering, or just what it was he knew at the first trial. The crash had been ruled suicide. Leah found that hard to believe, but there was nothing she could do about it.

Gretchen had plenty of other witnesses to call. Two retired officers came forward and gave testimony about the fabled good old boys network that protected cops like Brad, covering up bad behavior because he was a member of the Hangmen. They named names, confirming what Leah had thought: Chief Wilcox, Detective Patterson, and Lieutenant Racer were Hangmen. Wilcox and Patterson were reportedly on leave considering retirement. Terry Racer had been suspended pending a review.

To date five people had come forward to say they had complained about Brad's brutality and their complaints were ignored. Two of those complainants filed federal lawsuits against the department. Jenna found a pattern of abuse that internal affairs ignored when it concerned certain officers. There were two other officers besides Brad, but they had already retired and so far, none of their complainants had sued.

This saddened Leah. As hurt as she was by Brad's behavior, she'd long ago forgiven him. And a part of her still loved the good Brad. Now, because Jenna had done a thorough job, his memory as a solid cop, a medal of valor recipient, would be destroyed. But she had to consider both sides. The first serious complaint against Brad to be buried had occurred a year before Leah met him. The inevitable what-if questions came to mind:

What if he had been held accountable then? What might have been different?

Like so many questions in her situation, these would never be answered.

For this trial, besides the change of venue, Leah testified. During her testimony, one of the hardest questions asked of her was why she'd never filed a police report if Brad had been abusive.

"Didn't you attend hours of training on domestic violence? Didn't you file many reports documenting the domestic violence in other households? Didn't you know that if Brad was truly abusive, the activity would only escalate if you didn't say something?"

"Yes, I knew all those things. But it wasn't that simple—"

"Because the abuse didn't happen—isn't that right? You made up the story after the fact."

Gretchen's objections stopped the line of questioning. Leah feared that couldn't fully explain all that was going on in her head four years ago. She tried. Yes, she knew beyond a shadow of a doubt what abuse was, but that it could happen to her did not compute at the time. And Brad was one of the good guys; she'd looked up to him long before they were married. Even in spite of the slaps, the punches, and the arguments, she couldn't reconcile her Brad, the hero, with a man who was an abuser. And because of her own pride, it was impossible to consider herself a victim.

Leah wasn't certain she'd gotten her point across. She'd taken the stand with Gretchen's blessing and full support. It was important that this jury heard from her own lips just how scared she'd been that morning that Brad would kill her. When she finished, two of Brad's cousins were ejected from the courtroom after yelling, "Liar!"

Now, a week later, after only hours of deliberations, the jury had reached a verdict. Today there were hate stares aplenty sent her way from half the courtroom. That area was packed with Brad's family and friends—those who had not already been removed for disrupting proceedings. Generally, a disruption was along the lines of someone screaming out that Leah was a murderer, a liar, or a name more profane.

Brad's parents, Blanche and Harden Draper, and his sister Ivy were front row every day. Harden had a permanent scowl, Blanche looked heavily medicated, while Ivy appeared to want to be anywhere else but court. Assorted family members and friends filled in the seats behind. They all vented their fury at Leah to any reporter who would listen.

"Why do you insist on reading what they have to say?" Leah's father had asked one day during the trial when he saw her with the newspaper. "They're bitter and lashing out."

"They lost their son. He was their pride and joy."

"He was an abusive so-and-so."

"Dad, they'll never believe that. He was their only son. I remember all the dinners at their house—to them he could never do any wrong."

"They want to make your life miserable."

"And they could have, four years ago. But I'm in a different place now. While I wish it hadn't happened, I've made peace with the shooting. I feel sorry that the Drapers will never know peace."

Leah felt light-years removed from the woman she was the night she followed her husband and found him doing something she believed was illegal. As she thought back to that woman, she barely recognized her. Today, she did have supporters. Her father and Chaplain Darrel had been at the trial every day. Included along with her training officers, she saw a few of her teammates from her college basketball team. There were also women present from the battered women's advocacy group that Gretchen represented, No Violence at Home.

She glanced toward Chaplain Darrel. He gave a slight tilt of his head. Seeing him gave her strength, in the same way seeing her father did. Chaplain Darrel had helped her through the toughest time of her life.

All the friendly faces couldn't dim the sorrow she felt at not seeing the one face she really wanted to see. She'd hoped against hope he'd be there. They'd been corresponding for two years, and she believed she'd been reading his heart. He was a good man, a real man. His last letter told her about the opportunity for a new smuggling task force. He'd been lobbying to get a new one formed for at least a year. He was a sergeant now, and her heart was happy for him. He deserved the promotion. Leah knew he'd just not been able to take the time off right at the moment.

He'd wanted to visit her in prison, and she'd stopped him. It surprised her how much she wanted to see him now. Technically she was still in custody, and if she lost this trial, she wouldn't see the light of day for years. But Clint had become so real to her, so close to her, she'd wanted him here even if she was about to face defeat.

Leah turned back to the front and banished all thought of defeat from her mind. The last time she appeared in court she'd been emotionally devastated by the fact that her husband was dead, and she'd killed him. Leah had been oblivious to the proceedings. She'd stayed in a shadow world for months until she met the prison chaplain. Now she was fully aware of everything going on around her and anxiously awaiting the end of this second trial and the verdict of the jury.

The bailiff called for everyone to rise as the judge entered the courtroom. Leah stood and watched the men and women of the jury enter the court single file and take their seats. Several looked her way and smiled. A good sign?

After they were seated, the judge called the court to order. She spoke to the jury, asked about the verdict, and reiterated the charges. Leah barely heard the legalese. Her heart was pounding so loud, she was certain everyone in court could hear. She knew all of this was out of her control, that ultimately God controlled the outcome, but nervous anticipation threatened to swallow Leah and she gripped the armrests tightly, knuckles turning white.

Then, from what seemed like miles away, the jury foreman pronounced the verdict: *"Not guilty of all charges. The defendant acted in self-defense."*

Her side of the courtroom exploded into cheers.

The other side exclaimed loudly in disbelief and was warned by the judge to calm down.

Leah closed her eyes and offered a prayer of thanksgiving. To say she was relieved and happy would be an understatement. But a negative niggling thought plagued her: What next? After Brad's death and the pain and bitterness that obviously still existed in his family, could she really live a normal life? Could she really go home again? Leah couldn't answer those questions. But she knew she had to go home. Too many questions remained unanswered there. Especially after she considered how Larry Ripley had explained away that late-night mysterious meeting to the trial jury. Leah had paid particular attention to what Larry and Grant Holloway had to say on the stand.

"Ms. Radcliff testified that she witnessed Brad Draper take what she believed was a payoff, in the early morning hours of August 6, while you and Richard Chambers watched. Is that what she saw?"

"No, no, that's not what she saw. I just picked up a rent payment, that's all. Officer Draper and his partner merely stood by

to make certain it all went well. The help of these officers was approved by their sergeant."

"Why did your renter pay in such a way and so early in the morning?"

"Lots of my tenants pay in cash. I'm always working so nothing was strange for me."

Gretchen couldn't shake Ripley. Holloway wasn't as forceful as Ripley, but he repeated the same story. Leah had studied him closely. He resembled the man she'd seen that night. She couldn't say positively one way or the other if he was the man and that bothered her, raising doubts in her mind.

But one of the last things Ripley said erased some doubts for Leah.

"Would his wife finding out about this 'out of policy' meeting, as you called it, cause Officer Draper to become so enraged that he'd want to harm her?"

"No, not Brad."

Initially, she'd believed that and been devastated that they'd fought over such a trivial matter. Now, after thinking about it for four years, none of it made sense, and she knew beyond any doubt Larry was lying.

CHAPTER 35

C lint didn't get home until noon. He'd kept the pup with him, and when he got back to the station, one of the K-9 officers gave him some food and a kennel, then let Clint give the dog a quick bath where they bathed the working dogs. After being fed and washed, the dog curled up in a crate and went to sleep. Clint went inside the station to deal with the blow of a compromised operation.

By the time he and his team had finished at the farm, their clock had run out and the Russians had to be booked. The men quickly lawyered up and were not talking in English or Russian.

Still the operation in Sams Valley wasn't a total bust. The barn revealed three truckloads more of marijuana, fentanyl from Mexico, and a collection of stolen goods, from guns and ammunition to cigarettes and assorted electronics. The smugglers might have been tipped off and fled, but they hadn't had time to get rid of the goods. From what Clint had overheard and read when he arrested the two men, the farmhouse had been a sort of way station. Goods were separated and trucks assigned routes: north, east, and south.

Anger built over the leak and the fact that they'd not caught anyone, and he vowed to catch the leaker. He needed sleep to clear his head before he could sit down and consider a list of suspects. For the moment he had to console himself with putting a financial dent in the operation. At least now they had a better idea of how the smugglers worked.

Carrying the dog under one arm, he picked up his newspaper on the way to the front door and came up short when he read the headline: *Former Police Officer Radcliff Not Guilty—Self-Defense.*

"Look at that," he said to the pup. "This jury saw the truth, and I missed being there for the verdict."

The pup stared at him, finally, without a trace of fear in his eyes. Clint leaned against the door to read the article. The picture on the front page was of a smiling Leah hugging her father. Clint felt a jolt at the sight of her. Besides the shorter hair, even in the small newspaper photo she looked so different from the beaten woman who had told him to stay away from her and keep out of her life. He skimmed the story, a recap of what he knew all too well.

The joy he felt for Leah flushed away the disappointment over the raid. This was answered prayer. Leah had been railroaded. In the months after the conviction, when Clint thought about her sitting in prison, he'd felt guilty for telling her to trust the system. Now, however, his advice was borne out. There had been a painful hiccup, but the system came through—albeit helped out by a lot of prayer.

Leah was a free woman. He knew she planned to come home

and searched the article for some hint about her next step but found none. Clint had wanted to visit her in prison, but she'd asked him not to. He'd respected her wishes and truly felt a great loss that he'd not been there in court. Should he call her? He could call Randy; maybe that's what he'd do. He'd gotten to know her so well over the months through their correspondence, excitement rose in his chest at the thought of hearing her voice.

He unlocked his front door and went inside. Holding the pup in one hand and the phone in the other, he hit Randy's name. The call went immediately to voice mail.

"They are probably really busy," he said to the pup, swallowing the disappointment he felt. In the article on the front page, Leah gave no comment except to say that she was thankful and appreciative of all the people who had stood behind her.

But there was an interview in the article with someone who had no problem giving comments. Harden Draper, Brad's father, complained that a grave injustice had been done. In his mind Leah was a cold-blooded killer and she would always be. Clint knew there was no moving forward for the Drapers. He felt sorry for them. Would that impact Leah's plans? He hoped to see her come home, but would that be possible? She was a cop who killed her cop husband because he tried to kill her. Could she really come home and pick up where she left off?

Clint didn't know the answer to that question, any more than he knew what on earth he was going to do with a puppy.

CHAPTER 36

Southern Oregon in November is often cold, rainy, snowy, and gray. This November Leah got two out of four. Bone-chilling cold and gray, depressing skies. She drove south down Highway 62 through Prospect toward Trail. She'd not been down this road in probably four years, and the knot in her stomach grew tighter the closer she got to home. It was the long way home, for sure. If she'd shot down Highway 5 from Salem, she'd have pulled into her father's driveway by now. But she was coming from Bend, Oregon, where Gretchen was based. The defense team had held a celebration for her at their office and surprised her with the used car she now drove.

The reason for the party was twofold: to celebrate her release, but also to delay her trip home so she could outsmart all the news media. She'd barely made it out of the courtroom after the not-guilty verdict.

As she neared Lost Creek Lake, Leah slowed, hands suddenly clammy and sweaty on the steering wheel. Though she'd been over this a million times, fear rolled through her in a wave. *Maybe this is a mistake. Maybe I shouldn't go home.*

Doubt joined the fear and hit her like the fists of ten professional boxers. Other than her father and maybe Clint, no one would be happy to see her, no one wanted her home. She knew that after reading the paper and letters to the editor.

She pulled over, heart racing, thinking of her father and Clint. Would her coming home just make their lives more complicated? Selfishness reared its ugly head. More than anything she wanted to see Clint. She wanted to be face-to-face with the man whose letters had been a refreshment, a window to life in freedom, though not a lifesaver—God had done that. Leah could admit now to herself that she'd fallen a little in love with Clint through his letters, and she was ready to see him, hear him, and find out if there was any chance he felt the same way.

Traffic sped by. Leah rested her head on the steering wheel and went to the only help she could count on—she prayed. The irony did not escape her; the last time she was home, she'd screamed that prayers didn't work. The verse that came to her was her life verse, from the book of Joshua, chapter 1, verse 9. *"Have I not commanded you? Be strong and courageous. Do not be frightened, and do not be dismayed, for the Lord your God is with you wherever you go."*

The day she'd climbed, shackled, onto the bus that would take her to Coffee Creek Correctional Facility, she didn't believe she'd ever to return to southern Oregon. If and when she was ever free, she'd wanted to run as far away in the opposite direction as she could. Her life had ended there, that day on the bus. She could not conceive of any future in the place where she'd been born and raised.

But a change in her heart and soul brought on a change in her mind. Before the second trial had even begun, she'd known she needed to come home. There were so many unanswered questions about Brad and exactly what had been going on four years ago. Leah needed answers. That was one reason she became a cop in the first place: she was insatiably curious and hated loose ends. Besides that, she was different now. When she looked in the mirror, she no longer saw that dependent woman, the woman who needed Brad to validate her. She had other reasons to live her life now.

Her heart rate slowed to normal, and while the fears didn't go away, they faded enough to where she could pull back onto the highway and continue her journey. Before long she crossed the bridge over Lost Creek Lake. The familiar vista brought memories flooding back.

Brad's boat on the lake, the hours spent fishing, water-skiing, racing from end to end, laughing, the wind in her hair, his arm gently resting on her shoulder. Cooking their catch on an open fire. Enjoying the awesome, rugged beauty of the Oregon outdoors.

She wished she could stop the memories with the good ones. But it didn't work that way. The bad ones were there as well, and they bubbled up like acid, scouring the good ones away and burning her heart all over again.

This was when the if onlys started. If only she'd said something after the first punch. If only she'd taken the advice to leave, advice she'd given so many other women during the course of her career. If only she'd confided in someone, anyone, about what life with Brad was really like. If only she hadn't confronted him that night. If only she'd grabbed his phone instead of his gun.

It was a constant battle for Leah. Regrets were as useless as ice cubes in a snowstorm. And it tired her out to keep fighting them. As she turned off the highway toward home, she knew she had to ignore the regrets. There was nothing at all she could do but move forward. The past was lost forever; she had the years ahead to look to and live the best life possible.

She stopped at the base of her father's driveway and took a deep breath as a Bible verse from the book of Joel came to mind. Leah knew it well. She clung to it as if her life depended on it: *"I will restore to you the years that the swarming locust has eaten, the hopper, the destroyer, and the cutter, my great army, which I sent among you. You shall eat in plenty and be satisfied, and praise the name of the Lord your God."*

Leah continued up the familiar gravel driveway. For the five hours on the road she'd not shed a tear. But as her father's modest manufactured home came into view and she saw the legion of yellow ribbons tied everywhere, flitting in the cool breeze, and the huge banner that read *Welcome Home, Leah*, she couldn't have stopped the tears if she tried.

The number of cars told her this would be a party.

Am I ready for that?

Too late. The front door opened, and her dad stepped out, and right behind him was Clint Tanner. Leah thought her heart would stop. She flushed with pleasure; he was more handsome than she remembered. Strength fleeing, she quickly wiped her eyes with her palms. Could she really get out of the car and face him?

There was no choice—they were coming for her. If she didn't get out, they would get her out. Swallowing, she opened the door. As she stepped outside the car, her father grabbed her in a tight embrace and the tears started anew.

Then Clint was in front of her, and before she could think, he pulled her close in a hug. "So good to see you home," he whispered in her ear, his warm breath sending shivers down her spine, the sound of his voice musical.

"It's good to be home," she whispered back, relishing his strength and the scent of his aftershave. It was a moment alive with electricity, connection, bonding, and Leah felt no small sense of loss when it had to end and she was pulled away into a house filled with well-wishers and supporters.

Her father led her through the house, where everyone wanted to greet her and say hello. She was conscious of Clint following, but in the small double-wide, with the large crowd of people, she lost him. Then there was food to eat, a toast from her father, and soon she was swimming in well-wishes.

When she caught a glimpse of Clint again, he was talking to someone. She saw blonde hair and stepped forward to get a look at the profile. Jenna Blakely, Gretchen's PI. They seemed very well acquainted. Something in Leah twisted, like the shank the day she was stabbed.

They've been working together all these months, she realized. *They've probably become friends, good friends.*

She turned away and gulped some punch. It was schoolgirl silly to think Clint had feelings for her. He was an anchor to reality for her, not the other way around. Time to toughen up, she thought. Clint and Jenna were a good match, better than Clint and someone who was now an ex-con.

She felt like a deflated balloon, tired and all wrung out. What was here for her after all?

CHAPTER 37

L eah Radcliff winning a new trial had battered the city
   for months, and Clint knew that her exoneration would
   likely rock the city more. However, after the not-guilty
   verdict he was in no way prepared for just how hard the
   rocking would be. The verdict knocked Table Rock off of
   its very foundation. The decision turned the city and the
PD upside down. Wilcox and Patterson had both applied for
early retirement. Lieutenant Racer was fired. Interim chief TJ
Haun spent more time at city hall than the PD as the council
tried to strategize. The city was in full damage control mode.
The question everyone was asking was not *if* Leah would sue,
but for how much.

   The verdict had also affected his new task force. After
the raid at Larkspur Farms, organization and deployment of
TRuST was put on hold indefinitely, frustrating Clint to no

end. Because of the resignations, the firings, and the nervousness in city hall, the powers that be wanted to adopt a wait-and-see attitude.

The two Russians were freed on bail, and while ICE had placed a detainer on them, Oregon was a sanctuary state and the detainer was ignored. When they failed to show up for their arraignment and bench warrants were issued, he doubted they'd ever see them again. So instead of making plans to take down a multistate smuggling operation, Clint was back on day patrol as supervisor and free to watch the ripples of Leah's exoneration roll through the city like a large-scale tsunami.

As he dressed for his shift, Clint thought back to the welcome home party three days ago. It was one of the best days of his life, finally seeing Leah after months of just reading her letters and imagining what it would be like to have her back in his life. She looked thinner, somewhat more wary, but she was home and he hoped their relationship would progress. He felt that through the correspondence he knew her well, well enough to have developed strong feelings for her. The next step was face-to-face. One question did hang in his thoughts: How did she feel about him?

He wished he'd had more time to talk to her that night, but there were so many well-wishers. Admittedly, he'd felt like a teenager facing his first crush—awkward. And she was tired. He could understand that; after all, a lot had happened in a few days. Clint could be patient and wait. He didn't want her off-balance. He wanted her on a firm foundation when they finally had a face-to-face and he told her how he felt.

He did wonder if she'd try to get her job back. She'd never said in any of her letters. It wouldn't be easy. He remembered the weeks after the indictment. Things went sideways fast. Within the department, sides had formed. There were Leah believers and Brad believers. Tempers ran high at the PD. Flaws and all, Draper was a cop, a high-profile one, and he was dead. No one could understand him being abusive. Leah was a cop too, but why didn't she say anything if he was hitting her?

Being a cop was a double-edged sword. Most cops Clint knew hated to ask for help—especially from other cops. *Needing help* meant weakness, and most cops would not admit weakness. They were, after all, trained not to show weakness, to always be in control.

Would Leah face hazing like Vicki had if she returned? He hoped not. He hoped the people he worked with realized that an organization like the Hangmen was the polar opposite of law enforcement—it was criminal.

Cops were family; they watched each other's backs. The idea that you could count on your brother in uniform was comforting in a world growing increasingly anti-police. Unfortunately, there were always rogue cops. Wilcox, Racer, and Patterson proved that. And sometimes, like in any family, there was dysfunctionality. Clint saw that here with the hero worship of Brad Draper and the refusal to believe he was flawed.

Now, with several years of hindsight, among the rank and file at the PD there was an odd split. The guys still there who'd been tight with Draper grumbled, *"He was a true hero, and she shot him in his underwear. She should still be in prison."* And some new officers who had not even been here when Brad was were putting him on a pedestal built from secondhand stories and exaggerations. But there were enough officers who'd been scandalized by the existence of the Hangmen and the number of rules and laws broken to get the first conviction to counteract that sentiment. It was anyone's guess how many guys would boldly take Radcliff's side.

Clint fastened his keepers and closed his locker. As a believer, he knew things would work out for Leah, but he just didn't know how . . . or how long it would take.

"Sergeant Tanner?"

Clint stiffened. He hadn't heard the locker room door open and was surprised to look up and see two men in suits, men he didn't know, regarding him.

"Who are you?"

They both held up IDs. FBI agents Falcon and Cross.

"Do you have a minute to talk to us about your arrest of a few days ago?" Agent Cross asked. He was a younger man, with smooth dark skin and an unreadable expression. Falcon was older, white, with dark hair and a pockmarked face. Both men carried themselves like military veterans.

Surprised this visit wasn't about Leah, he said, "Sure, let me log on, and then we can go into the patrol office." Clint advised dispatch that he was on duty but out in the office for a bit.

"We would like to know if there is anything else you can tell us about the Russian nationals you arrested," Cross said as Clint closed the office door.

"Not really. It's all in my report."

"You speak Russian?" Falcon asked.

"Not well. I understand a lot more than I can speak. Never could get the accent right."

"Where'd you learn?"

"Kyrgyzstan. I lived there for five years when I was a teen. My parents were . . . uh, are missionaries." The two men exchanged glances, and for a second, Clint felt as if he were on the hot seat. "What's going on? I do something wrong?"

Falcon opened a folder that he held in his hand and pulled out a photo. "Have you ever seen this man?"

Clint took the photo. It was a grainy surveillance photo of a large, bearded man wearing workman type clothing, reminding

Clint of a uniform for a moving company in the valley. He studied the photo for a moment. The man was familiar but generic. Hundreds of men wore beards in the valley—he could be any one of them.

He looked up to find both agents watching him. "I can't say I know who this is, no."

"The raid you attempted on the farmhouse—it didn't go well, did it?" Cross asked.

"No." Clint tensed. "It didn't. Somehow they were tipped off. Will you please tell me what this is all about?"

"This man is Colin Hess. He's a fugitive from justice, on our most wanted list. Ten years ago, he was an enforcer for the Russian Mafia. He murdered an undercover FBI agent, then fled." Falcon put the photo back in his folder and continued. "He disappeared without a trace, and we believed he was smuggled out of the country. We were wrong."

Clint frowned. "And now you're here looking for him? In Oregon?"

Falcon nodded. "The trail in Jersey went cold immediately after Hess disappeared. Since then nothing—no credit card, no Social Security number. Your team processed a lot of finger-prints from the raid last week. Hess's were all over the place."

"Whoa." Clint tried to wrap his mind around this, wonder-ing if that was why the Russians he'd arrested were in such a hurry to get to the phone.

"Hess has obviously been here for a while. You must have someone in your department who is a pipeline to him, someone who has been protecting him all these years." Cross stepped close. "We never believed he could disappear without help, so someone is helping him."

"Does he have connections here in the valley?" Clint asked.

"None that we've found—yet. Hess shot our agent in the

back of his head, then left a note for us, bragging that he'd never be caught. He's a vicious criminal." There was anger in Cross's eyes. And accusation.

Clint held his gaze. "It's not me. I thought we ended a prolific smuggling operation a few days ago. I'm angry about being sold out. If there is a leak here, I'll find it."

After a few seconds, Cross looked away.

"Are the men I arrested connected to the Russian Mafia?" Clint asked.

"From what we can tell, loosely. Whether or not Hess is still working for the Mafia, we haven't been able to determine. He's most likely running his own operation out here. We do know that he speaks several languages. He has an IQ at genius level. We don't believe he's a lackey—he's running the whole show."

"Do you have any evidence as to who your leak might be, who spoiled the farmhouse raid?" Falcon asked.

Clint shook his head. "I wish I did. But we were working under a time constraint, little or no sleep. Maybe we missed something. I've been going back over everything, but so far nothing sticks out."

"Until you find the leak, any investigation you conduct will be compromised. We are going to advise your chief that you stay out of it."

"What?" Now Clint was angry. "Those Russians were my arrest, and I will find their boss."

Cross pointed to a copy of the newspaper on Clint's desk. The headline was about Leah. "Your department is a cesspool of corruption, and it looks like it has been for a very long time. Stay away from Larkspur Farms and anything to do with this investigation, or you'll find yourself in our crosshairs."

The two agents turned and left his office, leaving Clint scratching his head. They'd all but said they thought he was dirty. He wasn't going to give up on the smuggling. Russians being involved only piqued his interest.

Clint gathered his kit and left for his patrol vehicle. Someone calling out his name stopped him just before he reached his SUV. It was Vicki Henderson. She'd ridden out a really rough beginning and was now the solid cop he'd thought she'd be.

"Sarge, can I have a word?"

"Sure, what's up?"

"What do you think is going to happen with Leah Radcliff? Do you think she'll try to get her job back now?"

"I don't know."

He truly didn't. He wished he did. In fact, he wished he could sit down with Leah and plan the future—one that had the two of them together. "I'm not sure that would be a good idea."

She stood up straight as if surprised by his answer. "Why not? She was seriously wronged."

Clint knew Vicki thought highly of Leah, no matter what negativity she might have heard, even more so when Leah's investigator actually helped her case. "Henderson, I feel for Leah—I really do—but even innocent I think it would be difficult for her to pick up where she left off. Consider your own experiences."

Henderson shrugged. "I made it, and I hope she does too. She got the short end of the stick. I want to see her fight to get her job back."

"The next few days will tell."

His phone rang and Henderson continued into the station. It was Chief Haun. Clint set his kit down and answered the call.

"Where are you right now?"

"About to get into my car. What's up?"

"I need you to do something for me. I'm in the office."

He disconnected. Clint stared at his phone for a moment.

The call was odd even for the normally terse Haun. A sick feeling folded inside Clint's stomach. This was probably about Leah Radcliff. He put his kit in the trunk, resigned to the fact that he just might not make it to the field this morning, and returned to the station.

Haun's office door was closed. Clint knocked.

"Come in."

Clint opened the door and fought to keep his expression neutral. Haun wasn't alone. Morton Fendle, the city attorney, was there, along with Rachel Clyburn, a high-priced private attorney Clint knew represented the Draper family.

The chief looked grim. "Sergeant Tanner, you know Mr. Fendle and Ms. Clyburn."

Clint nodded.

"We need you to serve a restraining order," Fendle said. He shuffled some paperwork and handed some sheets to Clint.

Clint took the paperwork. Rachel Clyburn watched him, a deep frown on her face. He could feel daggers coming from her, and he had no idea why.

Clint looked down at the paperwork and again fought to keep his face neutral.

"Do you have a problem with this task, Sergeant?" Clyburn asked, arms folded, posture tense and hostile.

Clint met her eyes. "Problem? No. Just a question."

"What's the question?"

"Is this really necessary?"

"Of course it's necessary." Clyburn's eyes narrowed, and she studied Clint. "You're very close to her father, aren't you?"

Clint nodded. "Not sure what that has to do with anything, but yeah, we go to the same church."

"Where do your loyalties lie?"

"I don't understand the question."

"I'll spell it out. Leah Radcliff murdered my client's son in cold blood. Now, after finagling her way out of prison, she has the nerve to return to Table Rock and flaunt her freedom while my clients are still grieving. You will admonish her to stay completely away from my clients, their property, and anything to do with them—is that clear?"

"I'll do my job."

"See that you do." Clyburn picked up a briefcase, nodded at the chief, and left the office, Fendle on her heels.

Haun arched an eyebrow at Clint, then shook his head. "Radcliff coming back is stirring up a lot of stuff . . . bad stuff."

Clint thought carefully about his next statement. He didn't know which side of this Haun was on.

"Chief, she had two trials. The first one found her guilty and sent her to prison, but it was deemed to have been flawed, criminally so. And the second trial found her completely innocent. She's free and clear. Are we going to compound that first injustice now?"

Haun stood. He was ex-military and had been a cop for twenty-five years to Clint's nine. Clint respected him.

"Tanner, I don't have any respect for a man who hits a woman. And I didn't really care for Brad Draper. But he's dead. She killed him, and even though that killing was found to be justified under the law, his parents and the people who idolized him are never going to get over it. They ignore everything negative that has surfaced about Brad." Haun rubbed his chin. "And the Drapers have the money to make her life a living hell now, innocent or not. I fully expect them to sue her in civil court for wrongful death. With this restraining order I believe they're firing the first shot and declaring war."

"That's not going to bring Brad back. And you and I both know the state cops are still investigating the prosecutor's office here because of the juror who claims he was paid to vote guilty. Patterson and Racer are under the microscope for various illegalities. Wilcox is also being investigated. I wouldn't even be surprised if they find themselves facing criminal charges somewhere down the line. The Drapers won't win this war. Radcliff was railroaded."

Haun gave a tilt of his head. "Birch is dead, so he can't be cross-examined to answer the charges against him or defend himself. And winning isn't the object. The Drapers only want to inflict pain in this war. If you and I are going to survive unscathed, we're going to have to be careful not to choose sides. All we can do is stand by and prevent collateral damage. But I guarantee you this: if you openly side with Radcliff, you risk becoming collateral damage."

He held Clint's gaze. He knew what the chief was saying was true. It wasn't fair to Leah, and he didn't like it, but it was true.

"After you serve the order, see that you file proof of service with the court, ASAP."

"Yes, sir." Clint turned to leave.

"Wait." Haun stepped around his desk. "The two federal visitors catch up with you?"

Clint leaned against the door. "They did." He recapped the brief, frustrating meeting. "Do you have any thoughts on who our leak is?"

"No, I don't. I almost don't know how anyone could have tipped them off. You moved as quickly as you could—not that many people even knew of the arrest. The Russians weren't booked or even in the system for thirty-six hours." He held his hands up. "Now the feds want to take it over."

"Are you on board with that? It's our case."

"Until we find the leak, it might be the best thing. And you know the smuggling isn't going to stop."

Clint nodded. Smuggling was a problem on the interstate. Most contraband was headed through Oregon, or in the case of pot, out of the state. It was lucrative and difficult to interdict. Clint left the chief's office thinking about Hess, wishing he could be in on the manhunt and not filing paperwork to make Leah Radcliff's life more complicated.

CHAPTER 38

C lint prayed as he drove up Highway 62 toward Trail, wondering how in the world Leah could pick up where she left off. He knew that she deserved to. He wanted her to. They'd talked about a lot of things back and forth in their letters, but never really her plans for life after prison. It was almost as if they danced around it. Now everything seemed to be aligned against her returning to a normal life.

He could admit to himself that his feelings for her had gotten stronger, especially after all the correspondence. Clint felt he knew her better now, and he liked what he knew. However, the feelings would stay buried, unspoken—they had to. Leah was in a very different place now. The last thing he wanted to do was disrupt her reintegration.

His head hurt when he thought about all that was swirling around Leah at the moment: the state investigation into what happened during her first trial, this mini war with the Drapers, the rumor that the state investigators were going to reopen the investigation into prosecutor Birch's death. And those were just a few of the big items. Leah would be way too busy for any personal relationship.

Clint considered Birch. He might have been a favorite prosecutor for the PD, but every single move he made was fraught with political calculations. Cops liked to gossip, and Birch and his connections were always a topic, especially when Birch picked and chose what cases to prosecute. The Drapers were big donors. When Brad's case came before him, he should have passed the case off to someone else, but he didn't.

His death was convenient for the Drapers, that was for sure. Was it really a suicide? Because of Leah's vindication and interest in the Hangmen, the crash was another favorite topic at the watercooler. Conspiracy theories abounded. Clint even heard someone say they thought Birch had been murdered. All of the scuttlebutt circled back to the Drapers.

Clint glanced at the paperwork beside him. When all the smoke cleared, would Harden Draper find himself behind bars? Time would tell.

As Clint made the turn toward Trail and Leah's home, he realized how glad he was that she was home with her father. Randy was someone else Clint had gotten to know well, someone he liked and respected. Leah would be safe there.

He turned onto the gravel driveway and felt strangely nervous. He wanted to protect Leah from the Draper family, not inflict more pain because of them.

+ + +

Not surprisingly, Leah didn't sleep well her first few nights of freedom. The bed felt soft and comfortable, and it was quiet.

Even at night prison was never completely without background sound—there was always facility noise or inmate noise. With the total silence at her father's house, Leah couldn't still her noisy thoughts. What surprised Leah was that her mind raced so quickly back to that night, the final confrontation with Brad and the ugly aftermath.

This was something she thought she'd put to rest. She'd let go of Brad, forgiven him and herself. But being back in familiar settings resurrected a waterfall of bad feelings. For two days she'd tried to ignore them, spending a lot of time outside, enjoying the cold and anticipating the snow that threatened.

After a third night of restlessness, Leah couldn't ignore the bad memories and she got out of bed, not wanting to fight a battle she had already won anymore. She refused to let all the nastiness bury her now that she was free and ready to move forward. She grabbed her father's Bible and opened to the book of Psalms. Reading a few verses here and there calmed her thoughts, steadied her heart. She would not go back to despair, self-pity, and hopelessness.

She looked out the window to see a light snow falling in the gray morning light. She thought of Clint and almost dug into her bag to retrieve his letters and reread every one. She couldn't let Clint become a stumbling block for her. If he was involved with Jenna, then she'd just be happy for him.

Sighing and fighting the darkness that threatened, she wrapped herself in a warm throw, sat in her father's recliner, breathed deeply, and closed her eyes, imagining she was wrapped in his arms and nothing bad could happen to her ever again.

CHAPTER 39

Clint was halfway up the drive when movement to the left caught his attention. He stopped the SUV and peered into the tree line. He expected to see deer or elk, something common here, but saw nothing. Thinking it was just his imagination, he'd shifted to continue up the drive when movement flashed again, and it wasn't a four-legged animal.

He put the SUV in park and got out. The person was wearing camo, but it was late November, and the pattern was easily picked out among the bare trees and fresh snow. Whoever it was moved quickly through the trees away from Clint and off the Radcliff property.

There was no way Clint could catch the person even if he had a solid reason to chase him. The figure was short—maybe a kid up to mischief? Whoever it was moved fast. Clint stepped off the drive and tried to think. *Which way was the person going when I first saw him? Toward the Radcliff home or away from it?*

He wasn't sure. All he'd seen was a flash of movement from the corner of his eye. An uneasy feeling gripped his gut. Back in the car, he pressed the accelerator and hurried for the Radcliff house.

✦ ✦ ✦

The smell of coffee brewing woke Leah. Part of her hoped the pampering could go on forever. Her dad loved making breakfast for her. Soon, though, she'd need to stand on her own two feet.

She was stiff from sleeping in the recliner, but she felt rested. And free. She could hear her father humming in the kitchen and that brought on a smile. Her mother used to joke that Dad knew the words to every corny musical ever made. Leah recognized the tune he was humming as "Oklahoma!" A funny song to sing when the world outside was white with a thin, fresh layer of snow, Leah thought as she got up and peered through the blinds into the backyard.

"You awake?" Dad appeared in the kitchen doorway, steaming cup of coffee in his hand.

"You bet. That coffee smells wonderful."

"Here you go, sweet pea. Does my heart good to be able to make this for you again."

Happy tears sprang to her eyes. She went to her father and hugged him around the waist.

"Careful, careful," he said, patting her back. "You'll spill this hot drink all over us."

Leah smiled, released him, stepped back, and took the coffee. She held the cup in both hands and looked her father in the eyes. "Thanks, Pop. Thanks for everything. It feels more wonderful each day to be home."

"It feels wonderful to have you home. Now, what do you want for breakfast today?"

+ + +

The red paint stood out against the backdrop of white snow like blood. Clint slowed his cruiser. Randy's work truck and Leah's compact sedan were plastered with the word *killer* in red spray paint.

He glanced over at the double-wide and noted all the front blinds were still closed. He wondered if Randy and Leah were up and if they'd seen this. It made him sad and angry. What a mess. He'd known the morning he saw Leah's bruised face there could never be any winners in this situation. And he realized that again when Leah was exonerated. She'd had to kill her husband to save her own life—how could she ever win?

Still, he'd prayed that something good would come out of the situation because he also knew God could work any situation out for the good of those who love him. But obviously someone—and he bet it was the Drapers—didn't want any good for Leah.

He got out of the patrol car and walked up to the front door.

+ + +

Leah opted for something simple for breakfast—bacon and eggs, scrambled with cheese—then sat at the table while her father prepared it.

"We got a little snow last night," she said, content to sip her coffee and watch her father cook.

"Just a dusting. It'll be gone by noon. It's been a wet fall—spring will be off the charts, I'm betting." He went back to humming "Oklahoma!"

When he finished cooking, he loaded two plates with bacon and eggs and sat down with Leah at the table. He gripped her hands, closed his eyes, and said a blessing. "Lord, I thank you for providing all that we need to eat this morning and I thank you for bringing my daughter home to me, safe and sound." He squeezed Leah's hands and then let go, opening his eyes and grinning. "I'm really glad you're here now, really glad."

The love in his eyes took her breath away. She had to swallow before speaking. "I am too, Dad."

They both dug into their meals.

"I noticed that you finished the patio out back," Leah said while they ate.

Randy nodded and swallowed his food. "Look forward to a lot of great barbecues once the weather warms up. By the way, yesterday I pulled a permit to cut down a Christmas tree. What do you think about doing that today? My schedule is clear."

Leah's fork stopped halfway to her mouth. Cutting down the Christmas tree was an annual ritual when she was growing up. They'd not been back in the forest to do that since her mother died.

She blinked. "Dad, we haven't done that in years."

He smiled, put his fork down, and placed his hand over hers. "I know. There's a lot of things we haven't done together in a while and I hope now to change all that. What do you say? Are you up for a trip to Prospect to cut down a tree?"

Her throat tightened; she cleared it and said, "Sure, Dad."

"Good, now finish your breakfast."

Just then there was a knock on the door.

"You expecting anyone?" she asked her father.

"Not this early."

She didn't miss the concern that creased his brow.

"I'll get it," she said.

"No, no. You finish your breakfast. I'll see who it is."

He left her in the kitchen. Leah felt her pulse quicken and she chastised herself for automatically thinking the worst. She gulped her coffee and followed her father to the door.

"Good morning, Randy."

Leah recognized the voice and held her breath. It couldn't be good news, but how bad would it be?

"Clint, I'd say it's good to see you again, so soon, but I fear you're not here with a snow report."

"Afraid that's true. May I speak to Leah?"

"She's eating—"

"I'm here, Pop."

He turned when she spoke, and Leah caught her first glimpse of Clint. He looked wonderful, standing there at the door in full uniform. Obviously he was here on official business. And like a badge bunny, Leah loved the sight of a man in uniform. She felt her face flush. He was more handsome than she remembered even from a few nights ago, especially with the dotting of white at his temples.

His eyes regarded her with an unreadable expression. He looked away first. "Hello, Leah. Sorry to ruin your first week home."

She stepped forward, trying to find her voice, clearing her throat. "That's okay." Cold air rushed in from the outside and Leah shivered. "Why don't you come in?"

He stepped inside. "I wish I was here now with better news or on a simple social call, but I'm not. First, I have to serve you with a restraining order." He held out some paperwork.

"A restraining order?" Her father tensed and stepped forward to peer at the papers.

Leah put a hand on his shoulder. "It's okay." She turned to Clint. "The Drapers?"

"Yep, sorry. Drawn up by Rachel Clyburn."

"I expected as much, maybe more. Took them three whole days." She took the TRO paperwork from him. She'd seen enough in her time on the force that she knew what it said. But still a jolt hit—this could keep her from getting her job back, if she decided that was what she wanted. She would have a chance in court—the Drapers had to show cause for the order—so she made a mental note to get the temporary restraining order to Gretchen as soon as possible. She didn't look forward to another court confrontation, because if they did show sufficient cause for the judge, she'd be under the confines of the order for three to five years. A judge could even deny her the return of her firearms.

"There is more, I'm afraid. I can't say for sure the Drapers are responsible for this, but you need to take a look at your cars." He turned back to the door and Randy stepped in front of him to open it.

Leah grabbed a jacket and followed her father and Tanner out the front door.

The cold air hit hard, but the bright-red paint hit harder. *KILLER.*

It was on her dad's work truck and the little sedan that No Violence at Home had gifted her with on her release.

Leah stood rooted, fearing if she moved, she'd break down, and she didn't want to do that in front of Clint.

Her father stepped forward, hands on hips. "This happened not too long ago. Look, they wiped snow off the vehicles to paint them."

"I may have seen the culprit," Clint said. "As I was coming up your driveway, I saw someone in camo running through the trees. He was too far away for me to get a good look. I can take a look around, maybe find some evidence."

"Why?" Leah asked, unable to keep the bitterness out of her voice. "It's not your jurisdiction. We're in the sheriff's area."

He turned to face her, his gaze a study in compassion; Leah saw no pity or falseness there.

"I can get ahold of a deputy to come out here and take pictures. You should report it."

"I—" Leah stopped, wanting to say, *"What's the point?"* Even if he could prove this was done by the Drapers, they would never be held to account. It had been a mistake to come home, she thought for the hundredth time. *"I should have driven a thousand miles in the other direction,"* she almost blurted out as anger and resentment threatened to swallow her whole.

Clint stepped closer and his presence had a steadying effect on Leah, sort of like the effect a good partner had on a cop when the call was bad and dangerous. He had her back. She clamped her mouth shut.

He hooked his thumbs in his gun belt. "It's important to document anything that happens like this, you know. And this is wrong. The guy who did this is beyond off base. The law exonerated you, Leah. There's nothing to be ashamed of. Do you remember one of the quotes I sent you . . . ?"

Clint's letters had made Leah feel free, even behind bars, because she could imagine and see in her mind's eye all the places and things he wrote about. They were a breath of fresh air. She nodded. "Agatha Christie: 'I learned . . . that one can never go back, that one should not ever try to go back—that the essence of life is going forward.'" Leah smiled. "I wrote that on a piece of paper and put it in my Bible."

Clint returned the smile and Leah was mesmerized. "Move forward, Leah."

The earnestness in his expression warmed her spirit and doused some doubts about coming home and all of the angst about the stupid spray-painted message. The 3D Clint from all his letters stood in front of her. She'd barely known him before all of this happened, and now she was certain that the only positive here was that she had gotten to know him better.

"I'd like to do that, but it looks as if some people will never be able to move on."

"Forget them," her dad said, throwing his arms up in frustration. The rancor in his voice surprised her, though she knew it shouldn't. "I refuse to let anyone ruin the rest of your life." Her father kicked some snow and stomped over toward the cars.

"I agree with your dad," Clint said, and Leah jerked around to face him. "Whoever did this wants to scare you, maybe make you leave the area. Don't let them bully you."

An indefinable expression crossed his face: support, caring—maybe something else. It made Leah want to reach out and touch his hand, but the moment passed. He stepped back.

"Thanks, Clint."

"I haven't done much but bring you bad news."

Leah inhaled, exhaled. "You've been a friend in the midst of bad news. There's a difference."

"Well, never forget that you're innocent. I pray now that the worst is behind you."

"Like I told you in my letters, I'm glad you didn't listen to me and kept praying. I know now that God listens, he hears every prayer, and nothing is wasted." She wanted to grab him in a hug but extended her hand instead.

"Good to hear. I'm sorry we didn't get to talk much the other night. Maybe after you're settled and you have some time, we can grab lunch? Catch up with what wasn't in the letters." He grasped her hand with both of his warm, strong ones and held it for a moment before releasing it. The jolt to Leah's system was electric.

"I'd like that. I know I'd like to hear more about your promotion and what's going on at the PD." She still felt the warmth from his grip after dropping her hand to her side.

He looked as if he was going to say something, but her dad interrupted, stomping snow off his boots.

Clint turned to her father. "Randy, you and Leah should both know that you can call if you need anything. You can also call Jack." He turned to Leah. "That's my sheriff friend. Your dad has his number."

"I appreciate that," her father said. He'd calmed down and walked back to the porch.

"Goodbye, Leah. Please try to enjoy your freedom."

After Clint left, Randy turned to Leah. "He's a nice guy, one of the good ones."

Leah nodded in agreement, a little chagrined when she remembered that morning they'd handled the domestic violence call. "Saint Tanner" wasn't even on her radar. Today, the same as when he'd helped empty her house with Dad, she found herself agreeing wholeheartedly. The warm feeling it gave her when he asked about lunch hadn't faded. It wasn't the first time she'd ever seen him, so it couldn't be love at first sight, could it?

Yet as strong as she knew her feelings for the man were, a question intruded: What about Jenna?

CHAPTER 40

Her father did the best he could with the cleanup, but both cars would have to be repainted. You couldn't see the word *killer* anymore, but it was obvious something had been there.

"Ruined the paint job on your new car," he said, wiping his brow as they stood on the porch.

"It's okay, Dad."

He faced her. "It's not okay . . . but we'll get past it."

"You're right; we will."

"Ready to go find a tree?"

She smiled and hugged her arms to her chest. "Yeah, give me a minute. Everything is so beautiful with the sun glinting off the snow." She breathed deeply. "And the cold air tickling my nose . . . This is wonderful."

He chuckled, patted her back, and went inside.

Leah relished her view. The light dusting of snow on the ground and trees dissipated quickly. Where there still was a covering, the clean, white snow was a refreshing sight. She thought of Nora, still at Coffee Creek with three more years to serve, and the conversation they'd had on Leah's last day as her cellmate.

"You get out, enjoy the outdoors, sunsets, sunrises, and think of me. Don't take nothing for granted, ever."

"I won't. And when your time is up, I hope you'll come visit and we'll drink coffee outside watching the sunrise."

"Sunset, honey. When I get out of here, I'm never getting up before 10 a.m. again."

They'd both laughed.

Leah had meant what she'd said. While she'd never miss Coffee Creek, she missed Nora. The woman had been a good and steady friend. As good a friend as she'd ever had. It never ceased to amaze Leah that she'd met such a friend in prison.

Sighing, she went back into the house to change for the trip to Prospect and Christmas tree hunting. Later, sitting in the four-wheel drive truck, traveling frosty paved roads and then snowy, bumpy dirt roads as they climbed to a higher elevation, Leah was flooded with a tsunami of good memories. Her mother had loved Christmas and spared no expense decorating. The tree was always the first box to be checked off.

"Mom liked to check boxes."

"What?" Her father glanced over at her.

"Mom. She always had a list and she always checked boxes."

He grinned. "She sure did. Boy, I'd forgotten. She was the most organized person I've ever known."

Leah laughed, joy marinating her soul as she remembered her mother. Sun Radcliff's parents had emigrated from South Korea before Sun was born. Leah's mother once told Leah she'd like to visit Korea, but she considered herself 100 percent

American. She always had a smile and she loved to chat with anyone. She'd never met a stranger.

"I haven't thought about Mom much lately," Leah said. "But now I remember her laugh and her joy at just living."

"I think about her all the time."

Leah turned to study her father. He had a nostalgic smile on his face. Her parents' relationship had always been warm and loving. It made Leah sad to think that even with their example, she'd settled for something less. But she wasn't going to stay sad. Even if it was just to honor her memory, Leah was going to emulate her mother.

She reached out and put a hand on his arm. "It's good to think about her and how much she loved Christmas."

"I agree. Let's make this the best Christmas ever."

Leah grasped her dad's arm with both hands and grinned. "Amen to that, Dad."

After finding a tree, the rest of the day was spent settling in, dodging phone calls from reporters, and simply appreciating freedom. That night, Leah slept soundly through till morning.

+ + +

The next day, while her father was in the garage pulling out all the Christmas decorations, Leah spent some time inside on the computer, catching up on the past. The house smelled of fresh-cut Christmas tree, and the five-foot noble pine in the living room was perfect.

She knew a lot had changed in four years, and she'd kept up with most of the big news. What she wanted to do now was read the local stuff, catch up on hometown happenings she might have missed. Gretchen would be over in the afternoon to discuss the temporary restraining order and her future options.

Duke Gill was now a county commissioner, Larry Ripley was a state senator, and Grady Blanchard was the sheriff of Jackson County.

She could be happy for Becky because of Grady, but the other two names bugged her. They'd both managed to escape the Hangmen stigma, probably because they weren't cops. But Leah knew they had to be just as involved as everyone else. Just as dirty as the dirtiest.

As state senator, Larry Ripley's district covered Table Rock, Medford, and the surrounding area. On his website there were hints that he'd eventually be running for a federal congressional seat. Time hadn't dimmed Ripley's rising star. He really hadn't changed much, Leah thought as she looked at his picture. Maybe a little grayer, a few more wrinkles, but the same superior smirk that she'd hated so many years ago.

She sat back and stared at the picture. How could people look at that face and think of Larry Ripley as sincere?

"What were you and Brad up to that night? It certainly didn't have anything to do with collecting first and last months' rent. Was it more about furthering your political career?" Leah asked out loud.

She then switched gears and went to research her department. She'd been an officer for a little over three years before the shooting, and Table Rock was a small enough department that she'd known everyone back then. Who was still in uniform that she knew? She could have asked Clint, but their letters were more personal, and she never wanted to seem as if she was simply pumping him for information.

Leah clicked on the department website and perused the roster. One name she didn't find was Richard Chambers, Brad's old partner, and she wondered what happened to him. He had not been called as a witness in her second trial. A lot of Brad's old crowd were still employed, though. Patterson was gone, Racer and Wilcox were gone, but Forman was still there. He was a night shift sergeant.

Of course Marvin Sapp and Vicki Henderson were still in patrol. And Clint was day sergeant. She also knew Interim Chief Haun and wondered if he'd be made permanent chief. Brad never liked Haun. "Too straight-arrow and by the book," he'd said. Leah had never had a problem with him. As she read the list of officers, she realized how narrow her focus had been when she worked. Only people approved by Brad were in her circle back then. But those outside of it were good people, good officers—she knew that now. He'd probably avoided anyone who would call him out on his behavior.

She also realized, with a great deal of regret, that she should have come forward the first time he hit her. When she thought about that, an uneasiness settled in the pit of her stomach. Why hadn't she?

During the last year of her incarceration, she'd been approached by No Violence at Home, the women's advocacy group Gretchen was associated with. Would she be willing to tell her story? Help make sure other women recognize the danger? That even when the boyfriend or husband says he's sorry and appears to be an upstanding member of society, there still needs to be intervention?

Leah had put them off, saying she had to think about it. She was still thinking. In court she'd told the jury she hadn't reported the abuse for all the reasons domestic violence awareness bulletins warned about: she thought it would stop, she didn't want to hurt his career, she didn't want to admit she was a victim, and she couldn't wrap her mind around the idea that she'd married an abuser, a man just like the men she often arrested. It wasn't until the worst-case scenario happened that she was forced to admit it: Brad was an abuser.

Would intervention have helped? Brad's personality was such that he never would have spoken to a counselor willingly. At least that's what Leah thought. And it was something she would never know for sure.

✦ ✦ ✦

"Absolutely, fight to get your job back." Gretchen was adamant. She'd come to Leah's home to work on the TRO and tie up all the loose ends in Leah's case: monetary compensation, return of firearms, and now something Leah really hadn't thought much about—getting her job back. "You shot someone in self-defense; you broke no laws."

"But I don't see how it will be possible to be an officer here again. The Draper—"

"Stop right there. They cannot dictate the rest of your life." She waved the TRO. "And this has absolutely no merit. Have you contacted them in any way?"

Leah shook her head.

"Did you plan to contact them?"

"No."

"They won't be able to show cause for such a broad order. Asking you to stay away from all of his property is asking you to stay out of Table Rock. They might as well ask you to stop breathing."

Leah closed her eyes. "So much pain . . . I hate coming home to so much pain. To them Brad could do no wrong. I don't want to hurt them any more than they've already been hurt."

"Leah, you have a big heart, a compassionate heart. But your former in-laws may soon find themselves in hot water for bribery. Birch didn't just go after you full speed ahead because he didn't like you; he was getting paid."

"Can that be proved?"

"Not yet, but my source at the state PD says they're working on it. If the Drapers get hurt more now, it won't be you doing the hurting."

She paused and Leah thought about that. In spite of their hatred toward her, Leah couldn't hate Blanche and Harden and Ivy. They had, after all, been family for a couple of years, and they were, at that time at least, good to her.

"Besides," Gretchen continued, "you still want to find out what Brad and Larry were up to that night, right?"

Leah looked up at her lawyer. "More than ever."

"Well, I think the best way for you to do that is to get your badge and gun back. A big fat lawsuit might be the only way to do that."

There was a knock at the door.

"Are you expecting someone?" Gretchen asked.

Leah shook her head, fear creeping into her gut. Her father had a gun safe in the garage with several different types of guns. She'd have to open it up and find something to help her feel more secure. Her guns been confiscated a long time ago, and while they'd planned to file a request to get them back, it wouldn't happen overnight. She shook away the fear, feeling a little silly and way too paranoid.

"Who is it?" she called out, stepping to the door.

"Larry and Grady."

CHAPTER 41

Holding his phone in his hand, Clint itched to call Leah. Seeing her briefly yesterday just to bring bad news was not enough. He wanted to have that lunch he'd asked about, talk to her, have the living, breathing letter writer in front of him. Was it too soon? he wondered, feeling a kind of anticipation and excitement he couldn't ever remember having. Maybe on his lunch break, he decided. He'd call then and set a date.

Date. The word gave him goose bumps of anticipation.

He put the phone in its holder and went into service, smoothly settling into patrol mode. As he traveled streets busy with holiday traffic and listened to routine radio chatter, his thoughts stayed on Leah. Henderson had asked if he thought she would try to get her job back. The question caught him by surprise. His knee-jerk reaction was that no, she shouldn't. But knee-jerk responses weren't always the best or wisest.

Why shouldn't she?

He tried to imagine what would have happened if she'd been exonerated at the first trial. She wouldn't have been fired, he didn't think. After all, she'd acted in self-defense, hadn't broken any laws. And as he thought about policy, he didn't see any failures in her actions, unless the failure to report that Brad had been abusing her could be considered a policy violation. While Clint didn't recall such a rule, officers were mandated to take a domestic violence report in the field. But their personal lives? Hindsight is supposed to be twenty-twenty, but right now he wasn't so sure.

Then again, her arrest and the unfair first trial had exposed malfeasance in the PD and beyond that Clint was certainly glad was gone. Racer and his good old boys, Birch and his corruption—if there was a silver lining, that was it. Clint would never defend a bad cop and believed his department was better for the firings and the retirements of bad guys. The Hangmen were a cancer that needed to be excised.

Mind switching back to patrol, Clint followed a truck that suddenly appeared and passed him on his right. He punched the plate number into his computer and waited for the return. The truck turned abruptly onto Carlyle, heading south toward Foothill. A wave of apprehension swept over Clint. He wasn't superstitious, but something about the truck bothered him. It was a rental out of Grants Pass. Clint radioed for backup, intending to stop the truck when he had another unit with him.

They continued south. Without signaling, the truck abruptly swerved to the right, exiting at Foothill. At the bottom of the ramp he could turn east or west. Clint grabbed the mike and prepared to give dispatch a new direction of travel. Backup would be with him in a couple of minutes.

The truck approached the stop sign at Foothill but never

came to a stop. The driver punched it and turned left, cutting off two cars and nearly colliding with a third. Tires squealed and horns blared as Clint activated his light bar and siren.

The truck sped east with Clint on its tail. The violations were so egregious that Clint bet the guy didn't think he'd be pursued. Vehicle pursuits were out of policy in the city of Table Rock. But right now they weren't in the crowded city center, so Clint would push his luck, praying that the guy did not turn toward downtown.

He'd keyed his mike to inform dispatch that the truck was failing to yield when in his peripheral vision he caught movement to his right. The huge, cold visage of a semitruck appeared at the passenger window.

Before Clint could even process what was happening, the semi slammed into the side of his SUV with the force of a bomb. That was the last thing he remembered as the world around him winked into darkness.

+ + +

Leah frowned, for the life of her not knowing what Larry Ripley and Grady Blanchard would want with her. At least Duke Gill with his toothpick-chewing, sardonic face wasn't present. That would have been really annoying. She turned to Gretchen, who nodded.

"I'll get it." A diminutive woman, slightly taller than she was round, Gretchen nonetheless had a great command presence. She strode to the door as Leah stepped out of the way.

"Can I help you?" she asked as she pulled the door open.

"We wanted to talk to Leah." That was Larry's voice.

"About what?"

"Who are you?"

"Her lawyer, Gretchen Gaffney. Anything you have to say to her you can say to me."

"I don't think so."

The years hadn't softened his tone of superiority, Leah thought.

"Our business is with her, not her—"

"Excuse me, we've gotten off on the wrong foot."

Leah recognized Grady trying to be diplomatic. He was better at it than Larry.

"We're old friends of Leah Radcliff."

"Look," Gretchen started but Leah cut her off and stepped to the door.

"It's okay, Gretchen." She looked from Larry to Grady and back again. "What is it you want?"

Larry arched an eyebrow. "Is that any way to treat old friends?" In person, Brad's best friend had not aged well. He looked ten years older, not four.

"You were never my friend, Larry, and you know it."

Larry's face folded into an expression of hurt.

Leah turned to Grady. He was off duty and in civilian clothes. Was that so he wouldn't be intimidating? she wondered. "I don't know about you."

"I think you do. I always wondered about you and Brad. I'm so sorry I never saw any of the warning signs."

That comment caught her off guard and made her take a half step back. It sounded so genuinely caring. But then she'd always liked Grady.

Completely prematurely gray now and balding, he was the same height as Larry but broader and soft in the middle. Leah remembered he was never very athletic, and the physical training required for police work had never come easy for him. Brad normally had no time for anyone he considered "without physical skill," or WPS. It was Grady's sense of humor that saved him where Brad was concerned. Grady had moved to Southern California and tried to be a stand-up comedian but failed. When he came back to the valley, "tail between his legs," as Brad would say, Brad helped him with the physical side of the testing process. Grady always credited Brad with helping him get hired.

Leah didn't want to think Grady was a Hangman, but after everything she'd been through, she couldn't help it. He was never a macho Neanderthal like other friends of Brad. At least, he'd always been funny and nice to her, not superior and irritating like Larry. Now he regarded her with a kind expression. She didn't want to lump him in with Larry, but seeing them here together was bringing up all sorts of memories. Not good ones.

"We only want to wish you well," Grady said.

"Both of us." Larry tried to step closer.

"I may believe Grady, but coming from you, Larry, all I hear is insincerity."

"I'm sorry you feel that way. I'm glad you're a free woman. You were a good cop. I know what a maniac Brad could be. I never believed for a second that what happened to Brad was not justified."

Leah did a double take. Larry had been Brad's best friend, his partner in crime, to coin a phrase. Was he saying now that he believed abuse was going on and he never tried to stop it?

"I find that hard to believe. And it certainly doesn't match your testimony. Admitting to perjury? Trying to convince me that you didn't belong to the Hangmen when I know you did?"

His eyes narrowed and he put his hands on his hips. "Careful with that, Leah. Your lawyer can tell you about slander and libel."

"It's not slanderous if it's true. You only escaped notice because you're not a cop." Leah crossed her arms and glared at him.

"Friendly warning: drop the Hangmen; they're done."

"Warning or threat?"

"Hey, hey, hey." Grady held his hands up as Larry turned away, seeming to Leah a gesture to try to calm everyone down. "This went south faster than the last lap of the Indy 500. We can't redo the past. You're free now. And I'm—we're—in a position to help you, you know."

"Help me how?"

"We know you deserve a settlement with the city," Grady said. "We can help ease you through the process."

"That's enough." Gretchen stepped in. "Any legal action my client decides to take against the city is none of your business."

Larry turned back, in control now, eyes on Leah, looking at her as if they shared some secret code. "All I'm saying is I think you deserve to be compensated for the injustice done to you, and we can help."

An idea struck and she held her hand up as Gretchen started to speak.

"How about helping me get my job back?"

It was Larry's turn to step back. Grady reacted as if she'd slapped him.

"We believe you're entitled to monetary compensation, but after all these years away, you really think you can be a cop again?" All pleasantness fled Grady's features like water running down a culvert.

"There's a lot of questions I want answered, so yeah, I want my job back. That wasn't rent Brad collected for you that night, Larry, was it?"

Larry backed further off the porch. "Like I said, leave it alone, Leah. You're free, with a lot of options. Don't choose the wrong ones."

"Is that another threat?"

"Advice from an old friend."

"Don't disturb the past, Leah," Grady said, gentleness in his tone. "Right now, you're a victim people can sympathize with. Don't make a mistake and become the goat again."

"What is that supposed to mean?"

"You're a bright girl; you'll figure it out," Larry said. "And you're four years older. Think long and hard before you go this route." He turned for the car, but Grady hesitated. He'd recovered his geniality.

"Leah, you've been through an ordeal no one should have to go through. All we're saying is think carefully before you make any big decisions." He turned toward Larry and their car. "Becky sends her love," he called over his shoulder before he got into his car and left.

Leah closed the door and looked at Gretchen. "That was odd."

"It was. They were fishing for something. I thought you weren't sure about wanting your job back."

"I wasn't. But now that it's something Larry and Grady don't want, I'll reconsider. My impression just now is that they want me to take a payoff and disappear." She walked back to the couch and sat. "So tell me, Gretchen: how do we go about getting me my job back?"

CHAPTER 42

After promising Leah she would work on petitioning the city for reinstatement, Gretchen left. With her dad off to work, Leah was alone and free, a word that kept echoing in her mind. Outside the day was gray and overcast, but it wasn't snowing. She wanted to take a walk. It didn't matter that it was cold. She was free and could go outside, and that was what she wanted to do.

Before she went out, though, she needed to stop putting off the chore of sorting through her things and finding her old favorites. During her first couple of days home, she and her dad had brought all her clothing from storage, but everything was still boxed up and she'd been procrastinating going through it all, instead wearing new clothes she'd bought in Bend. Her favorite warm pair of boots, jeans, and sweatshirt should be easy enough to find, she thought.

She found her boots first and then the jeans. The jeans fit loosely but they would do. It took longer to dig out her socks. In the process she came across an Oregon Ducks sweatshirt wrapped around something heavy. She unwrapped it and found a gun case.

Leah frowned. The sweatshirt was Brad's. She thought back on the day Clint and others removed her things from the house; the case and the shirt must have accidentally been placed in a box with her things. The case was only big enough to hold a single handgun, something Brad would have used to pack a gun if he was flying somewhere. She knew he'd had a case like this, but this one did not look familiar. It was heavy because it was a secure case, but she didn't think it was heavy enough to have a gun in it. Odd that an empty, strange gun case would show up in her stuff. She certainly didn't have a key to open it.

As she considered the case, the phone rang.

She set it aside, making a mental note to search for the key later, and picked up her phone, noting that the caller ID said *Wireless Caller*. She debated answering but in the end decided she wasn't going to hide. She punched the green phone button.

"Hello?"

"Radcliff?" It was a woman's voice, vaguely familiar.

"Who is this?"

"Vicki Henderson."

"Oh, what a surprise." Henderson had been at the coming home party, but they'd not spoken much. Leah had thanked her for getting fired because that had ultimately led to her own freedom.

"Wish it was for something good. I wanted to fill you in. Clint Tanner has been in a horrible car crash. It took forty minutes to cut him out of his SUV. He's in the Rogue Valley emergency room."

✦ ✦ ✦

When Clint came to, he couldn't move. He heard voices, felt pain everywhere, but couldn't move. And he couldn't remember what happened. Was he at work, at home? *Where am I?* he wondered. He tried to open his eyes, but the light was so bright. He squinted.

"Hey, he's coming around," a woman said.

"Sergeant Tanner?"

He blinked and the white blurry world came into focus. He was in the hospital. Why?

Again, he tried to move and couldn't. Before panic set in, he realized he was on a backboard, with a neck immobilizer, and everything hurt. What had happened?

"What?" Speaking one word seemed to take all his strength.

"You were in an accident—do you remember?" The same woman's voice spoke, close to his ear.

"Acc . . ."

"Yeah, didn't you see the truck?" Another voice. Marvin Sapp, he thought, but couldn't turn his head to check.

Clint tried to think back, but everything was so foggy.

"You have a concussion and maybe a broken arm . . . who knows what else," the woman said. "We're sending you to X-ray and then maybe to MRI to see if there's anything else more serious. If you understand me, blink your eyes."

Clint blinked.

"Great. Now just relax, and let us take care of you."

Clint tried to relax as he felt himself being moved by medical personnel. When he shifted his torso slightly, pain shot up his left arm. Yeah, broken, he bet. Why couldn't he remember what had happened?

+ + +

Leah had reached the hospital parking lot before it occurred to her that she might not be welcome. The call from Henderson had elicited an icy cold fear and brought up long-forgotten and horribly painful memories of the day she'd received the same kind of call about her mother. Sun Radcliff had died instantly in the crash and was long gone by the time Leah and her father reached the hospital.

How was Clint?

The thought of losing him like she'd lost her mother was something Leah couldn't entertain. As she made the drive to the hospital, she shoved it far to the back of her mind, relying instead on repeating Proverbs 3:5: *"Trust in the Lord with all your heart and lean not on your own understanding . . ."* Meditating on the verse had calmed her down by the time she reached the lot.

Now that she was here, though, she didn't care if she wasn't welcome. Nothing was going to keep her from Clint's side. There were four police cars in the emergency room lot, probably most of day shift. Who would be there?

There was nothing she could do but take a deep breath and face the gauntlet. This was about Clint. She locked her car and walked into the ER. The first two officers she saw were young; she didn't know them. They were leaving and passed her in the doorway. If they recognized her, they gave no indication. She continued on into the ER. The next officer she saw, she did know. Sergeant Erik Forman, Brad's old supervisor on SAT. He recognized her immediately, she could tell, and she stopped.

"What are you doing here?" His eyes widened with surprise at first, then narrowed as he glared at her.

"I came to see about Clint, if it's any of your business."

He stepped forward quickly enough to make Leah step back. "I'm making what you do my business. You killed my friend in cold blood and then lied about it," he said, voice low, tone dangerous. "Don't think you're going to come back here and pick up where you left off."

Leah kept her face blank. Out of practice, it was still her best cop face. "Are you threatening me?"

"Take it any way you want." He pushed past her and continued out the door.

"That could have gone better," Leah muttered under her breath.

She turned and saw Marvin Sapp come out of the double doors to the ER exam rooms. He smiled. "Good to see you, Mighty Mite."

Leah returned his smile as all the unpleasantness left in the wake of Forman melted away. Marvin's demeanor served to untie the final knot of fear about Clint that had encircled her heart since Henderson's call. He was too upbeat for Clint to be dead. Sapp had been in her academy class, and he used her moniker from those days. The nickname had nothing to do with police work; it was left over from her basketball career when the school newspaper called her Mighty Mite.

"Hey, Pinky." She stepped forward and gave as much of a hug as his vest and gun belt would allow.

"Good to see you, but surprised," he said. "How'd you hear about Clint?"

"Does it matter? How is he and what happened?"

He studied her for a moment. "He's okay, considering he should be dead."

Leah blanched at those words. "What on earth happened?"

"We're still trying to piece everything together. He was trying to stop a vehicle when a bobtail semi broadsided him on

Foothill. His rig must have rolled five or six times before it came to a stop against a tree. Fire cut him out of the patrol unit."

Shock rolled over Leah. "And he's okay?"

"Yeah, concussion for sure, broken arm. He's in X-ray now. Saint Tanner's nickname might change to Miracle Man now."

They both turned as the double doors opened again and Interim Chief Haun stepped out.

"Sapp—" He stopped when he saw Leah. Surprise crossed his features before he composed himself. "Sapp, coordinate with Forman. He's following up on a guy who claims to have witnessed the crash. See if you two can pin him down."

"Yes, sir." He nodded to Leah and left the ER.

"Hello, Chief," Leah said, not at all sure where Haun stood.

"Radcliff. I won't ask how you found out about Tanner. They'll be moving him to a room in a few minutes. X-rays and MRI were negative for anything more serious than a broken left arm and a lot of bruises. I'm telling you all this because I know you'll be asking. I notified next of kin, but they are all out of the country, so I expect for the time being, Tanner will need friends." He raised an eyebrow. "I assume you're one of those?"

"Yes, Clint was very good to my father while I—I was away."

Haun nodded. "I know he's definitely been on your side during this mess. He's headed to the third floor. I'm sending a rookie over to take first watch."

"Watch?" Leah frowned. "I thought it was a traffic accident."

"Traffic, yes, but it wasn't an accident. Someone tried to kill Sergeant Tanner—I'm sure of it."

CHAPTER 43

Clint felt much better when they took him off the backboard and removed the C-collar. They kept asking him
all sorts of questions, monitoring his level of consciousness, they said. He tried not to complain too much
when they cut off his uniform, but he was sore all over.
Besides the broken arm, he got seven stitches in his
head and a couple more for a cut on his jawline. The rest were
bruises—bruised ribs, hip, he could have told them without
having them look.

The firemen who cut him out of his SUV stopped by after
his X-ray. They said the curtain air bags saved his life for sure.
They considered him a miracle.

"Expected to find a dead cop," one of them said. "So glad I
was wrong."

The doctor had ruled out any bleeding on the brain with the

MRI, but he'd kept asking questions. Eventually Clint's head began to clear and the questions began to make more sense. The doctor said while Clint had sustained a concussion, he appeared to be recovering. They wanted to keep him overnight, and Clint had argued against that. After all, he had a dog to take care of. It was a battle he lost. Now, while he waited for the painkillers to take complete effect, Clint tried to think of someone he could call to look in on the little guy.

After he'd been patched and cleaned up, Clint found his memory of what had happened returning. The semi that hit him—it was deliberate. There was no cross street there; it had shot out of a driveway. As his thoughts cleared further and he thought about the truck he was chasing at the time, he realized he'd most likely been set up.

But why? As he asked himself that question, the door to his room opened, and in walked Leah. It surprised him how glad he was to see her. Worry shrouded her features, and Clint tried to square his shoulders—not wanting his physical condition to be a cause for her knit brow.

"I would hate to see the other guy." She smiled and the sight of it made Clint forget his aches and pains.

"He's really messed up." He tried a smile, but the tightness in his face reminded him of the stitches.

"Glad to see you're okay."

He tried to nod, but it hurt. "And I'm glad you're here. They're monitoring me because I had a concussion. Could probably tell them that my head is hard enough to survive even a semi."

"True," Leah said.

Whether it was her or the drugs, suddenly Clint felt a little giddy. "Hey, can I ask a favor?"

"Anything."

"Can you go check on my dog?"

"Dog? You never mentioned a dog in your letters."

"Just got him. The whole department is likely to be tied up on a manhunt. My house keys are in the bag at the end of my bed." He rambled off his address. "He's a little skittish—don't take it personally."

"What's his name?"

"I haven't picked one yet." He explained how he'd come to possess the dog. "He was the only worthwhile bit of contraband I confiscated during the failed raid at Larkspur Farms."

"Larkspur Farms?"

"Yeah, you know the place?"

"I sure do. I worked there one summer in high school. My mom thought physical labor would do me some good."

"Did it?"

"I liked the work. I loved the Hubbards; they were very special people. I picked summer peaches and some early pears before I had to go back to school. They taught me a lot about farming and gardening. They sold the place a little while after I left for college. I wish they were still around."

"I'm not sure who owns it now."

A nurse came in and checked his vitals, then lowered Clint's bed.

She faced Leah. "He needs to get some rest. We'll be checking on him throughout the night. You can come back in the morning."

"I will." She said her goodbyes, took his keys, and left.

Clint tried to relax. The nurse gave him a sip of water and it helped the dryness in his mouth. She told him they were still monitoring his level of consciousness. His LOC was fine as far as he was concerned. Trying to figure out who would want to kill him and why kept his brain active and alert.

CHAPTER 44

The image of Clint's battered face stayed with Leah. He looked as if he'd been in a bar brawl. She took solace in the fact that he was alert and talking. The urge to run a soothing hand over his forehead was strong. But when the nurse suggested she leave, she turned and left his room as requested. She looked at the keys in her hand, amazed he'd asked her to look after the dog. A thought came to mind: *He didn't ask Jenna to feed the pup.*

Haun said Clint needed friends now, and Leah was glad to be able to step in. She knew from his letters that most of his family, at least close family, was overseas in various countries as missionaries. His aunt was the person Leah most wanted to meet, but she was in Singapore or somewhere thereabouts. Leah wondered if that was who Haun had notified. Clint hadn't said—she should have asked.

An officer she didn't recognize sat outside the room. Leah nodded to him, but his expression was hard, not welcoming at all. Leah turned away and walked toward the elevator. She pulled out her phone to call Henderson and thank her for letting her know about Clint.

She dialed before getting on the elevator.

"Radcliff," Henderson answered.

"Thanks, Henderson, for letting me know about Clint."

"Sure. He and your dad are tight. How is he doing? Did he say anything about what happened?"

"No, he didn't. He's doing okay. They're keeping him overnight. Do you know any more?"

"A little. Accident invest is out at the scene now. Seems Clint tried to pull over a truck that we know now was stolen from Grants Pass. The semi that hit him was stolen from White City."

"What is going on?" Frustration built as Leah tried to grasp why someone would do this to Clint. "That's going to a lot of trouble. Why Clint?"

"I think it has to do with the smugglers he arrested a week ago. About the time you were in trial."

"Yeah, he told me a little about that, but it sounds as if they'd been released. Why try to kill him days later?"

"I'm just guessing. But someone sure went to a lot of trouble to try to kill him. Thank God they weren't successful."

"You said it." Leah shivered as she ended the call.

She got on the elevator deep in thought, wondering about these smugglers Clint had arrested. Was that really behind the attempt on his life? It didn't make sense. Smuggling was pervasive, sure, but to kill an officer because he made an arrest was a risky move for anyone and awfully personal. There had to be more to the story.

She remembered snatches of conversation she'd overheard

when Brad was on the smuggler apprehension team. They'd thought at that time a lot of smuggling was taking place with the Russian Mafia trying to take control of the entire West Coast. There was a large community of Russians living in the Sacramento area, and often stopping a truck registered in that area would result in an arrest.

But something wasn't right when Brad was on that team, she knew. In hindsight, there were other irregularities besides the payoff she'd seen Brad take. For one, Erik Forman was never really a supervisor. She'd heard Brad and others joke about that, calling him "Sleeper" behind his back. That team basically ran amok.

She was so involved in her own thought process as she stepped off the elevator and walked toward the exit that she almost didn't see him. She looked up in time to nearly bump into Harden Draper.

"You have some nerve." He was red-faced with anger, reminding Leah of a cartoon where the character has sparks flying off their visage. "Killing Brad wasn't enough—you also had to ruin his reputation. Now you're trying to ruin mine."

She stepped back, a confrontation the last thing on her mind. Harden was a big man. Though now soft and much thinner than she remembered, he still towered over her.

"What are you doing here?" he demanded.

"I didn't come here to argue with you."

"You should be sitting in a cold, dark prison cell. It's a travesty of justice that you can even show your face in this town. I should have you arrested for violating my restraining order." Both of his fists were clenched.

Leah stiffened and struggled with her own emotions— shock, fear, and a little shame. *"This one is the last of the true-blue heroes,"* he'd said of Brad one time they'd had dinner as a family. Harden always beamed over Brad. The memory hit her like a fist to the gut.

"I'm on my way out of a public place. You've accosted me."

"Now you're accusing me? How dare you. It's not enough that you murdered my son." Harden was borderline hysterical, and Leah could see several people watching.

She took another step back, but he moved closer, and for a minute she feared he was going to strike her. Yet as angry and hateful as Harden was, her own anger fizzled out and all Leah felt was profound sadness and pity. Brad had been born to him late in life and he'd loved his son so very much. If a son could be a father's idol, Brad was that to Harden. He could never do wrong in his father's eyes.

She said something she'd been wanting to say for a long time but there were always lawyers in the way.

"I'm sorry, Mr. Draper. I'm sorry I had to shoot Brad. If anything else had been possible at the time, believe me, I would have done it."

Time seemed to stop. Harden's face froze in fury, and it amazed Leah just how much Brad had looked like his father.

"Why, you—" He raised his hand and Leah tensed. "I'll see you back in prison if it's the last thing I do."

"Is there a problem here?" Another voice broke Harden's concentration.

The older man dropped his hand and turned to face the hospital security guard, a tall, thin man.

"Problem? Yes! This woman is violating a restraining order. I demand you arrest her right this minute."

"I'm just here to keep the peace. And, sir, I saw you approach her, not the other way around. Maybe it's time for the both of you to go your separate ways."

Harden scoffed at the guard. "You're not even a police officer."

Heels clacking across the floor made Leah turn, and she saw Ivy Draper striding toward them.

"Here you are, Dad. I've been looking all over for you." She gave Leah a dismissive glare and grabbed her father's arm. A pretty woman with a nervous personality, she always reminded Leah of Jennifer Aniston.

As long as Leah had known Ivy, she'd been firmly under her father's thumb. Sadly, she'd also been a bit under Brad's thumb. A memory surfaced: Years ago, Ivy had been sweet on Grady Blanchard. Brad boasted about putting an end to the relationship, saying his sister was just not right for Grady. Becky claimed she simply swept Grady off his feet. Whatever the truth was, Leah felt sorry for Ivy. It didn't seem as if she would ever have her own life.

Her father protested Ivy's attempts to move him along. "This Radcliff woman just violated the restraining order," he said.

"She did no such thing," the guard spoke up before Leah could. "Probably be a good idea if you take your father home."

"I resent that." Harden puffed up again. "Like I'm a doddering old man."

"It's okay, Dad. We'll get home and contact our attorney."

Reluctantly Harden responded to his daughter's tug and turned away.

"You'll be hearing from our attorney," Ivy threw over her shoulder.

Leah felt violated, and anger began to bubble up like acid.

"It'll be all right, ma'am."

"Uh, what?" Leah turned to see the security guard watching her. His face was vaguely familiar.

"This. You give 'em my name—I saw it all."

"Thank you. I appreciate that. But that's Harden Draper. He owns half this hospital. You might want to think twice before you step into this mess."

The guard smiled. "He don't scare me none. Name's Haynes, Michael Haynes."

Leah recognized the name. And in spite of the years, she remembered why she knew it and why he looked familiar.

"I know you. You were the witness on the Porter case."

He tipped his head to her. "Amazed you remembered. Sad day, that . . . I know you did all's you could for that poor girl."

The image of the battered woman, still clear and bloody, flashed in her mind's eye.

"If that were true, she'd still be alive."

He shook his head. "Don't do that to yourself. Alex was a sweet girl, but she never asked for help. People only get help when they ask for it." His radio crackled. "I got to go. You'll be okay?"

"Yes, I'm leaving."

"Remember my name if you need a witness."

She watched him walk toward the elevator.

People only get help when they ask for it. Truer words were never spoken.

CHAPTER 45

Clint's house was in a secluded neighborhood in Table Rock. Leah had only gotten one call in the area that she remembered, and it had been a natural death. A man had a heart attack mowing his lawn. She guessed Clint probably picked the house because the neighborhood was quiet.

She parked in the driveway. The small Craftsman-style house looked as cheerful as possible in November, when everything in Oregon seemed to turn gray. The lawn was tidy, and Clint had banks of rosebushes on either side of the front door. Leah bet they were beautiful when they all bloomed. He hadn't said much about the dog, except that it was skittish, so she opened the front door and entered carefully.

She stepped into a small living room, tastefully decorated, very masculine. *Funny,* she thought, *when I walked into Brad's house for the first time it reminded me of a dorm room. This place is cozy.*

Leah remembered everything Clint had written about his family, and she gravitated toward the pictures on the mantel.

"Both sets of grandparents emigrated from eastern Europe. For some reason that made my parents want to be missionaries there. They ended up in Kyrgyzstan."

He'd told her how he'd gotten the scar on his face and basically been banished from the mission field.

"I had to come home and live with my aunt GiGi. It turned out really okay. I love my aunt, and the move helped shape my future. It was with my aunt that I discovered being a cop was my calling."

A younger version of Clint was standing between a smiling man and woman. The man had to be Clint's father; the resemblance was striking. The woman had a kind but careworn face. From the picture it looked as though they were out in the country somewhere.

There were more pictures on the mantel, but Leah heard whimpering coming from another room and knew she needed to get on with the task at hand. She followed the sound and found that Clint had set up a kind of kennel in the laundry room. The source of the whimpering melted her heart. A small brown-and-white pup looked up at her with big, soulful eyes.

"Oh, you sweetheart." Leah knelt down, surprised when the little dog tucked its tail between its legs and backed up. She baby-talked the dog, holding out her hand for him to sniff. Slowly, tentatively, the pup came forward. It took some time, but eventually Leah was able to pick the dog up and cuddle him. She carried him out to the backyard and set him down to do his business. Watching him sniff here and there, she wondered what kind of dog he was. Small like a beagle, but big paws . . . Maybe there was some Lab in there.

It was cold outside, and Leah ran her hands up and down her arms watching her breath in the frigid air. She was ready to go back inside when the dog trotted up to her, tail wagging.

"All finished, cutie?" She opened the back door and the dog bounced in ahead of her. He went back into the kennel enclosure, turned, and looked up at her expectantly. Leah looked around for his food. She found a bag of puppy chow in the cupboard and filled up the little dog's bowl.

He ate with great enthusiasm, tail wagging furiously, and she chuckled as she watched. Faintly, the sound of traffic out on the street could be heard, a car door being opened. Leah didn't think anything of it, enjoying this puppy moment. A few seconds later the crash of a window made both Leah and the dog jump. She turned toward the living room, wishing she had a gun. Then she heard the sound of tires squealing as a car sped away.

On edge, Leah stepped into the living room. The front window was smashed to pieces and a brick lay on the living room floor amid shards of glass. *DEAD* was written on the brick in black block letters.

+ + +

"So why were you here exactly?" Erik Forman was the supervisor who arrived in response to her 911 call.

It had taken some time for Leah's heart to stop pounding so hard. This threat, coming on the heels of Clint's "accident," was no coincidence. "I told you. Clint asked me to feed his dog."

Forman glared at her as if he didn't believe her. Both of them were on the porch. He'd gathered up the brick, but it was a poor substrate for prints. Public service was on the way to board up Clint's window.

"The window will be boarded and the door can be secured, so we'll handle that from here."

"What about his dog?"

"What about it?"

"Suppose those guys come back."

"What, you think they were going to steal the dog?" He shot her a disgusted look.

"I just don't want to take a chance. In a way I'm responsible for the dog."

"I'm not animal control or a dog-sitter."

"Okay, then the dog goes with me. At least until Clint gets out of the hospital."

Forman rubbed his face with his hand. Leah could see the wheels turning. He wanted to find a reason to say no. He was here to secure Clint's property, and if anything happened to the dog, there was a slight chance he'd get in trouble for it. Forman was a trouble dodger. If he could deflect the liability to someone else, he would. And that's what he did.

"Take it. If Tanner blows a gasket, it's on you. We'll have extra patrols around his house till he comes home." He turned and left her standing on the porch.

CHAPTER 46

With the pup curled up on her passenger seat, Leah made her way out of Table Rock. She passed a flatbed with a crumpled PD SUV on it. There were signs the vehicle had been cut open by the Jaws of Life. She shivered. That had to be Clint's. It was a miracle he'd survived the crash. Was this really all about a smuggling arrest?

As she drove through the city she used to patrol, she took in the changes. There were a lot. Larry Ripley must have gotten the zoning changes he'd wanted because the neighborhood where his rental once stood was no longer there. It was now a large shopping complex with a sporting goods store, a market, and several other businesses. She pulled into the parking lot, wondering if it was a good idea to fight to get her job back.

Like the city, Leah knew she had changed a lot since that

night. When she worked as a cop, she'd taken nearly all her cues from Brad. It struck her how completely opposite Clint and Brad were. Clint was a true sheepdog. Being a police officer was his calling, a career where he could help people, rescue those in need. In hindsight she realized that while Brad could be a sheepdog, he was an officer for a totally different reason. The job was all about power and control for him.

Leah wondered about her own motivations for serving. Could she find a unique style on her own?

Before she'd taken the plunge and applied to become a cop, law enforcement had been a career in the back of her mind. Her mother was killed when Leah was sixteen. She never forgot the kindness and the professionalism of the officers that brought her and her father the news. But when she'd told her father she might want to go into law enforcement, he'd discouraged her. "Too dangerous," he'd said.

Eventually, when she got a full-ride scholarship to play basketball, her life goals changed. She worked hard at basketball and majored in business. At graduation she was offered a spot on a professional women's basketball team and was called crazy when she turned it down. But while she loved playing basketball, playing for a college team had taken all the fun out of the game. Winning was everything and she knew it would only be worse on a professional team. Besides, Leah was a homebody at heart. All the traveling involved with a professional team did not interest her in the least.

A year after she graduated, thoroughly frustrated by a job managing a UPS store in Table Rock, Leah circled back around to law enforcement.

"This isn't working for me, Pop," she'd told her father. "I want to do what I thought about when Mom died. I want to be a police officer."

"It still scares me," he said. "But I know you're unhappy where you are. So you have my blessing."

Leah was hired and sent to Salem for the academy. She loved everything about the police academy, the camaraderie, the work. She sailed through the physical part, aced the academic part, and graduated at the top of her class. Brad had caught her eye immediately. When she realized she'd caught his as well, the rest was inevitable.

As she sat back and thought about that Brad, the man she fell in love with, she had to ask herself why she hadn't seen his real self. What made him so angry that night? Was he corrupt? Was it the Hangmen?

She shook her head and sniffled because there were no ready answers to her questions. Finally she touched her forehead to the steering wheel and let the tears fall.

+ + +

Leah arrived home and got the puppy settled. She loved dogs and this pup was quite a character.

"Clint needs to give you a name, little one," she said as she watched him prance around in the yard. A lot of names went through her mind, but she wasn't going to presume that it was her place.

When it was time to go to bed, she brought the pup into her room.

"Could be a mistake," her father warned. "He'll keep you up all night, or you'll get too attached, or both."

"I'll take that chance."

In the end, it wasn't the pup that woke Leah up—it was the pounding on the door at three thirty in the morning. Even as she struggled up from the bed and grabbed a robe, she could hear her father already heading for the door.

"I'm coming. I'm coming."

Fear shot through Leah. She didn't like the sound of the pounding and hurried to be there when Dad reached the door. Emergency lights were flashing outside—she recognized the red and blue strobes. Thankfully, Dad didn't open the door right away.

"Who is it? What do you want?"

"Jackson County Sheriff's office. Open the door."

Leah stopped her dad before he could. She peered through the blinds. Three cars—a Table Rock unit and two county cars, from what she could see. She had to squint because of the brightness of the light bars. The mechanical sound of the emergency lights cycling though their sequence was so loud it was as if the cars were on the porch.

"Why? What do you want?

"To talk to you, Leah." She recognized Grady's voice.

"Why pound on the door like you're going to break it down if you just want to talk?"

"Do we need to do this through the door?"

"Yeah, we do until you tell me what you want." She turned to her dad and spoke loudly. "Dad, call Gretchen. Tell her it's an emergency."

He nodded and grabbed his phone.

She could hear voices talking in low tones on the other side of the door, but she couldn't make out what was being said. Her heart pounded inside her chest, and she realized that was probably what Grady wanted. Why else try a knock-and-talk at this time of the morning? Fear gave way to anger. What on earth was going on?

The emergency lights winked off one after another.

Finally Grady asked, "Leah, where were you tonight, about two hours ago?"

"In bed, asleep."

"Who can corroborate that?"

"My dad. What is this about?"

"We have a witness who says they saw you pour gasoline on the porch and set fire to Brad's house. It burned to the ground tonight."

"What?" Shock nearly made Leah pull the door open.

"I have Gretchen," her dad said, and more loudly, "I have our lawyer on the phone. Speakerphone."

Leah explained to Gretchen what was going on.

"Do they have a warrant?"

"Did you hear that?" Leah asked.

"At this point it's a knock-and-talk," Grady said. "Will you open the door and talk to us?"

Leah didn't need Gretchen's advice for that question. "No, I won't. You could have come by at a civilized hour, but my guess is you just wanted to intimidate and harass me. I'd have no reason to burn Brad's house down. I don't even know who owns it now. Was anybody hurt?"

"I'll ask the questions, Leah." Grady sounded decidedly frustrated.

"I don't know who says they saw me, but they didn't. I've been home since late afternoon."

There was more muffled talking.

"You've said enough," Gretchen said. "They need to leave."

"Will you come to the station and give a formal statement?"

"No," Gretchen said. "Say nothing else, Leah. I'll be back down there as soon as I can. All communication on this matter will be through me."

Leah started to relay the message.

Grady interrupted. "I heard. We'll get to the bottom of this, Leah, one way or another."

Eventually the patrol cars backed up and left the property, but the early morning peace had been shattered, which, Leah was certain, had been the point.

"If they really had a case, they would have had a warrant," Gretchen said. "My guess is that they couldn't get a judge to sign a warrant, so they improvised. I'm surprised this new sheriff would be part of such a thing."

Leah agreed.

"Are you sure he's not a Hangman?"

"He wasn't as far as I knew." But Leah was left thinking that maybe she'd been wrong, and Grady Blanchard was every bit as dirty as Chief Wilcox and the others were.

ey, are you finished goldbricking?"

Clint looked up to see his friend Jack Kelly in the doorway, backpack in hand. The first responding officers to his crash had removed his weapon and placed it in a gun safe at the station. Jack had retrieved it as well as a change of clothes for Clint. He wasn't the first visitor. Guys from all shifts, some off duty and some on, had been stopping by to show their support. Nothing brought the blue line together like a murder attempt on one of them. Cops rallied around their own.

"Not quite." Frowning at his friend's demeanor, he said, "You look like you just worked a double."

"In a way I did. Not sure if you've heard, but Brad Draper's house burned to the ground early this morning."

Sore and achy all over, Clint shifted in the bed. "What? How is that your problem?"

"I was working in Trail when it happened, heard it go out on the scanner as a fully involved house fire. I didn't know it was Draper's place until Blanchard logged on. This was about three in the morning."

"They called out the county sheriff for a fire in Table Rock city limits?" Stiffness forgotten, Clint tried to imagine where this was going.

"Yep, the long and short of it is, Sheriff Blanchard got an earful from Harden Draper, who claimed he had a witness who saw Leah set the house on fire. Wanted her arrested and thrown in jail."

"Leah!" Clint sat up, ignoring the shooting pain he felt from the sudden movement. "There is no way—"

"Relax, buddy; I know. But Sergeant Forman came rushing into Trail ready to break down her door. I headed him off until the chief could get there. Forman wanted to bring out the universal key. They had a private conversation. I don't know what is going on, but I fear . . ." He looked around as if to see if anyone was listening, then lowered his voice. "I fear Blanchard is compromised. Forman had us roll lights blazing up her drive to pound on the door, no warrant, only his statement 'Harden said.'"

Clint digested this. *Universal key* was slang for a battering ram. Forman had wanted to break Leah's door down.

"That's crazy."

Jack nodded. "We all went to her door. They pounded. It was snowing lightly, had been on and off most of the night. Both vehicles in the drive had a layer of snow on them. There was no way she was in Table Rock when the fire started. It's a forty-minute drive, so the car still would have been warm, and snow wouldn't have stuck."

"She wouldn't have burned the house down anyway. What happened?"

"They got her and her dad out of bed. Leah was smart; she never opened the door. Again Forman wanted to kick it in, but we had no grounds. She called her lawyer, and everyone stood down. It never should have happened. Draper pulled everyone's strings."

"Wow." Clint sat back, fully realizing that Harden Draper was bound and determined to make Leah's life miserable. "Maybe the Hangmen still have some teeth after all. Where is this going to end?"

"I don't know. All I do know is that Draper won't stop until he's made to stop. This impacts my department, though; Leah's lawyer filed a formal complaint."

Clint thought about that for a moment. "They made a mistake then. This will put the spotlight back on the Hangmen, I bet."

"It's put the spotlight on my department, which I hate. Whoever is behind this, Draper or that elusive fugitive the Feds told me about, this needs to stop."

"Then I'm going to find a way to make that happen."

"Be careful, Clint."

"I will be. Thanks for picking me up a change of clothes." He then remembered that someone was trying to make his life miserable as well. "Was there any other damage to my house besides the window?"

Jack shook his head. "Nope, just one busted-up window." Expression serious, Jack stepped close to the bed. "What is going on with all this? Who did you get so angry they'd want to kill you?"

He still couldn't shrug, so Clint said, "I got a threat after the whole Hangmen thing came out, but that was months ago. I certainly touched a nerve somewhere. About the only thing I am sure of is that I'm ready to go home."

"Have they given you a release time yet?"

"Just sometime this afternoon."

"Any more information on the crash?"

"Nothing on the suspects—they're in the wind. Accident investigation briefed me on their findings. The crash was definitely intentional. The semi was left blocking Foothill after it pushed me from the road. Witnesses saw the drivers of both the semi and the truck I'd been following get in a third car and flee west, toward the interstate. But descriptions of the men were vague, you know. They could be anyone."

"No real help."

"Right. I'll be off work at least three weeks. Probably off full duty and on light duty for longer than that."

"Do you plan on staying at your house?"

"Where would I go?"

"Ah, I recognize that look. You want them to try again, don't you?"

"You bet. This time I'll be ready, and they'll have the business end of a gun pointed their way, if they are so foolish."

Jack shook his head. "Be careful what you wish for. I think you should take a vacation somewhere, a place quiet and warm, take advantage of this forced hiatus."

"Was never much good at vacations. I hate being sidelined." *Besides,* he thought, *Leah needs me.*

"You need to rest, pal," Jack said. "Your department is working on it. And mine as well."

"There's a lot going on that I can work on without being too active." He told Jack about the visit from the feds.

"I hate to say it, but it makes sense. Let the suits take that over. They have the resources, and it sounds like they really want this guy Hess."

"I want him too. Even more if he had something to do with

running me off the road. But what I really want is a line on the guy who tipped the smugglers off."

"That's a puzzler. Since the Russians weren't even booked into the system, we need to look hard at my department and yours."

"Man, I hate to think of one of our own being a rat."

"It happens. Unfortunately, the right amount of money can change some people."

Clint couldn't dispute that truth.

"Text me when the doc signs your release," Jack said.

"Will do."

About three hours later Clint got the okay to get dressed, which he did, slowly and painfully. Fidgeting as much as he could without feeling pain, he was elated when the doctor came in and checked him out.

As he waited for Jack to return, Clint thought about all that was going on. He didn't believe the Hangmen had been stopped. Not with the death of Brad and not with all the negative publicity or scrutiny by state police. That was his mission now, to put an end to them once and for all.

CHAPTER 48

C lint surveyed the damage to his front window. It was a big picture window, so it would be a pretty penny to replace. Hopefully insurance would cover the bulk of it. The brick that did the damage was gone, placed in evidence, but the lab had left him a photo. *DEAD* was all it said. Heavy-handed threat, Clint thought. Almost childish.

He went into his bedroom and took his gun and gun belt out of the bag they were in. He removed his .45 from his gun belt and reholstered it in his off-duty belt. It was tough going with his left arm in a cast, but he could move his fingers and got it done. He then put on his off-duty belt. If anyone decided to make another attempt on his life, he'd be able to deal with them. Good thing his right arm wasn't broken.

His phone rang. It was Leah.

"I just called the hospital and they told me you got sprung before I could even visit again."

Clint smiled at the sound of her voice and flinched as his stiches pulled. "My loss at missing that second visit. How is the pup doing? Causing you trouble?"

Leah chuckled, the sound music to Clint's ears. He didn't remember hearing it ever before.

"This little guy is no trouble. Why haven't you given him a name?"

"I haven't had a minute to think about it. I figured he'd work himself into a name."

"I think you're being lazy. Cute guy needs his own moniker."

"Does anything come to your mind?"

"Nope, no help here. Your dog, you pick the name. Do you want me to bring him back?"

"Actually, I was hoping you'd be able to keep him a little longer. Just give me time to loosen up. Until after the weekend?"

There was a pause, and Clint feared this was a big imposition. "If you can't—"

"It's not that. I don't mind at all. As long as you're telling me the truth about the reason."

"What do you mean?"

"I mean, you're not asking me to keep him so that you can be free to try to investigate the attempt on your life."

Her insight surprised him. "I'm not moving well enough right now to do any serious investigating. But I won't make any promises once I feel better."

"At least you're being honest. He's a good guest. We can keep him as long as you need us to."

"Thanks, Leah. I appreciate it. Jack told me what happened this morning. How are you holding up?"

"Other than lack of sleep, I'm fine. Can I ask you a question?"
"Sure."

"Do you know who bought my—uh, Brad's old house?"

"No one."

"What?"

"The Drapers kept it." He paused, wondering if he should pass on the gossip he'd heard. "The rumor floating around was that the Drapers made it a shrine, a memorial to Brad. Not sure if it's true—"

"It probably is." Her voice had gone flat, with none of the exuberance he'd heard at first, and he wondered if he'd made a mistake in relaying unverified information.

"Harden idolized Brad. It wouldn't surprise me if that's exactly what he'd done."

"I guess that's my observation as well—they can't move on."

"No, they can't. But who would want to burn the house down and blame it on me?"

"Someone who doesn't want you to relax or slide easily back into your life here."

"Hmm. Gretchen called Haun first thing and got an apology from him. The supposed witness to the arson is in the wind. No apology from Grady yet. She plans on writing a letter to the newspaper."

"I like Gretchen." Clint didn't allow himself to think much about this next comment. "Now it's my turn for a question."

"Of course."

"Do you plan on getting your job back?"

The line went quiet and Clint was afraid he'd overstepped. "Sorry if that's not a fair question."

"No, that's not it. At first I was going to take my time, pray, discuss it with my dad. But the other day I had an odd visit from Larry Ripley and Grady Blanchard. They seemed completely against me getting my job back. So Gretchen is going to file papers next week to petition the city for me to be reinstated. The TRO could be problematic if a judge grants it."

"I have faith in Gretchen to make that a tough fight. But it will be a rough road, you know."

"I do. Honestly, when I was released, the biggest issue on my mind was to find out what was going on with Brad when we were married."

"The payoff."

"Yeah."

"Do you want some help?"

"Hey, you're convalescing. I'm not going to be a bad influence."

"Can you be an influence when I've already been out asking the questions you want asked? I didn't write you about my visit with Grant Holloway." Clint shared with her what happened to him when he went to talk to the insurance agent and also about the IA complaint that got erased.

"I'm glad it came to nothing," Leah said, and then she was quiet for a few seconds. "And Racer, Patterson, and Wilcox are gone. Do you think the Hangmen really have any more clout?"

"It sounds like Harden is still pulling strings. If he wasn't, Grady wouldn't have pounded on your door in the early morning hours."

"I'm still not worried about asking questions. They can't threaten me with an IA complaint. And I've prayed a lot about this. I need answers."

"Prayer is the first, best weapon for any fight," Clint said, smiling into the phone, glad Leah could see that now. "They may make it impossible to get your job back."

"Maybe you're right."

"I am. We need to be patient, I think."

"One thing I learned in prison was patience."

"Give me a couple of days to heal up. Then we can ask together. You can drive; how's that?"

"Fair enough. I think I have some stuff to do with Gretchen anyway. But promise me you'll take it easy until then."

"Promise."

+ + +

After the conversation with Clint, Leah knew she needed to stay busy or her patience would dissolve. It was time to finish sorting through her things and find a key for that odd gun case. Besides the boxes of miscellaneous stuff she had piled in the spare room, there was also a storage unit she'd have to visit. But there was no rush for that.

With the pup on her heels, she started to open up boxes. Her summer wear she left boxed up. All of her winter gear she laid out so it would be easy to get to. The gun case was problematic. Curiosity made her start searching pockets, hopeful she'd find a key and get the thing open.

She'd gone through almost everything—still no key—when a knock at the door made her jump.

The pup looked at her with big brown eyes.

"Sorry about that, little guy. I told my dad I'd be okay. And I will be." She picked the dog up and walked to the door. "Who is it?"

"Agent Falcon, FBI."

Frowning, she peeked out the side window and saw a man on the porch in a long winter coat. He had a folder wedged under his arm and he wore dark gloves.

"Can I see some ID?"

He dug into his jacket and held up a federal ID card.

"What can I help you with?"

"Any way I can come inside and discuss this?" The agent rubbed his gloved hands together.

"I'm a little gun-shy."

"You have nothing to fear from me. I'm on your side."

"How so?"

"The Hangmen. I want to get to the bottom of that group. There's more to it than a social club. And it may have some bearing on what I am here for."

Leah thought a moment. She couldn't mistrust all law enforcement for the rest of her life. Especially if she wanted to be in law enforcement again. Still, she let him stand on the porch. "What do you know about the Hangmen?"

"Not as much as I'd like."

She hesitated. "I need to call my lawyer."

"I spoke to her yesterday. Please confirm. It's cold out here—hurry."

Leah punched in Gretchen's number.

"I apologize, Leah. Yes, he did call me. You have my blessing to talk to him."

Leah opened the door and poked her head out. "Would you like some coffee?"

He nodded. "You bet."

She led him back to the kitchen and started a pot. "I'm surprised you're investigating the Hangmen. I thought the state cops had the case."

"They weren't the reason I was originally sent here," Falcon said. "I'm here looking for a fugitive."

As they waited for the coffee to finish, the agent told her about the fugitive, Colin Hess. While he never mentioned Clint's name, she recognized that he was talking about the raid on Larkspur Farms and Clint's smuggling arrests.

"What does all that have to do with the Hangmen?"

"Answer my questions and I'll answer yours," Falcon said.

The coffee finished and Leah poured two cups, nodding for Falcon to proceed with his questions.

"Before your husband's death, he was assigned to an anti-smuggling task force, wasn't he?"

"He was."

"Did he interdict much smuggling?"

Leah frowned. "He made some arrests, yeah. I'm still not seeing what this has to do with your fugitive."

Falcon opened the file he had with him and pulled out some papers. "Your husband hit our radar unexpectedly. Six years ago, he paid off his mortgage in full. Out of the blue he came up with $275,000 in cash."

Leah had to think for a minute. "His parents are wealthy. Maybe the money was a gift?"

"You didn't know the house was paid off?"

Leah shrugged. "We never talked about money. Except that I was not to touch his. I made my own and that's what I spent. I assumed he was still paying on the house."

"He made good money, but not that good. That was quite a chunk of cash, and there's no indication anywhere it was a gift from his folks." He paused and Leah felt her brain freeze. What on earth had Brad been into and up to?

"Our fugitive disappeared with an estimated $500,000 cash, maybe more," Falcon continued. "He's been well hidden, so we believe he purchased a new identity. He had the money for it; he just had to find the right person or people to help him. In your court testimony you said you saw your husband take a payoff."

"That's what I thought I saw."

He pulled a photo out of the folder. "Is this the man you saw?"

Leah studied the grainy photo. There was something familiar about the figure, but she couldn't say for certain it was the man she'd seen that night.

She shook her head, then stood. "Let me show you who I saw." She went to the other room and grabbed her sketchbook.

Opening it up to the page where she'd drawn the bearded man, she put it on the table in front of Falcon. "This is the man I saw that night."

Falcon arched an eyebrow and studied the drawing. "You did this?"

"I had a lot of time to work on the sketch. From my memory of that night, that is the closest I can get."

"It's a good drawing. It could be our guy; height looks about right. But he'd have bulked up a lot. A possibility." He studied the drawing thoughtfully for a moment before handing it back to her. "Nothing your husband ever said gave you pause, maybe an inkling that something was not right?"

Leah shook her head, a little numb. It was bad enough she'd married an abuser. Was he also sheltering a fugitive cop killer?

"Is there anything you can think of, in retrospect, that might give us a clue to what your husband was involved in?"

"Ask Larry Ripley or Richard Chambers—or Grady Blanchard for that matter."

"The new sheriff?"

"Yeah, he, Brad, Larry, and Duke Gill were tight back then. Larry and Duke are Hangmen for sure. I don't know about Grady or Richard."

Falcon sat back and rubbed his chin.

"Have you talked to Richard Chambers?" she asked.

"He won't speak to us. He lawyered up and we don't have enough to issue a warrant. The other names you've mentioned have given us boilerplate statements basically saying they don't recall."

"I know that they know what was going on. To borrow a saying, they were all thick as thieves back then."

CHAPTER 49

After he finished talking to Leah, Clint considered his promise to her to take it easy. The gun on his hip said that he wouldn't, but did he have a choice? Alone with his thoughts, he poured a glass of water, picked up the pain pills that had been sent home with him, and sat in his recliner, trying to get comfortable. He hated taking pain meds but knew he wouldn't get any sleep if his whole body ached. Later would be soon enough, he decided.

As he sat in the quiet room, partially dark because of the boarded-up window, it sank in that someone had tried to kill him, and they'd come very close to accomplishing their wish. Fear vibrated through him—fear and a little shame that he'd not been more careful. Taking off after that truck had been foolhardy. He'd told Leah to be patient. Could he follow his own advice?

He was glad she called; it made him change his focus. Clint reflected on the three Leahs he knew: the beaten, lost Leah that horrible day; the questioning, growing Leah from her letters; and the free woman, a believer now, committed to uncovering the truth. She had a foundation, he realized. She understood how important prayer was. Every time he learned something new about Leah, Clint found himself drawn even more to her, the desire to learn everything there was to know about this amazing woman overpowering.

He also realized his own foundation needed to be firm, his own guidance clear.

His Bible was on the end table next to his chair. He picked it up and let it fall open in his lap to one of his favorite passages, Ephesians chapter 6. Clint reflected back to how Leah's faith had been destroyed by the indictment and how his faith had been devastated by her conviction. She'd come full circle and her faith was strong. Where was he? He'd felt renewed when she won her appeal and thought he was back on solid ground when she was acquitted.

I thought it was all over, he mused. *That things were right again and everyone could move forward.*

I was wrong.

Like so many years ago when he'd lost the fight to save the girl in Kyrgyzstan, thinking that it was all up to him, only to learn painfully that it was up to God and God hadn't dropped the ball, Clint realized he'd been taking everything upon himself again. Leah, the smugglers, the Hangmen—he wanted to protect one and defeat the others all in his own strength. He'd forgotten what he just told Leah, that prayer was the first, best weapon in every battle. He didn't think he could have stopped the truck, but the truck was definitely a wake-up call. Whatever happened with Leah and the Hangmen,

Clint needed a strong faith in God's work and ability, not in his own strength.

He prayed for clarity, forgiveness, and the wisdom to recognize which battles were his to fight and which battles he needed to leave to prayer. He began to read Ephesians chapter 6 and didn't realize he'd fallen asleep until much later when something jolted him awake. He blinked in the darkness as pain roared through his body. He would need to keep his promise to Leah and take it easy, he thought, as he slowly stood and limped to bed.

+ + +

Over the next couple of days, he mostly kept his promise to take it easy, but he wasn't going to do nothing. He fired up his computer to uncover any information he could about the two Russians he'd arrested and Larkspur Farms.

While he worked, he made sure it was obvious that he was home and working. If the guys wanted to try again for him, he'd give them the ride of their lives.

He had no luck whatsoever finding out any more information about the Russians. Once they were released, they disappeared. What he'd learned the night they were arrested was about all there was. Larkspur Farms was also a mystery. He vaguely remembered the couple Leah had mentioned, the Hubbards. They'd been running the farm when he came to live with GiGi. Known for their peaches and pears, they set up a booth at every farmers' market and sold their produce. After they sold the place, Clint didn't know who bought the farm.

He sat back in his chair, trying to remember, but it was at least six or seven years ago those people went bankrupt and left the farm. Eventually he found an article about the couple leaving the valley, saying that the family couldn't make it any-more; the farm wasn't paying the bills.

Clint thought he'd read that the place had been bought by a pot farmer. An hour later, after a painstaking search, he did find a new owner. LHR, LLC, had purchased the farm at auction for peanuts. But whatever the corporation was, it never developed the farm; it simply maintained the buildings until letting the property go into foreclosure a few years later.

Was Harden Draper somewhere in the mix? Clint won-dered. He had extensive real estate holdings. It would be no problem for him to buy the farm and hide the smuggling. Clint wouldn't be surprised if somewhere down the line, there was a connection between the farm and Draper.

+ + +

Monday morning, Gretchen filed a petition to the city for Leah's handguns to be returned. She'd owned three at the time of her arrest: a .45 caliber—her duty weapon—a 9mm, and a small five-shot .38. She also filed for Leah to be reinstated. Citing her firing as "without cause," she additionally asked for back pay spanning from her arrest and dismissal to the present.

"That's a lot of money," Leah said, shaking her head. "Is that request really necessary?"

"We need to get them to the table, so yes. This is the open-ing round of negotiations." Gretchen turned to Leah, eyes ear-nest. "What happened to you was wrong on so many levels. The Hangmen perverted the justice system. I believe in the system. This wrong needs to be righted."

"I agree. Justice has to matter for everyone or it matters for no one."

"I've also written an op-ed for the local paper about the

sheriff coming to your door in the middle of the night. That too was wrong."

"I'd be surprised if they print it. Harden Draper and the publisher are great friends."

"I told them if the word didn't get out locally, there were some cable news outlets who would be interested."

There was no way to know how long they would have to wait for a response to the two petitions. They stayed in the courthouse because there was also the matter of the temporary restraining order demanded by Harden Draper scheduled to be heard in the afternoon. Because Draper was trying to slap an extreme risk restraining order on Leah, it was important that she win the case and have the judge deny the TRO. If the order were put in place, Leah could be denied her guns. If she was denied her guns, she would not get her job back. Unfortunately, the judge hearing the TRO case was Judge Revel.

"I wish it were a different judge," Leah lamented to Gretchen.

"We have to count on him being impartial."

When Leah and Gretchen arrived in the courtroom, Harden was already there, along with Rachel Clyburn and two other lawyers. Leah also saw Blanche and Ivy. Ivy's appearance shocked Leah. Normally a pretty woman, today she looked haggard and as if she wanted to be anywhere else. Blanche looked heavily medicated.

If looks could kill, Ivy, Blanche, and Rachel had just committed a homicide with Leah as the victim.

There were several other people in the courtroom petitioning for restraining orders—all domestic violence related. When the judge called on Harden, it was hard for Leah not to imagine a secret look between the two men. She knew they were close. While they never socialized directly, she and Brad had attended several parties where Revel was also present. She held her breath while Harden stood to give a statement.

"Judge, this woman murdered my son in cold blood. Add to that, someone closely resembling her burned down the last remembrance I had of my son, his house with all of his possessions inside. She's unstable. I don't want her near my family or anything that belongs to me. And she should never be allowed to own a firearm of any kind."

Gretchen silenced Leah with a glance before standing to rebut Harden. "Your Honor, in the first place, my client has been exonerated and we have no wish to rehash the circumstances of that case. And in the second place, my client has made no effort to contact Mr. Draper or anyone in his family. Further, Ms. Radcliff has always been an upstanding member of the community. There is nothing unstable about her or her past, and we have already petitioned the city for her reinstatement as a police officer."

Harden snorted audibly. "There is no way this vicious individual should be a police officer in this city or any other!"

Leah knew they were in trouble when Judge Revel did not admonish him in any way.

"I understand there is a history here. And it is my opinion that when there is a history, the court should err on the side of caution."

Gretchen started to speak up, but Revel silenced her immediately.

"There will be order in my court." He shuffled papers. "I find the complainant has shown cause for this order."

Gretchen put a hand on Leah's shoulder.

"However, the order is rather broad. I will narrow the parameters. The respondent is hereby ordered to stay away from the petitioner's primary residence and person. This shall also apply to co-petitioners Blanche Harden and Ivy Harden. Additionally, the respondent is also ordered to surrender any firearms. She will not be able to possess, purchase, or borrow any firearms for the entirety of this order . . ."

He droned on and Leah barely heard. She almost felt as bad as the day she'd been convicted of murder. This was wrong. Judge Revel quashed any hope she had of working as a police officer in Table Rock. The injustice of it weighed down on Leah. But she held her head up. She refused to let Rachel Clyburn or Harden Draper see how deep this dagger had struck.

CHAPTER 50

Blindsided, Leah left the courtroom in a daze. She'd believed the judge would see through the TRO. For someone who'd never been in trouble before, she certainly had struck out almost every time she stood before a judge.

"I'm sorry, Leah," Gretchen said as they drove back to Trail. "I didn't see that coming. The only positive is that Revel did lessen the scope of the order. He might believe that he split the baby. If Draper had gotten all he'd wanted, you'd never be able to set foot in Table Rock again. I'll try every avenue available to me to fix this."

"It's not your fault." She ran her hands through her hair. "Maybe this is for the best. I really only wanted my job back because it was obvious Larry and Grady didn't want me to have it back. Maybe it's not to be."

"You were unjustly deprived of your job, Leah. That was wrong, and so was this."

Leah started to say something bitter but didn't. Something Chaplain Darrel said once stuck in her mind.

"Life isn't easy, not for anyone. The difference is how people respond to the difficulties. You have prayer to fall back on now, and prayer works. Use it."

After Gretchen dropped her off and left, Leah tried to pray. It was difficult to concentrate and cut through the self-pity. Resolving not to cry, she opened her Bible to the book of Psalms, settling on 91. After a while she felt better. Refusing to give in to self-pity and bitterness helped her to focus her prayers. She wanted God's will in every issue facing her at the moment.

Sighing, almost wishing she were back in prison so she could talk to Nora—almost—Leah knew she needed to call Clint. She wanted his broad shoulder to lean on, his wise counsel. She punched in his phone number and stuffed down the disappointment when he didn't answer. It went to voice mail. Clearing her throat and working hard not to be whiny, she said, "Hi, Clint. How are you feeling? I hope you're mending and taking it easy like you're supposed to. . . . I wanted to bring you up to date. I just got slapped with a three-year TRO. If you feel up to talking, give me a call."

She hung up and said to the dog, "I hope that didn't sound lame."

Setting the phone down, she walked to the front door and opened it to check the weather. It was a beautiful sunny day but still in the low forties. Goose bumps rose on her arms immediately. She took a deep breath, shut the door, and went back inside to grab her jacket.

"I don't want to be cooped up in the house," she said to the dog. "I've been cooped up places too long already. Time for a walk."

Whether it was the word *walk* or just the fact that Leah was talking to him, the pup began prancing around and that made Leah smile.

She took the little dog outside, praying and thinking while she walked. Her father's lot was an unfenced five acres with plenty of trees. She breathed deep, enjoying the fresh, chilly air. The dog took her mind off the TRO hearing. Every so often they'd reach a patch of snow not yet melted and she'd pause, enjoying the show as he ran through the white stuff. He was a real cutie, and she knew it'd be hard to give him back to Clint. But the dog couldn't occupy her entire thought process.

Do I really want my badge back? she wondered.

She thought of the women she knew in prison, how being there had changed her perspective on people in jail. To Brad, everyone on the other side of the badge was scum. Unless someone like Larry or Duke found a way to get on his good side, Brad considered most people beneath him. Leah realized there were times when she'd agreed with him. The thought shamed her now, as she remembered Nora and Donna and the women in the basketball clinic.

Nora would be the first person to say that she belonged in prison, but not because she was subhuman scum. She was a person, a child of God, who made a mistake and was paying for it. Leah knew, at that moment, she could be a different cop, a better cop. The fight to get her job back was worth it, and she would pray and try with all she could to make it possible again.

Just then the pup caught her eye and she laughed out loud as he lay down in the snow and wriggled his little bottom back and forth.

The snap of a twig caught her attention. She jumped when

the figure of a large man loomed in her field of vision. It was Richard Chambers, Brad's former partner.

"What are you doing here?" She took two steps back.

"I came to talk to you." Looking older and somehow bigger than she remembered, he was breathing hard, probably from trekking through the forest.

Leah felt naked without a gun and stooped to scoop up the wet, squirming puppy. "Why are you sneaking up on me?"

"Because I don't want to be seen talking to you."

"What do we have to talk about?" Leah took another step back, wishing she hadn't walked so far from home.

He came no closer. "I heard you're trying to get your job back."

"So what if I am?"

"Are you going to leave the past in the past?"

"What's that supposed to mean?"

"I mean are you going to try and settle scores, get even?"

Leah stared at him. "For being wrongly convicted? I think the state cops are going to do that for me. A lot of people are being investigated for what happened to me."

He said nothing.

"If you mean, do I want to get to the bottom of what the three of you were doing at Larry's rental? You bet I do. Did you come here to enlighten me?"

"There are some doors you shouldn't open."

"Is that what you and Brad were doing with Larry that night? Opening one of those doors?"

"You're free. He's dead. Leave it alone."

Leah held the puppy close. "I can't. It made Brad angry enough to try to kill me. I will find out what was going on with your help or without it."

"Even if it costs your life?"

"Are you threatening me?"

He shook his head and stepped back. "You kick a hornet's nest and you're going to get stung. Take what just happened to Tanner as a cautionary tale."

"What does Clint have to do with what you and Brad were doing?"

"Just leave it alone, Leah. I always liked you. And I knew Brad . . . well, let's just say I knew he had a dark side. It's my respect for you that made me bring you this warning. Take it to heart."

Leah started to say something, then stopped. Chambers turned on his heel and took off through the forest, back the way he came, toward the road, which was about a mile and a half away. Leah noticed he was limping.

Maybe he'd meant to warn her away, but he'd done just the opposite: made her more curious. How in the world was what Brad did four years ago connected to the attempt on Clint's life?

CHAPTER 51

B y Monday afternoon, Clint was tired of the computer. Computer searches and wading through pages of legal documents was not his forte. He knew he'd have to find a lawyer to dig through all the legalese he kept running into. He stood, grimacing as his body reminded him that he'd been in a serious collision a few days before. The only lawyers he knew were the ones he worked with, prosecutors and defense attorneys. He wasn't certain he wanted to go to any of them. Gretchen might help, but her plate was full helping Leah.

As he shut down the computer, he tried to convince himself that the stiffening and soreness in his body was easing. The cast on his wrist left his hand free, and he could make a fist, provided he didn't squeeze very hard. He pushed his physical limits because he had to get out from behind a desk. He'd promised

339

Leah they'd do some investigation together and he wanted to keep his promise.

He thought of her as he closed his eyes. His feelings toward her were getting stronger. Every time he saw her, he wanted to pull her close and never let go. And though he'd promised himself not to say anything until he was certain she was on solid emotional footing, he wanted to tell her how he felt—now.

It seemed as if he'd been waiting forever to do so, and he was running out of patience.

Clint opened his eyes and switched gears: figuring out who the leak at the department was. When he made the arrest, anyone working that night—if they were paying attention—would have known about it. What not everyone would have known was that he'd sequestered the Russians and planned the raid.

Clint reviewed the list he'd made of everyone on duty that night, crossing off the ones who would only know about the arrest. He then highlighted those who were most likely to know he'd delayed the booking and planned a raid. He was beyond dismayed when he finished the list. It contained only eight names, four from his department: the watch commander at the time, Lieutenant Glick; Vicki Henderson; Marvin Sapp; Erik Forman; Judge Olson, who'd signed the search warrants; two jailers from the sheriff's department; and his friend Jack Kelly.

Clint knew and trusted every one of those people with the exception of the jailers. He called Jack.

"I'm sure of everyone except the two sheriff personnel."

"Way ahead of you, buddy. I pulled the phone logs for both of them. No calls out on their cell phones or jail phones. It was a busy night; they had a combative drunk to deal with and they were short-staffed. I don't believe either one of them was the leak."

"I'm sorry to hear you say that."

"Why?"

Clint read the rest of the names on his list.

After a pause, Jack said, "I hope you're not truly considering me."

Clint sighed. "No. But everyone else on the list is also above reproach."

"What about Forman?"

"He's a jerk, but he lost a cousin to human traffickers several years ago. Hates all types of smuggling. I can't see him moving to the dark side. I could be wrong, but I'm going to have to tread carefully here."

"Let me know if I can help. I want to find the problem as well."

Clint ended the call and went to work. Erik Forman was the obvious choice, he admitted to himself. *But is that because I don't like him?* Clint asked himself.

True, Forman had been in trouble. After it was discovered he'd been sleeping on duty when he was supposed to be supervising SAT, and he was suspected of altering time cards, though that was never proven, he was suspended for fourteen days and came very close to being demoted. But in the years since then he'd seemed to be minding his p's and q's. Still vocally loyal to Draper, which was more obvious now that Leah was free.

Was Forman part of the Hangmen? The same question could be asked of Glick. He was Harden's generation. Clint made a mental note to ask Leah if she knew.

"I can't let my personal feelings about Forman enter into this," Clint said as he stood and began to pace. After a minute he sat back down. He wrote a word or a phrase next to each name.

Erik Forman—most likely suspect, too likely?
Lieutenant Glick—old-timer, stable, by the book

Vicki Henderson—good, solid officer, but young and to my estimation completely without guile
Marvin Sapp—excellent cop
Judge Olson—respected judge

Why would any of them leak?
Is there someone or something I'm missing?

He knew he'd have to go down the list one by one, be thorough, not emotional, and figure this out—after all, someone had just tried to kill him. There was as good a chance the attempt on his life was connected to the smuggling as it was to his work on Leah's behalf. Clint had to find the leak to save his own life. But even if he picked a name, how did he prove that was the leak? Confront? Let the FBI know?

He found himself wondering if Leah might have any insight. He liked the way she thought. And maybe he was too close; an uninvolved pair of eyes might see something he couldn't. He picked up the phone and noticed he'd missed a call. The ringer had been turned off. It was Leah's number.

He played her voice mail and frowned when she mentioned the TRO. It made him angry. Harden Draper didn't want her to be a cop again, and a TRO that denied her guns would do that. He punched in her number. It went almost immediately to voice mail.

"Hmmm," he muttered under his breath and, a few minutes later, called again.

✦ ✦ ✦

Leah put the dog down and started back home, unsettled by Chambers's unannounced visit. She reached into her pocket to try Clint again and realized she'd forgotten to bring her phone with her. She'd not had a phone to carry with her for a long time, and it was difficult getting back in the habit. Clint should know about the odd visit. He surely knew if Chambers was no longer a cop. Watching the dog as he sniffed and pranced ahead of her, looking back every so often to be sure she was following, eased some of her angst. He was a sassy little dog with a lot of personality, and she found herself clicking through likely names in her mind as she walked. *Spicy, Sparky, Sassy* . . .

The manufactured home came into view, and so did an SUV Leah didn't recognize. She stopped, wary now. The pup was a short ways ahead of her, but when he turned and saw she'd stopped, he came trotting back. Leah scooped him up and stepped behind a tree, peering around it to ascertain who was in her driveway.

A man—not Chambers, and she didn't think it was Larry Ripley either. He turned and she breathed a sigh of relief. It was Marvin Sapp.

Leah stepped out from behind the tree. "Hey, Pinky, what's up?"

Sapp jerked around, obviously startled. "Leah! I've been knocking. Your car is here. I got worried."

"Just out with the dog." She walked toward him and watched as he calmed down and smiled. "Were you thinking something happened to me?"

"Ah, Mighty Mite, I know you've made a lot of enemies. And Clint told me what was painted on your car." He gestured toward it. "Call me a paranoid cop."

"I get it. Hey, can I ask you a question?"

"Shoot."

"What ever happened to Richard Chambers?"

"That's a little off-the-wall. Why do you ask?"

"Not so off-the-wall. He was Brad's partner. I expected to hear from him. Maybe see him. But he's not even on the department's website."

"He blew out his knee really bad. Foot pursuit of a robbery suspect. Took a medical retirement about two years ago. Last I heard he was living out in the Applegate." He pointed toward his car. "I heard about the TRO. That's got to hurt. What say we go inside and commiserate for a bit? I brought a six-pack."

Hmm, Leah thought, *it's all over the valley already that I won't get my guns back.* She'd forgotten how fast stuff traveled on the PD gossip superhighway.

"No beer for me. I'll make a pot of coffee if you like."

"What? That doesn't sound like the Mighty Mite Radcliff I knew. You never turned down beer."

"Losing your freedom changes a person."

"Not just one? For old times' sake?"

He stepped toward her and suddenly Leah felt uncomfortable. But was it Marvin or the fact that she really had changed and had no desire to pick up old, bad habits? Drinking had been a big part of her relationship with Brad.

"No—" She stopped, and they both turned as a truck pulled up the drive.

"You expecting someone?" Marvin asked.

"No, but that looks like Clint's truck." She frowned. "He should be taking it easy, not driving around." *What on earth is he doing out here?* she wondered, even as pleasure at seeing him flooded through her.

"I guess that's my cue to leave. Take care, Leah." He backed toward his car as Clint slowly climbed out of his truck.

"Hey, I can make coffee for all of us."

"You know what they say—three's a crowd."

Clint nodded toward him. Marvin met him and they shared a brief greeting. Strangely, Leah was relieved that Marvin decided to leave. *Have I really changed that much?* she wondered.

And even though she knew that he shouldn't be out driving around, she was glad to see Clint.

+ + +

Clint's anxiety faded a bit when he saw Marvin Sapp. He knew Leah and Marvin were academy classmates and Sapp had been concerned about her from the beginning. He'd been the first officer on scene that fateful morning. Maybe Leah was just visiting and had her phone off.

Clint had raced over after calling her five times and getting no answer. Now that he saw he'd overreacted big-time, he hoped Leah wouldn't be annoyed.

Working not to show Sapp or Leah his angst, he kept his tone light. "Hey, Marvin, what's up?"

"Nothing much, Sarge, just out saying hello. Kind of wondering what you're doing up and about."

"Not really good at sitting around on my butt."

"I get that." Sapp glanced back toward Leah. Clint followed his gaze and saw that she had the dog in her arms.

"I'll be on my way, then," Sapp said. He climbed into his car, turned around in the large driveway, and left.

Clint walked stiffly to where Leah stood and stifled a smile. She looked so perfect there, holding the pup—they were made for each other.

"Don't you answer your phone?" he asked casually and with a smile.

"Sorry; went for a walk. I didn't have it with me. Just not used to having one in my possession." Then he saw realization dawn in her eyes. "Wait—you're here because I didn't answer my phone?"

"Busted. I played your voice mail and tried to call you back. Worry can be a reflex."

"Well, I guess it's a good thing you're here. I wanted to talk to you."

As they walked into the house, she told him about the TRO and its parameters.

Clint shook his head. "I can't believe it. Makes me wonder more about Revel. Was he a Hangman?"

"I don't know. I know he and Harden are close."

"Gretchen's on it, right?"

"Yeah, she is. But it was a shock. On top of that, I had a strange visitor."

Once inside the house, Leah set the puppy down, and he bounced and wagged his way over to Clint. He grinned.

"So glad you didn't forget me." He picked the pup up, turned him over in the crook of his bad arm, and rubbed his belly, to the dog's obvious delight. But as with most pups, he had to test the world out with his teeth, and he sank them into the sleeve of Clint's flannel shirt.

"Hey, Buster, that's enough of that," Clint said as he disengaged the teeth and set the dog down.

"Buster? Is that his name?"

"I guess it is. It fits." They both watched the dog as he squirmed in and around Clint's feet. "Buster Brown . . . I think it fits like a glove."

Leah laughed, and Clint liked the sound.

"You're right. He is a Buster! Tons of personality, this guy." She knelt down and gave him a belly rub.

"Who was your visitor?" Clint asked, stepping reluctantly back into the real world.

Leah stood. "Have a seat."

He sat, absentmindedly playing with the dog when he buzzed by for attention, while Leah told him about her strange encounter with Richard Chambers.

"He said he didn't want to be seen talking to you—by who?"

"He didn't say." Leah shrugged. "Marvin just told me that Chambers retired on a medical."

Clint nodded. "Officially, I guess that's it. Chambers was lost after—well, without Brad. He was always a follower. Then SAT was disbanded. He floundered and never did much good police work."

"What truly happened with SAT?"

"It's close to what you probably read. Forman wasn't really a supervisor and all the guys were off doing whatever they wanted. You probably already knew this, but Brad was for all intents and purposes the real leader of the squad, and they didn't do much smuggling apprehension."

"I really had no inkling then. I guess I had blinders on. I'm getting the big picture now."

"Racer covered for Brad in everything. Brad was the pied piper everyone followed. He did a little police work, but only if he thought the arrest would burnish his image. Without him SAT was counterproductive."

Leah nodded, remembering how Brad loved accolades. "After they discovered all this, why wasn't Forman fired?"

"He almost was. But there was a lack of solid evidence. He ended up with a two-week suspension without pay. Since then, other than the fact that he's as warm and fuzzy as a porcupine, he's been doing his job."

"He learned his lesson?"

"Apparently."

"Chambers insinuated that what happened to you is some-how connected to what I saw that night and my wanting to look into it."

"That's a tough one. I can't see a connection."

"Makes me more convinced that I need find out what was really going on that night."

Clint looked at her, saw the determination in her face. Though he didn't know her personally then, he remembered how years ago, when he'd watched her play basketball, her dogged determination had always impressed him. The women she'd played with and against were all taller than she was. Back then, he'd wanted to meet her but feared coming off as some sort of creepy groupie. He didn't believe in fate, but he did believe she'd come back into his life at this time, as a friend, for something important, and he prayed to know what that was.

"Do you have any theories about that night?"

Leah sighed. "It was a payoff for something. I was certain at the time. Brad was given the money—he stuck the barrel of his gun in the guy's face, for heaven's sake. But I wasn't certain it was for him. That night I . . ."

She paused, and Clint thought he saw her wince. "What?"

"The memory of that night still stings once in a while." She swallowed and seemed to steady herself.

"Do you not want to talk about this?" Clint's heart went out to her. Bottom line, even though it was years ago now, she'd had to kill her husband. Could that memory ever be erased?

She gave a wave of her hand, and he saw the darkness leave her eyes. Her footing firmed up, and Clint felt his admiration and respect for her grow as she continued.

"I'm okay. That night my question for Brad was 'What was the payoff for?' I'm certain it wasn't first and last months' rent for Larry. I thought it might be some kind of political payoff. However, something came up recently that makes me doubt that theory." She told Clint about the FBI agent, Falcon, paying her a visit.

"Oh, you only got one, and he was on your side." Clint

rolled his eyes, still remembering how angry the agents had made him. He told Leah about his experience. "They told me to keep my nose out of my own investigation."

"What they told me about Brad surprised me. I can't see him sheltering a fugitive." She paused; Clint saw sadness shade her features. "But then I couldn't admit that he was an abuser."

"The man you saw give Brad the money that night wasn't the fugitive?"

"I don't think so. There was a generic resemblance, I guess. I couldn't say definitively that they were the same person. But it wasn't Grant Holloway either. I really need to talk to him."

"Are you sure you want to go there now?"

"What do you mean?" She stared at him.

"You've been out of jail a week. Maybe take a breath?" He smiled.

"From the man who should be resting at home after a near-fatal traffic accident."

He saw the amused twinkle in her eyes. Would what he had to say change that? There were hard questions he needed to ask Leah. Was she ready?

"Point taken, but I have to ask you something. Maybe you won't like it, but I want to help, and I need the answers to these questions."

"I'll tell you everything I can."

"Did you believe Brad was a dirty cop the night you followed him?"

irty? No. I knew he was up to something." She paused, remembering all the angst that night. Her fears. Her suspicions. "I thought—affair."

"I can understand that." Clint nodded, thoughtful, and Leah felt compelled to go on, but she needed a prop.

"How about some coffee or tea?" she asked.

"Nothing for me, thanks."

"I'm going to make a cup of tea." Leah went to the kitchen, needing to move, memories swirling inside her head. How much should she tell Clint? The word *everything* echoed in her thoughts and she realized that was right. She wanted more with Clint, and he needed to know everything. There would be no secrets or wondering in this relationship.

"Brad saved me, you know," she said, looking out the back window as she filled the kettle.

"How?"

"In field training. Don't know if you remember the fiasco

at Duster's Creek, when we were cleaning out the homeless camp—gosh, almost seven years ago now."

He shook his head.

"I was one of the officers who wandered into a combative group of crackheads. I was almost finished with field training and it took me by surprise. One of them sucker punched me, broke my nose. And also broke my confidence."

"Stuff happens."

"I know that now, but back then I was cocky. I'd graduated top of my class and thought field training would be a breeze. After that hit and three days off injured, I wavered, considered quitting. Maybe I wasn't cut out for the job. Then Brad took me under his wing. Worked with me on my weaponless defense. I was in awe of him. There was good there."

Clint nodded. "I don't doubt that. We all have two sides to our natures. Sometimes it's a battle to keep the ugly side down. I was there the day he saved that woman in the river." He hiked a shoulder. "I'm not a strong swimmer, and that water was icy cold. I didn't want to make the situation worse by getting in and becoming a victim myself. Brad never hesitated."

Leah's throat thickened as memories of the good Brad flooded her thoughts. She held Clint's warm hazel eyes. "That's why it's so important to me to find out went so wrong that he'd try to kill me." She swallowed the lump and kept her composure.

"I wish I had an answer. Maybe there isn't one. Could you live with that?"

Leah considered the question. "No. I want answers."

"No doubt." Clint flashed a smile. "You were tenacious on the court—why would it be any different now?"

Leah liked his smile and her mood improved. "Finding the truth is driving me forward. Getting my badge back will be the first step. I'm praying that Gretchen can get the TRO rescinded."

The kettle clicked; the water was ready.

As Leah poured water over her tea bag, more memories from life with Brad surfaced. Not good ones. Life with him was so complicated. All the stuff that went on—she knew now their relationship had never been healthy and the back-and-forth that led her to follow him, to check up on him, was a result of the competition and codependency between them. Right now, she could see all the issues clearly. Even the abuse she put up with and rationalized away for two years. Why couldn't she see that then?

Buster was sprawled out in the center of the living room, sound asleep. Clint and Leah had moved to the kitchen and were seated across from one another at the table.

"So I guess you could say Brad and I didn't have the best of marriages."

"I'm not judging. And you don't need to share any details with me. Our relationship moves forward, to the future. We're not going to be beached on the past—deal?" He held out his good hand.

Our relationship. Leah held his gaze, saw the warmth and compassion there. She felt so connected to Clint, so safe.

She gripped his hand. "Deal."

"Good."

Leah let go of his hand and pushed her hair up off her forehead. "With Brad I was always walking on eggshells. We spent a lot of time with his parents. Harden is every bit as controlling as Brad was, even more so. Blanche had a saying: 'Let the men do their men things.' It meant that we never questioned them; it was just the way things were."

"Sorry to hear it."

"I always wondered if anyone at the PD guessed, if there was any gossip."

"Not that I heard. I know people were stunned that morning.

No one knew what to make of any of it. I think that's what made it easy for the trial to become a travesty."

"I made that easy by never saying anything."

"Don't blame yourself. The reason I wanted to know what you suspected and why you followed him was because I wondered if you knew what was happening in SAT, if you ever heard him discuss smuggling operations."

She frowned. "Falcon asked me almost the same thing—did Brad interdict much smuggling. I didn't have an answer."

"Do you think it's possible Falcon is right, that he was actually making it easy for smugglers rather than stopping them?"

Leah sighed. "A year ago, I would have said no way. But now . . ." She shrugged. "I guess anything is possible. Brad was a lot of things; he did bend the rules. Things had to be his way. I do wonder, though, what would have been in it for him to turn a blind eye to smuggling?"

"Maybe a piece of the action? The money Falcon mentioned."

Leah sat back. "Brad was never obsessed with money. He was quirky about it, but—" she shook her head—"I can't see him going to the dark side to enrich himself personally."

"Let me guess: he was more about control," Clint said with a wry smile.

"Yes, that was Brad. He needed to be in control."

"Maybe it wasn't personal profiting. Maybe it was all controlling things for the Hangmen."

"That would make more sense than the other, I guess. I'm still trying to wrap my mind around the thought that any cop would shelter a cop-killing fugitive."

"Maybe he didn't know. Hess has to be in the valley under an assumed identity."

That didn't fly for Leah. "Brad wasn't stupid. He liked to say he had his finger on the pulse of the whole valley."

"Maybe he did and that's why his house was burned down."

"What?"

"I've been thinking about it. Maybe there was something in the house they were afraid would be found. You say you want your job back and the house burns to the ground. I hate coincidences."

"There was a bar top with all the Hangmen names carved in it."

"Burning the house down for something that could be sanded over seems a bit extreme. There has to be something bigger."

"Harden never lost possession of the house. If something was there, don't you think he would have found it by now?"

"Maybe. Harden might have looked and come up empty."

She redirected the conversation. "Larry Ripley is who I think of when I think of Brad's house and the Hangmen. Do you remember the day you helped me retrieve my belongings?"

"I'll never forget it. You threw a pizza at me." He grinned and Leah had to laugh, even as she blushed.

"Okay, before that. When we got to the house, just before we went in, Ripley drove up."

"I vaguely remember that. He wanted something, correct?"

"Yeah, he said he wanted a gym bag. Ivy told him to pound sand. What if there was something in the gym bag and it was still in the house or Ripley thought it was?"

"You think Larry burned the house down?"

Leah set her tea down. "I don't know, but I need to show you something."

She went into the other room and retrieved the gun case. "This was in a box of my stuff, wrapped in one of Brad's sweatshirts." She handed it to Clint. "Do you remember putting it in a box?"

He took the case and frowned. "No, I don't. This isn't yours?"

"No, and as far as I know, it wasn't Brad's either. I bet it's what Larry was looking for."

"Thought he said he wanted a gym bag."

"I would guess he said that because *gun case* would have raised eyebrows. Larry is the consummate liar."

Clint turned the case over with his good hand. "No key?"

Leah shook her head.

"This is a nice case. It'll be difficult to open without a key." Like most cops he carried a utility knife on his belt. He took the knife out and struggled to pull out a small tool with the hand that stuck out of his cast. He held the knife up. "You'll have to help me; I need two good hands."

Leah moved her chair close to him, their shoulders touching. "What do you need me to do?"

"Hold the case steady."

Leah reached over with her right hand, elbow pressing into Clint's chest. She was almost sitting in Clint's lap. His warmth seemed to envelop her, and Leah bit her bottom lip to concentrate on the job. Her left hand on the other side of the case, she pressed down, holding it steady while Clint worked the tool on the knife into the lock, his head down, breath tickling her hands.

"You don't mind if I break this, do you?" he asked.

"No, uh, of course not."

He worked on the lock more. Leah had to press down hard on the case to hold it still. Suddenly the lock popped open and Leah felt a jolt of happy success. She sat back, still conscious of his nearness, heart racing a bit. Even with the bruises and the stitches, he was very easy on the eyes.

Clint turned toward her and smiled.

For the briefest of seconds, Leah felt the urge to lean forward and kiss him. The light in his eyes was warm, and they sparkled, full of—could she say love?

His eyes never left hers. He set the knife down and took her hand in his good one. "It was easier than I thought. We make a good team."

Leah felt as if her heart would beat out of her chest. He leaned toward her, and she reciprocated, closing the distance between them.

There was knock at the door and the moment was shattered. Leah jumped and the pup woke up.

She pulled her hand from Clint's. "Busy here today," she said as she stood.

"You're not expecting anyone?"

"No."

"Before you open the door." He stood, blocking her exit, and opened the case. Leah tore her eyes away from him and looked inside. There wasn't a gun, just a small computer storage drive.

Clint held it up, expression thoughtful. "What do we have here?"

"That doesn't look familiar."

He handed it to her, and she put it in her pocket. The visitor knocked again.

As Leah made her way to the door, Clint trailing after her, she could see it was Becky Blanchard.

Leah opened the door. "Hi, Becky." The pup bounded toward the door and Leah scooped him up just before he connected with Becky's legs.

Becky smiled and stepped in as if to give Leah a hug, then stopped when she saw the pup. Then her eyes lit on Clint.

"Oh, I didn't know you had company. I, uh, I missed your coming home party and just wanted to welcome you home. I even got a babysitter."

"Thanks." Leah shifted the wiggling dog under her arm and indicated Clint. "Have you met Clint Tanner?"

"Not in person, but I know he's the hero cop. Two years later my husband is still talking about your intervention at that convenience store." She smiled brightly and shook Clint's hand, frowning at the cast. Leah thought she saw Becky stare at the case, which he had tucked under his arm. "I had no idea that you two were friends."

Something about that statement hit an off chord with Leah, but she wasn't sure why. "Come in, Becky."

"I don't want to interrupt anything."

"Coffee or tea with friends, nothing to interrupt."

She stepped inside, and Leah followed her gaze. Becky was still looking right at the gun case.

"Grady has a case just like that," she said. "I thought you couldn't have your guns back, Leah."

Clint held the case up. "It's empty. We were discussing what a case like this could hold."

"A valuable gun, I bet," Becky said. Something about her demeanor bothered Leah. "Interesting the kind of discussions you have." She sniffled and almost sneezed. "Oh, I'm having an allergic reaction to that dog. It was nice to see you, Leah, and to meet you, Clint. But I have to run before I start sneezing all over the place." She flashed a big smile. "We have to get together for lunch, like old times." Becky turned and was gone.

Clint pushed the door closed and looked at Leah, eyebrows raised. "Was it something I said?"

"That was just odd."

CHAPTER 53

Clint considered Becky's hasty departure. It reminded him of Jack's suspicions about Grady Blanchard. *His wife is the driving force in that relationship. "Grady is a different person when she's not around, a better person. Funny and lighthearted."*

He wished he knew Grady better and had better insight into Becky. She'd bolted like a scalded cat. He thought he knew why, but it wasn't making much sense.

"How well do you know her?" he asked Leah. His full attention returned to her as warmth and attraction flooded his being. Being this close, hearing her heart had held him completely captive until the knock on the door.

"I'm tempted to say pretty well, but I might be wrong," Leah said. "She was really the only friend Brad approved of. She came to visit me in prison a couple of times. She went out of her way to do that."

"Hmm." Clint could acknowledge that was true. But he couldn't let this alone. "She recognized the gun case."

"What?" Leah stared at him.

He held the case up. "She's seen this before. Maybe this belonged to Grady or Duke." He could see skepticism in Leah's face.

"That's a leap. I still think it's Larry's. I want to know what's on the thumb drive." She made a move to get a computer, he guessed.

"Wait." He put a hand on her arm. "I don't think you should plug that into your computer."

"Why not?"

"Call me paranoid, but maybe there's a virus on there, and if you don't have the password, all the information gets erased. I can't see anyone locking it away in a gun case unless the contents were valuable. We should get it to a computer expert we trust."

"Meaning you don't want it to go to the PD."

"I hate to say it, but no."

"What about Falcon?"

Her brown eyes were warm, sharp, and focused, and he was sure he could get lost in them.

"The FBI." Clint rubbed his chin. "That might be a good idea. They would certainly have the resources." Inside he found himself wondering if even the FBI could be trusted. But the reality was, they had to trust someone.

Just then his phone rang. He checked the number. "It's Jenna. Let me see what she has."

Leah nodded and turned away.

Clint answered, "What's up?"

"Where are you?"

"With Leah at her house. Is something wrong?"

"Brad Draper's uncle, the one who works for the state police, has been suspended."

"What?" Clint faced Leah. "You have to hear this; I'm putting it on speaker."

They both listened.

"Turn on the news. State cops are having a press conference. They formally reopened the investigation into Prosecutor Birch's suicide. They found evidence that Brad's uncle, the handling officer, was negligent and may have falsified his report. They no longer believe Birch's death was a suicide. It's murder."

+ + +

Leah felt shock reverberating all around as she turned on the TV by reflex. She'd met Brad's uncle. He seemed the only agreeable and grounded Draper in the family.

Clint finished his conversation with Jenna and stood next to Leah as they watched the last part of the press conference. The state cops didn't spell out all of their evidence, but it was obvious they'd decided that the jury tampering investigation going on from Leah's first trial was related to Prosecutor Birch's death.

"Was Birch a Hangman?" Clint asked.

"I don't know. He was a good friend of Harden's." She crossed her arms. "It was good of Jenna to call."

"She's been working hard on this case for months." He smiled. "She's almost as determined as you."

"You two are close."

He shrugged. "I've known her a long time. We met at a training class years ago. She's sharp as a tack and a great investigator."

Leah nodded. "Can I ask you a question?"

"Of course."

"It's just that, well . . . after corresponding with you for two years, I've come to know you, and I like what I know. But if you and Jenna—"

"Stop." Clint stepped forward and looped his right arm around Leah's waist, gently pulling her close. With the fingers on his casted arm, he held her hand.

Her other arm went naturally to his shoulder and her head tilted back as she looked up into his eyes. They seemed to smolder with emotion.

"Leah, there is no 'me and Jenna.' I told you in my letters that I had a crush on you in college. I did. I do. You are the only woman in my heart and my mind right now."

"Oh" was all Leah could manage as Clint's grip tightened and he leaned closer.

"I've wanted to be this close to you for such a long time," he whispered as he pressed his lips to hers.

Leah relaxed and leaned into the kiss, amazed at the warmth and fire in his embrace, feeling as if the entire ugly world disappeared and there was only her and Clint in amazing bliss.

CHAPTER 54

After Clint left, Leah found herself humming one of her father's show tunes and walking on air. They were in sync, each feeling the same way about the other. *Yes,* she thought, *the future does look good, job or no job.*

They'd agreed to turn the drive over to the FBI, and Clint was on his way to deliver it to Agent Falcon. Leah had wanted to go with him, but the next stop for Clint was his own house. He'd admitted to her that he'd overdone it just a little bit and needed rest. And he said he'd call her when he got there.

While she waited for the call, Leah fidgeted. The pleasant warmth she felt from the kiss faded slowly. To keep busy, she decided to finish with her belongings. She'd sorted everything already; now she needed to organize and put away. As she worked, she wondered what the ramifications would be now that Brad's uncle was in the spotlight. Harden would not be happy—that was for sure. She shivered at the thought of Birch's death possibly being a murder. She'd liked Birch years ago—or at least she knew Brad had liked him.

She was bending over a box when a thought flashed in her mind and she stood up abruptly. Cutting through the clouds of pleasant emotions regarding Clint, Leah realized how serious this was if the city prosecutor had been murdered because of her case. Was he killed to keep investigators in the dark about what had gone on in the first trial? Did the Hangmen kill him? Two different people had tried to kill her in prison; was that also the work of the Hangmen?

All of a sudden being isolated at her father's place didn't seem like such a good idea. Richard Chambers had snuck up on her easy enough.

So Leah did something she hadn't wanted to do because it would be a violation of the protective order. She went into the garage to her father's gun safe. She unlocked it and removed a 9mm handgun. She then loaded two clips, put one in the gun, racked a round in the chamber, and took the items to her room.

Protective order or not, Leah would be prepared the next time someone surprised her on her father's property.

It was nearly dark by the time Leah finished organizing. Tomorrow she'd tackle the storage unit. She turned on lights and checked the time. Her father should be home by now. She picked up her phone and thought about calling him.

"Am I being paranoid?" she asked Buster.

He didn't answer, simply wagged his tail and shuffled his feet. Leah realized it was time to feed him. She picked up his bowl and filled it with puppy chow. Just then her father's headlights swept by the front window and she sighed with relief. When he walked inside whistling a tune she recognized from *West Side Story*, Leah chuckled.

"Hey, Dad."

"Hi, sweet pea." He came to where she stood and kissed her cheek. "How's your day been?" he asked.

Thinking of Clint, Leah grinned. "Best day since my release."

"Glad to hear it." He filled up a glass with water. "I heard about Dave Draper on the radio. It surprised me, but maybe it shouldn't. The whole Draper family is corrupt."

"Yeah, and because of that I took a gun from your gun safe. I want to keep it in my room."

"Fine with me. You know how to use it."

She walked back into the living room in time to see a vehicle pull into the driveway. It was a white BMW. Not a common car in the valley. Leah tensed, wondering if she should retrieve the gun. Her jaw dropped on the floor when she saw Ivy Draper in the driver's seat. What on earth was up?

CHAPTER 55

As Clint left Leah's house and headed back to Table Rock, he felt giddy, a looseness in his brain, almost like the day he'd gotten the concussion. Finally telling Leah how he felt had lifted a huge weight from his heart—and finding out she felt the same way caused all the indecision and uncertainly to disappear. It was a game changer—Leah cared for him too.

Daylight was fading, but to Clint, everything was bright. Every so often a grin split his face. He'd dated women before, but never had the depth of emotion affected him like what he felt toward Leah. She was the *one* and he prayed for a way forward, for all of this controversy and unsettledness to be resolved. Hopefully the drive he had in his pocket would do that. It was a leap, true, but there was a reason it'd been hidden away in a locked gun case.

Falcon had been skeptical at first, but after Leah explained everything, he agreed that the FBI techs would be best suited to look into what was on the drive. Clint still didn't believe Falcon was on his side, but he did believe the agent was on Leah's.

It was just getting dark enough for headlights, and when the vehicle behind him turned its on, Clint did a double take in the rearview mirror. The truck was awfully close. How long had it been behind him? He'd turned off the highway a couple of miles ago to take back roads into Table Rock and now wished he had paid closer attention to the vehicles around him. He couldn't make out the face behind the wheel and realized if it was a tail, the driver wasn't taking any pains to hide it. Clint recognized what a poor choice he'd made turning off the highway.

He sped up and the truck behind him did likewise. Clint slowed, waving the truck around him, but the truck stayed where it was.

Why would someone follow me into Table Rock? Clint wondered. This two-lane highway was straight and flat. There was no way to push him off the side like they did on Foothill—then he realized that in about two miles, if they did try that same tack, he'd end up in the icy Rogue River. Was that the plan?

Chewing on his lower lip and thankful for hands-free, Clint called Agent Falcon just as the truck behind hit him with high beams. He told the agent what was going on.

"Where are you?" Falcon asked.

"About six miles out, closing in on Duster's Creek bridge."

Just then Clint saw the truck swerve left as if it was going to go around, but Clint tensed. He recognized the move. The guy was going to try to smack the left side of the bumper in a PIT maneuver and cause Clint to spin out of control.

If that happened, there was no way he'd be able to control his truck without two good hands.

"Tanner, what's going on?"

Clint couldn't answer. He sped up and abruptly jerked his truck to the right, off the road, smashing through a fence and barely keeping control of the vehicle as the follow truck screeched to a stop. Apologizing in his mind to the farmer whose fence he'd obliterated, Clint shifted into four-wheel drive and took off across the field as fast as he dared. Thankfully the ground was mostly level and there was no dust. Provided there were no impassable gullies, he could make it back to the roadway past Duster's Creek bridge. It was a short two miles into town by then and he'd avoid the PIT.

In his rearview mirror, he could see that the truck behind him had taken a minute to turn around and follow the surprise path Clint had taken.

"You still there, Falcon?" Clint asked, grimacing as the bouncy path he was driving took its toll. Every bump and bruise screamed at him. There was silence from the phone and Clint didn't try to get him back. He concentrated on controlling his vehicle and staying ahead of the truck on his tail.

He thought of Leah, wondering if she was in danger. Torn between calling her and needing to concentrate on the road ahead, Clint prayed that this was all about him and she was fine.

+ + +

Leah opened the front door and stepped onto the porch as Ivy got out of her car.

"Ivy, what brings you out here?"

Ivy jumped. She looked as far from comfortable as a person could. She stopped about five feet from the porch and stared at Leah. Finally she said, "I've come to you for help."

Leah let the surprise show. "How can I help you?"

"I know you have a storage drive that my father wants."

Nonplussed, Leah frowned. "And if I do?"

"My father plans to kill you and Clint Tanner to get that drive back."

Shocked now, Leah held her hands out, palms up. "You're telling me this because . . . ?"

"I know you have no reason to trust me. Becky was just here, at your house, wasn't she?"

Leah nodded.

"She saw the gun case they've been looking for and came over to my parents' to tell my father about it. I overheard the conversation. Brad hid the storage drive in the case a long time ago. It was his insurance policy."

"Insurance for what?"

"Brad stored stuff on the drive that gave him leverage. My dad has dangerous business partners. Brad controlled them. When you killed him, my father lost control. He wants it back. Becky claims to want to help him, but I don't believe a thing she says. I think Brad has things on the drive about her."

Leah had to think. "You know how crazy this sounds?"

"Any crazier than the Hangmen controlling law enforcement in Table Rock? Any crazier than you going to prison for killing a man who I'm sure was trying to kill you?"

Leah stared at Ivy.

"Brad tried to kill Melody. Why do you think she left?" Tears fell from Ivy's eyes. "Melody was always going against him. She resented that my father favored Brad over both of us. She was Brad's thorn in the side. He beat her half to death and my father said nothing. I never had her courage. I never talked back. But I can't stand by and watch them kill Grady. They plan to get the drive back, then kill you and Tanner and frame Grady for it. I heard it all."

Leah felt as if the ground shifted beneath her. Fear threatened to split her in two. "I—"

The ring of her phone interrupted a response. It was Falcon. She held her hand up to stop Ivy from saying more. "I have to take this."

"Radcliff, where is Clint Tanner?" Falcon was abrupt.

"What? He should be with you. He left here—" she looked at the time on her phone—"probably twenty minutes ago." Leah's hand felt numb. Ivy just watched.

"He called me, said someone was following him; then the call dropped."

"Did he say where he was?"

"Coming up on Duster's Creek bridge. I see that on the map. It's a back road, farmland and such—"

"I know the area." Leah tried to think, tried to beat back the panic. "Did you call him back?"

"I did. We didn't connect. He should have been here by now, no?"

"Yes, he should have." The area around Duster's Creek bridge did have dead spots for cell phone coverage. But Clint should have been in Table Rock by now, dead spots notwithstanding.

"I'm going to head out that way, try to follow his path," Leah said.

"All right, me and my partner will head out from this end and hopefully we'll meet you and him in the middle."

Leah lowered the phone.

Ivy's expression was annoyingly knowing. "That was about Clint Tanner, wasn't it?"

The phone seemed frozen in Leah's hand. "Yes, it was. Someone was following him after he left here."

"I bet I know who. Leah, you have to trust me," she pleaded.

"We have to do something. Maybe we're not friends, but I care about Grady. I don't want him dead."

✦ ✦ ✦

Clint struggled to control the truck and felt he was losing. The topography of the field made him turn north, taking him farther away from Table Rock. He was above Duster's Creek bridge now, in the farming area outside the city limits. The truck following him was minutes behind him.

He came to an irrigation ditch and slowed. Even with four-wheel drive, this would be tricky. He angled the truck into the ditch and then punched it, roaring up and out, right into a fence post. The truck bounced and groaned, freed from the water, then tangled and stuck on the post and a mass of barbed wire.

He tried to work the truck out of the mess and couldn't.

"Think, Tanner, think," Clint talked to himself. He had to get out of the truck.

He opened the door and stopped, not wanting to be caught with the drive on his person. Quickly he opened the glove box and yanked his Bible out. He shoved the drive into the pocket that bulged with all the church bulletins he never threw out. After putting the Bible back in the glove box, he prayed that God would protect it and got out of the car.

The headlights were almost upon him. Clint knew he needed to move fast. Conscious of every ache, he headed for the edge of the field where there was some tree cover. Once behind a tree, he tried to redial Falcon, only to see that he was in a dead zone. It was anyone's guess where he'd get cell coverage. Clint took stock of his surroundings, looking for landmarks. Off to the right he saw one, an old water tower that used to say

Table Rock but now only said *a e oc* . If he remembered right, the tower could be seen from Marvin Sapp's backyard. A ray of hope brightened in his heart and he started in the direction he believed would take him there.

Clint trudged downward as quickly as he could. Even in the low light, he started to see backyards. He had a good sense of direction and knew he was close, but he needed to call Marvin to be sure.

"Yes." He gave a fist pump when he saw that now he had a signal. He found Marvin in his contacts. "Marvin, it's Clint—you home?"

"Just got here. What's up, buddy?"

"I'm in a bit of a bind. Can you step into your backyard and shine a light?"

"What?"

"I'll explain when I get there."

"You're coming here? Uh, okay, I guess."

Clint waited. A few seconds later, he saw the light. "That's good, Marvin. I'll be right there." Sweating even in the frigid temp, Clint made his way down the hill to Marvin's house. A minute later he was at the back door.

Marvin met him there. "What is going on?"

Breathing hard, Clint wiped sweat from his forehead. "Long story. I need to make a phone call."

He stepped into the house and pulled his phone out of his pocket. Just as he was about to hit redial for Falcon, he felt a hard poke in his back.

He turned; Marvin held him at gunpoint. Realization dawned.

"Sorry, Clint; you'll have to give me the phone and your gun."

Breath slowly returning to normal, Clint complied. "You're the leak."

"Nothing personal; I like you. I just like money more. Now have a seat while we wait for my colleagues to arrive. They were happy to hear that you called me." He motioned with his gun and Clint sat down in a chair in the living room.

"The Hangmen?"

"No, people we work with."

"You're a Hangman?"

"I am."

"Why?"

"Why not? It's a little bit extra for a guy like me. I was flattered when Brad asked me in."

"Why pretend to be Leah's friend? You called me in after the shooting."

"I like Leah too," he laughed. "Oddly, she did us a favor that day, killing Brad. He was a control freak. Everything is spread around a little more evenly now that he's gone. If it were up to me, I'd have left her alone, might even have given her a medal, but it isn't up to me."

Clint quit trying to process Marvin being a traitor and tried to think of a way out of this mess. Best to keep Marvin talking.

"Is that what the Hangmen are about, making money?"

Marvin nodded. "You were never going to beat the smuggling, Clint. We have it all wired, with a lot of important people everywhere. You're a good cop and you tried, but everything is aligned against you."

"Was it the Hangmen who tried to kill me?"

"No, the people we work with. I told you—nothing personal; it's business."

"So that's what this is now? Business to kill me?"

Just then Marvin's front door opened, and two men came in. A tall, blond, bearded man Clint felt he should know but couldn't place, and another man he recognized, one of the Russians he had arrested. Gregor was his name, Clint remembered.

"I want the flash drive," the bearded man demanded, looking straight at Clint.

"What flash drive?"

He turned to Marvin. "You search him?"

Marvin shook his head. "I just took his gun and phone."

"Stand up." The bearded man motioned to Clint. When Clint didn't move to stand right away, he pulled a gun. "Look, it will be just as easy to shoot you and search your dead body."

Clint held his gaze and slowly stood. Something about the man seemed familiar. He looked like Grant Holloway, but his expression was too hard and angry.

Gregor stepped up and searched Clint none too gently. He removed Clint's wallet and tossed it next to his phone. When he finished, he turned to the bearded guy. "Nothing on him."

"Sit back down," Marvin ordered.

Clint sat back in the chair, tense, watching and listening.

The bearded man turned to Marvin. "Ivan is searching the truck. Maybe he left it there."

"It would be easier all around if you just gave it to us," Marvin said.

Clint said nothing.

A few minutes later the door opened again, and Clint recognized the second Russian as Ivan. He was breathing hard; obviously he'd been running.

"Nothing in the truck; I even cut open the seats. He didn't hide it there." He spoke in Russian and Clint winced. He'd loved that truck.

"The girl must have it," Ivan said, and Clint nearly came up out of the chair.

Bearded Man chuckled. He also spoke in Russian. "You

understood, and that bothered you, didn't it? If the girl has it, Duke will get it. He's probably got the girl as we speak."

Clint gripped the armrest tight with his good hand, praying Leah was not in Duke's hands.

"If he holds nothing, can I kill him?" Ivan asked.

"Stop with the Russian," Marvin protested. "Speak English."

"Ivan's ready to put this man out of his misery," Bearded Man said.

"Not in my house, he's not."

"It's not going to happen here anyway. We need the drive. No one dies until we have the drive. Period. Once we have the woman, the rest of the plan will proceed." He regarded Clint with eyes so dark they resembled pools of oil. They were devoid of emotion or compassion, and Clint knew that if this man had his way, he and Leah would soon be dead.

CHAPTER 56

I vy was certain Duke was on his way to pick Leah up.

"He's going to try and convince you to go with him to the farmhouse of your own volition."

"And if I refuse?" Leah asked, still wondering whose side Ivy was really on.

"My father told him not to take no for an answer. He plans to end everything at the farmhouse—I swear, Leah."

Leah exchanged glances with her dad, who looked as unsure as she felt.

"I'll hide your car," Randy said. "If what you're saying is true, and Duke does show up, at least he won't know that we're on to him."

Randy went out to pull Ivy's BMW around behind the barn.

Leah invited Ivy to take a seat. "Why are you on my side all of a sudden?" she asked.

"Because I realize we have a common enemy. I did hate you

once, after you killed Brad. In reality, you made my life easier, finally; you set me free. Brad and my father are bullies, and they have taken from me my entire life." Her voice broke and she chewed on a fingernail that looked raw to Leah. "First Melody and then Grady. I doubt I'll ever see Melody again. I don't want to say the same about Grady."

There was no time to talk about Melody, though Leah had questions. She focused on Grady and Ivy.

"Even if he's married to someone else?"

"Grady and I were just starting to date when Becky set her sights on him and Brad told me to stay away. Becky manipulated him. Recently they've been fighting. When she and my father were talking, I heard her say she's had it with Grady because he's not tough enough."

"Why would Becky be okay with her husband being murdered?"

"Becky thought she could make Grady like Brad. But Grady is good inside. He'll never be a bully."

"You're wrong. I know Becky—she loves Grady." Leah could not see where this was going.

"You weren't dating Brad yet when Becky and Duke came to town. They helped resurrect my dad's business when Costco nearly bankrupted him. They brought that stupid Colin with them—"

"Wait, what? Colin? What's his last name?"

"I don't know. All I know is that the three of them—Colin, Becky, and Duke—came to my father with a business proposition years ago. Everything went wrong after that. You think you know Becky, but she puts on an act. She's ruthless and cold like her brother. Grady came to your house in the middle of the night after Brad's house burned, didn't he?"

"He did."

"My dad ordered him out here. He's got something on Grady. I don't know what. He didn't kick your door in like my dad wanted. They think he's weak. They're trying to control everything."

"Who is *they*?"

"My dad, Becky, Duke, Larry Ripley. My dad calls the valley his domain. He has Ripley where he wants him and other people in various parts of the government, but Grady is the weak link."

Her father interrupted. "Leah, we have more company."

Leah walked to the front window and saw Duke Gill climbing out of a car.

Ivy paled. "I told you," she said. "He's going to try to take you to some farm where they can kill you and blame it on Grady."

Leah looked at her father, who shrugged. "I already didn't trust Duke. He's too close to Harden."

She nodded. "Go back in the kitchen, Ivy. We'll deal with this."

Ivy complied.

Leah retrieved her dad's handgun and put it in the waistband of her jeans at the small of her back and opened the front door. Duke had stopped short of the porch. He was texting.

"What are you doing here?"

He looked up. "You never could be civil to me, could you?" The toothpick hanging out of his mouth bounced as he talked.

"Spare me the victim act. I'm on my way out. You'll have to move your car."

"You're not going anywhere unless it's with me," Duke said, rolling his toothpick from the left side of his mouth to the right. He also shifted so that Leah could see the gun on his hip. "I hear you have something that belongs to Larry."

"What would that be?"

"The gun case," Duke said. "According to Larry, it was in Brad's house. He thought he lost it when the house burned down, but now we know that isn't what happened. Becky saw the case."

"If he had a gun case in Brad's house, why would I know anything about it?"

"Spare me the stupid act." He smirked and glanced at his phone when a text message pinged.

Leah casually put her hand behind her back.

Duke shoved the phone in his pocket and held his hands up. "The case is all I want."

Leah fidgeted, thinking about Clint and what Ivy had said. If they didn't have the thumb drive, they didn't have Clint. Where was he? She needed to be out looking for him, not sparring with Duke. Time to be blunt.

"I don't have it."

"Where is it?"

Leah shrugged.

He motioned toward his car. "Why don't you come with me and explain to Harden where it is?"

"I'm not going anywhere with you."

Duke stepped toward her, right hand reaching for his gun.

"That's far enough."

Leah heard her father, but she didn't turn. She also heard the distinctive sound of a shotgun shell being racked into the chamber.

"I know how to use this. You pull that gun on my daughter and you're dead."

Duke dropped his hand, angry surprise crossing his features. "Randy, relax; no one here is threatening violence."

"I don't care what you came for or what you want. You leave my daughter alone."

Duke twitched and the shotgun boomed as Randy fired a warning shot. Everyone ducked.

"I ain't playing." He racked another round. "I called the sheriff. He'll be here shortly, and we'll settle this mess once and for all."

Duke smiled and folded his arms. "That's fine with me. I have no problem waiting for the sheriff."

Leah did not miss the smug expression. She fought the urge to turn back to her dad and ask him what he was thinking. Maybe he thought Jack would come, and she prayed that was what would happen. They couldn't trust Grady. But what would Grady say if Ivy told him what she'd heard?

A few seconds later a sheriff's car roared up the drive. Leah tensed.

Grady stepped out of the car. He seemed surprised by what he saw. "What's going on here, Randy, Leah?"

"What's going on is me, your county commissioner, is being held at gunpoint." Duke spoke up before Leah could. "I'm ready to place both Randy and Leah under citizen's arrest for this affront."

Leah glanced toward her father; he didn't lower the shotgun. The ball was in Grady's court.

He made his side clear when he unsnapped his holster. "Randy, put the shotgun down."

"No, Dad, don't."

Grady looked at her, surprise in his eyes. "Haven't you learned your lesson, Leah? You want to get your father in trouble too?"

"Duke threatened my daughter," Randy said. "He's the one who should be arrested."

Duke laughed outright, holding his hands out, palms up. "He's got the shotgun. Fired it too. You can see for yourself what's what, Sheriff."

"Randy, I insist—"

"Don't do this, Grady." Ivy stepped out onto the porch.

Grady's eyes went wide. "Ivy, what in the world are you doing here?"

"Trying to save you. Becky's betrayed you."

Leah tuned Ivy out, concentrating on Duke. She saw his eyes narrow and his features fold into fury.

"What are you talking about?" Grady asked.

"My father sent Duke here to pick Leah up and take her to Larkspur Farms, didn't he?"

Duke flinched; his hand strayed toward his weapon. Leah drew hers and held it down at her side.

Grady didn't answer Ivy; he seemed speechless. His attention stayed on her, though. Leah saw a lot of emotions cross his features.

"Ivy, shut up," Duke ordered.

"I won't shut up. They plan to kill you, Grady, and make it look like Leah or Tanner did it. You'll be the hero—dead, bu—"

Duke drew his weapon. Leah brought hers up on target as he raised his. They fired at the same time. He jerked right and she missed. Before she could fire again, her father's shotgun boomed on her left and Grady's handgun boomed on her right. Duke was hit before he found cover. He slammed into the car, dropping his weapon and falling to his knees.

Leah dropped to one knee and turned toward Grady. But he was no threat to her. He'd reholstered his gun and jumped up on the porch toward Ivy, who was down. Everyone had been a second too late; Duke's bullet found its mark.

Returning her attention to Duke, now flat and not moving, Leah ran to him and picked up his gun.

"You'll regret this," he said, holding his bleeding midsection. "Becky will see that you regret this. Tanner is already dead."

Leah looked away and shuddered as fear threatened to choke the life out of her. *Clint could not be dead.*

She looked back down. Duke's breathing was labored, and he closed his eyes. The phone in his pocket pinged with a text that wasn't going to be answered.

"Can you watch him, Dad?"

He nodded, a little pale, but Leah knew he'd be fine.

Leah turned toward the porch, where Grady cradled a bleeding Ivy in his lap.

+ + +

"What's taking them so long?" Marvin asked.

Clint watched the man he'd thought was his friend fidget. The bearded guy was as cool as a cucumber. He'd been texting someone; now he waited for a reply. Clint was now certain that the bearded guy was Colin Hess, the FBI's fugitive. Nothing else made sense.

"Duke might have to convince her. He's probably doing a lot of talking." He stood, and Clint didn't miss the glance between Colin and Ivan. "Let's get started for the designated spot."

"We're supposed to wait," Marvin protested.

"I just texted to let them know there's a change in plans." He looked at Clint. "Stand up."

"Where are you taking me?" Clint asked as he stood.

"You'll see." He pointed to Ivan. "Tie him up. I don't think handcuffs will go around his cast."

"I have rope in the truck." Ivan darted out of the house.

Colin tossed his car keys to Gregor. "After he gets the rope, you go, set things up."

Gregor caught the keys, nodded, then headed out the door.

Hess moved slowly toward the counter. He picked up Clint's gun from the counter where Marvin had set it. In one smooth move with no hesitation or wasted motion, he pointed it at Marvin and shot him in the head.

Clint flinched as blood sprayed all over him and Marvin's body dropped to the floor.

"I hate loose ends," Colin said, smiling. "Thank you for killing him for me."

"Because you used my gun, that's going to be your story? That will never fly." Clint spoke confidently but inside he felt anything but confident. Marvin lived far enough away from his neighbors that it was doubtful anyone would have heard the shot. Hess was as cold a crook as he'd ever dealt with, and he was armed. Clint wasn't.

"I think it will. After all you were quite upset when you found out he was your leak. It makes sense that you would kill him."

Ivan came back inside with a length of rope and secured Clint's hands behind his back.

Hess grabbed Marvin's car keys. "This way," he said. "You're going to steal your friend's car."

Clint had no choice but to climb into the back of Marvin's SUV. Ivan sat beside him and Hess got behind the wheel.

Clint felt helpless . . . but that didn't stop him from praying. Foremost in his prayer was that Leah avoid whatever fate Hess had planned for them.

CHAPTER 57

L eah called 911 as Grady tried to comfort a bleeding Ivy.

"They want to destroy you," Ivy whispered.

"Quiet, Ivy. Save your strength," Grady said as he pressed the gauze pack Randy had given him to Ivy's shoulder. Her wound was bleeding a lot.

Duke had breathed his last while Leah tried to stop his bleeding. She'd barely ended the call with 911 when another sheriff's vehicle pulled up. It was Jack.

"Sorry it took me so long, Randy—" Jack's eyes widened as he took in the scene before him. He rushed up to the porch. "What is going on, Leah?"

"It's a long story. Grady will have to tell you; I have to find Clint."

Jack tore his eyes away from Ivy and back to Leah. "Where is Clint? I've tried to call him and got nothing. That's not like him."

As quickly as she could, Leah told him what happened.

"Larkspur Farms?"

"Ivy says that's where Grady was supposed to take us. My guess is that Clint is already there."

"He is," Grady said without taking his eyes off Ivy. "They want something you have. I was supposed to go along with you and Duke to the farm so they could talk to the both of you. They felt my presence would put you and Clint at ease." He looked up, tears in his eyes. "That's what they said, just talk." He returned his attention to Ivy.

Jack took Leah's arm. "You can't go running off by yourself."

"I won't be. The FBI is looking for Clint as well. Now I can tell them where he is. I'm going to call as I go."

"And I'll be with her," Randy said. He'd been helping with Ivy since Duke was beyond their help.

"No, Dad, you need to stay here and explain this mess. How Duke got shot."

He started to argue but Grady interrupted.

"I'll go with her, Randy. Please stay and look after Ivy." He pointed to the pressure bandage on her shoulder.

Randy acquiesced and took Grady's place.

Grady wiped blood from his hands.

"Grady, you—" Leah protested, not sure if she could trust him.

"I'm part of this. I never wanted to be, but I am. I can tell you and the FBI guys everything that was supposed to happen."

Leah studied the man. He was shaken, that was for sure.

"If you're lying, Grady . . . ," Randy said.

Grady turned to him. "I promise to do what I've been sworn to do. I'm a parent too. I'll protect Leah."

That seemed to mollify Randy.

"All right, follow me. I'll call Falcon and tell him that we are on the way." Leaving Jack and her father to deal with Duke and Ivy, Leah climbed into her father's truck, since her car was blocked in.

The ambulance arrived as she started the engine. Leah was confident everyone would be taken care off. She headed down the driveway, Grady behind her. She didn't get a chance to call Falcon; he called her.

"We found Tanner's truck." Falcon's words almost made Leah's heart stop. It started again when he explained how they'd found a broken fence line, almost by accident. They followed the trail and came upon Clint's truck stuck on a fence post.

"Somebody searched it," Falcon said. "They ran a knife through the seats and tossed out everything in it. No sign of Tanner though."

"I know where he is." As quickly as she could, Leah told the man what had just transpired.

The line went quiet.

"You still there, Falcon?"

"I am. I'm just a little speechless."

"Try this on for size: Ivy claims that someone named Colin is the heavy muscle behind everything."

"You believe her?"

"I believe she's in a position to know a lot."

"She could be setting you up."

"How? She just got shot for telling me what she knew."

There was silence again as she made the turn for Sams Valley and Larkspur Farms. She'd be there in ten minutes.

Falcon came back on. "My partner and I were reviewing the list of addresses we have, of people we wanted to talk to or have already talked to. Marvin Sapp lives near here. Is it possible Tanner would go to his house?"

That gave Leah pause. Clint would go to Marvin's if he got

away from his pursuers. Relief was quickly replaced by fear. If he had gone to Marvin's, why hadn't he called?

"I'm staying the course for Larkspur Farms."

"Radcliff, if he's there with Colin Hess, you're heading for trouble. Will you wait for us to get a handle on things?"

She didn't answer him. All she knew was that she had to save Clint, no matter what.

+ + +

Even in the dark it didn't take Clint long to figure out where they were going. Larkspur Farms.

The place was still sealed with police tape when the SUV's headlights flashed across the front door. There was another vehicle in the drive, off to the right. Hess got out, as did the driver of the other car. Clint squinted in the dark, but he couldn't make out the face. Then he heard a raised voice.

"*Why did you want me out here in the middle of nowhere? Can't you handle this yourself?*"

He frowned in the dark. That sounded an awful lot like Harden Draper.

Ivan opened the door and walked over to Clint's side to pull him out. Clint stepped out and was face-to-face with Draper. And the man wasn't alone—Becky Blanchard was with him.

"Where's Grady?" Colin asked.

"He should be here, but he's not answering my texts," Becky said. She offered Clint a frosty glare. "There was a shooting at the Radcliff residence. I heard it on the scanner. A female required medical attention. Maybe he took care of her there."

Clint stiffened and fought the urge to throttle Becky. If Leah was shot . . . No, he wouldn't entertain the worst-case scenario.

"I don't like maybes," Colin growled. "If he killed her there, he's ruined the plan. What about Duke?"

"He's not answering either. But he can handle things. I'm not worried. We'll figure something out. Get Tanner inside."

"I still don't know why I needed to be here for this," Harden complained. "I paid you all well to get the drive back. You could have brought it to me in the comfort of my own home."

Ivan grabbed Clint's arm to pull him into the house. At the same time, Colin swung a clenched fist and hit Harden with a sucker punch on the left side of his head. Harden went down like a sack of potatoes.

Clint stopped and stared in shock only to be jerked along by Ivan. He heard part of the ensuing argument as he was dragged into the house.

"Was that really necessary?" Becky asked.

"Yeah, for me it was. He was getting on my nerves. We're tying up loose ends, aren't we?"

"Now you have to carry him inside."

Clint couldn't hear the rest as he was taken to the back of the house, to the very room where he'd found the puppy. Ivan grabbed a chair and put it in the middle of the room. He jerked Clint toward it, and Clint realized he was going to be untied and then retied to the chair. But not with rope. Ivan now had a roll of duct tape.

This would be his only chance to break free, and he knew he couldn't waste it. Ivan stepped behind him and began to undo the knots. Bracing himself for the pain, Clint prayed the Russian would undo his good arm first, and that was just what Ivan did. As quickly as his sore, battered body would allow, Clint twisted around, catching Ivan by surprise. He looped his good arm around the Russian's neck even as the man tightened his grip on the rope around the cast.

Clint squeezed his bicep and forearm muscles over Ivan's carotid arteries as the man struggled to gain leverage by pulling on the cast. The pain in his bad arm was intense, but Clint held on and squeezed. As Ivan lost the battle, his grip weakened. In minutes, the Russian went limp.

Clint let out the breath he was holding and slowly lowered the man to the floor. He took the rope around his cast off and secured Ivan with the duct tape as quickly as he could. Ivan had a gun in his belt, just a five-shot .38, but Clint was happy for the weapon. He had to get out of the house before Ivan sounded the alarm. He wouldn't be unconscious long.

Opening a window, Clint paused when he heard raised voices.

CHAPTER 58

When they reached the driveway to the farm, Leah pulled over and waved Grady to a stop. She wanted to talk to him. They had to have a plan.

"He might even already be dead." Grady's voice was grim.

"What?"

"Clint. All you might find here is a body."

Leah stared at Grady. All the life seemed to have gone out of his eyes. Blood spotted his uniform shirt, but his face was white as a sheet.

"Colin is ruthless. So is Becky, for that matter," he said.

"When all this is over, you'll have to tell me how you ended up with Becky when you obviously still care for Ivy."

"Secrets, Leah. Secrets." Profound sadness now colored his features. Leah was dying to know what he meant. But they had to get moving.

Grady stopped her once more. "If I don't make it out of this, I want my parents to take my son."

Leah nodded. "How do you want to do this?"

"Becky's been texting me. I just answered her and told her I'm on the way. I expect everyone to be in the farmhouse, so I'll do my job."

"What do you mean?"

"I mean I'm going to arrest them."

"On your own? That's suicide."

"What would you do? Rush in, guns blazing, to save Clint?" His empty eyes held hers and for a minute she had no answer.

"I know a back way in. I picked peaches here one summer. And I have the element of surprise," she said.

"Well, you do what you have to do, and I'm going to do what I have to." He turned to get back in his car.

Leah grabbed his arm. "Don't you get Clint killed."

He jerked his arm away and got back in his patrol car. With a growing sense of dread, Leah watched the car start up the drive.

When she climbed back in the truck, her phone rang. It was Falcon.

"Where are you?" he asked. When she told him, he said, "Don't go anywhere. We just kicked the door in at Marvin Sapp's house. He's been murdered."

"And Clint?"

"His wallet is here, no sign of him."

Leah banged her head back against the headrest. "Then you can't ask me to just wait until they shoot him. Grady already went up the drive. I couldn't stop him."

"At least wait until we get there."

"I can't, so you'd better hurry."

＊ ＊ ＊

Leah drove a little farther up the road. She found the back road to the orchard easily enough, but it was overgrown with a chain across it. She grabbed her father's tire iron but soon realized she didn't need to use it. The lock had been broken, then set back onto the chain to look closed.

Not having time to wonder about it, Leah got back in the truck and drove through. She traveled up the rough, overgrown road, apologizing in her mind to her dad for all the scratches. When she believed she was too close to the house for headlights, she turned them off.

Then she came to a spot where she could go no farther. There was a truck blocking her way. She put her vehicle in park and shut down the engine.

Her father had a couple of different flashlights in his work belt behind her seat. Leah grabbed a small one, gripped her gun, and got out. She walked around the parked vehicle and put her hand on the hood. It was warm; whoever had driven it here hadn't been here long.

Leah didn't recognize the truck but she wasn't going to let that stop her. She started for the house. The trail was as overgrown as the road, and since all the pear trees were gone, there wasn't a lot of cover for Leah. There were blackberry bushes scratching and scrabbling at her clothes.

As she approached the farmhouse, she could see lights on in two rooms. No one should be able to see her, though, unless they were looking. She was above the house now, and looking down, she counted two SUVs and one sheriff's vehicle. Where was Clint? What was Grady doing?

Movement off to the right caught her eye. She brought her

gun up. When she was sure she had her target, she flicked the flashlight on.

A large man squinted and turned toward her, gun in hand.

"Richard?" Leah said as she tried to process who was standing in front of her.

"Turn that light off," he hissed between clenched teeth.

Leah did and lowered her gun as well. Richard did the same.

"What are you doing here?" Leah whispered.

"I could ask you the same thing, but there's no time. I knew something would happen after Uncle Dave was caught. Their house of cards is imploding, and they will jump ship." He started toward the house.

Leah stepped in front of him, making him stop. "Are you ready to tell me now just what is going on?"

"As much as I can, Leah, but we have to hurry. If Tanner isn't dead already, he will be soon."

+ + +

Becky was yelling.

"You're going to have to wait, do you understand? Grady is on his way. I'm sure Duke will follow." The tone she took with Hess was like a mom scolding a toddler.

"I'm past trying to stage a scene to look one way or another. Things have gone sideways. It's time to cut our losses."

Hess's voice was level and calm. Clint strained to hear him.

"We're not leaving until Duke gets here, no matter what." Becky sounded more on edge, less in control.

Footsteps pounded, moving away, Clint thought.

"Grady is here now." Becky's voice was farther away from the room Clint was in. *"He's probably got Radcliff."*

Clint tensed. Then Hess said, *"He's by himself."*

If Grady was here, whose side was he on? Clint wondered.

"What do you think you're doing, Grady?" Becky said. *"Where's Radcliff? You couldn't handle one simple task?"*

"She doesn't matter anymore. I've had enough. I'm placing you all under arrest. And once you're booked, I'll turn myself in."

Derisive male laughter. Clint looked back at Ivan, who was stirring but still not fully awake. In his head he counted the number of people on the other side of the door. He could help Grady if Grady was really trying to do the right thing. Becky and Hess—it would be two on two. But one thing bothered him. Where was Gregor?

"Blanchard, you coward. No way you're taking me anywhere. Put the gun down and we'll let you walk away." Now Hess was angry.

Colin Hess would not go willingly; Clint knew that.

Ivan was beginning to move around now. Clint turned and saw the surprised anger in his eyes as the Russian came fully awake. He doubted they would hear him scraping around as they argued.

"Where's Duke?" Becky asked.

"He's already in custody."

"What do you mean?"

"I mean Radcliff took your big bad brother down."

At the mention of her name, Clint's heart rate spiked. *Leah is alive.*

"You'd better be lying." Becky's voice was cold and flat.

Clint tensed; something was going to happen.

"Ivan, get out here," Hess yelled. Then the gunfire started.

✦ ✦ ✦

"I saw them take Clint into the house." Chambers turned toward Leah.

"How long have you been here?"

"I told you—since I heard about Dave Draper. I knew they'd come back here before they left." His breath was visible in the frigid air. "They hid stuff in that barn that Tanner didn't find when he did his raid. You want to know what was going on that night all those years ago? I'll tell you." His voice low, Leah had to stay close to hear him. "Brad did take a payoff, but it was Larry who talked him into it."

They worked their way down toward the house.

"It was all about that trooper who got killed. That wasn't supposed to happen."

"You mean your smugglers weren't playing nice?"

"You could say that. Brad was furious. He was ready to chuck the whole thing, kill Hess, or turn him in. Larry convinced him not to be rash." Richard grunted in disgust. "I was hoping he wouldn't listen to Larry, but he did."

He faced Leah. "I wanted it to stop, but I'm a coward. Then you killed Brad, and I thought things would be over. But it only got worse. Hess took everything over. He's calling the shots and he's a killer, stone-cold."

Leah had to take a minute to process this. She'd come close to inadvertently exposing the smuggling operation. Brad had a chance to do the right thing and didn't. But then so did Richard. It made her angry. But anger wasn't going to change anything.

"So you retired and got out, put your head in the sand."

"I'm sorry, Leah. I knew what Brad was; I just didn't have the courage to back you. They would have killed me. They tried. I didn't destroy my knee at work. They let me live but promised if I ever set foot in Table Rock again, I'd be dead. I was in too deep myself. I'm no angel."

"And what about now?"

"I hate Hess. When your lawyer started poking the Hangmen

nest, I started keeping tabs on him. Things are getting way too hot. Then the FBI got here, and now Dave Draper's in trouble. He'll fold like a cheap suit."

He turned away and continued walking. "Hess has money and IDs galore in that barn. I saw one of his men head down that way. Hess is getting away over my dead body."

They were almost to the house when the first gunshots rang out. Fear didn't paralyze Leah; it made her move. Passing Chambers, she prayed as she ran. *Oh, Lord, please let Clint be alive.*

She skidded to a stop when she saw someone coming from the barn, running up the well-lit drive. He was holding a long gun and he wasn't FBI. His attention was on the house, and it gave her a chance to get the drop on him. She darted behind an SUV.

Behind cover, gun on target, she almost yelled, "Freeze!" Deciding against it, not wanting to make that much noise, she was trying to think when Chambers opened fire on the running man. He hit him several times. The rifle fell to the ground and so did the man, face-first in the driveway.

So much for not making any noise.

+ + +

Clint opened the door, trying to remember the layout of the farmhouse. After several rapid-fire shots, the gunfire had stopped.

Gun up, Clint tiptoed down the hall.

"Poor, stupid Grady." Becky's voice sounded mocking.

He stopped. Where was Hess? Everything was eerily quiet now. Clint remembered that the kitchen was off to the left. He had a sense that someone was on the other side of the door.

He lowered his shoulder and dove left into the doorway, straight into Hess. The big man went down with Clint on top of him. Clint lost the handgun he'd had, but so did Hess. Clint landed a right hand to the fugitive's face and felt the satisfying crunch of cartilage as he broke the man's nose.

Hess cursed but was barely stunned, and he countered with a hard left to Clint's battered rib cage. Something cracked and the pain blinded him, taking Clint's breath away. He rolled off of Hess and was trying to regroup when outside, more gunfire sounded. Clint wondered if the FBI had made it to the party.

Hess got up quickly and retrieved his gun, wiping blood from his nose.

He landed another kick to Clint's midsection, and all Clint could do was roll up into a ball and try to catch his breath. He looked up at Hess and prayed that Falcon or someone would find their way here. The only thing that gave him peace was the knowledge that at least Leah knew how he felt about her.

"Is that Gregor shooting outside? At what?" Hess called out.

"I can't see, and I'm not going to stick my head out the door," Becky responded. She rushed into the kitchen. "Just shoot him and let's get out of here through the back. We have to get Duke."

"Grady said Duke was in custody."

"So what? He's my brother. We're not leaving him."

Hess laughed. "He shouldn't have gotten caught. If you think I'm going to try a jailbreak, you're crazy."

From his position on the floor Clint could see the fury in Becky's face. It seemed to turn purple.

She directed her venom toward Hess. "We saved your butt; we made certain you had a place to start over and prosper. You are not going to desert Duke now."

Hess jerked his arm from her grasp, shoving her into the

wall. "I'm gone. They're never going to catch me. You're on your own."

He turned toward Clint, pointing the gun. Clint held his breath, waiting for the kill shot, then jumped when a gun fired. But he wasn't the one hit.

Becky fired her gun at least five times, hitting Hess every single time. The big man went down with surprise on his face and was still. Clint's nose burned from the acrid smell of expended rounds. He thought he heard sirens but decided it was his ears ringing from the gunfire.

Becky glared down at him. "Get up," she fairly snarled, features feral and crazed.

Clint rolled over slowly and pushed himself to his knees.

"You're going to help me get my brother out of jail."

"No, he's not."

Clint looked up in surprise and Becky turned.

Leah stood in the dining room, just outside the doorway. Pointing a gun. To Clint's pain-addled brain, she looked like an angel, bathed in light.

"Drop the gun, Becky."

"I thought you were shot. I heard it on the scanner." Becky didn't drop the gun.

"It was Ivy. Duke shot her."

"Ivy?" Becky looked as confused as Clint felt. What did Ivy have to do with any of this?

"Yeah, he shot Ivy and Grady shot him."

"What?"

"He's dead. You're not going to break him out of anything."

"*Dead?* You killed my brother?"

Clint could smell Becky's smoldering anger like he could smell the gunfire. Rising from the floor as fast as the pain allowed, he lurched into her. Her gun went off, the shot wild.

Becky screamed. He tried to hold her and couldn't.

She wrenched herself from his grasp and lunged toward Leah. Leah was ready with the signature quickness of a point guard. She caught Becky's right arm and stepped aside, using Becky's momentum to her advantage. Twisting Becky's wrist just the right way, Leah dropped to one knee, pulling Becky down, face-first.

Leah had her wrist in a picture-perfect twist lock as the door slammed open. Clint recognized Falcon and then Cross on his heels. The FBI agents took custody of Becky. Leah dropped her gun and rushed to Clint's side.

Clint relaxed into her embrace and the pain in his rib cage dulled somewhat. But every breath hurt, and he knew something was broken.

"How did you know to come here?" He leaned partially into the doorway. He saw worry crease her features and tried to smile. Breathing was agony.

"I'll tell you all about it. After I call for paramedics."

"I don't need paramedics," he said. "I just need you." That was the last thing he remembered.

CHAPTER 59

L eah rode with the medics as they hurried Clint to the hospital. Collapsed lung, they said. She could tell he was having trouble breathing. She prayed and held his hand.

Falcon had Becky Blanchard and Richard Chambers in custody. Leah hoped they'd open up and tell the authorities everything. Richard might, but Becky was doubtful.

Leah had already pieced things together in her mind. Harden had sold his soul to the devil to keep his businesses alive. Hess found the perfect spot in Table Rock because of the Hangmen. He was able to expand and grow his illegal business by paying Harden tribute. In return, Harden's Hangmen kept him safe.

Clint told Falcon where he'd left the flash drive. Leah was hopeful that it would help button things up. But right now, her only concern was Clint. As soon as they got to the hospital, he was taken into surgery, and she had to wait.

She called her father and discovered Ivy was alive and holding her own at a different hospital. While in the waiting room she watched as the cable news channels began reporting what had happened at Larkspur Farms.

"Three people are in custody, and three are dead, including Jackson County Commissioner Duke Gill. Four more remain hospitalized in unknown conditions. According to the FBI, the late-night callout was the culmination of a two-year investigation that branched off the Leah Radcliff shooting incident. People will remember Radcliff was . . ."

Leah tuned the rest out and got up to pace. Richard, Becky, and a man who was found tied up in a back room were the ones in custody. Hess, Duke, and the man Richard shot were the three dead, with Clint, Grady, Ivy, and Harden being the four hospitalized.

Leah had seen Harden on the floor of the farmhouse. At the time she'd thought he was dead but had since learned that while he'd suffered a head injury, he was alive. After all the trauma of the last few years, Leah wondered if Harden would stay that way to face justice. And what would happen to Larry? Would he weasel out of his part?

"I'm truly sorry I never came forward. The thin blue line deserved better than me," Richard had said to her before she left with Clint.

There were a lot of people who could say that.

"Thank God it's over," she whispered.

"Miss Radcliff?"

She turned. "Yes?"

"He's out of surgery and in recovery now. Everything went well. His prognosis is good."

"Thank you." Leah collapsed into a chair, tears of relief falling.

Later, they let her sit beside him as he slowly woke up. Without hesitation she gently ran a soothing hand over his brow. Outside, the morning sun was rising and she could see snow falling.

"Hey, is that you, Radcliff?"

Leah turned to see Clint regarding her with a dopey half smile on his face. She dropped her hand to the side and gripped his. "Yeah, Tanner, it's me."

"We have to stop meeting like this."

She laughed as the stress and fear faded. "You have to stop ending up in the hospital."

He chuckled. It was weak, but it sounded good.

"At least you don't have to ask me to look after your dog. My dad's got the little monster; he's driving Dad crazy."

"We'll have to work on that, train Buster to be a good dog."

"I agree."

"There's a lot we'll have to do together . . . always together. We make a good team."

She squeezed his hand with both of hers, happy tears falling. "Copy that, Clint Tanner."

This will be the best Christmas ever." Leah grinned as she put the last touches on the tree. The house smelled of roasting turkey, and also cinnamon and nutmeg because of the apple pie she had baking, and a steady, light snow was falling outside. It really felt like Christmas.

Randy gave her a hug. "Beautiful tree."

They were waiting for their guests. Clint was expected, along with Jack, Vicki, and their dates. The dining table extended from the kitchen, and Randy was itching to carve the turkey, fidgeting and humming "White Christmas." Even Buster got in on the act, dressed in Christmas finery, a big red bow on his collar.

The knock on the door was early, but Leah was ready. She flung the door open, her smile dying on her lips. "Falcon, what are you doing here?"

He grinned. "Merry Christmas to you too."

"Uh, merry Christmas. Come on in. I thought you were back in DC." She stepped aside to let Agent Falcon in.

"Smells great. Wish I could stay." He handed Leah a manila folder. "Here's the preliminary report. I thought you deserved a copy."

She took the folder. "That was fast. The government usually takes its time."

"There will be more. Becky Blanchard finally started talking."

"You trust what she's saying?"

"What we can corroborate. Turns out she had a mile-long rap sheet under the name Rebecca Gill. We knew Hess was a killer and that he had an unidentified partner."

"It's Becky?"

"Most likely. She and her brother were Hess's silent partners on the East Coast. They came to Oregon twelve years ago. Harden Draper's business was in danger of going under—too much competition from the big box stores. They had cash and a business plan. Hess stayed in the shadows, but he made things work. His connections to the Russian Mafia kept goods and money flowing for Draper."

That Harden Draper's business was a well-hidden smuggling operation had rocked the city of Table Rock. He'd survived to face the music, and Leah couldn't help but feel sorry for him. He was likely to die in prison with all the charges he was facing. Brad, his uncle, and all the well-placed people in important positions had covered for him for years. Judge Revel had even been caught up in the investigation. He'd retired abruptly and was waiting to be charged.

"I can read all of this for myself, and you could have mailed it. Why come out here on Christmas Day to hand it over?"

"There were some salient details I wanted to tell you in person. We learned that Draper did order the attempts on your life at Coffee Creek. Hess set things up. Both the women who attacked you were pressured and their families threatened."

Leah digested this. One of the women was dead; the other would be in jail a long time. She almost wished Hess wasn't dead so he would spend his life in a cage.

"And the storage drive was a gold mine," Falcon continued, "but it might not tell the whole story. The records kept on it were five years old."

"Meaning that anyone added to the Hangmen or Hess's operation in the intervening might stay hidden?"

"Yep. And we lost Ripley."

"What?"

"He skipped bail." Falcon held his hands out, palms up. "We believe he fled the country. He's made the most wanted list. There will be more charges after we complete the review of the storage drive."

Leah shook her head in disappointment. Larry had been indicted for perjury for the testimony he gave in Leah's trial. Grant Holloway turned state's evidence. He owed Hess a great deal of money due to a gambling debt. Since Holloway had the misfortune of resembling Hess, Larry decided to use it to their advantage. Ripley made up the story he told in court that Holloway was the person Leah saw collecting rent.

"Larry the weasel is gone, a fugitive. Duke is dead. A state senator and a county commissioner, not to mention cops and judges." Leah shook her head. "How is Table Rock ever going to survive this?" She'd already heard the city council talk of disbanding the PD and hiring the sheriff's department to patrol Table Rock, like they did Shady Cove and White City.

"Because there are still good people around to step into the spaces created by the indictments and make things right. Jackson County needs a new sheriff, for example; maybe you should throw your hat in the ring. You'd be in a position to help Table Rock rebuild, even more so if they do decide to disband the PD and hire the sheriff's department."

"Hear, hear," Randy called out from the kitchen before resuming his humming.

"I was only a cop for three years."

Falcon shrugged. "The sheriff is an elected position, part politician, part cop. Besides, you've got life experience that can't be bought. Think about it." He tipped his head. "And merry Christmas."

Leah set the folder aside after Falcon left. A few minutes later, Jack and his girlfriend arrived with Clint in tow.

Jack's girlfriend was a pleasant surprise. The woman in his life was Melody Draper. She'd been hiding in plain sight in Klamath Falls. Since Jack had grown up in the valley, he knew her well already. When he came across her in Klamath Falls, he kept her informed about Brad and her family. She'd left Table Rock to escape Brad and never contacted anyone, fearing if she did, Brad would find out and find her. That fear kept her away even after Brad died. It was only after she learned of her father's indictment that she felt safe enough to come home. From what Leah had heard, Ivy and Melody had a great reunion. They recently checked their mother into alcohol rehab.

Grady, sadly, did not survive. Whatever secret he'd had that kept him on Harden Draper's leash had died with him. Leah made certain the authorities knew about his wishes regarding his son.

Clint had spent a week in the hospital after surgery for a punctured lung, thanks to Colin Hess's kicking. He'd been released a couple weeks ago, but Leah was still glad he caught a ride with Jack and Melody. Melody resembled her mother, though she looked happier and more alert.

"Hey, long time no see," Clint said with a grin.

Leah returned the grin; she'd been at the hospital every single day. When she stepped up to give him a gentle hug, he pulled her close and tight.

"It's not that I don't like it, but I don't want to hurt you."

"Not possible," he whispered as he pressed his lips to hers. Leah gladly would have stayed like that, but Jack cleared his throat.

"No mistletoe there, guys."

Leah stepped back, blushing. Clint's eyes were warm and filled with amusement.

After Vicki and her date arrived, and they were all gathered around the table, Buster at Leah's feet, her father proposed a toast.

"To friends, family, and a God who handles all the details."

"And prayer," Leah chimed in. "To prayer, the first, best weapon for every battle."

"Hear, hear," Clint said. After the toast, he turned to Leah. "Now what's this I hear about you wanting to be sheriff?"

Leah started to protest but saw his eyes dancing with loving amusement, not mockery.

Then Jack joined the fray. "You've got my vote."

Conversation exploded around the table, and all Leah could do was sit back and bask in the glow of love and friendship and wonder, *What would it be like to be the sheriff?*

Turn the page for an excerpt from *Crisis Shot*, the thrilling first book in the Line of Duty series.

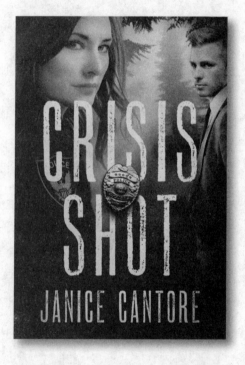

Available now in stores and online

Join the conversation at

1

"999! 999—" Click. The voice cut off.

Commander Tess O'Rourke was halfway to the station when the emergency call exploded from the radio. The frantic transmission punched like a physical blow. A triple 9—officer needs help—was only used when an officer was in the direst emergency.

Adrenaline blasted all the cobwebs from Tess's brain. Dispatch identified the unit as 2-Adam-9, JT Barnes, but had no luck getting the officer back on the air.

She was early, hadn't been able to sleep. Seven months

since Paul left and she still wasn't used to sleeping alone. After a fitful four-hour nap on the recliner in the living room, she'd given up, showered, and decided to head into work early in predawn darkness, at the same time all hell broke loose.

Tess tried to get on the radio to advise that she was practically on top of the call and would assist, but the click and static of too many units vying for airtime kept her from it. Pressing the accelerator, Tess steered toward Barnes's last known location.

A flashing police light bar illuminating the darkness just off Stearns caught her eye. She turned toward the lights onto a side street, and a jolt of fear bit hard at the sight of a black-and-white stopped in the middle of the street, driver's door open and no officer beside it. It was an area near the college, dense with apartment buildings and condos, cars lining both sides of the street.

She screeched to a stop and jammed her car into park as the dispatcher wrestled to get order back on the air.

Tess keyed her mike. Voice tight, eyes scanning. "Edward-7 is on scene, will advise" was her terse remark to the dispatcher.

She drew her service weapon and bolted from her unmarked car, cold air causing an involuntary inhale. Tess was dressed in a long-sleeved uniform but was acutely aware that she was minus a vest and a handheld radio. As commander of the East Patrol Division in Long Beach, her duties were administrative. Though in uniform, she wore only a belt holster, not a regular patrol Sam Browne. It had been six years since she worked a patrol beat as a sergeant in full uniform.

But one of her officers, a good one, was in trouble, and Tess was not wired to do nothing.

"JT?" she called out, breath hanging in the frigid air as her gaze swept first the area illuminated by yellow streetlights and then the empty car.

The only sounds she heard were the gentle rumble of the patrol car engine and the mechanical clicking of the light bar as it cycled through its flashes.

A spot of white in front of the car caught her eye and she jogged toward it. Illuminated by headlights were field interview cards scattered in front of the patrol unit as if JT had been interviewing someone and was interrupted, dropping the index cards.

Someone took off running.

She followed the line of cards between two parked cars and up on the sidewalk, where the trail ended, and then heard faint voices echoing from the alley behind an apartment building. Sprinting toward the noise across grass wet with dew, she rounded a darkened corner and saw three figures in a semicircle, a fourth kneeling on the ground next to a prone figure.

"Go on, cap him, dawg! Get the gat and cap him!"

Anger, fear, revulsion all swept through her like a gust of a hot Santa Ana wind. Tess instantly assessed what was happening: the black boots and dark wool uniform pants told her Barnes was on the ground.

"Police! Get away from him!" She rushed headlong toward the group, gun raised.

In a flood of cursing, the three standing figures bolted and ran, footfalls echoing in the alley. The fourth, a hoodie partially obscuring his face, looked her way but didn't stop what he was doing.

He was trying to wrench the gun from Barnes's holster.

Was Barnes dead? The question burned through Tess, hot and frightening.

"Move away! Move away now!" Tess advanced and was ignored.

Sirens sounded loud and Tess knew help was close. But the next instant changed everything. The figure gave up on the gun and threw himself across the prone officer, grabbing for something else. He turned toward Tess and pointed.

She fired.

A NOTE FROM THE AUTHOR

One of the first incidents of domestic violence I encountered when I was a uniformed police officer happened like this: I was new, low seniority, and working the police station business desk. We processed bails, took walk-in reports, and generally handled nonemergency situations. A young woman entered the lobby. She was obviously pregnant, and she had a black eye and bruised face and neck. She approached me and gave me a name, asking if the man was still in custody. (At that time, arrestees stayed in the city jail for up to three days. When time ran out, they were either released or sent to county jail, depending on the charges.)

I found the name in the booking log and saw that the man was in custody for domestic violence. He'd been arrested the night before. I gave her the information, and she told me she was dropping charges and that she wanted him released. I asked why, since she was obviously injured. She told me that she was fine, and the rent was due, so he needed to be released. Nothing I said would change her mind. I sent her up to the detective division. Since they were the ones responsible for filing charges, they were the ones who could drop them. (This was before laws that made it possible for the state to be the victim and keep the batterer in jail no matter what the victim said.)

Eventually the man was released. Sadly, this was not an isolated incident, and though new laws have helped some, too many women stay in abusive relationships. Sometimes the perception is they can "fix" the abuser; other times there is a perception they can't escape, or they need the abuser. Abusers escalate; they do not de-escalate unless forced to. The first man I arrested for homicide in my career had just shot his live-in girlfriend. Their problems and his abuse were well-known to neighbors and family, and the abuse only ended with her death.

Domestic violence affects women and men in all walks of life. The relationship that should provide the most comfort and protection is often the most painful. A heart change is the only thing that will stop abuse, and until the abuser is changed at that level, women and men need to do what will keep them safe. My prayer is that anyone in an abusive relationship would come to realize their worth in Christ. As a much-loved child of the King, they do not have to accept abusive behavior from anyone. Pray and ask for help. Resources are available. You are not alone.

ACKNOWLEDGMENTS

Thanks to Darrel Wiltrout, a prison chaplain and man of God who shows the love of Christ to the least of these by example.

ABOUT THE AUTHOR

A former Long Beach, California, police officer of twenty-two years, Janice Cantore worked a variety of assignments, including patrol, administration, juvenile investigations, and training. She's always enjoyed writing and published two short articles on faith at work for *Cop and Christ* and *Today's Christian Woman* before tackling novels. She now lives in Hawaii, where she enjoys ocean swimming, golfing, spending time on the beach, and going on long walks with her Labrador retrievers, Abbie and Tilly.

Janice writes suspense novels designed to keep readers engrossed and leave them inspired. *Breach of Honor* is her twelfth novel. Janice also authored the Line of Duty series—*Crisis Shot*, *Lethal Target*, and *Cold Aim*—the Cold Case Justice series—*Drawing Fire*, *Burning Proof*, and *Catching Heat*—the Pacific Coast Justice series—*Accused*, *Abducted*, and *Avenged*—and the Brinna Caruso novels, *Critical Pursuit* and *Visible Threat*.

Visit Janice's website at janicecantore.com and connect with her on Facebook at facebook.com/JaniceCantore and at the Romantic Suspense A-TEAM group.

DISCUSSION QUESTIONS

1. As a police officer, Leah Radcliff handles domestic violence cases from time to time, but she's unwilling to label her own situation at home as such. What makes her so reluctant to see Brad as an abuser? What does this tell you about victims of domestic violence?

2. Clint Tanner's scar is a physical reminder of a time he tried to be a hero. What does his dad remind him of after that event? What advice does Clint take to heart?

3. Leah struggles to maintain a positive outlook on life after being sent to prison. What snaps her out of her funk? How do you change your attitude when the world around seems dark and gray? What sorts of things improve your mood?

4. As Clint wrestles with the injustice of Leah's conviction, he encounters corruption within the police force. What consequences come as a result of this type of abuse of power, both in this story and in real life? Is it possible to have authorities who adhere to a moral code—and how is that moral code defined? Or is the promise of power too heady?

5. What advice does GiGi give Clint about getting involved in taking down the Hangmen? When you face a problem that seems too big for you to handle, what do you typically do?

6. After a rousing game of one-on-one, Nora makes an observation that gets Leah thinking: "Here we both are, guilty of crimes." How does this idea change Leah's perception of the women in prison? What does that statement say about choices we make in life?

7. Chaplain Darrel tells Leah, "Life isn't easy, not for anyone. The difference is how people respond to the difficulties." How does Leah respond to what life throws her way? How does her response change over the course of the story? What positive examples can she point to? How do you react when life feels too hard?

8. Leah's return to sketching becomes a metaphor for the state of her soul: "first blurry, ugly, and misshapen, then later clearer and more defined." Read Isaiah 64:8. In what ways is Leah being shaped and more clearly defined throughout this story? Where do you see God molding your life?

9. Even after giving Leah advice to leave matters in God's hands, Clint realizes he's been taking everything upon himself again. Is there something that you have a hard time surrendering? How do you identify those moments and relinquish control?

10. Leah believes "justice has to matter for everyone or it matters for no one." What does that look like for her? How would Clint define justice? What about the Hangmen? How does this statement work in real life?

11. Clint tells Leah, "We all have two sides to our natures." Do you believe everyone has both inherent good and bad within them? Why or why not?

12. Leah is initially on the fence about returning to her job. What convinces her to try to get it back? Is that a good reason to pursue that goal? Where do you see her going in the next few years?

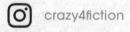

By purchasing this book from Tyndale, you have helped us meet the spiritual and physical needs of people all around the world.

Tyndale | Trusted. For Life.